OVER

THE TIGHTROPE

By Asif Ismael

Publisher: J.R. Sarmoun
Cover Design: Gary Val Tenuta
Interior Design by Scribe Freelance | www.scribefreelance.com

ISBN: 978-0-9967158-0-5

Printed in the United States of America

If I survive this life without dying, I'll be surprised.
— MULLA NASRUDDIN

Contents

Chapter 1

Yage

IT WAS A BALMY SATURDAY NIGHT late in October of the year 2050. The southbound A-train arrived fifteen minutes late at Columbus Circle, forcing me to make a run for it as soon as I hit the street. Breathless when I arrived at Yage Yoga Center—a sprawling New Age complex off the Westside Highway—I was just in time for the ceremony. A tall, dark complexioned girl at the reception desk welcomed me with a bright toothy grin.

"I'm registered for the nine o'clock ceremony," I said, trying to catch my breath.

"Name?" she asked, gazing at the hologram that sprang from the glass countertop.

"Ismaeel."

"Please read and sign the disclaimer," she said, pointing to an iPad near my hand.

I stared at the form as it zoomed out of the screen and floated in front of my face. Big bold red letters declared:

I VOLUNTARILY ASSUME FULL RESPONSIBILITY FOR ANY RISK
OF LOSS, PROPERTY DAMAGE, PERSONAL INJURY, OR DEATH.

I swallowed hard and scribbled my name on the indicated dotted line.

"The ceremony hall is on the 7th floor," the girl continued, fluttering her eyes and using that soft, oh-so concerned voice New Agers all seemed to be blessed with. "From the elevator turn right; the entrance to the hall is at the very end. Locker rooms are on your right. Yours is 786. You've got five minutes before they close the doors," the girl added, having already moved on to the next person in line.

Thanking her, I dashed to the elevator and punched number 7.

If the lofty claims made about Ayahuasca were true, tonight could be a night of discovery for a skeptic like myself; someone who'd written their doctoral dissertation to refute the existence of any spirit worlds albeit in my own case, of the Islamic variety: *Al-Jannah* or Paradise, where the pious would be served with virgins of incomparable beauty, and *Al-Jahannum* or Hell, where the sinners would be roasted alive many times over in a raging inferno. I'd titled my thesis: *Paradise and Hell: Metaphors in the making of the Muslim Mind.* In the paper I'd argued that these binary worlds were mere metaphors, a theoretical construction, and a work of creative imagination of human mind, and that these worlds and their infamous inhabitants had no external existence of their own.

In the locker room I hurriedly changed into my white ankle-length cotton tunic with long sleeves, the traditional Arabian robe or *thobe*; my loose-fitting dress for the occasion. I hadn't worn the thing in over a decade but it was still loose on me. Clutching my yoga mat, I pushed open the large mahogany door and entered the large circular candlelit hall. The space was designed to look like the inside of a jungle hut and was large enough to hold a hundred people.

The walls and conical roof were covered with thatched straw stuffed behind wooden planks. The place smelled of pine and the air was distinctly pleasant to breathe, thanks to the higher concentration of oxygen that was supposed to enhance a deeper experience. This process had been thoroughly explained in the two-page email YYC sent me at the time of enrollment.

Thirty or so people, mostly in their 20s and 30s and dressed in white clothes, sat on their yoga mats meditating with their backs against the walls. In the center of the room, perched on a long wooden bench, was a man draped in black robes. The man's long flowing black hair covered his shoulders and was held in place by a black headband. Beside him, on a large stone block, stood three pitchers and a number of clay cups.

A tall black girl, dressed in a burgundy-colored robe tapped my shoulder and smiled as she handed me an orange-colored purge-bucket lined with a sealable vomit bag. Then she led me to the far end of the room and showed me my designated spot amid a whispering sea of attractive young bodies.

To be honest, more than wanting to get a glimpse of the supernatural world of the shamans, which I believed to be the work of a brain on hallucinogens, I'd been drawn to Ayahuasca because of the *the purge:* the legendary cleaning up of subconscious trash clogging mind, body, and soul. I was prepared to puke my guts out, as long I could rid myself of my past demons; demons inherited from my father.

"Tonight we're really lucky to have Don Miguel here to conduct the ceremony," she whispered. "His trips are the best."

"Nice!" I said, staking out a spot against the wall. Positioning my bucket at arm's reach, I unrolled my yoga mat. A redheaded girl sitting about ten feet to my right gave me a conciliatory nod as I hit my mat, as if to acknowledge some shared secret.

Don Miguel spoke for a few minutes in heavily accented English. He was giving last minute instructions: breathe deeply; keep a straight back, keep your eyes closed; stay focused on the intention. The clearer the intention, the deeper the experience, and don't hesitate to raise your hand if you think you need more than a cup. Let your mind ride the *icaros*, the shaman chants, the cantos for travel into the spirit world.

When Don Miguel stopped speaking, five of his cohorts, three men and two women clad in black robes, joined him in the center of the room. As soon as they sat down on the floor in front of him there came the sound of rain; each drop landing with a distinct plop as if falling on a tarp overhead. One of the women started to hum softly.

After a few minutes, Don Miguel began pouring a thick dark liquid into the little cups that were carried on trays to the participants by two male assistant shamans.

The drink stank of putrid earth. I closed my eyes, held my breath, and knocked back the pernicious brew in one gulp. The bitter aftertaste had a long, lingering finish of rotten leaves with just a hint of ground insects. As soon as the concoction hit my stomach I dry-heaved and my torso spasmed violently. I gripped my bucket in my lap, but thankfully the nausea subsided after a few seconds. I closed my eyes and my mind started to drift on the hypnotic chant as it faded into the rhythmic patter of gentle rain.

Chapter 2

Grasshopper

IT WAS *THAT* CHANCE ENCOUNTER with a girl named Petra that had awakened my interest in Ayahuasca. I'd met her in *Grasshopper*, a candlelit cannabis cafe in the West Village. Grasshopper was one of a handful of businesses that had managed to thrive in the aftermath of Isis, a Category 4 hurricane that had pounded Lower Manhattan with a twenty-foot storm surge eight days earlier. Modeled after a warren of subterranean caves, the cafe attracted the usual sorts, including insomniacs working on advanced degrees in the arts and humanities and insomniacs much like myself. Like all hipster enclaves everywhere, Grasshopper was also a great place to meet interesting chicks who were more than willing to help you brainstorm your academic thesis. And more.

The night I met Petra, Grasshopper had been packed as usual for a Friday night. With my cup of spiked latte in one hand and my tablet in the other, I drifted to the back of the cafe looking for a quiet corner to hunker down for a couple of hours and plunge undistracted into my thesis.

Petra was sitting alone. How could I not notice this stylish bespectacled girl with smooth coppery skin and long brown hair trailing over her broad shoulders? I approached her with a closed-lip grin.

Striking up conversations with girls had never posed much of an obstacle to my social life. I was thirty-years-old and gym-fit. With my perpetual five-day stubble and tousled black hair, I'd always been well received. And I had to admit I was a handsome bastard.

I'd quickly discovered that Petra was a psychoanalyst-in-the-making, and that she specialized in Psychedelic-Assisted Psychotherapy. Having completed her Masters in Clinical Psychology, she'd been gathering ideas for her doctoral proposal.

Once I got the hint that she was lesbian, the conversation stayed pretty much focused on our respective academic endeavors. She thought my thesis was ambitious and seemed to delight in telling me that. I responded by saying hers was intriguing so the conversation continued to flow. As the night progressed, fueled by a few more spiked lattes, the conversation turned into a highly invasive psychotherapy session—my psychotherapy session.

"You seem more like a poet to me," she said, studying me over the top of her glasses. "Or a writer with the moral compass of a player! The Department of Religion is the last place I'd expect to see you hanging out in," she added, pushing her square framed glasses back over her upturned nose. Her eyes sparkled with excitement and I was the perfect captive audience.

"Appearances can be deceptive." My lips curled in a smile. "Perhaps the Department of Religion is where my demons reside."

"Now we're getting somewhere!" she said, folding her arms under her breasts. "Demons! My specialty."

I just shook my head and stole a glance at her deep cleavage, which had become accentuated by the push from below. All I could do was focus on her next query.

"Let's see. What made you choose the topic of your thesis— Paradise and Hell?"

"It's complicated!" I added and we both laughed.

"Okay, so uncomplicate it for me." Resting her elbows on the table she leaned toward me.

I drained my almost empty cup, rubbed my forehead, and thought of how best to answer her.

"Well, I've chosen this particular topic because it's a matter of identity; my identity apart from my dad's. Really though, it had been the only option that would give me the power to stand up to my father on his own turf: religion."

"Very insightful," she said with a smile, encouraging me to elaborate. "Tell me more about your dad."

Where to start?

"Well, the whole of my dad's life has been about some future life to be lived in the next world. This world doesn't mean much to him."

"Your father must be true ascetic."

"Not when it comes to women. The women of this world and the next—and he likes money."

"How interesting!"

"And, he won't settle for anything other than the highest level of Paradise when he dies—and when he wasn't thinking or talking of Paradise, he was projecting all the gory scenes of Hell on the screen of my impressionable young mind. He delighted in pummeling me with stories of the horrible punishments awaiting those who strayed from *siraat e mustaqeen*, the so-called straight path. He saw me as a sinner who was ruining his chances of entering into Paradise. That's all he talked about. Jannah and Jahannum. Paradise and Hell..." I paused and took a deep breath. She was listening to me with rapt attention.

"I can't tell you how much he enjoyed describing the torture in the grave at the hands of Munkar and Nakir—the two fearful angels," I said. "Those were my bedtime stories."

Petra's brows furrowed and eyes seemed genuinely concerned and troubled. "What a traumatic childhood!"

"Now you understand why I chose this particular topic for my dissertation."

"Yeah, understandable. It's therapeutic and highly personal," she said, nodding. After a moment's pause, she continued.

"But what I don't understand is what makes you so convinced that Paradise and Hell aren't real?" she said.

"Because they just aren't," I snorted, thinking we were back to square one.

"See, deep inside, you're a man of conviction. But you try so hard to project to the world the image of a man of logic, a man of the intellect," she spoke slowly, enunciating each word as if rendering a final verdict. "If you're so convinced that your father's so-called Next World isn't real, then what exactly is the difference between you and him? Like him, you're just believing as well."

"You're being pretty judgmental," I said, now feeling annoyed at her audacity.

"Goes with the territory. Self-discovery can be a bitch," she added, and I sighed in reluctant agreement.

"Things would be much simpler if I could afford a shrink," I said. "Midlife crisis can be a bitch too."

"You don't need a shrink, and you're too young for any midlife crisis. You haven't earned one! Besides, you can do it yourself."

"How?"

"Ayahuasca, the psychedelic brew from Amazon, that's all the rage—"

"I don't do drugs—and I've got no experience with psychedelics."

"For your information, yage isn't really a drug—it's more like a medicine, which the shamans have been using for centuries for healing. And if I were you, I'd totally experience the spirit world before I presumed to write a paper about it," she said.

"I think we're getting confused here. The spirit world you're talking about is way different from the kind I grew up with," I said. "My spirit world is either *Jannah*, a Muslim Paradise that's filled with virgins, streams of milk and honey, fruit-laden trees, and nonalcoholic beverages; or *Jahannum*, Hell, where a blaze awaits those who've strayed from the straight path; where sinners quaff bottomless goblets of boiling pus and get marinated in huge vats of their own piss. You know, stuff like that. Between Jannah and Jahannum, there's no intermediate world. No middle ground for someone like me."

"That's all the more reason to seek the truth," she said. "But remember, the spirit world can terrorize you if you aren't properly prepared. The bad trip could certainly be seen as a journey through Hell."

"Exactly! It's nothing more than what you make of it. Paradise and Hell don't have any tangible existence of their own. This is what my dissertation is all about," I said.

She was clearly in a combative mood. I sensed that she was used to winning most arguments and expected to bag this one too. I poked the tip of my index finger against my forehead.

"It's all in here," I said slowly through clenched teeth, trying to make her understand. "Nowhere else. The human mind on a trip; that's it. Either with the aid of hallucinogens, or just numbed and damaged by indoctrination. We see what we've been trained to see since childhood. It's the mind, stupid!" I rolled my eyes and shook my head.

"You may think I'm crazy, but I see a halo around you right now. It's a little spooky," she said, her eyes looking dreamy all of a sudden.

"What? A halo? Where did that come from?"

"I'm very sensitive to the vibrations around people," she said. "There's a very special kind of energy about you."

"Oh really. What else do you see?"

"Big holes. Your vital energy is leaking away constantly. Like from a wound."

"Jesus Christ!" I roared, and a few people looked in our direction. The girl was weirder than I'd thought.

"It's the childhood trauma which has left holes in your being."

"I think it's the system we live under which saps our energy," I said, meaning every word of it. "The modern life."

For the past six months, I'd been working twelve hours a day in the university library with three triple espresso breaks per shift. On weekend nights I was driving a Yellow Cab and squeezing in a break here and there. The harsh reality of doing a self-funded PhD had only begun to dawn on me lately.

"You're stuck in the system—your present—because of your past." She was becoming more and more relentless.

"When are you going to start taking patients?" I needed another stiff cup of coffee.

"You're too muddled. You're fighting the tide, and you need clarity. The quickest and the surest way for you is Ayahuasca. Once you're able to see with your inner eye, everything will make sense," she said, shoving a five-dollar bill under her coffee cup.

"Good luck, Ismaeel. It was nice taking to you." She got up and left without looking back, leaving me scratching my head.

I ordered another latte and brooded over her words and what I really wanted from life. I leaned back, closed my eyes, and let my mind drift.

I felt like an empty canister bobbing along a sewage pipe toward a recycling plant. My future struck me like a candle, slowly and unpleasantly dwindling into nonexistence. I became more and more uncertain of my next steps, thoughts that had crossed my mind before but which I had put off, mainly because of my irredeemable financial troubles.

Before I got recycled in the modern machine, I needed to travel; bike across continents; write a travelogue, and perhaps one day visit my country I had once loved because of its natural beauty. I wanted to hike and camp out in its magnificent north. Most of all I needed to make an attempt to patch things up with my father, regardless of our differences. He still lived in Lahore, in Faisal Town, the place where I'd been born. Abba was my only known living blood relation.

Last year, after having done my Masters with the Department of Religion at Columbia, I'd gotten my first U.S. passport. I'd even had it stamped for a multiple-visit entry from the Caliphate of Al-Bakistan. But at the last minute I'd dropped the whole plan. It was turning out to be way too expensive a trip to even contemplate. Besides, I wasn't sure I really was ready to see my father after all these years.

Chapter 3
Khidr

I HAD NO IDEA HOW LONG I'd been sitting there zoning out and tripping to the *icaros,* the chants. The patter of rain had transformed into an undulating wave of crimson dots, while the vocal ribbon of colors coiled upward in helical formation like the strands of DNA. My stomach gurgled, and it dawned on me that I could see the inside of my stomach where an orangish liquid formed pools in its folds like prehistoric shale in a network of antediluvian canyons. This orange liquid was now seeping through every hidden cave of my body, saturating the earth of my flesh like a spring thaw, like what people described when they talked of LSD.

Suddenly alarmed by this vision, I opened my eyes. Don Miguel's head seemed to have become elongated and was pushing backward at an unnatural angle. I turned and stared at my neighbor. Her fingers were impossibly long and pointed and moved with a creepy fluidity, each with a life of its own. The walls of the hall were swollen and pulsed as though we were cradled in the womb of a living thing. At that point, another wave of nausea threw my stomach into spasms. I squeezed my eyes shut and grabbed for my bucket. The redhead next to me was retching loudly between tormented sobs. The purge had started.

My ears began to buzz with a crescendo of vibration and my chest pounded with a distant drumbeat. It sounded just like a *dhol,* the barrel-sized drum beaten at the Sufi shrines of Punjab on Thursday nights. My father had always forbidden me to visit these shrines. Sufis, the mystics, were heretics according to him, and he had no tolerance for their antics. For him they represented the adulteration of the true teachings of Islam as contained in the Quran and *Hadith*, the latter being the saying of the Prophet, a corpus four times thicker than the Quran if combined with *Sirah*, or the deeds of the Prophet.

I began to breathe deeply, thinking about my intention. I wanted to know if Paradise and Hell were real. And I wanted to purge my demons. As soon as I thought of this intention, it sprang visibly before my eyes like a rope of shimmering colors that stretched to infinity. The rope coiled itself around me and began pulling me out of my body. In a panic I opened my eyes and looked at myself. My white robe seemed to have lost its fullness. A realization hit me: I wasn't in my robe. I screamed but no sound came out of my mouth. In the next moment, I was engulfed by a vast dark stillness.

I had no name, no body, and no feelings. I was just an awareness floating in a cozy dark womb. I had no idea how long I remained suspended there, and then slowly, drop by drop, I began to take form again.

I was back in my body, walking up a steep green slope. The air was luminescent and exquisitely fresh and the sky was radiant purple but without the sun. My legs had a mind of their own as they carried me along, pushing me higher and higher toward the top. I knew with some strange certainty that someone was waiting for me up there.

I was breathless when I reached the tabletop summit, my ears filled with the ringing sound of an old-fashioned bicycle bell. About a hundred or so feet away, a wiry little man stood next to an old-fashioned green bicycle that was leaning on its kickstand. He was waving at me. Filled with curiosity I marched toward him. I was about ten feet from him when he called out my name.

"Babu Ismaeel!"

How the hell did this strange-looking fellow know my name? And where did this babu thing come from? Babu was the word used by the village people of Punjab for an educated city dweller.

Dressed in a white kurta over a white dhoti, the traditional dress of rural Punjab—an unstitched cloth wrapped around the waist and legs and knotted at the waist, resembling a long skirt—the fellow was barely five feet tall and wore a huge white turban. His eyes were extraordinarily bright and he was wrinkled like the parchment of an ancient scroll. The wizened old face had a fine, white stubble.

"Hope is the engine which drives the universe forward," he said in lilting, fluid and unaccented English.

Tongue-tied, I merely nodded. The intensity of his gaze made my legs tremble, but I wasn't afraid of him, exactly.

"Right person, right time, right place makes what we call action; everything else is merely a reaction." He played with the brass bell on the handlebar of his green bicycle making it ring three times.

I remained quiet, still wondering who he was and how he knew my name.

"Babu, your intention and ours have met across time and space and made this moment possible," he said. "I am Khidr," he declared as he stepped forward and extended his right hand. "Chaacha Khidr."

He had only one tooth in his mouth and it stuck out from his lower lip like a shark's fin. The skin of his hand was smooth as silk.

"I'm so honored to have met you Chaacha Khidr," I said, not sure if I could believe my ears. Was this the vision of al-Khidr out of legend? He was known as the mysterious prophet, the eternal wanderer, and the hidden initiator of those who walked the mystical path. He had been known to have coached even Moses in divine mysteries.

"Just call me Chaacha," he said. His crisp voice, like his brilliant eyes, was in sharp contrast with his ancient tottering appearance. There was certainly nothing green about him. Al-Khidr was known as the Green One, always wearing a green robe. This man was thoroughly Punjabi looking, as opposed to the Hebrew Prophets.

"Yes, Chaacha." I nodded as I clasped the tight-gripped leathery hand. Since the word Chaacha meant uncle in Urdu language, the old man had to be from Pakistan or India.

"Babu, you're going to help us clean up a big mess," he said.

"I am?"

"Yes," he said. "You'll be leaving for Pakistan shortly. It's vital that you leave as soon as possible."

"Pakistan!" I shook my head in disbelief. "I don't have the money for that kind of travel."

"Once you land in Lahore, we'll contact you," he said, ignoring my protest.

"Fine," I was fully aware that I was in the grip of an Ayahuasca vision that would evaporate as soon as the chemical burned itself out in the circuitry of my brain.

"Fate has chosen you for a huge task. Looking at you, I can see that fate has chosen wisely."

"Chosen me for what?"

The old man climbed onto his bicycle, his feet barely reaching the ground. I saw he was wearing a golden pair of khusa with upturned toes.

"It's a mysterious world we live in, babu," he said. "Better start preparing."

Before I could fire off any more questions, he started pedaling away. He quickly picked up speed and in a few seconds he turned into a vertical streak of brilliant light against the purple sky. Then he was gone.

I was left with an overwhelming sense of loneliness in this oppressive vastness, which was broken only by soft rolling mounds of green. Overpowered by convulsions in my stomach, I collapsed on the grass and began retching.

In the next moment everything vanished. It was pitch dark all around. As I bolted upright in panic, I nearly screamed when I felt a hand grabbing my shoulder.

"Open your eyes," I heard someone say nearby. Somebody else was strumming a guitar in the background.

When I opened my eyes I was staring into the face of Don Miguel. The black headband across his forehead was soaked with sweat, and every muscle of his face was alive with movement in the flickering light of the candle. I was sitting with my back against the wall, my breath now calm and silent.

The head shaman squatted next to me; the vomit bucket in his hand was shoved against my chest. It had collected most of my purge. The rest made my robe feel sticky and wet against my skin. I smelled horrible.

"Are you feeling okay?" one of the Don's female assistants nearby asked gently.

"He's fine," said Don Miguel. His face pulsed with so many emotions it was hard to guess what was he feeling or thinking.

The truth is I was feeling fine and was determined to tell them: it was one hell of a trip. But I couldn't put these words together into a sentence.

"You've just met with your destiny, Ismaeel," Don Miguel said without moving his lips.

That was the most astonishing thing; he had somehow transferred his words directly into my mind without actually speaking. I wanted to say something, but was again lost for words. It was shocking to hear my name, his voice speaking in my head. How the hell did he know my name? I doubted he would bother remembering the names of every participant in the ceremony. How could he possibly know what my vision had been? Perhaps it was just a boilerplate statement to keep the crowd mesmerized by their respective trips.

"Hold on to your breath. You're not done yet," Don Miguel said as he and his assistant got up and moved on to attend another participant who was slumped on his knees and elbows. The guy's head was completely inside a bucket.

I closed my eyes and let my mind take me wherever it wanted to go. The guitar was incredibly soothing and gradually faded to complete silence.

I was completely at peace. After a while I was given another cup to drink, which went down effortlessly this time. The second cup didn't lift me off, literally speaking, to the other world like the first one had;

neither did it facilitate a meeting with any strange beings. But it did take me into my past and gave me new perspectives and insights on secrets long buried there. Most of these visions were gloomy and involved tense interactions with my father. I had just one fleeting glimpse of my deceased mother lying beside me in bed paralyzed. I was one year old when she died of polio.

As Abba's sole heir I'd been a complete disappointment. His presence had hovered over my childhood like a storm cloud, unpredictable and full of thunder and lightning. My defiance and resolve had only earned me shame and guilt. For the first time in my life, thanks to a little earthen cup of Ayahuasca, I saw my rebellious stance as sign of having a healthy soul that refused to submit to Abba's twisted worldview.

The sacred vine of the Amazon truly was helping me transform my pain and guilt into self-awareness. I began to understand my father's limitations. There had never been anything personal in his actions and thoughts. He'd just been regurgitating what had been fed to him; a narrative manufactured and perfected over centuries and never questioned or critically analyzed. I felt sorry for him really. He was a prisoner, a victim of indoctrination. I wanted to forgive him. And I wanted to see him.

The remainder of the night passed with blazing speed. As the sunlight streaked into the hall from a window facing east, it was hard to believe I'd been sitting in this place for the last ten hours. People were stretching, yawning, and beginning to stagger to their feet. They approached Don Miguel one-by-one for a farewell handshake and he hugged each of them before they left the hall.

My neighbor, the redheaded chick, got to her feet and threw herself into my arms, giving me a good three minute long hug. I patted her head without saying anything. There was nothing to say.

I approached the shaman feeling unstable on my feet.

"Thank you, Don Miguel," I said. "It wasn't as bad as I was expecting."

"A great task has been given to you, Ismaeel. Make yourself available to it, no matter how strange it may appear."

"How do you know, if I may ask, what kind of task I've been given," I asked.

He tapped the headband over his temple and looked me in the eyes.

"The people of the spirit world have their own special methods of communication," he said.

"What do you recommend I should do?" I said, recalling my encounter with a strange looking man who'd ordered me to start preparing for a trip to Pakistan.

"Learn to shut off your analytical mind from time to time. All wisdom is in learning how to go with the proverbial flow," he said, giving me a warm smile.

"Provided you know what the flow looks like."

"You'll know," he assured me. "You'll learn to recognize it."

I nodded and headed toward the exit. I couldn't wait to take off my robe, which reeked of putrefied soil. I longed for a shower with that special kind of urgency I had previously reserved for getting laid.

The locker room was buzzing with activity. The night's excursion had left people dazed, disheveled, and keeping to themselves. After taking the most invigorating shower of my entire life I put on my clean clothes; a pair of red chino pants and a gray fleece top. By the time I stepped out on the street, it was seven-thirty in the morning.

The sky was blue, the air balmy, and traffic was light since it was Sunday. I began walking toward Columbus Circle to catch the northbound A-train. My body was stiff and disoriented and I felt like I was re-entering the real world after a long absence. My mind was still not fully obeying the practical commands of my brain, as though it sought to drag me deeper into the past.

I'd left home at the age of eighteen. That was twelve years ago, the summer of 2038 to be exact. My father, a mid-level bureaucrat turned entrepreneur with his hands in every pie, was fifty-two at the time and had just married Sophie, his seventh wife. She was a beautiful, willowy fifteen-year-old girl from the Kalash tribe that occupied the picturesque valley of Kafiristan in the shadow of the Hindu Kush range in the former Republic of Pakistan. Sophie was also my first love. It was a love that had blossomed long before Abba ever laid eyes on her.

My father was always careful not to exceed the four-wife-limit at any one time in order to remain within the good graces of the Sharia Court. My mother Jannat was Abba's first wife. Like so many, she had fallen victim to a perfectly preventable disease. Abba regarded the polio vaccination programs provided by various global humanitarian agencies as part of a western conspiracy. A scientifically engineered genocide, he'd call it.

I'd met Sophie while Abba and I were spending summer vacation in Kafiristan the year before I left home. It was Abba's third trip to the region and he'd fallen in love with the idea of converting the whole Kalash tribe, the kafirs, or the unbelievers, to Islam. These hardy mountain folk were the descendants of the armies of Alexander the Great and his march through the northwestern Indian Subcontinent toward the fertile plains of Punjab in his quest for immortality. The truth of this could be seen in the light-skinned faces, pale brown hair, and blue eyes so frequently seen in the far-flung and isolated valleys of the North.

Under the inspired and persistent leadership of Abba, Kafiristan became Nuristan, the Abode of Light. This whole Kafiristan affair had boosted Abba's prestige in a land that was destined to become the Caliphate of Al-Bakistan. Most of the ancient tribe of Kalash became extinct overnight. Those who resisted were killed. Many fled, taking refuge in the mountains. Women and children were captured and distributed as slaves among the affluent. Abba took Sophie for his own, even though she never accepted Islam.

Within a month of her wedding, Sophie ran away in the middle of a dust storm that enveloped the city of Lahore in an opaque crimson haze, bringing the city to a standstill for three days on end. She was never found despite Abba's best efforts. She'd had the courage to bolt for freedom and she'd inspired me to do the same. It took me a month of mustering up courage and a lot of soul searching before I, too, said farewell to Abba and his world. I had left without telling him goodbye. He was somewhere in the north at the time. But I'd left him a courtesy note, letting him know he wouldn't be seeing me for a very long time and not to waste his time looking for me. I said I'd come back when the fates chose and not a day before. Sophie was gone but never from my mind, for in every woman I'd had since, I'd look for her trace, her reflection, her taste.

At the time I left home Abba was living with his two wives: Safa and Marwa, his fifth and sixth wives respectively. They were in their twenties and were quite attractive. Up until Safa and Marwa, I'd been an only child; the sole heir to Abba's expanding fortune. Since I turned out to be a complete disappointment, Abba had desperately wanted another son in whom he could see himself. This son would be just like him; somebody who'd carry the mantle and further his mission to help spread the light of his faith and in the process ensure him a suitable palace and a prime piece of real estate in Paradise. I had no idea if he'd another child since my departure.

After saying goodbye to Pakistan it'd taken me two years of hitchhiking across ten countries and three continents before I finally arrived in the United States. I was twenty years old. As luck would have it, I won the Green Card lottery and became a legal resident the following year.

I'd spent most of the next decade in libraries with a series of odd jobs to support me through college. I'd dived deep into the study of religion in order to understand its science, and the mysterious power it held over people like Abba and countless others throughout the centuries.

Abba saw me as a rebel without a cause; a pitiful excuse for a son who was sure to ruin his chances in the next world. He often publicly voiced his great regret at having invested so much time and energy into someone who turned out to be all but a complete failure.

When I was ten, my father had seen to it that I committed the whole of the Quran to memory and became a hafiz. For that he'd procured the best tutors money could buy and he tolerated nothing short of perfection from me. By the time I became a certified hafiz, something great happened: my father's growing political connections and popularity got him sidetracked.

Abba was seen less and less in Lahore, where he'd owned a chemical factory, and became more visible in Islamabad. Freed from his watchful gaze, within a year or two I'd all but forgotten most of the holy text.

He'd found out about my lapses and had taken this neglect of mine rather too personally. To my father, and all men like him, this was an unpardonable sin of the highest magnitude and an affront to all things decent. From that breaking point our relationship had slid downhill until it hit rock bottom. It had never recovered.

After getting off the A-train at 110th street, I ducked into a bagel shop on Cathedral Parkway. The toasted bagel with cream cheese and a black coffee tasted heavenly as I listened to the Beatles' "Yesterday" floating toward me from somewhere in the kitchen. In order to prepare myself for last night's trip, I'd abstained for two weeks from the staples of modern life. No coffee, cannabis, tea, beer and alcohol, meat of any kind, salt, spices, or dairy. I had forgone Internet, TV, and social media. To complete my transformation into an ascetic zombie, I'd also forced myself to stop hankering after women as I hung around the coffee houses near campus.

Savoring my breakfast, my mind quickly latched onto my encounter with the bright-eyed, ancient looking man clad in his dhoti. The sound of the bicycle bell, the conversation we had, the task he'd talked about, and the manner in which he had turned into a streak of light before being swallowed by a vast green emptiness; all remained vividly fresh in my mind and I realized I was smiling at the memory.

The more I puzzled over the experience, the more I became convinced that my so-called task somehow had to do with reuniting with my father. I thought of my financial constraints that prohibited even contemplating such a trip. Perhaps Abba would help me out. After all he was a very rich man.

Something had certainly changed within me on a fundamental level during the Ayahuasca trip; something extraordinary that was beyond the pale of any rational analysis. To be able to think of my father in a compassionate way was absolutely new to me, but it was the proof of a major shake-up in my psyche. Suddenly, I wanted to have a cup of tea with my Abba in the front lawn of the house of my childhood while we soaked up the warm late afternoon sun.

Ayahuasca had not only heightened my curiosity about the spirit world, it had also made me think about Paradise and Hell in a new way. Petra had told me that by insisting Paradise and Hell were nothing more than the work of the imagination I'd been acting out my personal convictions, all the while secretly believing otherwise. Maybe she was right. Perhaps I'd been unable to break free from the internal fight I'd been having with my father all these years. It seemed as if I'd lived my entire life as a reaction, while regarding myself as a man of action.

Chapter 4
The Note

"**Y**ESTERDAY" HAD STUCK IN MY MIND and I'd been whistling the haunting tune throughout my leisurely walk home. My steps halted as I stood at the front door of the one-room apartment I occupied courtesy of University Apartment Housing of Columbia. The door was ajar. Someone had broken in. I entered slowly and looked around. Finding no sign of activity I tiptoed further inside, tensed for fight or flight.

The place smelled of cinnamon and tobacco, though not my cinnamon and tobacco. Instead of taking anything, the intruder had left a Styrofoam cooler on my kitchen counter. It was the kind used for shipping medicines on icepacks.

A large brown manila envelope with my name scrawled across it in heavy black marker lay beside the cooler. Inside the insulated container, wedged between two icepacks, was a finger- sized plastic vial filled with a pinkish fluid. Its label read: Single Dose OPV. The brown envelope contained a business-class ticket on Khalifa Air's Flight 786. The flight departed at 9.00 pm from JFK on Monday, the following night. My eyes narrowed as I read the destination: Lahore, Pakistan, arriving 6:00 pm Tuesday night. It was a one-way ticket. Also in the envelope was a bundle of worn Dirham bills, ninety-nine of them; about a thousand dollars' worth. Also included was a handwritten two-page note in a beautiful flourished script.

Dear Ismaeel

 Knowledge, like a rare metal, is a precious commodity, and the price to gain the direct knowledge of Paradise and Hell is way too steep to be afforded if you are a mere mortal. However, there are methods known only to a select few— who are called the guides—who alone could unravel such mysteries. They exist to help those who seek with sincerity and an unwavering intention. Time has come for you to prepare yourself for the most important journey of your life. You'll be contacted once you arrive in Lahore.

 Your father is a well-connected man and a highly regarded entrepreneur in the Caliphate. Obviously, his business is now a household name. We know that you are estranged. Please know that regaining your father's trust is the path to success of our mission, a mission whose details will only be revealed to you when you are prepared to take action—at the right time, at the right place.

 You are to call your father tonight at midnight. It will be 9:00 am where he is. Let him know that you'll be flying to Lahore to see him, and that you have missed him very much. The two of you have a lot to discuss.

 Some basic reminders: Your greatest enemy will be fear, and the greatest distraction desire or lust. Doubt causes paralysis and resentments shackle one with chains. Anger burns what is vital, and impatience slows things down. Curiosity can have you killed. To succeed you must learn how to conquer these conditions which afflict all people. You will be tested every step of the way.

 If you have understood the above and still wish to continue on the Path to High Knowledge and undertake such a demanding journey, you must take the polio drops after reading this note. Your immune system needs to be optimal by the time you land.

Do not attempt to overthink or make sense of matters from here on, for it may prevent you from choosing the right course of action at a crucial point in time. We'll be monitoring your progress closely once you land. Failure is not an option, and obedience thwarts many a catastrophes. Your success will ensure your entry into the most ancient of the circles of the Elite.

Pir Pullsiraat

PS: Arrangements have been made to make you completely debt free, hence financial issues should be the last of your worries.

At the bottom of the note was Abba's mobile's number—next to his name: Haji Ibrahim. He hadn't changed his number in all these years. Maybe that was an encouraging omen.

Bloody hell! I let out the breath I'd been holding for the last several seconds and continued to stare at the note, numbed with shock. This couldn't be happening. It seemed like some kind of over-the-top psychedelic spy movie.

I read the note several times, my confusion mounting with each read. Pir Pullsiraat. Weird name! Pir meant guide, and Pullsiraat that mythical tightrope, which I had always imagined to be a steel cable hung high above the fire pit of Hell which, after death, every believer had to traverse barefoot. Most would fall off, except the true believers and those who died in the way of Allah: the martyrs. I had imagined the other side as being the lush rolling mounds of green as far as the eye could see, and beyond that the real paradise.

The more I tried to make sense of this baffling missive, the more restless I became. I paced back and forth in my tiny apartment as my mind raced over the possibilities in play. Then a thought occurred: I was doing exactly what I wasn't supposed to be doing; trying to make sense of things, things I supposedly couldn't understand anyway. *How about: Let's see what happens?*

Morning gave way to noon and by then I'd read the note so many times that I'd memorized it. The writing radiated a power which made me feel small and greatly agitated. Unable to sustain a state of hyper-arousal my wakefulness progressed to the point of collapse. As soon as I hit the bed, I was taken by a deep, dreamless sleep.

When I woke up, the room was dark. Feeling disoriented, I glanced at my watch. It was 10:30 pm. I bolted upright, thinking that the note and its accompanying items left on my kitchen counter by the intruder must be part of an ongoing vision from the last night's trip, the lingering effects of the sacred vine.

But the cooler was still there on the counter and lying next to it was the opened brown manila envelope. A feeling of enormity and inevitability began to envelope me.

I got up and read the note again in hopes new revelations would hit. Nothing. Everything was happening so fast. It was all so freakish, and totally bizarre. Who really were these people and what did they want with me? It was clear that my encounter with Chaacha Khidr wasn't merely my mind conjuring under the influence. The note had blown me away. It'd made a hole so big in my conception of reality that I felt bodily transparent.

Did they pick the right person? Or was I just being given a crash course in conquering my weaknesses, my fears and doubts? Now I was impatient and curious as hell. Obedient I was not, and Abba could testify to that. Free from lust, most definitely not, since I'd gotten it genetically.

One thing was for sure: my long-repressed sense of adventure was out of the barn and kicking up its hooves. Pushing the envelope had never been something I was afraid of—even though it had often ended in regrets. The bottom-line: I was intrigued; hell, I was hooked!

There was something happening here and I wanted a seat for the whole ride. Not to mention the debt-free deal which was, of course, way too sweet to pass up. More important, I wanted to find out what the hell my father was up to these days. On top of the list was that he was the key to the success of my mission. Whatever the mission might be. It was time to take the polio drops.

I snapped the end of the vaccine vial, took a deep breath, and emptied the contents into my mouth. A faint bitterness spread across my tongue. I opened the fridge and pulled out an icy bottle of Heineken and let beer kill the unpleasant aftertaste. The next two took the edge off the growing sense of unease that gripped me as I watched the hand on the clock edging slowly toward the fateful midnight hour and my phone call.

I plopped down on my ragged loveseat in a horizontal position and stared at the ceiling, my head resting against the armrest. A spider lay motionless in its tiny hexagonal hammock, waiting for a wayward victim, a moth that circled overhead. The filaments of the web were radiant and I gazed in amazement.

The wind rose suddenly, howling and rattling the windows. I shivered, noticing the temperature in the room had dropped. Stepping over to the window I peeked through the blinds. There was something unsettling in the air. It was snowing and had already covered the sidewalks and the parked cars that lined the street below!

I returned to the loveseat and began watching the moth. It was banging against the walls every few seconds, but it managed to stay clear of the spider's deadly trap. A part of me felt like that moth; about to be engulfed in the gossamer threads of an unseen world. But the other part of me was all spider, having been duly sent the nourishment I needed from the beyond. I emptied my mind and waited for midnight to arrive.

The moth was still fluttering about the room when my watch showed five minutes to midnight. It was unbelievable that I had been staring at the ceiling for the last hour and a half. Time to call Abba. I felt rested, energetic, and ready to take on my assignment. I took a deep breath, and studying the note, I dialed Abba's number.

"Hello!" he answered in the old familiar intense tone of voice.

"Abba? It's—it's Ismaeel."

After a long pause I heard his breath becoming irregular.

"I don't know if I should believe my ears," he muttered. He didn't sound particularly happy to hear my voice.

"I thought I'd never see you again," he added, sounding anxious and distant.

"I'm sorry, Abba. I've thought of calling you many times, but..."

"But what?" he barked.

"Abba, I miss you," I said drawing a deep breath and cringing.

"Where are you calling me from?" he demanded, sounding genuinely puzzled.

"New York City, Abba—I'll be in Lahore soon."

"What? You're coming to Lahore?" he sounded stunned, an understandable reaction.

"Yes, Tuesday night. My plane lands at 6:00 pm."

"Which Tuesday?" he sputtered, his voice clipped and tense. "You never fail to surprise me!" I now recalled that my father had never been particularly fond of surprises.

"This coming Tuesday, Abba—in two days."

"Is everything all right?"

"Yes. I just miss Lahore, and I miss being with you," I said, gritting my teeth as I spoke. I didn't remember having ever said this to him before and it didn't sound particularly believable now.

"Are you well, Ismaeel?"

"One hundred percent," I assured him.

"It's a very different place here, from what it used to be," he said. "I hope you know the requirements for the entry. They are very strict on immigration these days."

"I think I'll be fine," I said, rubbing my cheek and feeling my week-old stubble. To get through immigration, the length of my beard had to be the size of a grain of rice. That much I knew, having read it in the news somewhere a while back.

"I think I'll make it," I added, smiling to myself.

"I'll send my driver to the airport. His name is Wali."

"I'll just take a taxi, Abba."

"This isn't the same place anymore."

"Oh? Is it really that bad?" I was kind of taken aback by the obvious alarm in his voice.

"It's bad all right, but it's not terrible. Most of what you hear about our country is all western propaganda," he said. "The Jews!"

"I know, I know," I said. "The Zionists."

"Zionists or Jews, they're all the same—they're the killers of our Prophet—disliked by the Almighty the same."

Horrified by his reply, I remained silent.

"Why are you coming?" Now his tone was calm but deliberate.

"We'll talk about it, Abba—when we meet."

"I won't be in Lahore until Thursday. So you'll have a couple of days to yourself to get settled in and get over the jetlag. Wali and Ghulam Rasool will be in the house to look after you."

I was happy to hear that Ghulam Rasool, the cook, was still around. His kind face, warm smile, and the delicious concoctions flashed through my mind. I had never met Wali before.

"Thank you, Abba—it's very kind of you."

"It's fine. It's fine. Wali will pick you up from the airport. But please, and this is very, very important. You must remember—do not discuss religion with him, at all. Avoid the subject completely. In fact, do not talk to anyone at the airport. Understood?"

"Yeah, sure, I'll keep that in mind." A knot was forming in my stomach.

"You can't help it, at times," he added almost as if to himself.

I remained quiet.

"Good, then, Inshallah, we'll meet on Thursday evening," he said curtly. Then he was gone.

I guess it's really happening. I stared at the phone, thinking there was no way on this earth that I could ever hope to gain my father's trust, and certainly not on his terms. But this trust was deemed a critical key to this nebulous success I was tasked to so ardently seek. The thought of visiting my native country, now the Caliphate, filled me with a mixture of terror and excitement. *Shouldn't be a problem adjusting to the current norms*, I consoled myself. After all I'd spent eighteen years of my life there—albeit as a rather poor example of a Muslim. I'd never once set foot in a mosque in America. And if I still considered myself a Muslim, it was as a culturally self-hating Muslim.

I craved a cigarette. Though I'd quit a couple of months ago cold turkey, I was really feeling it tonight and got up and started to pace again, fighting the urge to go out and score a pack of smokes at the 7-11 down the block. Maybe I should get my laundry done. I needed a clean thobe for the trip. I discarded the idea, because I knew if I went out I'd be buying cigarettes. And then I remembered I had another similar robe somewhere in the back of my closet. I'd kept it as a souvenir since I'd been wearing it when I left home: a faded blue denim jellaba splattered with a patchwork of red, blue, and yellow squares. Abba hated it.

"Only a heretic would wear this kind of robe," he told me more than once, thus providing me a good reason to wear it even more often.

I tried it on in front the mirror. It used to hang loosely on me but now it fit perfectly. With my stubble it made me look like a dervish. I'd get a new one once I got to Lahore, but since I'd need to change my attire before we landed in the Caliphate, I'd need to carry it with me on the plane. Change the clothes, change the man, or woman. So went the prevailing mindset. I'd heard stories of women flocking to the bathrooms during a flight to change their identities from chic urban dweller to pious Muslimah before landing on their grandparents' home soil.

Since I had no idea how long I'd be gone, I threw whatever I thought I'd need for a week or two into my suitcase. By the time I finished packing I was exhausted. As soon as my body hit the bed I was out.

I stood in a vast courtyard lined with white marble tiles. It was dusk and I was staring at a massive white tent in front of me. Four pencil shaped pillars stood at the tent's four corners. The place looked familiar, but I couldn't tell what it was or where I'd seen it before.

In my hand I held a weightless ball of white light. An intense glow emanating from the sphere filled the whole area with dazzling brightness. A man wearing a black cloak and black turban, his face concealed by a veil, approached me. He stopped about twenty feet from me.

Against the light his shadow stretched from his feet to the top of the tent, like a band of darkness. The light from the sphere spilled out of the courtyard into the surrounding area of the building; then the man vanished like mist at sunrise.

I opened my eyes. I was perspiring profusely and my shirt was drenched with sweat. It was 1:00 in the afternoon. Being a light sleeper, it was unusual for me to have slept for such a long time without getting up even once. Something extraordinary was in play here. Something inexplicable yet palpable.

For one, I was disoriented as to time. I had this vision of the present moment like a portal into a timeless dimension, where a limitless worlds churned about, each being a distinct entity, each staying clear of the other, and I existing in all worlds simultaneously. I shook my head in an attempt to dispel this strange vision.

Must be the after-effects of Ayahuasca. Sitting on the bed as I wiped the sweat off my forehead and tried to clear my thoughts, the dream came back to me. It was vivid as hell. It had all seemed so real! I could still see the huge courtyard, the white tent, the cold marble beneath my bare feet and the intense white glow of the sphere's light upon my skin.

My curiosity to know the realities of Paradise and Hell had hit a new high. I wanted to know what mission Pir had been talking about but worried whether I really was prepared for this weirdest of the journeys one could possibly imagine? But I also had a certainty that by taking the polio vaccine I had already accepted fate and taken the plunge.

Chapter 5
Khalifa Air

To GET TO THE AIRPORT I'd taken the Air-train from Manhattan to JFK. Throughout the ride I couldn't help but marvel at the newfound clarity of my vision, the vividness of colors, a certain sharpness about the world around me which I had never appreciated before. The weather was perfect and I was dazzled by the luminous edges of the clouds under the shocking blue of the sky, the radiant city skyline receding from my view, the untold stories etched on the human faces, the gestures betraying people's inner thoughts, and the stark three dimensionality of space which I'd ordinarily taken for granted, wrapping everything in its fold.

Feeling giddy from my heightened senses I arrived at the airport two hours before takeoff. The flight was completely booked. A burqa clad air-hostess stood at the doorway of the wide-bodied Airbus A500. Peeking through the narrow slit in her veil, her big black kohl-lined eyes looked resplendent. I froze, hypnotized by the beauty of those luminous orbs, and wondering if the original purpose of burqa had been to enhance the power of a woman's gaze. A nudge on my back made me step forward. What was the old saying about eyes, souls? They sure had that right.

The woman looked over my boarding pass and pointed me towards the Business Class with nothing more than a sweep of her eyes. Reluctantly, I headed toward my seat but couldn't help glancing back a few times, hoping to catch another glimpse of her.

The piercing loveliness of those eyes had looked right into me and I was overcome as if by some strange potion. Unfortunately she had moved on to the next passenger who hadn't even glanced at her veiled face.

There were about twenty or so comfortable, dimly lit private cabins on the craft, each stocked with the predictable amenities. The air smelled of fresh roses, with a hint of cinnamon. I slipped into my own cabin and took off my backpack. Inside the cabin I detected a waft of jasmine. Either my olfactory sense had been heightened like everything else in my perceptual field, or the atmosphere was exactly the way Khalifa Air had intended, I wasn't quite sure.

I turned around and froze. A full-lipped girl in glossy red lipstick and wearing a red airline cap stood smiling at me. She was probably in her early twenties with long silky straw-colored hair trailing down her back to her waist. The young woman wore a tight maroon colored suit, but no blouse under her jacket. By the time she spoke, the eyes of a certain air-hostess in Economy Class were nothing more than a distant memory.

"Good evening, sir. My name is Alina. I'm at your disposal for the duration of the flight," she said reaching around behind me, touching the middle of my spine with her fingers.

"What's going on here?" I stammered, realizing I'd been holding my breath for several moments. I felt ashamed for uttering such a dumb response to her greeting.

"I understand your confusion sir. You're flying with us for the first time. Is that correct?"

"Right."

"Sir, this is the business class. Burqa wearing hostesses are for the economy class only."

"But aren't we all flying to the same country?" I asked as I eased into my seat. Again I vaguely detected the stupidity of my question.

"Sir, I'm from Latvia and am with a company hired by Khalifa Air to serve the business class. We aren't required to cover up, sir—because we aren't Muslims." Her lips almost touched my ear lobe. My heart fluttered imagining the scope of the "amenities" which were to unfold once we took off. The whole thing was so far out.

"What would you like to drink? No alcohol, of course," she said softly. I scratched my chin and looked into her eyes, thinking my journey perhaps had kick-started on a wrong note. I wished lust would have been the last thing to focus on, or at least until I'd landed in Lahore.

"I'm fine for now," I said, looking around to see whether our conversation was being overheard.

"Are you by any chance a Shia, sir?" she said, lowering her soft voice.

"Why do you ask?" I was struck by the oddity of her question. And a little apprehensive.

"Well—if you are, and would like to enjoy our complimentary full-service spa, you can register for the *Mut'ah* contract for the duration of the flight. Fourteen hours to be exact. I can bring you the register if you like. It's kept in the cockpit."

"I'm neither," I mumbled. I couldn't believe what she just said. *Mut'ah* or temporary marriage had been allowed in the Shia sect of Islam, where the duration of such contract must be specified and agreed upon in advance.

"What do you mean, sir?"

"I'm neither a Shia, nor a Sunni." I tried to figure out the practical ramification of this obscene perk reserved for the Business Class passengers. "Well, sir, for this flight, you're required to be one or the other."

She had to be kidding me. Was this a test of some kind? Suddenly America seemed located in another time, a place where I once used to live, a long long time away.

"Would you help me decide?" The girl had surely charmed me so I surrendered to the game. I was curious to see how far this would lead.

"I personally don't like the paperwork, sir, if my humble wishes are to be considered," she said with a playful toss of that golden hair and a smile that was anything but submissive.

"Well then, let's fly Sunni!" I said, replying to her smile with a grin.

"An excellent choice, sir. Once we take off you are invited upstairs for relaxation and massage."

"I'll keep that in mind," I said, smiling and admiring the view as she turned and slipped out of the cabin.

The entire flight was resplendent with wonders and unexpected amenities of exceptional quality. I didn't even want to guess how much all this was costing whoever was footing the bill, but one thing was certain: I had failed my first test when it came to conquering my lust. Though I'd successfully refrained from having the "full-service massage," I'd succumbed to the happy ending part of it. For the rest of the flight I had this nagging feeling that I shouldn't have done that. After all, I was on the Path to High Knowledge, and indiscretions had no place in such endeavors.

I had slept much of the latter half of the flight and was awoken before landing by my lovely Latvian hostess, Alina.

"Sir, you may now change into your mandatory attire." She helped me to sit up. "We'll be landing soon. I hope you've enjoyed your flight. Thanks for choosing Khalifa Air." She slid the cabin door open to leave.

As she left the cabin I slid into my blue denim jellaba and prepared for touchdown into the land of my birth. The side-pocket of my robe, its only pocket, was large enough to accommodate my fat wallet and my cell phone. I'd carried my ticket and passport in a neck pouch that dangled in front of my navel. I was planning to tuck the pouch under my robe once I was through Immigration and Customs.

At the immigration counter, the officer holding a handheld scanner passed it over my face before a word was spoken between us.

"Unfortunately, you can't enter the country," the immigration officer intoned grimly, his heavy lidded eyes staring at me with contempt.

"You'll have to be quarantined for at least three days," he continued, as though the injunction amounted to some sort of personal triumph. "Until your *beard* satisfies the proper criteria for entry."

He eyed me with tight-lipped disapproval while fingering his own twenty plus pious inches of wooly growth. Except for his eyes and forehead, the man's face was covered with jet-black hair. The tip of his beard trailed across my passport where it lay on the counter. Clearly, I was now in a land where size definitely mattered.

"Unless of course, you wish to pay the fine?" he added, his lips curled in contempt.

"I'll pay the fine, sir. How much?" I asked, not taking my eyes from his. It secretly pleased me when he was the first to look away.

"Three thousand Dirhams," he stated in a voice clipped and bristling with pride. "For each day your beard must grow to meet the legal requirement; so—" He paused, inspected my face, his eyes narrowed. "For you, it will be ten thousand in total; nine for three days, plus one thousand for handling-charges."

"Thank you sir," I said, peeling ten one thousand Dirham notes, roughly equivalent to a hundred dollars, and offering the bills to him.

I exited the immigration area and headed straight for the baggage carousel. I'd definitely landed in a foreign country. All signs were in Arabic, now the official language of the Caliphate. In the good old days, they'd at least had the courtesy to put Urdu translation beside Arabic. Such courtesies, and others as I'd soon discover, were long gone.

A recitation of the Quran poured from the intercom system and drowned everything in an aura of otherworldliness. At the Customs window a fiery looking officer with a bulging belly and jet-black dyed beard looked me over from head to toe. A matchbox-sized copy of the Quran dangled from his neck on a gold chain.

"Carrying anything we should know about?" His mouth widened in a mischievous smile.

"No sir. Please feel free to check anything you'd like."

He had me open my suitcase. Fumbling through my clothes, he

extracted my shaving kit. Unzipping the bag, he pulled out my razor and held it in front of my face.

"What, exactly, is this doing here?" he inquired as if discovering the most heinous piece of dangerous contraband.

"Did you keep this shamelessly petite little beard just to get into the Caliphate?" he demanded. His nostrils flared but he never took his eyes off me as he plunged his hand deeper into my shaving kit again like a diver searching for sunken treasure. This time he pulled out a half empty tube of Colgate toothpaste.

"This brand is haram, forbidden in the Caliphate!" he hissed.

"It's just toothpaste—for God's sake." I hissed.

"It contains alcohol and pig's fat," he declared, shaking his head like he just couldn't fathom what he was seeing and what on earth it was doing in my bag. He looked infuriated. Probably my tone had pissed him off.

"Please feel free to throw these things away. I apologize." I said, sensing trouble.

"Recite the fifth Kalima, then the third, then the first and then the sixth—in that order," he demanded. He reared up and folded his arms across his broad chest, weaving back and forth in front of me like a cobra. His two black eyes bore into me. I could tell that whatever patience he'd had was dwindling.

Suddenly, I felt embarrassed—for once being a hafiz, the person who was supposed to recite the entire Quran solely from memory. The memorization of six Kalima, the standard Arabic phrases mostly taken from Hadith (the saying of Prophet), had long been part of the syllabus of grade three education in Pakistan. Now all I could remember was the first Kalima, called *Shahadaa*, the shortest but the most important one, the one whose utterance was all one needed to be a Muslim instantly.

"I could recite the first," I suggested, breathing out a sigh.

"Three thousand Dirhams for each Kalima that you've forgotten. Eighteen thousand Dirhams in total," he said, extending a huge open palm toward me and rubbing his fingers together.

"Wait a minute," I said. "What's the total number of Kalima we're talking about here?" I reached into the pocket for the cash. I knew there was an ancient controversy, if there were six Kalima or five.

"Ten thousand Dirhams in addition to the eighteen. The additional fine is for not knowing how many Kalima there are in total," he said, narrowing his eyes. "Now you owe me twenty-eight thousand Dirhams."

"It's kind of steep."

"I'll let you go for twenty-five."

By the time I left the Customs window my wallet had lost one-third of its bulk. The Customs officers at Lahore Airport had been known for their heavy-handedness, but they were now operating on a whole new level.

I walked out of the luggage area and rolled my suitcase toward the exit and the pick-up and delivery area. My eyes scanned a thick knot of noisy jostling bodies of bearded men. Many were drivers with names of travelers written on cards dangling from their chest.

No sign so far of Wali, my dad's most trusted right-hand man who was supposed to drive me home. In the hallway, a ten-foot long water bottle hung from the ceiling by chains. It was labeled *Paradise Water*: Your only reliable source of clean water, Khalifa Inc.

A large crowd had gathered to my right beneath a flashing red neon sign that read Judgment Day Bar. What the hell was this all about? With mounting curiosity, I edged my way toward the entrance. About a hundred or so men crowded the doorway under the flashing lights.

"What's going on here?" I asked a young man in his twenties who stood next to me.

"Today we're having both a stoning and a beheading at the same time, under one roof," he said, giving me a nudge in the ribs.

"Really?"

"Usually, it's just one or the other," he said shoving himself deeper into the crowd, presumably to get a better look at the show.

"Good Lord! Why at the airport?"

"Can you think of a better public place than an airport?" he asked, looking at me suspiciously. "Did you just say, Good Lord?"

"No—Mashallah—Alhamdolillah. Jazakallah." I sputtered. "I'd better get going."

"Wait! What kind of Muslim are you?" he stammered. "You're not going to watch the beheading? It's how we kill the infidels in Islam, it is the preferred way! Stay, brother! It will make your faith strong!" he cried with excitement. But I was already rushing for the door.

"I'm in a hurry, some other time!" I shouted over my shoulder. "My father's waiting for me outside," I said. The guy emerged from the crowd again and stood by my side staring at me.

"Actually, if I remember correctly we have front row seats for next Friday's hand-chopping ceremony at Charing Cross." I had no idea how I came up with this excuse.

"On Friday, actually they do hangings after the Jumma prayers," he said smugly, as though he had a box seat for all the hot events on the Sharia calendar.

"Where have you been living?" He stroked his properly bearded chin and looked me over from head to toe, as if considering what to do with me next.

"Yeah, well, I've been away for a while. On business. It'll take a few days to get used to the system again." Rolling my suitcase out the door I continued scanning the crowd for a placard with my name on it. The light was dimming, the sky turning purple at the horizon. I almost lost my balance when my eyes caught sight of a whole bunch of camels hobbled in the taxi stand. I gaped at a passerby.

"Do you see what I see over there?" I said, pointing towards the camels.

"Yes. The taxi stand," he said, giving me a curious glance. As if it was obvious.

"That's not what I meant. I mean, do you see what's inside the taxi stand?" I said.

"Taxis," he said. He looked at me like I was from another planet and then, shaking his head, he walked away.

It was only when I got closer to the camels that I realized they really were taxicabs. Yellow cabs of Lahore! Each cab was fitted with the replica of a legless camel on its top.

As I tried to figure out the practical use of this contraption, I was surrounded by a dozen or so people of various ages each trying to snatch my suitcase. One kid had his hands on my backpack, aggressively yanking on the strap to dislodge it from my shoulder. Tightening my grip on the handlebar of my suitcase, I shouted.

"Hey, hey—get away! All of you," I yelled, realizing they were all either cab drivers or worked for one. "I don't need any damn taxi; I've got my own driver!"

"What's going on here?" I heard a loud voice bark over my shoulder. A tall lanky man wearing a Kalashnikov over his shoulder approached. The guys jostling for my suitcase melted into the crowd and I held my breath.

Before I could say anything, the armed man hoisted my suitcase and dislodged my backpack. The suitcase hung in his hand like a child's toy. The backpack was slung over his shoulder; the shoulder that wasn't sporting a high powered military grade weapon.

"Are you Wali?"

"I'm Sher Khan. You're coming with me."

"But I'm waiting for Wali," I insisted, growing increasingly more uncomfortable by the minute.

As if he hadn't heard me, the fellow started to walk away, taking my luggage with him.

"Jesus Christ!" All I could do was follow. "This must be some mistake, Sher Khan," I insisted without effect.

Someone shouted at my back. "He's a Christian."

Shit! I quickened my pace, berating myself for having uttered something out of habit.

Not looking back, Sher Khan entered the taxi stand. Keeping at about five feet from him I followed him. He approached a taxicab and pulled a latch located on the camel's belly. The camel hump swung skyward, revealing a luggage compartment. He threw my suitcase into the camel's belly, brought the hump down, and secured it with a sharp click.

"Amreeki babu," he said, opening the door of his cab for me like a spider inviting a fat fly into its web.

"Alhamdolillah, someone is picking me up. You should have told me."

His face loosened upon hearing the magical words of Arabic.

"Babu, only Sher Khan can guarantee full security of his passengers. I swear by Allah, I'll kill the bastard who dares mess with you." He rubbed his hand down the length of his Kalashnikov like it was a favorite hunting dog.

"Jazakallah! I'm very, very grateful for your kindness, Sher Khan. I would love to have you as my driver one day. Inshallah! But tonight, someone else is supposed to be picking me up. Can I have my suitcase back, please?"

"Once the suitcase has been loaded, it doesn't come out until the destination comes," the man said, gazing toward the sky.

"Look, I'll give you some money for the hard work you've already done carrying my stuff to your taxi—Inshallah! Once again, please take my suitcase out of the trunk and give it back." My patience was getting shorter by the minute.

"Have you got dollars?" he chirped, his eyes lighting up, and I suddenly realized how much taller he was than I.

"I'll give you one thousand Dirhams," I said, realizing that I didn't really know the value of the currency here. But I did know that I'd been stripped of thirty-five thousand Dirhams out of the ninety-nine I'd in my possession at the time of landing.

"Babu, you've come from Amreeka, but you behave as if you're from Afghanistan."

"How much do you want?" I stammered, glancing around.

"How much you're carrying?" He took a step toward me. I looked for help. I didn't want to lose my entire cash. To my amazement, a sizable crowd had gathered around the taxicab-stand—at least twenty or thirty people were standing about twenty feet from us. They'd all been keenly watching my exchange with Sher Khan. I waved at them.

Inside I felt ashamed for being too quick to offer him the money for my kidnapped luggage. That was nothing short of an admission of weakness. Weakness, I knew, didn't play well in these parts; not back in my day, and sure as hell not now.

Sher Khan was now standing next to me, rubbing his palms. Feeling helpless I slid my hand in my pocket and looked toward the crowd. And there he was! Holding the placard with my name on it, Wali had just joined the crowd. Ignoring Sher Khan, I broke into a sprint towards Wali.

"Wali! Wali," I shouted.

The man clearly stood out from the crowd. Wearing an orange-colored jellaba that almost glowed in the dim light of dusk, he raised his arm and waved in my direction.

"Sir Ismaeel ji, what are doing here in the taxi stand?" he asked. He was maybe in his late fifties, his back a little hunched, his bony shoulders drooping. He also sounded annoyed.

"I'll explain. First thing: that man took my suitcase," I said, pointing towards Sher Khan's taxicab.

"And you let him? Sir ji!" He threw the placard on the ground and approached Sher Khan, his shimmering robe flowing gracefully around his lean frame.

I was sure that robe was meant to glow in the dark. Wali stood next to Sher Khan, his right arm on Sher Khan's shoulder. From where I stood, it looked like they were negotiating some sort of deal. Sher Khan looked down at the ground, rubbing his temple from time to time. Then it was over.

Sher Khan nodded once then went to his cab, dragged my suitcase out of the metallic camel's hump and angrily slammed it shut. He ambled over to where I was standing and dumped my suitcase on the ground in front of me. Then he disappeared into the knot of bystanders.

Wali hauled my suitcase to his car, a shabby light green Corolla, which was parked not too far from the taxi stand. It was hard to believe that Abba, who always loved cars, would be driving this piece of junk.

Wali placed my suitcase in the camel's hump and opened the rear door for me.

"Welcome to Lahore, sir ji."

"Thank you Wali. It feels so nice to be back in Lahore." It wasn't entirely an inaccurate statement. I had run away from Abba, not from Lahore, the city I loved for its energy, food, and parks.

The first thing I noticed as we pulled out of the airport was all the billboards plastered with pictures of men with wild unkempt beards.

"Sir ji, when was the last time you have been to Pakistan?" Wali asked, lighting up his *beeri*, a dried rolled leaf filled with tobacco flakes, the poor man's cigarette. We were on the Airport Road, heading towards Fortress Stadium.

"Twelve years," I said looking at the billboard where a handsome looking elderly man with a long salt and pepper beard stood tall, his arms folded across his chest. He was surrounded by four burqa-clad women, all with remarkably beautiful eyes.

"So many women available to one man!"

"It's not that there are so many women, it's because the men are in short supply."

"Why are men in short supply?"

"You'll soon find out," he said, cutting sharply to the right to avoid a big crater on the road.

Chapter 6
You Know Who

WE HAD STOPPED at the traffic light. Wali turned on the stereo and the bright jangling strains of a Bollywood musical filled the car. The car had a pair of powerful woofers in the back that rattled with the deep bass waves.

"Wali," I yelled so he could hear me. "I thought music wasn't allowed in Pakistan anymore, especially Indian music," I added, bringing my face closer to his ear so I wouldn't have to scream over the singer's high notes.

"Sir ji, pay attention to the lyrics. It's not what you think it is; it's a *naat*."

"What did you just say?" I said.

"It's a *naat*," he said, turning the volume down.

He was right. It was indeed a *naat*.

"Oh, so music is allowed as long as it's in praise of Muhammad," I said.

As soon as I uttered the name, Muhammad, Wali kissed the tips of his fingers and started mumbling a prayer, his face unreadable and his eyes shut. Then his face turned red and flecks of foam appeared on his lips. I stared in alarm, not sure what to do.

The traffic light turned green. Oblivious to his surroundings, Wali kept his eyes shut while his lips trembled. Cars behind us started honking. Without warning he threw open the door and leapt out into the street. He left the door hanging wide open and cars swerved to miss slamming into it.

Ignoring the cacophony of shrill honking, Wali knelt on the ground and went into prostration, *the sajda,* his forehead and nose on the dusty asphalt. I looked back through the rear window, my heart pounding. Cars behind us had started retreating in reverse. The traffic was moving again, leaving our parked vehicle behind. By the time Wali got up from the ground and sunk back into his seat beside me, the light had turned red again.

"What was all that about?"

Without saying a word, he opened his glove box and took out a round, palm-sized object. It was a clasped knife. He pressed its one end and an evil looking blade sprung out. I could tell it was razor sharp and the thing must have been as long as my forearm. I jerked back in my seat, eyes bugging wide open.

Wali turned toward me and grabbed a hold of my collar. His eyes bulged; two angry pools of black fire. Without a word he pressed the sharp cold steel against my sweating throat. I tried hard not to swallow.

"Wali, what's wrong?" I sputtered. "What's happened to you? Take it easy buddy, relax," I pleaded. The whole thing was way too freaky and had happened so fast I barely had time to register the shock.

"You have uttered the name of *You Know Who* without the salutations; and, and—this is a terrible crime that's punishable by death," he groaned, pressing the blade harder against my throat.

"Wali, come back to your senses man!" I barked. "What's wrong? Come on; let's get going, look, the light's green. Let's go, please. We can talk about this over a cup of tea in the Fortress Stadium. I can explain." I hoped to have sounded convincing and unfazed by his sudden outburst but, inside, I was tasting my first dose of real fear since I landed.

Sweat poured from my forehead as I recalled my father's words: 'You'll be safe with Wali. He's the only one I trust who can deliver you safely to my house.'" I also recalled his warning me not to speak with Wali about religion under any circumstances.

"I've beheaded four idiots like you," he bellowed. "I did it right here where you sit on your stupid butt; and you will be my fifth," he said. The traffic light had turned red again.

"Aren't you done then? I mean, four's a pretty decent number. Come on, Wali, be cool buddy," I said, hoping this nightmare would end soon. "My father's not going to like it if you kill me."

"Mufti Sahib says, if I can personally behead seven kafirs in total, my place will be assured in the highest Heaven," he said, his eyes glazed and his face flushed with exultation. He wasn't the same Wali who'd picked me a few minutes ago at the airport. He started looking crazier by the minute.

"It's been getting more and more difficult to encounter enemies of faith like you," he continued, not even looking at me in the eyes. "As far as your father is concerned, he'd be glad to see you killed after what you've done. He wouldn't even attend your funeral."

"Wali—please! Have mercy. I'll do anything you say. Remember that old hag?" I said, suddenly recalling something that might break his concentration.

"That old woman who used to throw trash on *You Know Who's* head every time he'd pass by her house."

Without a word Wali withdrew the knife from my neck and laid it in his lap though he continued to hold his face close to mine and looked into my eyes. The terrifying fury that seconds before distorted his face had melted like ice.

"So you know the story?" he asked, his voice normal and composed. "Then you damn well know that the story of the hag cost me the seventh Heaven!" he roared with renewed fury.

"Fifth, Wali, fifth," I corrected him.

"You gotta get to fifth before getting to the seventh." Wali picked up the knife and I stiffened for a renewed assault, but he just shook his head, snapped the blade shut and tossed the thing into the glove box.

"On what level do you start getting the virgins?" I inquired, trying to move the conversation in another, hopefully less inflammatory, direction. I was actually genuinely interested. After all it was a matter that concerned Paradise. And my hard-to-control lust.

"I've got to ask Mufti Sahib about this," he said, lost in thought. "But I suspect you start getting them right after you drink the sweet water of Hoz e Kauser, directly from the hand of *You Know Who*," he replied, nodding with satisfaction.

Ever since I'd been a child I wanted to see Hoz e Kauser—a pond filled with sweet water at the gates of Paradise—just to see what it looked like. It was even mentioned in the Quran.

"I heard Mufti Sahib say the virgins come flying towards you when you have drunk enough water and your thirst is quenched," he explained as though sharing a treasured memory.

"Can we start driving please?" I said, fixing my collar, feeling satisfied at my performance. I had successfully handled fear. My handlers should be pleased with me. For some odd reason Faisal Town seemed worlds away. "Do you remember where we're heading—in this world I mean?"

"Fortress Stadium, of course. Sir ji, you'll have to fulfill your promise. A true believer never breaks his promise, even when it's about as small a thing as a cup of tea. In fact, I was thinking of stopping at the stadium myself and having a cup of tea."

The signal turned green. It seemed we'd been standing for all eternity. Something was still terribly wrong with my perception of time. Good thing I had the watch.

"Maybe you can help me buy a nice present for Abba," I suggested. "I left in such a hurry; I didn't have time to bring him anything from the U.S. Now I feel terrible. I'm seeing him after such a long time; I have to give him something special."

The night descended faster than I expected. The air was still pleasantly warm. I noticed with amusement that almost all cars had been fitted with fake camel bodies on the top. It was an odd spectacle but it had its use: an extra trunk.

"Wali, please don't be offended, but what made you do *sajda* after I mentioned *You Know Who*?"

"Sir ji," he began, shaking his head. "Your knowledge of Islam is so depressingly poor that a true Muslim will have no remorse or hesitation killing you on the spot after hearing such a stupid question."

I refrained from asking Wali for further clarification. The last thing I needed was another scary confrontation with this guy, one that would probably prove fatal for one of us. At the moment, I was the only likely candidate for extinction in the car.

I couldn't believe my father would actually send a man like Wali to pick me up from the airport. Did he want me dead? Ever since I had boarded Khalifa Air almost nothing that had transpired made any sense whatsoever. And here I was: doing it again; trying to make rational sense of things.

By the time Wali pulled into the Fortress Stadium parking lot it was already dark. The shops, embedded into the circular wall of the stadium, were lit by gas lamps. Wali parked the car not too far from the main entrance of the stadium. I remembered the place well; it used to be a popular hangout with the college crowd, and for families to dine out and shop at some of the nicest boutiques of Lahore.

"Sir ji, remember this; it may save your life," Wali began. "If anyone utters the name of *You Know Who*, you should immediately close your eyes and quickly send a blessing. You should know what I'm talking about: I'm talking about *drood*, the blessing sent to all the prophets of the line of Hazrat Ibrahim *alaihis-salaam*."

"Yeah—I know that part," I said.

"But what you obviously don't know," Wali continued, lowering his voice and gripping my arm firmly, "Is that right after saying your *drood*, you do the *sajda* and recite the first Kalima thirty three times. Why?" he asked, pausing to study my face. When I didn't answer he continued.

"Because, it's the law. If you ever get caught ignoring this law, you will be killed on the spot. And remember: most people around here have only gotten to the third or fourth Heaven—they're stuck there, searching for ways to break into the higher Heavens.

"And since their fate for all eternity depends upon it, people won't hesitate for a second to behead you—that's how it goes here nowadays. You just remember that."

"Understood! Wali, you are a true friend," I said, patting him on the back, and wondering: what else did people around here do? Besides trying to ascend to the higher Heaven.

"Sir ji, I don't know why, but I like you," Wali said shaking his head as though I was a mystery beyond all comprehension.

"What could possibly be better than constantly thinking about the Next World—the real world? It's like being in a state of permanent worship."

"Excellent point, Wali," I said, nodding as though I completely understood. I didn't.

"I mean, do you really believe for one minute this world of ours is worth living for?" he asked. "Do you think any of the things of this world should hold any attraction for a believer? This world is a trap, sir ji. A trap!"

After several moments of awkward silence we finally got out of the car. An eerie sort of calm permeated the air, the kind that descends right before a monster storm breaks. I saw hordes of robed men with hairy faces entering the stadium through its massive gates. The stadium was lit by floodlights mounted on the poles that bathed the whole area in a weird sickly glow.

A stray dog ran past me; it looked like a beagle. It was being chased by a huge cat the size of a panther. The cat leapt in the air and landed on the dog, pinning it to the pavement. Then it proceeded to maul the poor dog in a flurry of claws. The dog howled as the cat sunk its teeth into its throat. The cat's powerful jaws gripped its victim, shaking it once, twice, until it was dead. The victor dragged the corpse of the dog away and was gone.

"A clear sign the Day of Judgment is upon us!" Wali exclaimed in triumph. He seemed to really enjoy watching me witness this most spectacular aspect of nature.

I'd landed in a very strange place. Something incomprehensible, something very bad, had happened to this country and its people. The whole place seemed to shimmer like a phantom in some parallel universe.

By now the crowds streaming into the stadium had swollen considerably.

"Night cricket, I guess?" I asked.

"Oh, much more thrilling than night cricket," Wali said, as we walked toward the entrance. "Let's grab a cup of tea and get into the stadium. I promise you'll have fun."

"Don't you think we should go to the house?" I asked, getting bad vibes. Very bad vibes. "I had a long flight and I'm pretty beat."

"No one is waiting for us at home. Your Abba ji is in Islamabad at the moment. He's not going to be in Lahore until Thursday."

"But I—" I tried to protest but he chopped the air with his hand and cut me off.

"Your Abba ji has instructed me to show you around, to get you fully oriented to this place in his absence," he declared in a voice that warned he would tolerate no further breaches of protocol.

I had no interest in watching a night game, or spending any more time with Wali, for that matter. Right now all I wanted was to get home as soon as possible, lounge in my bed, and think about what the hell I'd been sent here for.

"Can we first buy some gift for Abba?" I suggested, hoping to distract Wali from whatever festivities were about to get underway.

I knew there was no gift in the world that was going to send us running back into each other's arms, but I was hoping to at least begin the thaw. According to the note, I was to be contacted shortly after I arrived, though I had no idea what form contact might take.

"Your wish is my command, sir ji," Wali said, touching my arm and pointing toward the shops.

We passed a line of stores and headed toward the tea stall. I stopped to look at a sign on the sidewalk: *SALE!* It read in bright red letters the items on sale in the store were listed in proud detail:

Top of the line Martyr Vests! All sizes! We proudly sell only Mujahid brand. Accept no imitations! Remote Control Detonation 4-packs also on sale. Martyr Vests for Children. Graduation Gifts! Exploding Toys! And much more! Come inside and see!

Another sign by the store's entrance read: *Pellets for quick stoning. Stones with special grips. No Refunds after use.*

Every sign I read seemed more and more bizarre and I had the sinking feeling entering the shop would be the start of just as bizarre an adventure.

"This is a good place to find some nice gift for your Abba ji," Wali said, his voice dripping with excitement.

He'd been watching me closely as I read the list of merchandise. As I stood at the entrance of the shop utterly speechless, Wali slipped inside and made a beeline for the men's Martyr Vests. I saw him pick up one of the grotesque garments. He glanced back and forth at me and the vest, then held the thing up in my direction. What the hell? This must be a dream. Closing my eyes I shook my head from side to side, and wondered exactly what sort of gift Wali wanted me to present to my father.

Chapter 7
Mujahid Vests

I STOOD ROOTED TO THE SIDEWALK, unable to force myself to go inside. Who wouldn't be a little jittery around that kind of merchandise? Wali had disappeared from my view.

The area was now quite crowded. Outside the shop bearded men strolled along the sidewalk in flowing Arab-style robes and keffiyeh and agal on their heads. Trailing a few steps behind them were their women, completely concealed beneath black burqas. Women outnumbered men by ten to one. Some burqas didn't even have the slit for the eyes, only small fabric screens.

I made a mental note of the surreal, or rather drastic, changes in the culture I'd become immersed in since landing just a couple of hours ago. This was a brave new world of Islam, about which I hadn't had the slightest clue, and which seemed ready to blow itself up any minute. I wondered what exactly was this brand of Islam that was being practiced in this godforsaken place; where it came from and how.

Wali appeared in the shop's entrance and gestured for me to come inside. Before I could step one foot into the shop, I was knocked aside by a man and his wife and their three teenaged beardless sons. They streamed into the shop—the parents first, followed by the three boys, about a year or two apart in age. I fell into step behind the last boy and entered the shop.

Lit by gas lamps, the shop was tiny and densely crammed with items stacked in the aisles up to the ceiling. Martyr Vests of all sizes and colors covered one wall and also hung from the ceiling on hangers.

The shelves overflowed with curious goods: stones, wicked looking scythes, swords with Arabic inscriptions, curved daggers with handles studded with jewels, tangled heaps of cheap-looking plastic tasbih rosaries, delicately carved glass perfume bottles, ammunition belts, plastic tubes, books on Islam, incense, bolts, nails, nuts, and copper hooks all lying around in no visible order. It looked like the prop department of a very bad movie.

The owner was a large man about seventy with tiny silver wire-frame glasses perched on the end of his nose. He sat on a three feet high wooden ledge, the size of a queen size bed, amidst a pile of vests. Stacks of colorful prayer mats and rugs decked the periphery of the ledge. His face was a mask of concentration as he absently combed his fingers through his henna-dyed beard that trailed into his lap. He looked like some wild mountain warlord sitting in a teashop. I had to pull my eyes away from this colorful spectacle before he noticed me staring at him.

The man was sewing what looked like fist-length red colored explosive tubes into the lining of one of the vests. Next to him was a long glass counter with an old-fashioned cash register. Behind the counter stood a boy of ten or twelve who was sorting boxes of ammunition and eyeing newly arrived customers.

Between me, Wali, the family of five, the proprietor and his shop-boy, the place felt uncomfortably crammed with people. Wali had made a place for himself at the far end of the counter by shoving a pile of vests out of his way. I squeezed between him and the tallest boy of the family.

Wali pointed toward something behind the shop-boy's head. It looked like some sort of rock—flat on the bottom, roundish on top, dark rust in color. It had sharp spines on top and looked like a cross between a porcupine and a soccer ball. The shop-boy took it from the shelf, using both hands, his face strained as if in pain.

Keeping the rock held aloft, the boy leaned over the counter as Wali took the thing from him and weighed it in his hand. Without warning he shoved the rock into my hands. I gasped and almost dropped it on my foot. It must have weighed at least twenty pounds.

"A perfect gift for your Abba ji," Wali announced proudly.

"What's this supposed to be?" I asked, staring at him.

"Sir ji, it's from Maidan e Arafat, the place where every soul will rise one day. It's an imported item. The finest quality!"

"So?"

"Sir ji, I think this is a most excellent present for your father. Tell me if I'm wrong: but what better present can there be than this rock for doing your *wudu* every day? It must have been around there for thousands of years."

The *wudu* or ablution with water before each of the five daily ritual prayers, or *namaaz,* was an integral part of one's faith. But when water wasn't available a stone could be employed instead. In that instance one would touch the stone and then follow through the same motions as if doing ablution with water. This dry *wudu* was called *tayummum.*

"This precious stone was touched by the blessed air of Maidan e Arafat. It is from the place chosen by the Almighty; the very place where He will raise the dead when the horn is blown on the Day of Judgment," Wali explained.

"Oh, I understand!" I assured him. The last thing I wanted to do was to offend Wali again, or for that matter, anyone else in this shop.

Smell of danger floated on the air like incense; the unmistakable odor of ammonium nitrate, used in explosive devices, mixed with the stench of my own fear-laced sweat.

"But aren't rocks and stuff used only when there's no water available to do *wudu?* What's that called? *Tayummum,* right?"

It felt good displaying what little knowledge I had. I moved the rock around, shifting its prodigious weight in my hands. The spikes bit into my palms and hurt like hell, but somehow I managed to keep a cheerful mask of curiosity on my face.

Everyone turned around and stared as if I'd said something wildly inappropriate. Had I? I just couldn't tell in this place. I felt glaring eyes sweeping over me, judging my all-but-naked face with its pitiful little illegal beard.

"Sir ji has just landed from America," Wali announced, casting his eyes over the crowd. Sure, it was only eight people but it felt like an angry mob.

"Sir ji is looking to buy a special present for his Abba ji," he continued as though a satisfactory explanation might mean the difference between getting out of this place in one piece, and not.

"He forgot to buy something before he left America; so happy he was at the very thought of seeing his Abbi Ji after a long separation. Mashallah!" he concluded.

I wasn't sure if Wali was mocking me, or just trying to be helpful. One of the teenage boys, standing right next to me, had slipped on one of the Mujahid Vests. He'd chosen a slick black number crisscrossed with red stripes and green tubes tucked neatly into loops sown into the webbed lining. I wondered if they were filled with some homemade explosives.

The shop-boy placed a mirror on top of the counter and adjusted it so the boy could admire himself. He tried to turn around so he could check himself out from all sides, but he couldn't budge an inch. He was pressed up against me tightly, I was next to Wali, and Wali was still pinioned against the wooden ledge next to the counter. The boy's father nodded approvingly.

"Cool design," the kid said, nodding and all grins. Was this kid real?

Wali distracted me as he whispered, "Sir ji, no one uses water here for *wudu* anymore—not in Lahore. Not anywhere."

"What?" I said. "Why?" I whispered.

"Because there is no clean water available. The water out of the tap is all mixed up with sewer. It stinks."

"So how do people get by without clean water?" I said, whispering. "I mean, what do they use for drinking and cooking?"

"We use Paradise Water for that purpose," he replied. "And in the tapwater we put Pinky."

"Pinky?"

"Gentian Violet, sir ji. It kills the germs and some of the smell, but it still doesn't make it drinkable."

My head reeled with the implications. I remembered the huge bottle filled with clear water hanging from the ceiling at the airport labeled Paradise Water: *Your only reliable source of clean water, Khalifa Inc.* Then I noticed something else in the air; something distinct from the smell of ammonium nitrate wafting off the Mujahid vests and permeating the shop; something ominous. I was brought back to my senses by a female voice.

"Let's try another size," the boy's mother said to the henna-haired proprietor. "Show us some nice ones. This one is a bit tight around the chest—and look at the fabric, it feels so cheap. Surely you can do better," she said as though she'd just suffered an unforgivable insult.

"And I want a better price. This is too much for such shoddy workmanship."

The old man grabbed a cane that was fitted with a copper hook at one end. Without bothering to stand up, he raised his cane over his head and started sorting through dozens of vests that dangled from the ceiling. His hook grabbed a hanger with the desired vest.

Then he released the hook and carefully eased the vest down the length of the cane a few inches at a time. It was quite an elaborate procedure, one obviously developed with great care over many years. I didn't dare to breathe until that vest was safely cradled in his lap.

"Baji ji, we also make videos, for a nominal fee of course, in the next shop. You get a discount if you buy a vest from us.

"Just imagine your son opening his eyes by the exalted pond, Hoz e Kauser, filled with sweet water of Jannah. How blessed he is to be given the water by the seal of the prophethood, Muhammad, peace be upon him, himself."

All movement came to a sudden halt. Only the white hot flame of the gas-lamp hissed on unaware in the ominous silence. The rock held in my hand slid a notch down along my belly. Everyone closed their eyes and started moving their lips with ferocious speed.

I closed my eyes, but kept one eye slightly open to see what was happening. The shop-boy was the first to go into sajda. He disappeared behind the counter. I was shoved back by Wali who was trying to make room for himself to do his prostration. The henna-bearded proprietor bent all the way down while still sitting on the ledge. His forehead rested on the tubes of explosives he'd been sewing into the vest.

The couple, both heavyset, managed somehow to maneuver themselves into a kneeling position. The two younger boys had already hit the floor; one piling on top of the other as their foreheads struggled to touch the cement floor. The whole thing almost looked choreographed.

The boy with the vest remained standing; his too small vest still zipped up and strapped in place. He shoved me out of his way as he scrambled toward the ground. The shove was hard and I barely managed to avoid crashing on top of Wali's spine—thanks to the weight of the rock pressed against my stomach. I looked around, desperate to find a place to get rid of the rock.

The counter-top had no space; besides, it was glass and would never hold the weight of the rock without shattering. The holy rock from Maidan e Arafat suddenly grew heavier manifold and I had to bend backward to counter it. I froze in panic when I looked down.

To my horror, the detonation loop on the boy's vest had gotten hung up on one of spikes of the sacred rock in my hands. The boy, in his desperation to find a place to rest his forehead, and without having the slightest idea what he was doing, kept tugging on the loop.

Clearly I was holding him back from doing his *sajda*. I thought of dropping the rock, but it would have landed on the boy's back, fracturing his spine. Smoke rose from the vest and a pungent odor filled my nose. I shut my eyes and prepared for extinction. My mind sank into an image of space, a black, vast, cosmic wilderness.

But the blast, and the cosmic wilderness, didn't arrive. I opened my eyes. Everyone was still down on their knees. A thin ribbon of blue smoke rose from the vest close to the boy's armpit. The ninety-nine seconds, provided each recitation of the first kalima took three seconds, seemed to have lasted an eternity.

My fingers, white-knuckled and locked onto the heavy stone like a death grip, cramped violently. Then everyone jumped up, patted their clothes and coughed as the acrid smoke clogged their throats.

Before I got a chance to put the rock away, vest-boy's father slammed my head down on the counter next to the mirror. The man dragged a monstrous dagger from somewhere inside his black robe and rammed it against my throat. This was getting old fast.

Following their dad's cue, the three boys drew their own knives and pressed them to my throat. In the mirror I could see four furious sets of eyes and teeth glowering at me.

From under a pile of vests, the shop-owner pulled out his own blade that was about the size of a bayonet and stuck it in my face, while the shop-boy fumbled with a Swiss Army knife. I longed to let go of the rock but it would have smashed my toes, so I held onto it.

"This kind of auspicious opportunity doesn't arise every day," the dad growled, locking his eyes with mine, his nose flaring. I almost thought he was going to start hyperventilating. "As soon as I knew he had come from America," the father continued, grinning with twisted rage-filled delight. "I knew he'd have no respect for our religion. I think I'll let Saad, my youngest son, enjoy the honor of killing you," he said, dragging his dagger away from my neck and nicking the flesh. I didn't know what these people would do if they actually smelled fresh blood. I was terrified.

There was a sudden flurry of activity behind the father. The woman, his wife, had unveiled her eyes and was shoving her sons out of the way. In her hand she clutched a huge butcher knife, the *toka*. Pushing her husband out of the way as well, she advanced towards me.

Suddenly I realized the immense benefit of death by explosives. Hopefully it was pretty painless. In a matter of seconds you'd cross over to the other side. I regretted not having a Mujahid vest of my own under my robe. I'd have gladly taken every slathering asshole in this shop with me straight to Heaven, or even to Hell for that matter, as long as they'd be going with me. It'd be a stupid waste for my life to end here and now getting slaughtered by people I'd always thought of as nothing more than angry villagers.

"Now everyone, hold your horses, take a deep breath and listen to me," Wali shouted from behind me. "It's a fine thing to desire Paradise above all else, but you are just too eager to get there. You have all failed to notice that sir ji, Ismaeel, couldn't even find a place to do his *sajda*. Sir ji kept looking for a space for himself."

"Yes! Alhamdolillah! Wali is absolutely right. I was looking for a clear space," I said. "Also, what is that weird smell, and where's all that smoke coming from?"

"This smell is common in places where explosives are stored," henna-beard replied with an impatient flick of his hand. But at least he took his knife from my throat and laid the wicked-looking blade down on the counter.

"No, it's more than just that," I said, trying to muster some courage from somewhere. "Look what happened," I hissed, raising the sacred-rock with great effort and holding it under the medley of knives still rammed against my throat. The loop of the small-sized Martyr Vest was still hooked on the spike. They all stared at the rock, eyes wide and their mouths gaping.

"Corruption has eaten like a worm into the very bones of this nation," Wali moaned. He seemed genuinely disappointed. "They can't even sell a properly working vest. Mujahid Brand indeed!" The knives were lifted off of my neck and then disappeared. Only the woman kept her hand gripped on her blade and lunged like a tigress towards the shop-owner to slide her huge knife across his throat. The man glared at the woman but didn't flinch. I had the uncanny feeling that henna-beard could have taken this woman down any time he wanted.

"So you sell second rate merchandize in this store? Mujahid Brand I doubt it. It's good we found out before we laid down our hard-earned money. We'll be back," she roared in indignation.

"All these vests are fake Mujahid Brand. I could already tell that from the quality of fabric," the woman growled, pulling the vest off her son and shoving it into henna-beard's hands.

"Thieves!" she continued with a shriek. "May Allah roast you in Hell's fire! My son would have been humiliated with a misfire like this. What's your name?" she screamed, pressing the *toka* deeper into the man's neck.

"Bibi ji, I'm sorry. Sister. I think maybe the vest got left out in the rain and ruined by water."

"I'm asking your name," she roared through clenched teeth.

"Muhammad Sadiq."

As soon as I heard the name Muhammad, I immediately lowered the rock down to the floor, closed my eyes, and plunged towards the ground. I was not going to miss my turn on the floor this time around. I said my kalima 33 times, as required by the law of the Caliphate. I counted them slowly and deliberately on my fingers.

When I stood up, I realized that no one had joined me on the floor. No one had attempted to prostrate. They all just stared at me like I was beyond all hope. Without saying another word, the patriarch of the party shook his head in disgust and the family headed for the door as they looked at me with palpable contempt. All disappeared from sight.

"How much for this beautiful sacred rock?" I asked, trying to dissipate a cloud of embarrassment. I'd done something incredibly stupid, that much I knew, but I just couldn't figure out exactly where I went wrong and how.

"Twenty five thousand Dirhams," the shop-boy said. "You want me to wrap it up for you, sir?"

"No, no, don't trouble yourself," I said, peeling off a stack of bills, and realizing that I was quickly running out of cash.

Once out of the shop, we took turns carrying the sacred rock to the car.

"Oh, Wali. What a narrow escape!"

"Death comes at the appointed time, sir ji—no point wasting time thinking about it." He opened the camel's hump and pushed my suitcase to one side. He then gently placed the rock into the boot like it was a sleeping infant and then clicked the hump shut. "Sir ji, you paid too much money for the gift—way too much."

"I had no choice, after what happened?"

"Sir ji, you don't go in *sajda* when you hear the name of a regular person whose name just happens to be Muhammad," Wali explained in a serene voice.

"What about now?" I said. "Right now you just mentioned that name. What should one do in this case?"

"That's a very good question, sir ji. I'll have to ask Mufti Sahib. Let's grab a cup of tea and watch a little bit of the game."

"Wali, I think we should push on," I whined. "I'm telling you I'm utterly exhausted."

"Sir ji, if we watch the game inside the stadium, you'll catch up on many important things going on in this country. What you must learn and understand very quickly. Otherwise, you'll remain confused, as well as in danger, for the rest of your trip. I'm under the order of your father to get you oriented and keep you safe."

"Wali, I need to think. I need to sit alone for just ten minutes and think in peace," I pleaded.

"Thinking will get you killed here real fast. This is a place of doing; a place of action, Sir ji. Life is all about action. Thinking kills action," Wali explained, his voice now that of a stern but kindly father or an elder brother.

Wali's words sounded shockingly familiar: *Do not attempt to overthink or make sense of matters from here on, for it may prevent you from choosing the right course of action at a crucial point in time. We'll be monitoring your progress closely once you land.* How the hell were Pir and company supposed to be monitoring my progress in this insanely bizarre place, where I was darn lucky to be still alive—thanks to the kid's counterfeit martyr vest that didn't fit properly.

"Tea is much better for you right now than thinking."

I really needed to sit down and gather myself. I needed to figure out what the hell was going on and how to navigate it all without getting my throat slit like an Eid goat. Why was all this happening to me? I knew at least part of the answer to that question. My father: he was the man to grab to unlock this whole damn mystery.

I opened my wallet and took out a 1000-Dirham note.

"I don't have change." I figured it was time to count my remaining funds. Having to pay twenty five thousand Dirhams for a piece of rock that almost got me killed was nothing but a huge rip-off. No wonder I was seething.

Wali strolled away, presumably in search of his precious tea, and I looked around for a bench where I could sit down but there weren't any. I supposed that must be haram too. The area had no electricity. There was no sound of generators either. The glow of the gas lamps imbued the air with stillness but it was far from peaceful and relaxing.

The stadium's interior, on the other hand, was aglow with floodlights mounted on huge poles. I sat down at the edge of the sidewalk. I was grateful for any place where I could rest my feet and think without the company of those who delighted in judging my right to continued existence at every turn.

Closing my eyes, I looked inward and tried assessing my bearings, which seemed to have gotten stuck in a maze with no outlets, a moth in the spider's web. I skimmed over the entire text of the Pir Pullsiraat's note from my memory. I was far from conquering anything that had been pointed out to me in that note. Never before in my life had I experienced fear like now, and I was overwhelmed with doubts. The ineffable mission I'd been tasked with seemed like a cruel joke. How was I even suitable for the task? I was resentful and I was angry—at myself for not thinking this whole thing through before I snapped the vial of polio vaccine. But for some odd reason I'd remained curious—a trait that would get me killed—as to what Pir and Chaacha Khidr were doing. Were they really monitoring me in this mess, and how? Suddenly a thought occurred to me: I was thinking too much, thus preventing myself from choosing the right course of action.

Oh Boy!

Chapter 8
Cricket

I SAT ALONG THE EDGE of the sidewalk waiting for Wali to return with our tea, feeling drained despite having had adequate rest and a sensuous massage in the Business Class of Khalifa Air. It was the jet lag and I was just dead tired, so I closed my eyes and rested my head on my knees. Memories I'd fought long and hard to banish from my mind streamed to the surface and I was too exhausted to resist.

Again I saw Sophie—technically now my mother because of a marriage that had lasted no more than a couple of days. She was strolling through a field of mauve flowers that bloomed each spring on the grassy slopes of the mountain not far from her home. Her long black skirt and red shawl with long knotted fringe fluttered in the wind as she walked.

In her delicate hands she carried a large trailing bundle of tiny purple blossoms, and a sprig of something green was tangled in the loose strands of dark golden hair that fell into her eyes. From where I sat on the slope, the guesthouse—where Abba and I, and his fourth wife Salma, were staying—seemed tiny where it lay nestled in the distant valley. With its little red tin roof, it looked like a matchbox toy waiting for a child.

For the last ten days, I'd hiked up here each morning to see my beautiful Sophie. It was an elevation of over a thousand feet above the guesthouse. Wind rustled through the tall, sweet-smelling grasses. Sophie was bathed in warm yellow light, her golden braids touching her pale cheeks. I remembered her full red lips, the taste of salt on her tongue. I cringed when I thought of her sleeping with my father, and wondered if anyone had ever heard from her again or if she was even alive.

Since those idyllic days of windswept fields filled with flowers and tall grasses, Kafiristan had been invaded by the Caliphate, and those beautiful slopes had run red with blood. The place was now called Nuristan. The irony of this ravaged land being called the Land of Light in these sad times was infuriating.

"Here is your tea sir ji—and your change," Wali said, jolting me from my reverie. He was already sitting next to me holding two steaming cups.

I shook my head to clear my thoughts and took the cup in my hands.

"That's exactly what I needed," I said, taking a sip even though it was too sweet and creamy for my taste. "You can keep the change."

"Never, sir ji. It's your money. And you're our guest." He shoved several 100 Dirham notes into my hand. I tucked the notes in my wallet without any further argument.

"Time for the game, sir ji," Wali said with a grin as he tapped my arm. "We don't want to miss the opening."

Reluctantly I got up and stretched my legs and yawned. The massive walls of the stadium loomed over the crowd as they streamed through one of its many gates. Holding our cups, we fell in line with the procession.

"How long are we going to stay?" I asked, trying to keep pace with Wali.

I knew that a typical cricket match could easily go on for hours and I was becoming more irritable by the minute. I knew what was coming. For me, irritability quickly passed into dangerous territory known as belligerence. I didn't want any of that while I was under Wali's questionable protection. How I longed for the comfort of my cabin aboard Khalifa Air.

"We'll stay only for one Over," he assured me. "It's a semifinal, sir ji—we must watch!"

"So what time do you think we'll get home to Faisal Town?" I asked, recalling that an Over comprises only six throws and shouldn't take more than fifteen minutes.

"Faisal Town?"

"Yes, Faisal Town," I replied, wondering if he was hard of hearing.

"There's no guarantee of anything in life. It may take an hour; it may take a day; it may take a week," Wali said. "Keep this in mind: we may never reach Faisal Town at all. Nothing ever happens without Allah's will." With his long strides and quick gait Wali was quickly getting ahead of me and I struggled to keep up.

"Don't we have to buy tickets?" I asked, wondering how much more damage this game was going to do to my wallet before I finally escaped from this damned stadium.

"We buy them on our way out," Wali said, holding his cup above his head and throwing himself into the wall of people.

I followed closely, not wanting to lose sight of him in this chaos. Trying to decode what he'd just said was a waste of time and I remained as clueless as ever.

Once inside the gate, we slowly pushed our way to the top of the stands. There were plenty of empty seats everywhere and loudspeakers blasted Arabic over the crowds. Almost everyone in our section wore a black headdress: a black turban or a black skullcap accompanying a long white robe. Curiously, some spectators wore helmets while others watched the field through their binoculars.

As far as I could remember, the Fortress Stadium had never been used for sporting events. Its grounds had been the home of the annual National Horse and Cattle Show, the Industrial Exhibition of Small Industries, and the Defense Day parades.

Wali hurried toward a row of empty seats and scrambled over the laps of a few angry spectators. All I could do was mumble a string of "sorry" as we pushed over the crowd. The teams were already out on the field and there were a lot more players than for any regular cricket match I'd ever seen. There must have been at least twenty or twenty five of them in the field at the moment. I took my seat beside Wali, looking at the two batsmen standing at the crease, both with bats resting on their shoulders.

Wali tapped my shoulder to get my attention. He was holding a six-inch long tube, the diameter of a flute, in his hand.

"What the hell is this?" I blurted. The tube was metallic and weighed half a kilo.

"*Doorbeen*, sir ji," Wali said. "Military grade telescope."

"What are the teams' names, and which side are we on?" Shutting one eye, slowly adjusting its focus, I pointed the high-quality spyglass at the field. The sight made me jump. Resemblance to any normal game of cricket pretty much stopped here. My flesh crawled as I focused on the bizarre scene down on the field, where each of the fielders was brandishing a long curved sword in one hand and a heavy, metal-banded shield in the other. The light from the overhead lamps splashed off the swords and threw the players into a "Danse Macabre" within an absolutely surreal scene.

"The semi-final is between the Karbala Cats and Wahab Squad," Wali shouted in my ear. "The winner will play the Badr Brigade."

For a moment, this whole thing felt like a dream. I looked at my hands, opening and closing my fists as I tried to push the fingers of one hand through the palm of the other. Nothing. No pain to wake me. This was no dream.

"Wahab Squad!" Wali boomed, stabbing the air with his fist. "Don't even think about supporting the kafirs of Karbala Cats when you're in a Wahab stand!"

I scanned our stand and spotted at least six men wearing Martyr Vests within a twenty-meter radius of where we sat.

"What's this game called, Wali?" I said, feeling my heartbeat quickening as I handed him back his spyglass.

"Cricket!" Wali exclaimed, his face beaming with pride.

"This can't be cricket!"

"Modified on the orders of Khalifa to reflect the principles our Khilafat is based on."

Unbelievable!

"Sir ji, our Khalifa ji has connections, you know, top floor," he said, winking and stabbing his index finger toward the sky. What can Allah have to do with cricket?

Khalifa, or the caliph, had been the absolute ruler of the country for the past eight years. He was a mysterious figure—had never been seen in public—and his spectacular rise to power had been attributed to his occult powers as much as to his campaign of terror, which he'd unleashed from his remote hideout in the Hindu Kush mountains in the north of Pakistan. He'd built his power on the model of Hasan Bin Sabbah, the legendary terror master of 11th century Persia, dispatching his highly trained assassins, *fedayeen*, to take out the country's key political and military figures. Rumor had it that he could talk to animals. He had been known for his fondness for cats.

"The tradition is, that one night Khalifa ji had a dream," Wali continued. "He was shown what the game of cricket should look like if it were to be according to the principles of Sharia. The next day, everything changed. Khalifa ji corrected the rules of the game and here we are," he explained with a broad sweep of his hand toward the field.

A handsome boy in his mid-teens squeezed through the crowd and approached us. Hanging from his neck on two cords was a tray stacked with *pappurs,* the spicy paper-thin crunchy tortillas. He was also wearing the ubiquitous Martyr Vest. The thing was torn in several places; loose threads dangled from the seams, greasy food stains covered the front, and a few of the explosive tubes were missing. A sight not conducive to eating.

He was lean-framed, a little over five feet tall, and stood right in front of me, one hand resting in the triggering-loop of his vest. Pulling on the loop from time to time, which made my hair stand on end, he just stared at me with his big bright eyes.

"No thank you," I muttered, keeping my eyes glued to his hand while my heart continued to pound.

"Get lost!" Wali said shooing him away. "Go sell your bhang *pappurs* somewhere else." As the boy wandered off he glanced back at me several times before being swallowed by the crowd. Bhang laced *pappurs* had always been a hot selling item during a cricket match in the good old Pakistan. I was glad to know that at least one tradition had persisted in the Caliphate.

"When one is at play, one must also be at worship. Do you understand, sir ji," Wali continued, his eyes narrowing as they bore into mine.

"That's brilliant," I said, not knowing what the hell else to say, but knowing by now it damn well better be in agreement. "And why are there so many fielders on the field, and what are those swords for in their hands?"

"The fielding is now done by the players of both teams at the same time, and—"

"That's impossible. How could both teams field at the same time?"

"Unlike the original western style game, suited only for sissies," he continued. "Now the fielders of both teams engage in a battle, real combat, as they compete for the ball. As they fight one another with their swords, the batsmen keep running between the wickets to earn swaab.

"Yes, sir ji, that's the major change Khalifa ji brought to the game," Wali said, beaming with pride at the accomplishment of his revered leader. "He replaced the system of runs with the system of earning swaab! Is that not brilliant?"

"Swaab!" Swaab or blessings were the points a believer earned by following the dicta of his faith. "What the hell does any of that have to do with cricket?"

Ignoring my question Wali pointed and I followed his finger with my eyes. There it was. The Swaab Board stood tall over the stands; the former scoreboard.

"How can players not get hurt when they battle for control of the ball?"

"Hurt sir ji? Hurt?" he roared, mocking me with a roll of his dark eyes. "It's an honor to die in the field, sir ji."

It took a moment to realize the game I was watching was a creative mixture of cricket and a gladiator arena of ancient Rome. The thought made me queasy.

"So they're real swords?" I asked.

"Sir ji, yes, ultimately, it's all just practice for the Final Battle, for the final victory."

"A Muslim killing a Muslim. That doesn't make a whole lot of sense to me."

"Sir ji, Khalifa ji says: whosoever dies in the practice battle will be given the exact same place in Paradise as those who die fighting real Jihad against the kafirs."

Taking a deep breath I asked: "How many players are on each side? At the start of the game, I mean?"

"Eleven at all times on each side. There are always about twenty replacements standing at the sidelines, ready and eager to jump in when one of their team is martyred."

"And how many die by the time the game ends, on average?"

"Three, four, sometimes as many as eight. I've even seen games with only one survivor. The others? Gone to Paradise!" Wali exclaimed, his eyes wide, his voice like that of an old storyteller recounting the early days of the community at Medina.

"How many Overs are there in a game?" My stomach had begun to churn. I shifted my weight in my seat and looked around. Two young men in their early twenties had just taken their seats next to me. By now, I wasn't surprised to see them wearing the martyr vests. Suddenly I was hit by a strong desire to eat bhang *pappurs*.

"Three Overs each—six Overs in total," Wali replied.

"Only three? The game must be over in a short time, then?"

"Sir ji, even in one Over, sometimes a team can earn as much as 100 swaab."

"Wali, can we go and sit somewhere else?" I said, eyeing the martyr-vests sitting next to me out of the corner of my eye.

"What happened sir ji?"

"Nothing!" I snapped nervously.

Sensing my anxiety, Wali chuckled.

"Don't pay too much attention to those vests boys wear around here. It's just a fashion statement to them. It makes them feel important."

"How do you know they're not real vests?" I asked, still not comfortable at all with their proximity.

"Actually, you don't." Wali pressed my arm. "Sir ji, just relax. Let's watch the game."

The wind had started to blow. For a fall evening in Lahore it was a bit chilly, but still pleasant. A bright sickle moon hung over the stadium in the dark sea of night and a star twinkled like a distant beacon guiding somebody somewhere. The sky brought me a feeling of reality. The spectacle was way too far out to be comprehended by someone who'd just landed in what was undoubtedly the most bizarre place in the whole universe.

The Karbala Cats' fast bowler started his run up and our side of the stadium roared in excitement. Halfway down his run, the man's robe filled with air and fluttered around his body like a parachute in the wind. The batsman, who wore no protective pads, missed the ball and it whizzed toward the wicketkeeper's hands like a bullet.

Wali stood up, blew a whistle, and then sat down again.

"Why do we buy tickets on the way out and not when we enter the stadium?" The question had been nagging me ever since Wali had mentioned it.

"Sir ji, why would anybody buy tickets going into a place, when he doesn't even know for sure if he'll ever get back out again?" Wali said without turning to look at me. His eyes were locked on the game and he didn't bother to elaborate.

I thought it best to keep my mouth shut as I tried to digest yet another new and harrowing piece of information.

"The vests you're seeing everywhere," Wali said, finally turning and looking at me. "They're good for cultivating courage. Khalifa ji says that courage is what we'll need in the end times—the times when everything blows up."

"How much do the tickets cost, Wali?" I asked. My hand unconsciously went into my pocket and searched for my wallet.

"One hundred Dirhams each," Wali said.

"Wali! I can't find my wallet!" I gasped in alarm. It took less than a second to realize that my cellphone was gone too.

"Not a leaf moves without His command," Wali said. "Him in whose hand is your life, which will also be taken from you one day."

"But this is serious! You've got to help me to find my wallet and cellphone," I cried, thinking of my passport. I checked to make sure the pouch was still on me under my robe and was relieved to find it remained hanging from its cord. "How the hell are we going to buy the tickets on our way out?"

"Relax, sir ji. We may not have to. Perhaps it was a sign," Wali said.

"Sign of what?" I demanded. A sign of death? I was more than a little irritated with this nonchalant attitude of his.

He said nothing but just sat staring at me. Then his face broke into a warm smile and he shook his head. I felt like punching him on his nose.

The *pappur*-boy wended his way back through the crowd and halted in front of the vest-wearing boys sitting next to me, a pleading look in his eyes. After some haggling, he succeeded in selling them some of his wares. The boy next to me, who had thick matted hair like a bird's nest, bought at least a dozen or so. He gobbled down most of them in a matter of minutes. I wished I had my wallet with me. I certainly didn't want to ask Wali for money for bhang *pappurs*. In truth, I really craved a spiked latte from Grasshopper.

The ball had been driven deep into the offside. The fielding pair ran along with the ball, the tips of their swords pointing toward the sky, their shields clutched tightly to their chests.

With a sudden surge of action, the two fielders locked swords and rammed into each other with their shields as they scrambled after the ball. The batsmen ran between the wickets. The rest of the players on the field started shouting *Allah hu Akbar*. The Swaab Board started to roll.

A roar spread through the stadium. The ball had come to a stop. The two fielders were locked in a ferocious battle, swords clashing and shields banging together as the melee continued. Both batsmen were dashing between the wickets while the two umpires stood erect and studied the fight through binoculars.

There was no question in my mind that this sword fight wasn't going to end well, and I wanted to get the hell out of here as soon as possible.

The kid next to me unfolded a piece of white cloth, kissed it, and then wrapped it carefully like a headband around his Afro-like hairdo. The cloth was inscribed with *shahadaa*, the first kalima, in black ink. The *pappur*-boy had again disappeared somewhere in the crowd. The whole thing was surreal, almost drug-like as time seemed to slow to an imperceptible crawl.

"Sir ji, we've earned 25 Swaabs!" Wali screamed. Tears ran down his face. And he was clearly swept away in some collective ecstatic euphoria. But my anger at him was growing.

"You're not paying attention, sir ji," he growled, his voice suddenly choked with rage. He was waving his arms in the air. His bright orange robe must be visible for miles.

Afro-kid with the white headband jumped up, straightened his vest and tightened its straps, and then sat down again. One of his companions pulled out a cell phone and started shooting a video of him munching his *pappur*. I pulled away to avoid getting caught on the video and yanked on Wali's sleeve to get his attention.

"Sir ji, you're missing all the best action. Come on, stand up here with me" he shouted down at me.

I did as instructed because it seemed the only way to escape being in that video.

"Wali, look! What are they doing?" I asked, jerking my thumb at the boys and their camera.

"He's having his friend make his farewell video. Let the kids play."

"What?" I yelled in disbelief.

"Sir ji, forget about them. Watch the fight; they're getting tired now—the real fun is about to begin," he shouted.

The pappur-boy materialized again out of the crowd. He stood next to Wali's chair, his tray now empty and his eyes glued to the boys shooting the video.

Ignoring Wali I looked at Afro-kid who was mumbling something in Arabic. The red light of the cellphone camera started blinking. And then something happened on the field and everybody gasped. The fighting pair had fallen to the ground, their robes splattered with red. A hush fell over the stadium, as the Wahab's fielder slowly raised himself off the ground, his sword held high in the air. The batsmen had stopped running. I looked at Wali. He stood motionless, his hands dangling at his sides. He'd stopped yelling his excited commentary at me and the team.

As soon as I looked back at the field I felt sick to my stomach. To my horror, the Wahab Squad's player had cut off the head of his opponent in one clean sweep of his sword. As he lifted the severed head above his head, his fist clenched over the victim's hair, our stand erupted in a roar.

"Sir ji, one down ten more to go!" Wali shouted at me amidst a deafening noise. "Not a single leaf moves without His command."

Then Afro-kid erupted next to me in a hysterical fit of giggles. I jerked away and almost fell on the ground.

The boy's friend, the one who'd taken the video, threw himself on the ground in front of me, also wracked by spasms of hysterical laughter. Soon they were both rolling around on the ground in a fit. The *pappur-* boy had drawn closer and was also laughing uncontrollably. I stood up to leave without Wali, but sat back down remembering I had no money to pay for my ticket at the exit gate.

As soon as the noise subsided a bit, someone shouted Allah Hu Akbar!

The shout came from nearby, flooding my mind with the no nonsense words of the pilot of Khalifa Air: *Duck without any shame or reservation when you hear, in a crowded place, a loud Allah Hu Akbar.*

I hit the ground next to Afro-kid, my mind reeling with the bloody images of the carnage I'd just witnessed.

Afro-kid stopped laughing like someone had flipped a switch; then he got up and jumped onto his seat.

"I've seen many like you!" the boy yelled in the direction of the shout. "I dare you! Let's just see who goes first?"

"Sir, I can tell you're not from here, but don't be afraid," a friendly voice whispered in my ear. "Why worry yourself when we know that death comes only at the appointed hour."

Shaking with fear I looked up and saw the cheerful face of the *pappur*-boy, his eyes peering at me with amusement. He was kneeling beside me with his hand on my back. I felt embarrassed getting a pep talk like this from a kid. Composing myself and wiping the sweat from my forehead I staggered to my feet, just as the headless corpse was being whisked away on a handheld stretcher by four black-robed men of the Karbala Cats. They were followed by two white-robed men supporting the shoulders of the injured combatant, who limped as he walked, the severed head swinging by his side

Afro-kid was still hurling insults at somebody in the back. The game resumed, and the stadium swelled once more with cheers, curses, and prayers shouted from the four corners of the field. I closed my eyes and wished I could just beam myself out of this hellhole. My trip so far had been nothing but an interminable nightmare of the highest order.

"Sir, the man shouting Allah Hu Akbar in the back is a big bluff. He's just trying to scare people. He does it all the time, at every game," the *pappur*-boy informed me.

"You sell bhang *pappurs* in a mad-house like this?" I stared at him.

"My *pappurs* save lives, sir. They make people happy; bhang calms people down and makes them forget."

"What's your name, dude?" I asked, admiring his cool attitude.

"Tarzan."

"That's an interesting name."

"Sir, there's going to be an explosion twenty feet from here in about ten minutes. Just so you know," he whispered in my ear.

"What! How the hell do you know a bomb's going to explode twenty feet from here, in ten minutes?" I was terrified at this new revelation.

"Because I was the one who planted it." He explained without a trace of guilt or worry on his young face.

"You just said, you were here to save lives and make people happy," I gasped, stealing a look at Wali. "Wali, can we get out of here?" I pleaded. Even in this open-air stadium I was feeling suffocated.

I looked at Tarzan, searching his face for answers and the admission that he was bluffing and just having some fun at my expense.

"Tarzan, my friend," I began nervously. "Where exactly is this bomb we're talking about, the one that's going off in ten minutes?"

"Eight," Tarzan said. "It's eight minutes now."

"Wali," I said turning to my companion and shaking his arm. "You gotta listen to me. We're getting out of here now!" I insisted. "Did you hear what I just said, Wali? Now!" I screamed.

"Sir, don't be afraid. It's just a shoe-bomb," Tarzan said.

"A shoe-bomb? What the hell is a shoe-bomb?"

"A bomb made of old shoes stuffed in a burlap sack."

"What!?"

"When it goes off, shoes come pouring down from the sky like rain."

"But it can physically hurt you, right?"

"It all depends where the shoe hits you and what speed it's traveling."

"Great!" I said, wondering what exactly was the purpose of a shoe-bomb.

"Why a shoe-bomb?" I sounded ridiculous.

"Sir, for a man, there's nothing more insulting than having a shoe land on your head," he explained as though I was a two-year-old.

"So you're a secret fan of Karbala Cats, eh?" I said, looking in Tarzan's eyes. "Planting shoe-bombs for them in a Wahabi stand."

"I plant my shoe-bombs on both sides, sir," Tarzan said, pointing at the stand across from us. "I do this everywhere," he explained, his dark eyes glistening with mirth. "After I blow this one, I'll go to the other side to finish off the day's work."

"Do you get paid to do this?" I said.

"Of course. From both sides. Sir, you can't eat two meals a day with one job. Everything here is so damned expensive."

Chapter 9
Emergency

I LOOKED UP AT WALI. Oblivious to his surroundings, he was standing on his seat absorbed in the game again. Afro-kid was jumping up and down on his chair along with everybody else. His head was flailing back and forth like a head-banger lost in his tunes. The shouts of Allah Hu Akbar had been replaced with a deafening wail of whistling and yelling.

I was convinced that surviving this blasted insane asylum of a game would be a matter of pure luck. Grudgingly, I took my seat. I grabbed the hem of Afro-kid's robe and gave it a couple of tugs.

"Sit down," I said, patting his seat. "Come on brother, sit down."

"Are you from America?" he said, looking down on me with big grin.

"If you sit down, I'll be happy to tell you where I'm from."

He dropped into his seat and offered me his hand. He was dark skinned, around twenty years old, and skinny as a twig. His hair was sticking out of his white headband like Medusa's snakes and he looked more than a little crazed.

"Pleasure to meet you!" I grabbed his hand and gave it a single shake.

"Yo, ma maan!" he cried, trying to sound like some urban home-boy and sort of succeeding.

He just sat there grinning at me and rocking from side to side. I looked around for Tarzan, but he'd disappeared.

Then it happened. My worst fear materialized. About twenty rows below us a huge fireball rose in the air and was followed by a deafening boom. A gust of hot wind hit my face and I ducked forward without thinking and tucked my head between my knees.

I heard screams all around me. When I finally looked up, I saw Afro-kid stretched out on the ground face down in front of me. Blood was pooling around his head on the concrete beneath my feet. Yet the game went on.

Below us, the site of the explosion was in chaos with people swarming over each other like ants as they scrambled to the aisles. The screaming became unbearable; overhead the loudspeakers blared louder, and the air reeked of gunpowder.

I reached over and grabbed Afro-kid's wrist in my trembling hand. He had a pulse. He was bleeding from an ugly gash over his right brow, but he was alive. His friend was nowhere to be found. I peeled off the kid's white headband and reapplied it over his laceration as tightly as I could. Next I got the accursed vest off him and shoved it out of the way. I had no way of knowing if it was real or just a 'fashion statement' as Wali described.

"Wali," I shouted. "Enough of the damn game. I'll see you at the car."

Hoisting Afro-kid's limp body over my right shoulder, I made my way down the stands and hurried toward the gate. Before I could reach the exit, a blast ripped through the air behind me. I kept walking without looking back. A smoking shoe hit the pavement about four feet in front of me. It was a military boot, its sole filled with holes.

"Sir ji, wait." Wali's voice bellowed over my shoulder. "The game was just beginning to heat up."

I turned around and stared at him. He was out of breath from chasing me through the stands and I was intensely relieved to hear his voice.

"Wali, I hope you have money to buy the tickets. I'll pay you back the whole amount. If we ever get to Faisal Town."

"I've got some money, but it might not be enough for all three of us."

As we stepped up to the ticket booth, another explosion rocked the stadium.

"Looks like the VIP stand, sir ji. Look over there." He pointed toward the far pavilion. A bluish gray cloud of smoke hung over the crowd.

"How many?" the ticket man demanded from inside a booth.

"Two," Wali said.

"And the one on his shoulder?" the man asked, shooting me with curious look.

"This one has crossed over," Wali said. "Alhamdolillah!" he added, sliding his hand across his throat.

"Yes. He's dead." I was pleased with Wali's quick thinking. I was never any good at lying.

The ticket agent gave me a piercing look. Then he shot up from his seat and marched out of his booth. Standing beside me he put his hand on the side of Afro-boy's neck. Shaking his head he went back into his booth.

"Two hundred and fifty Dirhams," he said, holding out his hand.

Without saying a word, Wali counted out the stack of bills and we made it out of the stadium without any further mishaps.

"Sir ji, if you had kept quiet, we wouldn't have had to pay the extra fifty."

"Why fifty for him? And not one hundred?"

"The injured pay half the price."

"Great! So they don't charge for the dead."

"He got suspicious when you chimed in," Wali said.

This game had shattered all my previous understanding of Pakistan, now an Islamic Caliphate. It was a terrifying place, to put it mildly. But what mystified me the most was the palpable, absolute fearlessness that pervaded the air. People had developed a complete disconnect with the fear of dying, not just in the stadium, but everywhere. They had embraced death as a way of life. I was shocked beyond belief when I saw that life outside the stadium was flowing along, business-as-usual.

"Wali, we have to take this guy to the nearest hospital." It seemed like the only right course of action to take. Where the hell was Pir Pullsiraat? When was he going to show up, if ever, and pull me out of this nightmare? Help!

Wali didn't say a word as we walked to the car. My shoulder ached under the weight of Afro-kid and I needed to set him down, soon.

"Sir ji, we should have left him behind in the hands of Allah," Wali said.

"Shut the fuck up!" I screamed at him. I was sick of all this shit; that freaky game, lunatics wearing martyr-vests like they were the latest Paris fashions and most of all, I was sick to death of this asshole Wali. I was furious at myself to be in this impossibly insane place. Was I really on some path to High Knowledge? Or was I just plain high? Spreading its tentacles, a deepening doubt grabbed my brain. Whatever happened to my mysterious mission, details of which were supposed to be revealed to me at the proper time? So far I'd been a rousing example of failure. And now I'd have to deal with this complete loser until we got home.

"You're taking me to the nearest hospital," I roared. "You got that?" I yelled, slapping Wali's back with the back of my fingers.

"Sir ji, who told you to pick him up in the first place?"

"Allah!"

"That tells me that you really don't trust Him, sir ji."

"Are you crazy?" I was gritting my teeth. "How can you say that?" It was impossible to explain anything to him.

"Because you didn't trust Him enough to take care of this boy without any interference from you," Wali said, taking long, hurried strides toward the car.

"He needs stitches, and a CT scan of his head," I stopped next to the car. My throat was parched and felt like sandpaper and I was horribly dehydrated.

"Wali, can you just get me some water?" I asked feeling the weight of Afro-boy on my shoulder. I couldn't wait to put him down.

"Water's hard to get these days, sir ji, as I explained already." He opened the rear door of the car.

I laid Afro-boy on the rear seat and shut the door.

"You mean you can't even get bottled water?" I said.

"Oh, the Paradise Water is in short supply as well, because the demand is so high, sir ji," Wali said.

"What about some sodas, cola, whatever. Right now almost anything will do."

"Sir ji, we've only got one kind of cola, Hoor Afza. It's nothing like Rooh Afza we used to get in the old days, but it does have its own unique flavor and effect."

"Would you please get me one? And please keep a tab on the money you're spending. I'll ask Abba to pay you back everything once we get home." Having to ask for money from this asshole must be a test of some kind. I was seething inside.

"Sir, ji, money is just a piece of paper. Don't worry about it," Wali said, shaking his head. "Although I wouldn't waste my money on a bottle of Hoor Afza. I always carry water with me in the car," Wali said. "You can have some from my bottle."

He opened the rear trunk revealing a pair of gas-cylinders lying side-by-side. They took up most of the trunk except for a foot-wide space in the middle. They'd begun to rust over and looked really old. One of the tanks had *Allah* painted along its side in red, and the other had the word *Akbar* in yellow. Wali stuck his hand between the tanks and pulled out a bottle half filled with water. The label read *Paradise Water, Khalifa Inc.*

"Big tanks you've got in there, Wali?" I asked, taking a swig from the bottle. The sight of these massive tanks had my anger dissipated like mist at sunrise. The water had a strange metallic taste and smelled of diesel.

"Yes, you're looking at a pair of custom-made martyr-tanks, sir ji," Wali said, beaming with pride. "Those silly vests are for the kids who wear them just to show off."

"Martyr-tanks?" The feeling of alarm returned as I took another swig from the bottle.

"Relax sir ji. They're just CNG tanks," he said, staring at me amusingly.

"Oh, compressed natural gas," I said, exhaling a sigh of relief. CNG had been used as a car fuel for ages in this part of world.

"Sir ji, there's a two-month waiting period to have your car fitted with these rockets to heaven."

"Rockets to heaven?" I asked. Clearly I'd missed something.

"I'll show you. Come," he said excitedly as he opened the driver's door and pointed.

"See these two buttons?" he asked, touching two red buttons located next to the headlight knob. One was inscribed with *Allah* and the other with *Akbar*.

"Press these two together at the same time and you're gone, sir ji." He snapped his fingers. "Vaporized! The West may be advanced in technology—but we know the secret of a direct flight to man's eternal dream, Paradise."

"A two-month waiting period!" In a flash I realized the logic of having an additional trunk on each car's roof. They needed the trunk for the CNG tanks, and a two-month waiting period meant that most of them were fitted with martyr-tanks.

"Sir ji, the man who designed these special modifications is a superb mechanic," Wali explained with great admiration.

"You can be one hundred percent sure that if you hit a pothole or bump into another car, or even get into a serious accident, the device won't blow," he assured me. "You must press both buttons together for five seconds to get the desired effect and begin your journey to Al-Jannah."

"Great security feature, for sure but you can explain the rest while we drive? We gotta move. The guy's going to die if we don't get him to the hospital soon."

I took my seat in the rear next to Afro-boy who was mumbling something, his head pressed against the window, and his knees rammed up against the back of front seat. Wali started the engine.

"Don't worry, we're taking you to the hospital," I said, placing my hand on his shoulder.

Wali gave me a glaring look, and I had no choice but to stare back. Obviously, he wasn't pleased at the prospect of having to take a detour just to help a stranger. As he put the car in gear I spotted Tarzan sprinting out of the stadium's gate, a burlap sack bouncing up and down on his shoulder. He halted for a second and looked around, as if deciding which direction to take off.

"Tarzan!" I yelled, getting out of the car and waving at him. I wasn't sure if he'd seen us.

As soon as he spotted me, he started running toward the car. Two other men in white robes were chasing him. Tarzan darted across the tarmac like a gazelle. Transfixed, I stepped away from the open car door. He tossed the sack into the back seat then jumped in the front seat next to Wali. I climbed back in next to Afro-boy and pulled the door shut.

"Wali, let's go." I shouted. "Come on. Go, go, go!"

Wali grabbed his head with his hands for a moment, and then we were speeding down the road out of the stadium. I looked out the rear window and saw the white-robed guys piling into a blue pickup truck.

"Sir ji, if you keep picking up whoever crosses your path, we'll never get to Faisal Town."

"How far is the nearest hospital?"

"Sir, the nearest one is KUH." Tarzan said, as Wali turned onto the main road. There was a bridge about a half-mile up ahead.

"Khidamat-e-Ummah Hospital, sir ji," Wali said.

"It used be Services Hospital, sir," Tarzan replied.

"Why are we going that far?" I asked. "What about all the private hospitals around Fortress Stadium?"

"Sir ji, they've all been shut down," Wali replied.

"Why?"

"Because there are no doctors to run them. They've all left," Tarzan replied.

"Where'd they go?"

"Some ran away to foreign countries," Tarzan replied bitterly. "And some—"

"Went to next world," Wali interjected.

"Sir, you can drop me once we're out of here" Tarzan said. He was trying to look relaxed, but his eyes kept darting back and forth between the mumbling Afro-boy, and the rearview mirror.

Chapter 10
Tarzan

THE TRAFFIC ON THE ROAD was light when we left the stadium. But like a bad case of acne, it was pocked with craters of all sizes and shapes. Wali drove expertly, cutting a sharp turn every few seconds to avoid the holes from ripping the undercarriage of the car. It was hard to sit still. I got thrashed around in the back seat with my head slamming against the roof every time Wali jerked the wheel. Viewed from the Mian Mir Bridge, the city of Lahore was steeped in murky darkness.

We passed a rickshaw with a CNG tank the size of an oil barrel bolted to its back bumper. I noticed Wali veered to the right, giving the rickshaw a wide berth. We were heading down the bridge when Wali glanced in the rear view mirror and cursed under his breath.

"We're being followed," he muttered.

I looked back and saw a pair of headlights tailgating us. By the time we came down the bridge, the blue Mazda pickup was right next to us on Wali's side of the car. The guy on the passenger side rolled his window down and started thrashing his arm up and down, yelling at us to pull over.

"Tarzan, who are these guys?" I demanded, my heartbeat speeding up. "What do they want?"

Before Tarzan could speak, Wali started yelling as he bore down on the wheel and floored the engine. The car kept ahead of the pickup truck.

"I told you sir ji," he bellowed, his face red with anger. "You don't just pick up people you don't know!"

"Everything happens because Allah wills it to happen, remember?" I said, bristling with pride when I saw him glaring at me in the rear view mirror. He opened his mouth to let me have it but then decided not to. I was quickly picking up the lingo and how to counter Wali's infuriating flood of religious mantras. I wasn't sure if I'd won this round, or if he'd just rip me a new rectum once we got home, or worse yet, report the whole incident to his master, my father.

Tarzan's eyes darted back and forth at the pickup while he dug around in his burlap sack. I grudgingly admired Wali's driving skills. He masterfully avoided holes and bumps without slowing down and we'd left the blue pickup a good hundred meters or so behind.

"What's going on, Tarzan?"

Afro-boy had begun to moan. The dark swelling over his eyes looked like it was about to burst.

"Sir, all I can say is that if you stop the car, we're all in deep shit," Tarzan said, taking what looked like a can of soda out of his sack.

"Sir ji, you've been away too long," Wali growled over his shoulder. "This country is a powder keg. You touch anything here and it blows up in your face."

"Sir, please tell him not to stop," Tarzan pleaded, gripping my arm so hard I cried out. "That pickup is fitted with a portable hand-chopper," he continued. "They won't only chop off my hand, but all of yours as well. Right here on the spot."

"Wali, is he telling the truth?" I gasped, feeling like I needed a breath of fresh air.

"Sir ji, yes," Wali explained as he swerved sharp to avoid the pickup. They'd overtaken us again and the driver was trying to run us off the road.

"Sir, many of my friends are missing one of their hands or feet," Tarzan explained, dousing all hope that maybe, just this once, the bizarre reference was just a harmless metaphor.

I looked away and shut my eyes. I thought I was going to vomit.

The kid had talked about a hand being chopped off like it was no big deal. Just like getting your ear pierced.

"And what do they do with the hands and feet they've chopped off?" I asked, regaining myself but still feeling nauseous. "What about the pain later, what about infection?"

The pickup had fallen behind but was gaining on us again.

"Sir ji, they take the parts as a proof," Wali said, looking in his rearview mirror "The more chopping you do, the greater the commission you make."

"Before they drive off and leave you standing wherever they found you, they hand you a roll of dressing, a bottle of Panadol, extra strength, and a bunch of penicillin capsules," Tarzan said.

"Khalifa ji says: Show kindness even to the criminals, once the punishment prescribed by Allah has been administered," Wali said. "Islam, sir ji, is all about kindness and caring for one another."

Just then the pickup pulled alongside us again and Wali let out a string of curses through his gritted teeth.

"Wali, what are we going to do?" I yelled. "Should we stop? They're going to run us off the road if we don't." As I completed the sentence, the pickup rammed us against the median.

"Let me think for a minute, sir ji," Wali replied, slowing down the car. "Remember, we haven't stolen anything, so we don't deserve a hand-chopping."

"Well, that's a relief."

Sensing Wali's intention, Tarzan lowered his side of the window. The cool air hit my face and it was exactly what I needed, except that it stank like hell; somewhere between an abandoned chemical dump and an *abattoir* on a really hot day.

The pickup was now only a few inches from the car, ready to ram us again. All its windows were down and I could see the barrel of a revolver next to a chubby-cheeked and bearded face staring at me bug-eyed from the back seat. It seemed like Wali had no choice but to pull over.

But then something happened that nobody saw coming. Tarzan twisted the top on the canister he'd pulled out of his sack and lobbed the thing into the open window of the pickup. The thing blew just as it went past the pickup's window. Smoke filled its cabin instantly. It swerved out of control away from us, its tires screeching. The truck hit the median and its front wheels slammed with a loud bang into a huge pothole as the impact popped one of the tires. The force knocked the truck off the median and it rolled end-over-end before landing on its roof in the middle of the road.

Wali floored the gas pedal and I was flung into the side door.

"What the hell was that?" I screamed. "Tarzan! Are you out of your fucking mind?" I was starting to hyperventilate as I stared at Wali in panic. "Wali, what in the hell are we going to do?"

"I really don't know, sir ji," he said, now perfectly calm and tooling along like we were on our way to a picnic. "I guess we'll do what Allah wants us to do."

"Well, in that case, we all know that Allah has already commanded me to take this injured man to the hospital," I said, meaning every word of it, as wind from the open window whipped my hair. I glared at Tarzan.

"What the hell was that for?" I asked, looking into his eyes. "Who were those guys? And dude, from now on, no more surprises that go boom, deal?"

"Those men were Commaqaadis," Tarzan said. "They're the only ones who drive those blue Mazda pickups."

"Commaqaadis?" I said. "You mean the cops."

"Sort of, sir ji," Wali chimed in. "A commaqaadi is half commando and half qaadi. Swift action. Swift justice. Right on the spot."

"Tarzan, why were they chasing you?" I said, giving him a piercing glare.

"Because they think I've got something they want," he answered with a sly smile.

"What do they think you've got, and why do they think it?" I inquired, wondering if I'd get a straight answer or just some hustle, religious or otherwise.

"I have a whole bunch of things." Tarzan said flashing his teeth in a smile that was anything but innocent. "It's hard to say which one they're after."

"What's in the sack, besides explosives?"

"Items of loot, what else?" Wali answered, swinging left onto the Canal Road.

The moon perched low in the sky above the Green Tomb Mosque. Lit by concealed floodlights, the luminous green dome looked like it was floating in midair. Suddenly I was hit by the stench of rotten flesh.

"Would you roll the window up?" Again I felt as if I was going to puke.

Tarzan did as asked, but hadn't answered a single one of my questions.

"The smell is from the water in the canal," Wali interjected.

"Tarzan. I asked you a question."

The kid just stared out the window.

"Hey! I'm talking to you, Tarzan."

"The raw material," he replied, turning to look at me with a puzzled look on his face like he had no idea why I was making such a big deal out of it.

"What raw material?"

"Shoes," he replied.

"And where'd you get all these shoes?"

This joker wasn't telling me the whole truth and I'd regretted bringing him on board miles ago. When I was exhausted and irritable, like now, I could be a real son of a bitch if I felt like I was being played, and I did.

"Wherever I can find them," he was muttering. "You can collect a lot of shoes at the scene right after a blast."

Afro-boy was now awake. Keeping his palm over his swollen eye he moaned incessantly.

I was beginning to understand the nature of Tarzan's profession. He was a scavenger. I could see him sprinting through the area of a blast with his burlap sack on his shoulder; pilfering bodies of the dead and injured for their valuables. It was hard to believe that somebody like Tarzan would limit himself to lifting shoes only.

"So what else did you collect tonight besides the shoes?"

"Nothing in particular, you know, the usual items," Tarzan said absently, glancing at Afro-kid. "What's the story on this guy? How did he end up here in your car?"

Before I could open my mouth to reply, Wali interrupted.

"Sir ji is from America. He believes it's his duty to solve everybody's problems."

"Oh Wali, just shut up," I snapped. "Keep your eyes on the road and drive."

I knew I was being rude to the guy but I no longer cared. He'd crossed the line with me so many times already I'd lost count.

The image of a smoke-filled pickup doing a somersault through the air kept flashing through my mind as we sped down Canal Road towards Jail Road. I wanted to tell Wali to stop the car and leave Tarzan and his burlap sack along the roadside. But I let it go. Maybe I was scared of him. Or maybe I'd begun to secretly admire him. That thing with the pickup and his smoke bomb really had been kind of awesome.

We took a right turn on Jail Road and headed toward the former Services Hospital. I'd seen more traffic in this area at 4:00 am, but now the place looked like a ghost town. Submerged in the dark, the buildings with their indistinct outlines looked like abandoned ruins. Our heads banged against the roof again as Wali hit a pothole.

"Wali, what happened to all the traffic and people? This place used to be humming with life, even late at night." I asked, chilled to the bone with the bizarre changes that had come over the place since the last time I was here—some twelve years ago. I supposed it was a rhetorical question, because I already knew the answer. I'd seen it all on the news as the chaos here in Pakistan replayed itself over and over again. And my few hours here confirmed it all in gory detail.

A decade ago, the country was not yet as isolated from the rest of the world as it was destined to become. The process was gradual, but irreversible. Lahore had experienced a succession of bloody riots that had cost hundreds of thousands of lives. It had all started as Jihad against the corrupt elite. The speed at which the riots engulfed the city had taken everyone by surprise.

From Lahore they spread to the rest of the country like wildfires consuming a forest in the hot dry season. Horrific scenes of carnage were seen everywhere; whole neighborhoods were massacred by mobs armed with everything from Kalashnikovs to farm tools and kitchen knives. Homes, state buildings, and marketplaces were torched and looted. The people had wanted Islam. They wanted Sharia and they were duly obliged when the terror master of Hindu Kush, the Khalifa, descended from his mountain perch and took over the country without having to face any resistance.

The poor, the destitute, the disenfranchised; these became the new powerful elite as the Sunni revolution spread and eventually devoured the whole country. Armed gangs of bearded young men wearing Arab-style robes invaded the affluent neighborhoods of Lahore.

A mass grave, dug for the Defense Housing Society—the rich and educated were seen as slaves of America—was said to contain more than five thousand heads. The beheading ceremony took place on the sprawling golf course of Lahore Gymkhana club. The headless corpses were burned at the site. But the heads, they were staked on spears and paraded to DHS as a spectacle for the adoring masses who cheered along the roadside while impromptu stalls sprang up selling food and souvenirs.

There were similar mass graves filled with heads in many areas of Lahore and other cities. The wealthy, and anyone else who had the means and a place to go, left the country. The masses swarmed into upscale neighborhoods and made their homes in abandoned houses and storefronts. Others set up permanent camps where they torched the spoils of looted museums in great bonfires that burned for weeks. In the subsequent months and years that followed the riots, there had been a complete reordering of society.

"Sir ji, people just went mad. The lava deep in their souls finally found its way to the surface," Wali said with a sigh.

Something monstrous had happened here; something far worse than anything televised on the nightly dinnertime news around the globe. Like some unearthly tsunami, it had washed through Pakistan until everything in its path had been obliterated, leaving only devastation in its wake.

"What happened to the water, Wali?" I asked. "I had no idea the water situation was so dire."

"Some say it was the water that made people behave like rabid dogs," Wali said, his voice strange and hollow. "If it weren't for Islam and our Khalifa ji, everyone would've died. Only Khalifa ji could guarantee peace and security, sir ji."

I remained quiet. Wali slowed the car and pulled into the emergency room parking lot of Khidamat-e-Ummah Hospital. I held Afro-kid by his shoulder and helped him out of the car and up the stairs to the emergency room. Tarzan followed me, his sack slung over his shoulder. Wali stayed with the car.

"What's your name?" I asked the injured kid.

"Omar Sharif." He stared at me with his good eye, and then began sobbing. He was wobbly on his feet and we had to help him walk.

The power was out in the hospital and its vicinity and only a few gas lamps and battery torches lighted the way. As we climbed the steps, my eyes fell on a glowing sign painted on the glass entrance door: *Death Visits at its Appointed Hour*. I pushed the door open and I staggered in with Afro-kid leaning against me and Tarzan behind us.

"Tarzan, you probably should have waited with Wali." We stepped into the entry hall.

"I need to use the toilet," he said, adjusting his sack over his shoulder.

"Well, if I don't see you again, good luck." I was hoping he'd get the hint and just disappear after he'd done his business.

"Same here, sir," he said. "If you ever need my help in any matter, you can count on me."

"Appreciated, thanks," I said, not fathoming what this guy could possibly do to help me that wouldn't land me in jail awaiting execution. But as they say, it's the thought that counts. All I wanted to do was finish with the hospital and get on with my life, whose purpose had been all but shattered to pieces by the events of the last few hours. I wanted nothing more than crashing in a bed and sleeping away until this nightmarish journey of mine was done and over.

Tarzan walked toward the rear of the building and disappeared down a dark hallway.

Afro-kid was able to walk normally, as long as I steered him in the right direction. I wanted to get him registered as a patient, hand him over to the staff on duty, and get the hell out of there.

We entered the waiting area, my arm still around the kid's shoulder. The place was lit by half a dozen candles and smelled of sweat and wax. A group of fully veiled women sat in a corner, indistinguishable from their shadows on the walls. After easing the kid into a chair, I went up to the reception desk.

A pair of large candles placed on each side of a bulky old-fashioned computer monitor looked like some kind of bizarre cyber punk altar, and I stifled a smile. A hand-written note taped to the side of the monitor said everyone was on break for namaaz of *ishaa*, the last of the five daily ritual prayers and the longest.

I heard a soft rustle of skirts as a figure in black materialized out of the darkness and glided toward the desk.

"We've got a possible concussion here," I said pointing to my slumped companion. "He's got a black-eye, a gash on his right brow the size of my finger and it'll definitely need stitches," I blurted out. "It's urgent!"

"Can't be more urgent than preparing for the next world," the figure replied in a soft sweet voice. Through a two-inch wide slit in her veil, her big, black eyes, expertly outlined with kohl, shone like lamps in the gloom. Suddenly the room felt stiflingly hot, and I was hit by a powerful déjà vu. It was as if I'd known those eyes all my life.

"Please! This guy needs to be seen right away," I pleaded, trying to think why the hell she looked so familiar.

"Haste is from the Devil, brother." I imagined her smile behind that veil, her teeth, her lips. I had no doubt in my mind that she was beautiful.

"How long before you start seeing patients again?" I asked, trying to keep my temper in check.

"Whenever the doctor returns. He's saying his *ishaa* prayer."

"Oh, good, it shouldn't take that long then?" I said, thinking it was getting rather late for the prayer of ishaa—even if one said all seventeen rakaat.

"After the prayer doctor sahib gives a lecture," she said.

"Lecture on what?" And for whom I wondered, having seen no one here besides this solitary enigmatic female and the three silent huddled figures in the corner.

"Doctor Tariq is a great scholar," she said raising her hand as though she were introducing him at a podium. "Doctor is writing a very important book on the principles and practice of Islamic medicine for the Ummah, the Muslims world over."

"Sister, my name is Ismaeel," I muttered slowly through clenched teeth and locking her eyes with my own. "I'm here with the patient. He's a boy of about twenty, and he needs medical attention," I continued, dragging it out so she'd see that I was neither playing, nor impressed with that holier than thou veil of hers.

"His cut needs stitches," I repeated, while she just stared unblinking at me. "Now, sister, can I entrust him to your care? Or not?" I added, allowing my irritation and sarcasm to flow unfiltered into the conversation.

"I mean after getting him registered and all?" I added. "Would you be so kind as to ask the doctor to see him whenever he's available for the affairs of this world?"

"Where's the patient?" she asked, her eyes sweeping the room.

"The one with the white headband," I said, pointing to the kid. "You know, the only male in the room besides me?"

"Do you live abroad?" she demanded.

"Landed this evening," I said. "Why?"

"America?"

"New York."

"Same thing," she said. She was in the mood to tease me. But I was in no mood to take it.

"Actually, it's not," I countered and wondered why I was adding to this ridiculous chatter.

"Why not?" she asked, blinking a few times as if I had startled her with some miraculous revelation.

"Because New York isn't the America you seem to have in mind."

"Bring the patient over. I'll register him," she said at last. "Meanwhile, you go and buy these items from across the road."

She handed me a photocopy of an invoice from some Shafaa Medical Store. I took the piece of paper from her and stared at it. The price of each item purchased was blacked out, as was the total billed amount. Looking at the list, I felt an imminent meltdown coming on. I was completely baffled and she obviously read that on my face.

"Without these items we won't be able to treat him," she explained quite seriously, all teasing vanishing from her voice. "The hospital doesn't carry any of these things. All patients have to buy their own supplies."

"All right, I'll be back soon," I said. Leaving Afro-kid sitting on the chair, I left the emergency room and made my way back to the car where I found Wali smoking a *beeri*. The broad smile on his face when he didn't see Afro-kid vanished when I handed him the invoice.

"Not again!" he said, shaking his head.

"Wali, I need to borrow some more money. Expect a large tip when we get home."

"Credit is the scissor which cuts the thread of friendship," Wali warned gravely.

I remained quiet. My mind was a jumbled mess of thoughts and images, none of which would make any sense in the world I lived in, but which seemed perfectly normal in this nut-house of a country.

"Okay sir, how much do you need," I heard Tarzan's voice over my shoulder. I jumped, startled to find him standing behind me.

It cost 15,000 Dirhams to get all the stuff on the list. Tarzan had accompanied me to Shafaa Medical Store and paid for everything without batting an eye. The way he laid down the cash, you'd have thought it was just pocket change.

The haul of medical supplies included a couple of packs of sterilized non-absorbable silk, syringes, a 50 ml vial of Novocain, a 4-oz. bottle of antiseptic solution, a roll of cotton, a box of 2x2 gauze pads, one roll of 4-inch dressing gauze, a tube of an antibiotic cream, and a vial of something for tetanus. In addition, I'd grabbed a couple of bottles of Hoor Afza.

"Good luck with that," he said with a snort and his eyes glued to the bottles of Hoor Afza.

"I shouldn't have bought them?" I asked, feeling confused.

"Sir, I think you can handle it," he said with a wink, heightening the mystery surrounding the innocuous-seeming beverage.

Outside the store, Tarzan stuck his hand in his pocket. He pulled out several 1000-Dirham notes and shoved them into my hand.

"Sir, keep this," he added with a smile and a reassuring nod. "You'll need it."

"I'm not taking your money, Tarzan," I said, trying to stuff the bills back into his pocket.

"No, really sir, it's okay."

"But I'm not sure if or when I'll be able to pay you back."

"Consider it a gift from a friend," he said, clasping my shoulder and giving it a friendly shake.

"No Tarzan, it's okay, really," I protested, feeling really awkward and embarrassed by my predicament. "I really appreciate your kindness."

"Sir, take it as a loan if you must," he insisted, shoving the notes back into my hand.

"Well, I will pay you back, Tarzan. You can be sure of that," I said, reluctantly taking the cash from him. "Thank you." My stomach felt queasy with a mixture of excitement and fear.

As I returned to the emergency room with the brown paper bag with supplies, the power came back on. The white fluorescent light painted everything with a sterile glow that burned my eyes. Afro-kid was no longer slumped in the waiting area. The trio of nondescript women was gone as well.

So was the mystery that had permeated the place; the swaying shadows on the wall, the murky darkness where anything could have been lurking, the hypnotic eyes of the reception girl. The glaring light had transformed her into just another professional woman seated at her post trying to do her very mundane job.

Just then, she was trying to reboot her computer while talking to an elderly woman seated on a stool next to her desk. When she saw me enter the room, bag-in-hand, she gestured for me to take a seat.

The receptionist struggled with her computer for a good five minutes, and then another ten, while the elderly patient sat waiting to register. I had no recourse but to sit patiently and wait for my turn.

When it was my turn, I walked up and put the bag of supplies on her desk. Then I dropped a couple of 1000-Dirham notes into the bag, making sure she saw me do it.

"Please make certain he's well cared for," I said, forcing a smile. More and more, my jet-lagged body longed for a place to crash.

"I certainly will."

"What's your name?" I was struck too late by the idea that it might be a grievous offense these days to ask a strange woman what her name was.

"Laila."

"You know what that means?"

"Darkness," she replied.

"Night," I corrected with a smile.

"Same thing."

"No, not at all," I shook my head, puzzling at her apparent obliviousness to the poetic beauty surrounding her name.

"Why not?"

"Night is not darkness." I longed to see her face.

"Do you want to see my face?" she asked softly.

The question sent an icy wave up my spine as she seemed to have read my mind. She locked her magnificent eyes on mine for several seconds before lowering them. Something warm and energetic filled my whole body.

"Maybe one day," I said, trying to compose myself and not knowing what else to say, what else was permissible.

"Or maybe one dark night," she said, again locking her eyes with mine and releasing a tinkle of soft, intoxicating laughter.

"We'll see," I said, turning on my heel and hurrying out of the room without looking back, my whole being aflame with desire.

Chapter 11
Hoor Afza

THE POWER WENT OUT AGAIN as I raced down the steps of the emergency room savoring the thought of having the entire backseat of the car to myself. Outside the hospital gate I looked for the car, but there was no sign of it or Wali. I just stood there, shaking my head and staring at the empty spot where the car had been.

What now? I wondered aloud.

Jail Road was deserted except for a pair of flashing red lights in the distance that moved closer as I stood there. Then I heard Tarzan's panicked voice.

"Sir, over here!" he shouted from the darkness.

As soon as I saw him, he turned and sprinted back up the steps of the emergency room.

"Come on!" he screamed. "Follow me!"

"Tarzan, where's Wali?" I demanded, running to catch up with him. The sense of impending doom had returned and was forcing its way through the fatigue. "What the hell's going on now?"

We took the steps three at a time and Tarzan flung open the door. Inside the hospital, Tarzan stopped to catch his breath. He peeked out the glass doors as if he was hiding from someone.

Two blue pickups, red lights flashing and sirens rupturing the silence, zoomed through the gate and screeched to halt in front of the stairs. Their headlights swept the steps we'd just vacated and I saw all the doors flying open.

"Come on," Tarzan said, trying to catch his breath. He started running again and there was nothing to do but fall in behind him.

"Tarzan, wait! Please! You've got to tell me what's going on," I begged, scrambling down the empty hall, like we were tethered by a leash. "Where the fuck is Wali?"

"You've just got to trust me right now! There's no time to explain," he yelled over his shoulder as he scrambled toward the rear of the building.

"Do I have a choice?" I screamed, my fear and anger rising to a new high.

"Not if you want to see the sunrise in one piece," he snapped.

We barreled down dark deserted hallways, made a couple of turns and then reached what looked like a dead end. Tarzan flipped his flashlight on and I saw the dead end was really a huge pile of junked hospital furniture stacked from floor to ceiling. Tarzan scrambled over rusted metal cabinets and disappeared into what looked like a closet while I was left standing in complete darkness.

"Would you talk to me for heaven's sake?" I demanded, leaping onto the pile and feeling it rock precariously beneath my greater weight. Staring into the closet I could see Tarzan standing on the other side of the heap, his flashlight illuminating the passage.

"Where are we going?" I muttered, dragging out each word so the kid knew I was serious.

"Faisal Town," he said from the other side. "Don't stop, keep going. You've got to crawl a few feet at the end."

I inched along on my hands and knees through a tunnel made of rusted hospital beds and broken furniture. It was like some twisted rabbit hole and I was definitely following a Mad Hatter.

By the time I emerged from the tunnel I was completely covered with a fine dust that I half expected to have magical properties.

We stood next to a door. Tarzan had his sack with him again and I couldn't imagine where he'd stowed it until now.

"Tarzan, how did you find this place?" I marveled at this wild hideout he'd discovered. He'd obviously scoped this place out before.

"I smelled it," he said, pushing the door open.

That sounded really weird, but I decided to let it drop because he clearly wasn't in a talkative mood.

We stepped into what looked like a large public restroom that'd been out of commission for months. The place stunk of pot, like somebody'd been smoking a joint just a minute before. Tarzan threw his sack on the floor and pulled out an old brown leather briefcase.

"Tarzan, if you're not going to tell me what the hell's going on, I'm leaving," I said, sounding lame even to myself. "Please, just tell me where Wali is. I'm tired, man!"

He didn't answer. Instead he handed me his LED penlight.

"I need some light here," he instructed. He'd taken a roll of red adhesive tape and a cigar-sized green tube from the sack. He positioned the tube over the number-lock of the briefcase, taped it down, and then pulled a lighter out of his pocket.

"I hate these number-locks," he muttered, putting the flame to a shoelace dangling from one end of the tube. "Go!" he shouted, giving me a hard shove toward the door.

I leapt through the door and Tarzan followed, slamming it behind us. He started counting. When he reached seven, a muffled blast shook the door. Tarzan pushed it open and we stepped back into the bathroom. The place was filled with billowing acrid smoke. Tarzan took the penlight from me.

I almost fell over when he pointed the beam of light at the floor. Bundles of 1000-Dirham notes were scattered all over the filthy broken tiles. The briefcase, minimally damaged, still contained the bulk of money stacked in neat rows. No more than a handful of the bills appeared to have been burned.

I stood speechless as Tarzan gathered up the bundles of money from the floor and carefully tucked them back into the briefcase. I sighed in frustration, wishing this whole thing to be just some jet-lag induced hallucination that would be over soon.

Reaching down to give him a hand I saw a palm-sized black leather-bound book lying under the sink. I picked it up and brought it closer to the light. Flipping through its pages I saw they were all blank and looked like some sort of graph paper with a dozen boxes to a page. The book consisted of thirty numbered pages.

"Keep this," Tarzan said, tossing me a wad of Dirhams and tucking a couple of bundles into his robe.

"I'm not taking any of that," I tossed the money back into the briefcase. I had no intention of risking life and limb for theft.

"What's in your hand?" he asked, clicking the briefcase shut. Except for its blown handle, the thing was undamaged. My admiration for Tarzan's expertise climbed a notch and I wondered where he'd gotten his education in these matters.

"Just a book of blank pages, looks like some kind of graph paper," I answered.

"Do you think it was in the briefcase?" he asked, stuffing the briefcase back into his sack.

"I don't know, maybe," I said, smelling the book for gunpowder. "It was just lying over there under the sink."

"It's not safe to pick stuff up that's lying around," he said. "Let's get out of here. Wali's waiting for us."

Tarzan put his sack on the floor and climbed onto the back of the toilet, holding his penlight in his mouth. Sliding his hands up the wall he grasped the sill of a large black window overhead. He released the latch and pale moonlight flooded through the open window. Sticking the penlight back in his pocket, he grabbed the sill, hoisted himself up and swung a leg through the window. He sat there straddling the opening and staring down at me.

"Sir, would you please hand me my bag?" he said.

"Okay, but where's Wali waiting for us?" I demanded. "Just tell me what the fuck is going on?" I suspected I wasn't going to learn anything more from this Mad Hatter until he was good and ready.

"You'll get your answers as soon as we're out of here," he replied.

"How the hell am I supposed to climb up?" I said, hoisting his sack over my head and shoving it into his hands.

"You can do it, sir—it's not that hard," he replied and then disappeared. My heart sank like a stone. I couldn't cope with the thought of getting trapped in some abandoned restroom slash drug den.

I had to admit though, I was curious about that book. Its blank pages had to mean something. It didn't look like an ordinary diary or notebook. Whatever else it was, I wanted it and decided to keep it. If I survived this long strange night, I'd figure out something to do with it.

Holding the book in one hand, I climbed onto the back of the toilet and looked up. It would take both hands to pull myself up to the opening. I laid the book on top of the water tank up on the wall, thinking once I'd climbed up the windowsill I could lower myself a bit and retrieve the book without any problem. What I didn't see was that the lid of the tank was missing. The book had fallen into it with a soft thud.

Shit! It's ruined.

Raising myself on my toes I put my hand into the tank and sighed with relief. There was no water in the tank, the book safely resting at its dry bottom.

I made it to the windowsill on my third try. With considerable effort I was able to drag myself through the opening and to straddle the sill as Tarzan had done. I reached down and tried to grab the book, but the tank was out of reach and I couldn't risk losing my balance and crashing to the floor. I'd no choice but to let the book go.

I jumped to the ground—a distance of about five or six feet below—where I landed on a soft patch of grass.

"Nice going, sir! See, it wasn't so hard," Tarzan teased, slapping me on the back. "Now, let's get out of here."

We walked over to the hospital's boundary wall, Tarzan leading the way as we crawled through a crack in the crumbling masonry. Outside the wall we turned onto a road lined by gated houses on both sides. They had front and back lawns enclosed within shoulder-high walls.

"We're right in the rear of Shadmaan Market," he said. "Wali's parked at the end of the street."

"How did you get him to move his car over there?" I asked, thinking of Wali's Teflon character, his imperviousness to any earthly persuasion.

"He's a tough nut to crack, that's for sure!"

"What did you say to him then?"

"Nothing—I just had to take over his mind."

Tarzan's answer made me stop in my tracks.

"How do you take over someone's mind?" I asked.

"We'll talk about it some other time, sir," he replied as he stopped walking and faced me. His eyes looked unusually bright in the darkness.

"Where the hell did you learn all this stuff from?"

"Jinns," he said casually.

Now he was pulling my leg. It was impossible to get a straight answer from him—that much I knew. I gave up and resumed walking.

"You're a rich man now," I said, as we walked toward the Shadmaan Road. "You don't have to sell *pappurs* anymore, or plant explosives in the stadium. Take a vacation or something."

"It's not my money! I have to deliver it to the boss."

"Oh, I thought you were self-employed," I said. "What about the bundles you stashed into your own pocket? Won't he find out?"

"That's my commission," Tarzan said with a toss of his head and a chuckle. "Pir Pullsiraat doesn't care too much about money matters himself."

The name, Pir Pullsiraat, stuck me like a bolt of lightening. Whatever had been left of my sanity was blown into pieces at that very instant. Bowing forward I rested my palms against my knees lest I passed out.

"Sir, are you okay?"

It took me a while before I regained my bearings.

"What! What did you just say?" I stammered, feeling as if I was waking from a dream.

Tarzan looked at me all puzzled.

"Pir Pullsiraat is your boss? I raised myself back up. "This is fucking crazy!"

"Yes, he is *the Man*, the head of the Resistance Movement, and he's waiting for us," he said, turning my budding understanding of him on its head.

"Waiting where?" I asked. So this was how I was supposed to be contacted once I landed. *You'll be contacted once you arrive in Lahore.* The whole thing was too impossible to accept, way beyond what my analytical mind could grasp.

"Shah Jamal," he said, his face lit by pride.

"And what's this resistance movement all about? Resistance against whom?" I asked, feeling the return of the alarm that'd dogged my trail ever since landing here an eternity ago and fearing his answer.

"Against the Khalifa."

Holy crap! This new revelation left me speechless, and realizing I was a pawn in the hands of players I knew nothing about. I had so many questions I didn't even know where to begin.

So if Pir'd been the head of the resistance movement against the Khalifa, then Abba had to be connected to the latter in some important way. *Please know that regaining your father's trust is the path to success of our mission, a mission whose details will only be revealed to you when you are prepared to take action.* Suddenly Abba, whom I'd been genuinely wanting to patching up with after my Ayahuasca experience, seemed more ominous than my childhood memories of him, which were all but terrifying. I remembered the brutal campaign he'd led against the hapless Kalash tribe of Kafiristan for not only gaining popularity and fame but also the choicest berth in Paradise.

Indeed the price to gain the direct knowledge of Paradise and Hell was turning out to be way too steep for a mere mortal like me. Shivering with a mixture of fear and excitement I braced for more disasters on *the Path to High Knowledge* I was supposedly treading at the moment.

The curiosity of meeting with Pir Pullsiraat had taken the edge off my fatigue, but now I was thirsty as hell. My throat stung like it was lined with sandpaper. Remembering the two bottles of Hoor Afza lying on the backseat of the car, I quickened my pace, my mind desperately trying to make sense of things. The only thing I was certain about was the fact that I'd failed miserably in all tests in every step of the way.

The power was still out in the area. Submerged in darkness, the houses looked like they'd been abandoned for years. The howls of numerous cats pierced the air, growing louder as they were joined by more of their tribe to go about their nocturnal rounds. An eerie glow from a crescent moon overhead bathed the scene in milky light and huge shadows crawled over every surface.

Among other things, my perception of time had suffered a blow as well. Good thing I had my watch on. It was quarter to one in the morning. My flight had arrived at 6:00 pm, barely seven hours ago. My journey so far felt like some never-ending dream barreling along out of control and tumbling toward a dark abyss. It could not be reality, as I knew it. Yet I knew this was only the beginning.

The landscape itself was surreal, irrational, and the oddity so pervasive that people had stopped noticing it. This certainly wasn't how they'd had behaved when I'd lived here.

"Tarzan, I need to use your phone," I said, thinking that perhaps I should give my father a ring, although I wasn't sure if it was a good idea to call him at this hour.

"The phone's dead right now. I took the sim card out."

"Why?"

"Orders from the boss. I think you should stay with us tonight at Shah Jamal. It's not safe moving around after dark."

"As long as Wali is willing to drive, I think I'll leave right after meeting your boss."

"Sir, you don't get to meet a person like Pir Pullsiraat every day."

"Oh really?"

"Pir has *powers*."

"Powers? What kind of powers?"

"We're not allowed to talk about those things," Tarzan replied solemnly.

Up ahead I could see the faint outline of a car and silently prayed it was Wali's.

"What if I don't want to come along with you?" I'd come to realize that asking Tarzan indirect questions was the best way to get information out of him.

"But I can't show up at Shah Jamal without you. You don't have a choice, sir."

The look on his face told me that if he had to drag my dead body back to Shah Jamal, he would. *Under orders from the boss* meant pretty much the same thing everywhere in the world and in all languages.

"Okay fine. I'll go with you—but just for a few minutes."

"That's great, sir," Tarzan said. "Pir will be happy to see you."

Wali was waiting for us at the end of the road as Tarzan had promised. He was lounging on the hood of the car smoking a *beeri* and gazing at the moon, his head resting on the windshield. Seeing us he jumped off the car and gave us each a hug like we were his long-lost relatives.

"Sir ji, I'm really glad to see you," he said, opening the rear door of the car for me.

I was about to slide into the backseat when I caught movement out of the corner of my eye. Crouching a few feet above my head on a branch of a tree was a huge black cat. Its long snake-like tail whipped back and forth as the creature studied me with fluorescent yellow eyes.

I froze. Before I could take a breath, the cat lunged through the air and landed on the roof of the car, snarling and baring long curved fangs. The creature was so close I could have reached out and touched it. I stumbled backward and Wali started banging on the bonnet with his fist. Startled by the noise, the animal jumped down and darted into the shadows.

"Damn! That was one huge cat!" I exclaimed. It was bigger than the cat I'd seen earlier pummeling a poor dog outside the Fortress Stadium. It was the size of a young leopard.

"We're seeing them more and more, sir ji," Wali said. "They've started attacking people."

"Where do they come from?" I asked, scouring the darkness and tensing in case the thing reappeared. "I've never seen anything like that before in my life."

"There used to be a lot fewer of them, but their population suddenly increased when the dogs disappeared," Wali said.

"What do you mean, the dogs disappeared?" I asked.

"They were all killed. Slowly, over time, all were exterminated. Now, Alhamdolillah, you hardly ever see a dog in this country."

"How could you possibly kill all the dogs in a country the size of Pakistan?"

"It was the order of the Khalifa ji."

"But why?"

"Sir ji, don't you know that dogs block the flow of Allah's blessing when they are present in an area; whether it's a small house or a whole country? There is a hadith which says that the angels of mercy won't come to you if there's a dog nearby."

"And people agreed to kill their own pets? That's horrible and kind of hard to believe."

"Well, if you're getting one free bottle of Hoor Afza for each dog you kill, that's pretty much all the incentive most people here need. Hoor Afza had just come on the market at the time the dog killing started." Wali explained the mass extermination of millions of animals, many of whom must be beloved family pets, like it was a nothing more than a new recycling policy.

"What's so special about Hoor Afza?" Now I was really curious about the drink, and my curiosity had only doubled my thirst.

"There's no point talking about it, sir ji. Why don't you try yourself and see what happens? You've got two bottles there in the car."

It seemed like the perfect time to try Hoor Afza. Quench my thirst and my curiosity at the same time. I got in the car, grabbed one of the sealed bottles of the mysterious beverage lying on the seat, and drank the whole bottle in one go. It was a mango flavored sugary soda drink with a peculiar, mildly sour but pleasant aftertaste. Wali and Tarzan exchanged glances when they saw me opening the second bottle.

"Anyone interested in Hoor Afza?" I asked, holding the bottle up. They both shook their heads. I gulped more than half of the second bottle in one swallow.

"Wali, we're not far from Shah Jamal, right?"

"Sir ji, it all depends on the road conditions," he said.

"Road conditions? We're not traveling on Karakoram Highway to China for God's sake! I could probably walk there in twenty minutes."

"Things around here have changed, sir ji. Have you ever seen Lahore this quiet before?" He was right. Shadmaan was empty and silent as a graveyard. There was absolutely nobody out on the street.

"Let's get going, Wali. It's already one o'clock," I said, feeling a pleasurable tingling sensation wash through my body. "Tarzan can lead the way. We'll spend a few minutes with Pir Pullsiraat at Shah Jamal and then go on to Faisal Town."

"Your wish is my command, sir ji," Wali said.

For the first time in a long long time I felt at peace. The prospect of meeting with Pir had lifted my otherwise ravaged spirits. I was happy just to be relaxing in the back seat of the car. I wouldn't have minded passing out here one bit. I leaned back in the seat and surrendered. The tension and foreboding that'd gripped me since I first stepped off the plane were replaced by a delicious indifference to all but the pleasure of lounging here in the back of this car. I watched Tarzan climb into the co-pilot's seat next to Wali. I smiled. They looked like a pair of old buddies.

I was beginning to understand Wali's attitude toward life. There was no guarantee of anything in this world—especially at one o'clock in the morning in Lahore, where my father's old car, equipped with a pair of martyr-tanks and a handy safety switch, could be the safest bet in town.

The road was a mess and the car bounced along as if the ground beneath us had been carpet-bombed. Gravel hitting the undercarriage of the car sounded like firecrackers going off under my feet. My arms and legs lay heavily as if made of lead and a warm cloud of euphoria lulled me like the lips of a Siren. I swallowed the last few drops of the second bottle of Hoor Afza and tossed it on the floor. I took a deep breath, held it, and then sighed.

I felt lightheaded, so I closed my eyes as another delicious wave of golden warmth washed away my body, the car, and my companions. A flurry of images raced across the screen of my mind. The vivid clarity of these scenes made me open my eyes in alarm. It was like watching a movie.

In the front seat, two heads bobbed up and down and sideways. I giggled. The heads looked so hilarious, like a pair of bobble-headed clowns. I recalled from somewhere that these heads were named Wali and Tarzan. I felt remarkably still, as if anesthetized, as the head named Tarzan swiveled around and gazed at me through huge dark eyes.

"Is everything okay, Sir?" a gentle hollow voice coming from the head asked.

"Yeah, I'm good," I said, laughing softly. I shut my eyes again and the images resumed their silent parade across the back of my closed eyelids. Clearer, sharper images now crowded my inner vision; the faces of my ex-girlfriends. I couldn't even remember the names of many of them. Everything seemed so absolutely real. But something wasn't right. With supreme effort I opened my eyes again.

"Guys, what exactly is in this Hoor Afza?" I said. "It's making me see things."

"Sir ji, with two whole bottles of that stuff in you, we're sitting here betting on how soon you'll spot a *hoori* sitting next to you back there," Wali said, shouting over the noise. "That's why it's called Hoor Afza."

"Spot a what? A, a *hoori*—you mean, the virgin of Paradise?" I said. "Are you kidding me?"

I felt elated. My aches were completely gone and my thoughts soared, except they were all about women. I was completely detached from my body; in it but unfettered, like a morning breeze drifting through a grove of sandalwood, a butterfly looking for nectar.

"Sir, this is why the boss forbids us to drink Hoor Afza," Tarzan remarked. "He says it's crap—number-two stuff."

"What the hell are you guys talking about? This is crazy!" I wondered what the number-one stuff would be like.

"Sir ji, don't waste time talking. Just relax, close your eyes and dream," Wali advised. "Enjoy it as long as it lasts."

My body started to flush and tingle in a soft embrace of liquid sensation. All my blood seemed to be rushing towards my loins. Just go with the flow, I thought, closing my eyes.

I saw myself sitting beside four girls whom I had dated while doing my Masters: Christen, Judith, Aisha, and Kim. They all wore bikinis and lay on towels spread over lush grass. I could do anything I wanted to with them. They were there just for me.

"Holy Shit!" I said loudly, grabbing my head.

"Sir ji, is she sexy?" Wali said. "When you relax, they look better and better by the minute."

"There are four of them, Wali," I said.

"It's a good practice for the seventy-two you're going to get up there," Wali said, winking and jabbing his thumb at the ceiling of the car.

"Sir, the drink brings out one's fantasies," Tarzan chimed in. "You see what you've been wanting to see deep in your heart."

"Don't tell me this shit is available to the public?" My loins throbbed and threatened to carry me over the edge. I struggled with the decision to either proceed with my Hoor Afza induced mental imagery and gratify myself with these four ravishing beauties simultaneously, or stop immediately by opening my eyes.

"Sir ji, now you know what I was talking about?" Wali said. He seemed to be having quite a lot of fun at my expense. The car hit a deep pothole and my head banged against the roof. My eyes shot open and I stared at Wali.

"Sorry, sir ji, I didn't mean to spoil your fun."

"Sir, two bottles of this stuff can drive anyone crazy," Tarzan said.

"How long does this shit usually last?" I asked, covering the obvious bulge under my robe with my hand.

"Long enough to cum once, or maybe twice if you get lucky," Tarzan snickered, turning around and ogling me. "It all depends how fast you can get it up again after the first time."

Wali looked at Tarzan and they both roared like a couple of teenagers.

"Don't talk like that in front of sir ji, Tarzan!" Wali scolded, his tone mocking and ready to erupt in laughter again. "Show some respect!"

"What if I keep my eyes open," I asked, ignoring their giggling fit.

"Sir ji, then what's the point of drinking Hoor Afza?" Wali asked. "Shut your eyes and go back to playing with yourself. We won't look. This time," he added, stifling another round of laughter.

"What happens to women when they drink this stuff," I said, shoving the bulge down between my legs.

"They're forbidden to even touch Hoor Afza, sir ji. No one in their right mind would sell that stuff to women. They put you in jail for things like that," Wali said. His voice sounded like it was bubbling up from the bottom of a deep well.

Drifting off again I wondered if I could control my trip vision and direct it to go wherever I wanted it to. I closed my eyes and conjured up the face of my beautiful Sophie. She was standing exactly where she had been when I'd first kissed her; by the waterfall. A rainbow formed on the curtain of mist as the water crashed over the boulders and roared down toward the valley below.

She stepped forward and brushed my neck with her soft fingers. Her lips parted. My mouth touched hers. She tasted like apricots.

Suddenly I was overwhelmed by guilt. I opened my eyes again. Somehow it didn't feel right to be thinking about her. Not like that. I felt angry at my father. Why in the hell he had decided to marry my girlfriend, of all the women in the world?

I closed my eyes. This time I'd just look at her, without touching her, possibly from far away. A lush green hillside opened before me; living, breathing, three-dimensional. I could even smell the little purple flowers and the tall grasses.

Once again, I saw Sophie standing in the distance as if through a pair of powerful binoculars. There was a bunch of wild violets in her hands. She wore her favorite long black skirt, and the red-fringed shawl wrapped loosely around her shoulders trailed down her back, tangling with her hair. She was gathering flowers as she waded through a field of mauve blossoms that spread over the green slope. Wind brushed through the golden grasses like a great unseen hand. All I could think of was her hair, bathed in the crimson rays of the setting sun.

About fifty feet from where she stood a dark shadow emerged from the tall grasses. I gasped when I realized that the shadow was a heavyset, dark skinned man wearing a black shawl. He crouched like a tiger, creeping closer toward Sophie as I watched helplessly from my self-imposed distance. Oblivious to her stalker, she knelt to pluck a bunch of wildflowers. That's when the man sprang forward and dashed toward her. Before she could flee or even cry out for help, he was on top of her.

Terrified, she screamed and beat the man's chest with her fists. But he was too big and powerful to be affected by her blows. He grabbed her by the waist and lifted her off the ground and then threw her over his shoulder. She kicked the air desperately but to no avail. The hideous intruder darted across the meadow carrying Sophie over his shoulder like a sheep to the slaughter.

The dark man came to a halt at the edge of a huge black hole in the ground. I opened my eyes. I was sweating, completely shaken. I knew beyond all shadow of a doubt the man had jumped into that hole. My Sophie had been taken into the Underworld!

I struggled to keep my eyes open until we reached Shah Jamal. It was a bone-rattling ride over a cratered road that was littered with rocks and debris. Though shaken by a vision so real I could still smell the flowers and see that hideous gaping hole, I was gripped in the moment by the crisis between my legs that had become almost unbearably painful.

I glanced into the front seat and saw Wali and Tarzan chatting away. As promised, nobody was looking. I rolled my robe all the way up to my waist. I reached down and wedged my right hand between my legs and rocked against the seat, making sure my cum stayed within my underwear. After a couple of minutes, my body shook with delight and I felt the warm wetness over my groins.

A few minutes later Wali stopped the car in front of the Shrine of Baba Shah Jamal. By the time Tarzan opened his door, about a dozen men dressed in black had the car surrounded. Their faces were masked with veils, rendering them almost invisible in the darkness that engulfed the shrine.

"Everybody out!" one of the men barked.

"Tarzan, this wasn't part of the deal. Now what?" I managed to whisper into his ear.

"Be calm sir," Tarzan said. "They're just doing their job."

We all stood by the car. The air was filled with the howling of cats. They were somewhere up in the trees, a lot of them. Their wailing filled the night like a song of death.

Entering the shrine's grounds I saw many people seated in groups around fires. A dense cloud of smoke hung over their heads and the pungent aroma of cannabis saturated the air. The cats were now silent as they watched from the trees.

Escorted by about half a dozen armed men, Tarzan and I walked past the fires. The men were all smoking hashish from rough carved pipes they passed from man to man around the circles. None bothered to even look up as we passed. They were lost in another world.

"Where's Wali?" I whispered.

"He's staying with the car." Tarzan said, his burlap sack hanging from his shoulder. "Sir, don't be afraid, they're going to blindfold you now."

Before I could speak, someone threw a piece of cloth over my head and tied it behind my neck, covering my eyes and my face. Then someone else grasped me firmly by the arm and walked me around in circles. We walked like this for a good five minutes before we descended a steep narrow stairway.

My shoulders rubbed against rough stone walls as we picked our way downward. I counted nineteen steps before my feet hit a flat surface. We walked again for a minute or two before we halted and my blindfold was removed. I was standing next to Tarzan on what looked like a rocky ledge. We were overlooking a huge courtyard filled with about thirty people; mostly boys in their teens. The men who had accompanied us had disappeared.

Lit by a dozen or so gas lamps hanging around the periphery, the courtyard looked like it floated in the air. Three tightropes were stretched across the courtyard, each tied to the apex of a pyramidal assortment of four metal poles set in a concrete base on either side of the court.

All three tightropes were in use by boys edging their way across the open space of the courtyard some twenty feet below; their arms spread wide, their faces strained with concentration. The rest of the boys stood below watching the action with rapt attention.

A man wearing a white-striped black tracksuit walked around beneath the tightropes, monitoring the boys' progress and barking instructions from time to time. He wore a red headband across his forehead and his long white hair hung limply down his straight back. He must be six feet tall and well built. I figured this must be Pir Pullsiraat.

We were gathered inside some massive building or subterranean cavern. No moon was visible overhead, but I couldn't see any ceiling overhead either. The man with the red headband turned and walked toward us looking straight ahead. Two of the huge black cats dashed across the courtyard and he stopped to scratch their ears and stroke their sleek fur. They flanked him as he walked, their tails raised in the air and their backs brushing the sides of his legs. They looked like two young black jaguars.

"Tarzan, where the hell are we?" I managed to whisper.

"We're inside the world of Pir Pullsiraat.

Chapter 12

Pir Pullsiraat

Pir Pullsiraat and his two cats disappeared beneath the ledge where Tarzan and I stood watching the action below. Down in the court, the tight-roping exercises continued. Somebody hoisted a bicycle up to one of the boys. The kid put the bicycle on the rope, and with one foot on the pedal he rode for a few feet, then crossed his other leg over and pedaled with both feet.

"Where did Pir go?" I asked.

"He's gone to change." Tarzan replied, tossing his burlap sack to the ground.

My underwear had begun to dry out, but not without leaving me with a gnawing guilt. This Hoor Afza fiasco had turned out to be the fitting tribute to my utter failure to overcome my weaknesses I'd been warned about at the outset of my journey. The Path to High Knowledge had me exposed to my bones.

"Well, well! If I may have the attention of the gentleman from the Big Apple." A deep musical voice reverberated through the air. I looked about in darkness to locate Pir, but didn't see a thing. I turned around. He wasn't there behind my back either.

Feeling unsettled I turned around again, and there he was, standing just a few feet from us, dressed in a luminescent green robe. Two boys, twins from the look of them, flanked him. Their eyes danced in the flames of huge torches they held aloft to light the way for their master.

Pir's face, glowing in the bloody golden light of the fire, looked like some sort of crazed ritual mask, yet it was a strikingly handsome face. His lean frame, chiseled features, and fine high cheekbones made it impossible to guess his age. He could've been anywhere from forty to sixty years old. His trimmed beard with streaks of white gave him a dignified, almost academic air. But it was those eyes; two white-hot searing probes that surveyed me from head to toe in one blazing sweep. I stood still, mesmerized by the shimmer of his robe. It was impossible to continue looking into those almost non-human eyes that bore into me and left me feeling more naked and exposed than when I'd had my robe hoisted up around my waist.

The red headband across Pir's forehead bore the Nike logo and kept his long white hair out of his face. He wore a pair of earbuds with two fine white cords disappearing into the side-pocket of his robe. I stepped forward dumbly, as if drawn toward him by a magnetic force. I was pretty sure he was seeing through me, and nothing could possibly be kept from him.

"I'm honored to be here, sir," I said, gingerly extending my left hand, not wanting to touch him with my right hand which had dealt with the urgent needs of my swollen manhood.

He took the offered hand and gave it a brisk shake with no sign of awkwardness. Before I could press his hand, it slid out of my grip like an eel.

"This is an amazing place! Your boys are doing great on the ropes."

"It's not a difficult skill to learn," the man said with a smile.

"Nothing's difficult when you're young, I suppose."

"Age doesn't matter," Pir replied. "It's all in here," he motioned, tapping his temple with his index finger. "Everything!"

"I know what you mean. Surely nothing is out of reach of man, for he is the best of all creation."

"Best of all creation?" he boomed. "I sincerely hope you don't believe any of that bullshit."

I remained quiet, having absolutely no idea what to say. Was he mocking me having known my real inner condition?

"Man's highest achievement is to elevate himself to the moral status of the animal kingdom. He must learn the nobility that's natural to all animals except man," he said staring into the flames.

"I've never heard of a noble monkey. Or a noble cat or dog."

"Just because you haven't heard of it doesn't make it any less true," he looked at me without blinking. "A pack of wolves doesn't punish, persecute, or kill another pack of wolves because they eat a different kind of meat." His voice was firm, yet calm. "Or have a different color of fur."

Feeling at a loss for words, I glanced at Tarzan who had a mischievous look on his face and seemed to be enjoying Pir's interrogation of me immensely.

"All of man's so-called higher intelligence," Pir continued after a pause during which he just stared at me until I began to squirm. "It is wasted searching for new and better ways to destroy everything that exists. No animal is capable of the level of moral depravity that is the trademark of humanity."

Sweat poured out of my forehead, my mind grappling with the shock of meeting with Pir Pullsiraat. Thankfully, he turned toward Tarzan before I could come up with a response.

"Let's see what you've got." Pir said, stretching his open hand toward Tarzan. Without saying a word, the boy pulled the briefcase out of his sack and placed it in his master's hands.

Pir turned the briefcase around and examined it from all sides. The strange twins moved closer to him to provide more light from their torches.

Pir turned the briefcase upside down and the bundles of banknotes fell out at his feet. I noticed he was wearing black military boots. He tapped the empty briefcase with his knuckles and examined it closely.

"What happened to the lock?" he demanded, scouring Tarzan's face with a fiery glance and sniffing the briefcase.

"I don't know. Probably got damaged by the blast," Tarzan replied, glancing at me for a second. I kept a straight face and didn't meet his eyes.

"Probably got damaged in the blast!" Pir cried, looking around. "So there was nothing else in it besides the money?" He let the empty briefcase fall on the pile of money at his feet. Clearly he knew the boy had tinkered with the lock.

Tarzan plunged his hand into the sack again and brought out a faded brown leather pouch with straps; like the neck pouch travelers wear around their necks for carrying travel documents. I felt my own pouch, which I'd tucked under my robe. It was there; my US passport was still on me.

"This may be what you're looking for," Tarzan said.

Pir's nostrils flared briefly as his eyes fell on the pouch Tarzan pressed into his large hand. The boy whispered something in Pir's ear and the old man smiled and looped the string of the pouch around his neck.

"You're sure there wasn't anything else in here?" Pir glanced at me but I just shrugged my shoulders. Obviously, he was looking for the book. The one I'd accidentally left back at the hospital. I decided to keep that bit of information to myself for the moment.

Just then someone called Tarzan's name from the courtyard below and broke the heavy silence.

"Go. Your friends are waiting for you," Pir said. "Just remember: I want you to spend that money you've got tucked under your robe wisely. That's your whole year's salary."

"What money?" Tarzan asked. His voice was calm and his face showed not even the slightest trace of his guilty secret. Damn, the guy was good.

"Get lost!" Pir yelled and Tarzan took off like a horse bolting from the starting line.

"Sir, Pir will take good care of you!" Tarzan yelled over his shoulder with a smile. Then he was gone, swallowed by a knot of noisy young men.

Pir smiled, looking me in the eyes. "My lieutenant!"

"I'm not sure I'd promote him any time soon," I exclaimed.

"I don't do promotions," he said firmly.

"He's a smart kid."

"Indeed. He found you much faster than I'd anticipated," Pir said as we started walking. "Let's talk in my room."

"What do you mean: he found me?" I sensed that there was a hell of a lot more going on here than was obvious. Anything seemed not only possible, but guaranteed in this strangest of the all imaginably strange places.

As we walked side by side, the torch-bearing boys at our sides held us within a golden halo of dancing light. The heat from the flames brushed my cheeks with pleasurable warmth, and I was lulled into a delicious peace.

Pir pulled out the pouch from under his robe and opened it.

"Here, I believe this is yours," he said, slapping my wallet into my hand.

I stopped in my tracks, shaking my head.

"That lieutenant of yours appears to be adept in quite a number of fields," I said, taking my wallet from Pir's hand. "Do you by any chance have my cell phone in there?"

"I'm afraid not," he said, shaking his head in a funny sort of mock pity. "But then, had my lieutenant not picked the pocket of the pick-pocket who picked your pocket, you wouldn't have your wallet either."

"If I may ask, sir, why am I here, exactly?" I felt Pir's eyes on me as if the walls were closing in. I was sure that Tarzan must have been tracking me ever since I left the airport. But how, given the fact he'd no transport?

"You mean, why are you here right this minute?" Pir said, bringing me back from my ruminations.

"Yes, right at this very minute?" I said.

"You're here because of me."

"And what exactly are you here for?"

"I'm here because of you," he replied, a shadow of mischief streaking across his face.

"Okay then," I continued, both intrigued yet quickly tiring of our little word game. "Why are both of us here at this moment?"

"Now that, my dear Ismaeel, is a most excellent question," he said, stabbing the air in front of my face with his fingertip. "We are both here because of Khalifa."

"That much I'd already figured out," I said. "That's not what—"

"I know you've got a lot of questions Ismaeel. But you won't be able to understand the answers if they're given to you at the wrong time. For now, you have to trust that you're among friends."

The words of that strange, ancient looking man with the bright eyes whom I'd met in my Ayahuasca vision rang in my mind like the tinkle of his bicycle bell: *Babu, you're going to help us clean up a big mess.*

"Were you with Tarzan when he blew the handle on the briefcase?" Pir was saying.

"Yes, yes I was."

"Was there anything else in the briefcase besides the money?"

"Not sure. It was dark," I said, knowing he didn't believe me. Without a doubt, Pir was after the black book.

"What exactly are you looking for?" I asked.

"It's the thing upon which Khalifa's power rests," Pir said. He led me through an arched doorway into what looked like a large rough-hewn cave strewn with tribal rugs over the dirt floor. Lit by dozens of candles set into small niches within the walls, the place was steeped in an otherworldly tranquility.

Pir gestured for me to sit down on one of the four chairs placed around a square wooden table in the center of the room. As I pulled my chair up to the table, my eyes fell on a red rose lying in front of me. Next to the rose lay a white porcelain ashtray.

A rustle over my shoulder startled me and I glanced up. My breath caught in my throat as I looked into the eyes of the boy who was holding a torch behind my shoulder. His eyes had vertical slits, just like the eyes of a cat. The boy averted his glance, looked straight ahead, and walked over to Pir.

"These are jinns," Pir said. He had a hand on the shoulders of his twin boys and beamed like a proud father.

"Jinns? For real?"

"Yes, for real."

"So all the big cats you see roaming around Lahore attacking people are jinns?" I asked.

"Very few of them. Most of those big cats owe their existence to Khalifa. He had them specially bred in a secret location in the mountains up north."

"This is crazy!" I said, recoiling in my seat, trying to fathom the logic behind this mass scale production of giant cats. "Is he trying to compensate for the loss of all the dogs he'd had killed?"

"Relax, lean back," Pir instructed. "You'll feel a lot better after having a cup of hot tea; it should be here any minute now." He dug a pack of Gold Leaf cigarettes from his pocket and offered it to me. "Would you like to smoke?"

"No, thanks," I said, resisting a powerful urge to take one. "All I want is to know why I'm here, that's all."

The boy holding the torch behind Pir's right shoulder brought his flame closer to his master's face and lit his cigarette.

"You're here to see your father, remember?" Pir said, removing his headphones. He took a puff of his cigarette and nodded at the boy a couple of time.

The boys padded out of the room, leaving the two of us sitting face to face in the dim light of the candles. Pir tapped the ash of his cigarette into the ashtray and then leaned back, eyeing me closely.

"Ismaeel, you're here for a very important reason. If you don't successfully complete the task we're about to give you, we won't be able to complete ours."

I remained quiet and tried to keep calm but my breath was shallow and fast. This was really happening!

"Do you understand what I am trying to tell you?" he said.

"Yes, I think so," feeling my heart pounding in my chest, and my guilt lifting off of me like mist in the morning sun. Despite all my shortcomings I was still a candidate for *the most ancient of the circles of the Elite.*

"Haji Ibrahim, your father, is one of the Khalifa's closest confidants," Pir's eyes still locked on mine.

"Not surprising," I said. "He was a businessman whose political ambitions were legendary and far-reaching. When I left home, some twelve years ago, he owned a chemical factory. But I suppose you know all this."

"Of course. He's still a businessman. But he's branched out a bit in your absence and no longer confines his activities to the typical chemical industry," Pir said.

"Not surprising. He was always an entrepreneur."

"These days your father's real money and power is in manufacturing martyr vests; and, as incredible as it may sound, it is currently the most lucrative business in the Caliphate." Pir's mouth stretched in a grin.

"What!" I bolted up from my chair and stood glaring down at him.

"His company manufacturers the most popular brand of these nasty little things; the Mujahid Vests," Pir explained. "They're in very great demand all across the country."

"You're telling me..." I stammered, and then stopped to shake the dizziness from my head. "You're telling me, that my father is the one who owns Mujahid Vests, the suicide vests!?" My body convulsed inwardly with disgust. "I think I'll take one of those smokes now, if you don't mind."

"Please sit down," Pir opened the pack of Gold Leaf, slid a cigarette out halfway and extended his arm toward me. My fingers shook as I pulled the cigarette out of the pack. He held up his lighter, flicked it once, and I drew in a deep drag.

"I can't believe it!" I said, coughing out the smoke.

"He produces the best martyr vests ever made," Pir said, his brows raised. "Please, sit down."

Ignoring his request, I took another hard drag on the cigarette.

The smoke burned my throat like acid and I went into a violent coughing fit.

"Have some water," Pir was holding up a glass to me. I didn't remember seeing any glass of water on the table when I first sat down.

I took a few sips and set it down.

"I don't think I want to see my father after all," I coughed, choking as I struggled to control my breath.

"Ismaeel, you're not only going to see your father, you're going to convince him that you're now a true believer," Pir said. "A devout and pious Muslim son he can be proud of."

"Ha!" I snorted in disbelief? "That mission is doomed from the get-go," I said in a hoarse voice. "That'd never happen in a million years."

"Oh yes, it'll happen all right," he countered. "And it'll happen long before a million years has elapsed. We're here to assist you and to make damn sure it happens."

"So, I've come all the way from New York to Lahore for this—to turn myself into a true believer?" I said. "What for?"

"To gain his trust," Pir replied.

"What makes you think I even want that guy's trust? What if I refuse to accept this assignment?" I said. "And, what if I take the next flight out of this madhouse and return to New York?"

"I'm not going to ask you again, please sit down, please," the Pir said in a voice that would brook no refusal.

Shaking my head I sank back into my chair, fuming from hearing about my father's business.

"You have to remember two things; first, as I said, your father is one of the most important men in the Khalifa's inner circle. Two, he's vulnerable when it comes to matters of faith. Nothing will please Hajji Ibrahim more than to discover that his only son and heir has finally rediscovered his faith."

"But that'd be a lie!" I cried, helping myself to another cigarette. "A great big fucking transparent lie. My father's a lot of things. Stupid isn't on that list."

"Remember Ismaeel, in love and war" he said with a curious twinkle in his eye. "How does the saying go, nothing is true, everything is permitted?"

"But I'm terrible at lying."

"You're a hafiz, right?"

"I was," I admitted, recalling those torturous years when I'd get up before dawn and head down to the cold dank madrassa for Quranic lessons in a language I didn't understand.

"For you, the Holy Book is the quickest and most direct route to the heart of your mission; your father's forgiveness and loving embrace—and by *that* I mean that you once again become an authentic and verifiable hafiz," he explained. The look on Pir's face assured me that he understood the irony of his words.

"But that's impossible! I'm meeting him on Thursday, in two days."

"You'll be amazed how quickly you'll be able to recall the whole book."

"I don't think so," I said, blowing smoke over my shoulder. "I've forgotten even my basic kalimas—except the first."

"What would you say, Ismaeel, if I told you that by the time you get to your father's house, you will once again be an impeccable hafiz?" he asked.

Suddenly, curiosity took hold of me, but with the realization that it could have me killed.

"I wouldn't mind having my memory improved," I said, feeling a surge of excitement. I was eager to experience the man's powers firsthand.

Suddenly, the flames flickered and the tinkling of a bicycle bell filled the air. A movement caught my eye. I turned and saw a man gliding across the room on an old green bicycle. I froze, feeling as if I was going to pass out. I was looking at Chaacha Khidr.

He was dressed in exactly the same clothes he had on when we met in that empty green wilderness under the purple sky on my Ayahuasca journey.

He stopped a few feet from the table, jumped off the bike, and kicked down the stand. He approached me with an extended left hand and a wicked grin on his wrinkled face. The incredible brightness of his eyes was at such odds with his decrepit look.

"Chaacha Khidr!" Pir cried out with delight. "We've been waiting for our tea for a long time now. I hope it's still hot," Pir said.

I wanted to get up, but my legs were powerless and almost buckled underneath me. I blinked, my mouth gapping wide open and my breath caught in my chest.

"Babu Ismaeel, very glad to meet with you again," Chaacha said in a crisp voice that could only have come out of the mouth of a very young man.

"Same here Chaacha," I managed to say, taking his hand.

He turned toward Pir.

"It's windy out there," he said, exchanging glances with Pir. "I almost got blown away by the winds," he added, taking a stainless steel thermos out of the wicker basket that hung from the bike's handlebars. As he put the thermos on the table, he stared at me for at least five seconds, his mouth stretched in a wide grin. His only incisor in his otherwise toothless oral cavity protruded from his lower lip like a shark fin. Definitely someone impossible to forget.

"Welcome to Shah Jamal!" he said. There was such warmth in his voice that I couldn't help but smile back at him and mouth my silent *thank you.*

He returned to his bike and took two white china cups from the basket. I noticed a burlap sack, just like Tarzan's, tied to the rear basket of his bicycle.

"Chaacha," Pir said in a scolding voice. "How many times have I told you to get a headlight for that bike of yours? I don't understand how you can ride around in the dark."

"Headlight? What for? I can see perfectly in the dark," Chaacha protested, standing his ground.

"I know your eyes are good Chaacha, but get the headlight anyway.

Not so much for you, but for everybody else, so they'll see you coming!" Pir said, teasing the old man as he poured the tea into our cups. Steam filled the room with the sweet fragrance of cardamom and other spices I couldn't place.

"How come you didn't bring any biscuits for our guest from America?" Pir asked.

"How could I forget those?" Chaacha asked, putting his hand in the basket again and retrieving a package of cookies. "I knew you'd ask me about biscuits. I brought your favorite brand: Barakat Biscuits."

Chaacha watched Pir peel back the wrapper on the package of biscuits and lay them on the table next to my cup.

Taking a biscuit out of the package I took a bite. It tasted of coconut and melted in my mouth, leaving an indescribable taste on my tongue. I took another bite, and then another. Pakistan, in the good old days, had been known for producing the best tea biscuits in the world. But this Barakat brand was like nothing I'd ever had before.

"Chaacha these biscuits are the most delicious thing I've ever tasted," I said, wondering if Chaacha Khidr was some thousand-year-old jinn. He certainly didn't look like he was from this planet. I had some strong suspicions about Pir Pull Siraat as well.

While we were enjoying our tea, Chaacha Khidr returned to his bicycle and untied the burlap sack and dragged it over to the table. Holding it upside down, Chaacha let the contents of the sack tumble out onto the floor. I spewed tea and biscuit out of my mouth in a wide arc when I saw the pile of objects at Chaacha's feet.

They were the disassembled parts of a man's body. A leg severed at mid-thigh; a shoulder attached to a piece of chest complete with jagged white ribs; a forearm with an attached hand whose middle finger still wore a ring with a large turquoise stone; a head with long curly hair and hairy face severed at the neck; and many other pieces that only a surgeon could hope to identify. The blood of the victim formed a dark crust over the torn edges of flesh.

I squeezed my eyes shut as my stomach heaved and I almost

vomited. I missed Wali, his benign company and predictable ways. At least, relatively speaking, things made a vague kind of sense when I was with him.

"Chaacha, please be a little more sensitive in front of our guest," Pir's voice was saying from somewhere. He sounded upset.

Do not attempt to overthink and make sense of matters from here on, for it may prevent you from choosing the right course of action, I chanted silently, remembering the instructions from the note and hoping it would keep the meager remains of my lunch inside of me.

"At my age, one doesn't have time for such trivial pleasantries," Chaacha's voice grumbled somewhere near his bike. "Our guest is a grown man. He can take it. After all, he's the one who's going to help fix it all."

I opened my eyes, feeling an acute sensory overload, the short-circuiting of my mental circuitry.

"There's such a thing as being delicate and subtle," Pir insisted. "Ismaeel has just arrived in our country."

"Delicate and subtle! I am fed up with being delicate and subtle. It's time for action. A military action." Chaacha Khidr roared as he squatted on the floor and stuffed the pieces of carcass back into his sack. My mind, frozen with shock, had indeed lost its ability to think straight.

I watched in a daze as Chaacha grabbed the severed head by its hair like it was a dead rat and flung it into his sack. I doubled over, the bile threatening to pour onto my lap.

"Ismaeel, please drink your tea before it gets cold—and don't mind Chaacha Khidr," Pir said.

I obediently followed Pir's command, hoping the tea would calm my stomach and wash the taste from my mouth. But the memory of that hairy head wasn't going anywhere.

"Chaacha, you may go now," Pir said, looking at the old man. "And please throw that mess of yours in the ditch."

"Not in the ditch—that would be a waste. I've got a much better place to dispose of him," he said. The old man looked at me and smiled, baring his shark fin tooth over his lower jaw. "Call me if Babu Ismaeel feels like doing a little sightseeing."

I had no idea what the hell these two disturbingly odd men were talking about. I just sat there, sipping my tea and slowly munching on more biscuits. When I put my empty cup down on the table, Pir refilled it immediately.

The tea and biscuits were the only decent thing that had happened to me since my arrival in Lahore. I felt a pleasant warmth spreading out from my stomach through the rest of my body. It washed away my exhaustion, the anxiety and nausea and all my unanswered questions.

Chaacha Khidr tied the burlap sack onto the rear of his bicycle and then mercifully rode away. After drinking my third cup of tea, I leaned back in my chair, finally feeling completely relaxed. I'd gobbled up about half a dozen biscuits already and wanted more.

"Never tasted anything like that before," I said.

"That's because this tea and these biscuits are not made in this world," Pir said casually.

"Then where are they made?" I said, keeping my tone polite.

"The Other Side."

"What's the proof?"

"You don't need proof if you see and experience it firsthand."

"And how that's done?"

"By learning how to tread the Pullsiraat," he said.

"Oh, the metaphorical tightrope. And you're the guide—Pir Pull-siraat."

"There's nothing metaphorical about Pullsiraat," he said, giving me a piercing look, his mouth stretched in a grin.

It was hard to digest what he was saying; and then a realization hit me: I was primarily here because of my intention, my own personal quest to know the realities of Paradise and Hell. I understood in a flash the words of Chaacha Khidr when I met him for the first time: *Your intention and ours have met across time and space and made this moment possible.* I had begun to get a vague sense of the scope of my mission.

"Unless you have direct experience, you can't and won't understand," Pir was saying.

Had I been utterly wrong all my life thinking Paradise and Hell as mere metaphors, figments of human imagination? Was he training the boys down in the courtyard to tightrope across the fabled wire? It was a far out thought, but nothing seemed far out anymore in this strange land where talk of the Next World was on everyone's lips. Everybody was either dying to get there, or helping others to get there. I longed for another cup of tea.

"There's more in the thermos," Pir said. As I helped myself to another cup, he continued to study me. Reaching into his pocket he brought out a palm sized piece of perforated paper, similar to a sheet of postage stamps. He extracted one of the small squares and laid it on the table next to my cup.

"This is your key to remembering the Quran, becoming a certified hafiz again," he said, tapping the tiny paper with the tip of his index finger.

"What am I supposed to do with that?" I asked, picking the tiny square of paper up off the table.

"Put it over your tongue. It may taste a little bitter at first."

"I don't do LSD," I said with resolve.

"It's not LSD—it's DSL. Think of it as a high speed connection to your brain that will allow you to download the lost data, very quickly," he said, smiling.

"Pir, I'm not exactly looking forward to recovering any lost data of my past," I said, shaking my head.

"We're talking about restoring a particular kind of data, not the whole of your past," Pir said.

"What if I develop a reaction to this stuff?" I thought of Wali. The poor old chap had been left with the car outside the shrine's walls beneath a tree swarming with jinns. He'd probably fallen asleep in the car by now. At least, I hoped so.

"I thought you'd welcome the opportunity," Pir said.

"I'm not sure, Pir."

"You've forgotten your intention."

"But what does it have to do with my intention—I remember my intention."

"I thought you'd just understood your purpose of being here," Pir said firmly.

"Not completely." I marveled at his ability to read my mind with such precision.

"You wanted to know if Heaven and Hell existed? And you also know there's a price for it."

"What if I can't afford it?"

"Obedience. You'll do what I tell you to do, the only way your intention and our task can move forward. You'll have to trust."

I felt super alert, without a hint of fatigue or exhaustion. I steeled myself and looked at the tiny square of paper.

"Thinking is the enemy of action," Pir reminded me.

He was right; ever since I landed I'd found thinking to be a pretty useless activity. If anything, grinding over everything in my mind had only made matters worse and done nothing to alleviate my confusion and uncertainty.

I opened my mouth, pressed the stamp over my tongue, and took the plunge of faith. After a minute or so the paper dissolved, leaving a mild bitterness in my mouth.

I sipped my tea and wondered about my future as a hafiz. It was a dreadful future in which I'd have to pose as a pious man of faith in order to gain the trust of my father, a man I never even wanted to see again. I was being forced to do something against which I had rebelled for as long as I could remember.

My part of the mission, it seemed, was becoming more despicable and offensive by the minute. I wondered what other terrifying commands and revelations would be in store for me. There was no doubt in my mind that this strange and powerful man, this Pir Pullsiraat meant business.

Chapter 13
Hell

THE TEA SUCCEEDED IN FLUSHING the bitterness from my mouth. From what other fantastical world had Chaacha Khidr procured this peculiar tea at such a tender hour? I was totally psyched about the big data recall, which Pir had called the high-speed connection for my brain.

How would it feel to remember the long-forgotten text whose every word had once been a jealously guarded treasure in the ground of my being?

Pir leaned forward, putting his elbows on the table. His dark eyes probed mine, searching for what, I could not guess.

"Chaacha Khidr is the real master of Pullsiraat," Pir said, blowing smoke in the air. "He's been traveling back and forth across the abyss his entire life—that's all he does."

"Then who are you?"

"I'm his deputy," he replied without further elaboration.

I felt he was pulling my leg.

"Is Chaacha a jinn?" I asked.

"No one knows what he is, except he's skillful and the best guide there is," Pir said.

"Is he the real Khidr?"

"Maybe you should ask him that question," Pir said, shaking his head and smiling.

"And Tarzan?" I said.

"Oh, he's all too human of course. He was just a baby when a jinn found him lying on Mall Road in front of the Governor's House. For one so small, he was crying and throwing his legs in the air raising one hell of a big fuss. He's human all right, but he was raised by jinns. He's got their fingerprints all over him," he said grinning.

"Ah, like the Tarzan raised by a family of baboons?" I said.

"Exactly."

"Are you a jinn too?" I asked pointedly.

"I'm a hybrid," Pir laughed, looking at me with an amused expression.

"What the hell's that supposed to mean?" I asked, trying to remember if I'd ever heard of jinns impregnating humans, or vice versa.

"You won't understand even if I explained it—not until you've got the necessary experience under your belt," Pir said.

"Necessary experience?" I said, feeling relaxed, lucid even. I had to admit that I hadn't felt this good in a long time. All I knew was that, whatever this *necessary experience* was, I wanted into the game.

"Necessary experience is only attained through what we call Direct Perception," he explained.

"And Direct Perception is . . .?" I prodded.

"If you take a ride across the abyss yourself, your experience of Pullsiraat will be direct, immediate, and unmistakable. And it'll save us both from a lot of the basic questions."

"Ride? I always imagined that Pullsiraat was some kind of wire that a believer walked over with his bare feet," I said. "How do you ride it?"

"On a bicycle," he said. "How else?"

"That's insane!"

"It was Chaacha's idea. For my part, I was perfectly happy teaching traditional tightroping to the select few," Pir said.

"How wide is the abyss?" I asked eagerly. My curiosity was racing and I could barely keep up with my own thoughts.

"I mean, how long is Pullsiraat?" I continued. "So it's a physical thing, not just your imagination?"

"Now just listen," he said impatiently. "The Abyss, and the way over it, changes according to the intention and capacity of the believer."

I realized he hadn't blinked in several minutes. His eyes looked like two bright mirrors suspended in the dark in front of my face. Was Pir trying to hypnotize me? If so, should I resist? Or surrender to the power of his gaze?

"What if you're not a believer?" I said, finding it hard to break eye contact.

"Those who know don't have to believe," he said. "I think you should avail yourself of the opportunity and go for the ride." He looked dead serious and made me very uneasy.

"Maybe another time. Wali, my driver, is waiting for me in the car. He must be wondering where the hell I am."

"That's what drivers are for, Ismaeel. They wait," Pir said.

I felt lightheaded thinking about crossing over some mythical abyss; traversing the fabled wire stretched over a pit of fire, on a bicycle!

"But don't you have to be dead first in order to experience everything we're talking about?" I asked.

"Yes. Typically. There are shortcuts for everything, my dear Ismaeel," he said, straightening his back. "And certain people know all the shortcuts."

"Certain people, like Chaacha?" I ventured, sensing some vague understanding of things coagulating in the belly of my mind.

"Fear has remained your greatest enemy, Ismaeel—a trip to Hell will really be helpful in your case," he said, slipping his hand into his pocket and drawing out three glass vials the length of my little finger.

He raised them to the light and I could see each vial was filled with a transparent liquid—one red, one yellow, and the third one green. He laid the vials on the table.

"What are those for?" I said, eyeing the delicate little receptacles.

"This is the shortcut," he said.

"The shortcut?"

"Crossing the abyss is an extremely dangerous affair," he explained. "One that requires years of discipline and training before you can even think of putting the first foot on the wire. The elixir in these vials contains a formula designed to reduce that time to a matter of minutes."

Pir seemed almost ruthless in pushing his concoctions on me so quickly. After all he'd only met me less than an hour ago. In comparison to the New Age shamans running sacred ceremonies in the yoga centers of New York City, Pir seemed to be operating on a whole new dimension. The man was clearly a master, but of what, I wasn't quite sure.

I touched the vials with my fingertips, rolling them on the table in front of me. After the marvels I'd already witnessed and consumed in this place, I could only wonder about the secret chemistry contained in these three vials.

"You must choose one," Pir said.

I picked them up and held them to the light of the candle, shaking them gently. They reminded me of a traffic light. Was I standing on the crossroads of life and death? Or on some threshold far more crucial to my existence than that?

"What are the chances that I won't make it back?" I asked, searching Pir's large fiery eyes for reassurance and finding none.

"There's no guarantee of anything in life."

"I meant probability. High? Medium?" I said trying to steady my voice. Pir just sat there.

"Low?" I hissed in a whisper. He just shrugged.

"Low to medium, maybe," he admitted, stroking his beard, his large bright eyes staring at me like those of the Sphinx.

The vials were pharmaceutical grade with tapered necks for easy snapping. I stared at them, massaging my lip with my finger. Red could be too hot to handle; while green may be too weak for someone like me. I smiled inwardly, like some psychedelic Goldilocks.

"Since I've got to choose one, I'll take yellow."

"Good choice," he said.

Keeping the yellow vial in my hand, I put the other two back on the table. As I rolled the vial around between my fingers, stalling as long as possible, I heard a faint drumbeat in the distance. It grew louder as if some spectral drummer marched through the unseen toward us.

"In life, Ismaeel, timing is everything," Pir said, standing up and walking over to the entrance of the room.

He stood there for a moment and then motioned for someone to enter. The drummer picked up his tempo as he entered the room. His *dhole* drum was the size of an oil barrel and hung from his neck by an old leather belt, its weight resting against his thighs. Pir came and sat back down at the table, sweeping me and my vial with his eyes.

"For the elixir to work, the crusted matter that's deposited on one's soul must first be polished until clean."

Before I could open my mouth to ask another question, the cadenced drumming rose to a deafening wall of noise that reverberated deep in my chest. For a moment I thought I'd heard this drumming before. But where?

The drummer had long black and henna-stained dreadlocks that hung to his waist. The guy made me think of a chunkier version of Bob Marley. Trailing behind him were the jinn boys holding their torches. The room swam with dancing red-gold light and the walls were alive with shadows moving in time with the drum's rhythms.

The drummer marched over to us, beating his dhole with such ferocity that his drumsticks blurred and all but disappeared. I grabbed the edge of the table to steady myself against the cacophonous vibrations that shook my eardrums. Pir raised his hand in the air and the man stopped immediately. In the absolute silence that descended upon us I could actually hear the crackling of the boys' torches.

"Ismaeel, it's time to break the vial," Pir said, sliding back into his chair. "And give me your watch."

"Why do you want my watch?" I asked, while sliding it off my wrist and handing it over. I noticed it was half past one. We'd started off from Shadmaan around one. It had taken about twenty to twenty-five minutes to get to Shah Jamal. Was it possible I'd spent only few minutes in Pir's company?

"Time will only complicate things for you," Pir said, dropping my watch into his pocket.

I took a deep breath and tried to empty my mind of doubts that had plagued me since Pir showed me the vials. I hoped I'd made the right choice.

One thing was certain: there was no point in trying to figure out where this whole thing was headed. I just had to trust him. I held the little vial in my fingers, feeling the cool smooth surface. Then I snapped the neck and poured the yellow liquid onto my tongue. I'd expected an unpleasant taste—like that of Ayahuasca—but the elixir was completely tasteless. It evaporated from my tongue, leaving a peculiar, but not unpleasant, dryness.

And that was it. The shamans had a long way to go in improving the taste of their jungle concoction. The contents of Pir's vial were smooth and delicate.

Then I glanced up and saw the drummer beginning to move his body, whirling slowly at first and then gaining speed. His dreadlocks whipped back and forth in a dense black cloud as he pounded the drum again. My body rocked involuntarily to the rhythm the drummer poured over us. I resisted the urge to get up and whirl around with the drummer like he was my dance partner from hell. The man was a gaping vortex of pure raw energy. I closed my eyes and allowed the wave of sound to sweep me over the edge.

Just twenty-four hours ago I was in Manhattan, a place that might as well have existed in another time, another dimension, for all I cared. I almost couldn't even remember the man called Ismaeel who had lived there long ago.

A long time passed. I couldn't even say how long, but it was long enough for me to have forgotten all about time and to become utterly absorbed in the moment. The drummer ceased his drumming. The man stood motionless, his sticks resting on the drum. Sweat poured from his face and he was heaving as he struggled to catch his breath. Pir raised his hand again and the man bowed and slowly walked out of the room, followed by the jinn boys with their bobbing torches.

I heard someone moving around behind me and turned to see Chaacha Khidr standing next to his bicycle, his arms folded across his chest. His eyes were bright as ever, and as before, they were locked on mine with a disquieting twinkle. He seemed to have materialized out of thin air. I had no idea how he had even entered the room.

"Ah!" Pir said, waving at the old man like he'd been gone for centuries instead of just a few minutes. "It looks like your ride's here. You may now request Chaacha to escort you across the abyss," Pir said.

Before I could reply, Chaacha said, "I hope Babu Ismaeel won't mind holding my sack as we cross over."

Clutching a burlap sack stuffed with human body parts and sitting on the back of a bike behind this crazy old man who probably wasn't even really a man anyway was not my idea of the best way to cross any abyss. Fortunately, my lifelong love affair with the unknown wiped out all trace of disgust, misgivings and bewilderment still lurking in me. "Not a problem!" I said with unbridled enthusiasm.

"Excellent!" Chaacha said. "There's no turning back now anyway, Babu."

"Chaacha, don't worry about me. I'm not turning back, not now, not ever," I assured him.

I got up from my chair feeling a delicious tingling vibration coursing through my body. It felt like somebody had struck me like a tuning fork. I was light as a balloon, filled with helium and ready to float away at the slightest tug of my string by some knowing unseen hand.

Chaacha had picked up the burlap sack and without any warning, lobbed it at me from a good ten feet away. I threw my arms out and caught the sack with my hands. It was so light it could've been filled with feathers. I fought the urge to think of what the sack really contained.

"Let's go, Ismaeel," Chaacha said wheeling his bike toward the entrance.

Pir stood up from his chair and we left the room together. The jinn boys were outside waiting for us, their torches illuminating the darkness.

We returned to the ledge overlooking the courtyard still illuminated by many lamps.

The boys on the wires were still practicing and I spotted Tarzan riding a bicycle across the middle wire. I wondered if he'd ever ventured to the other side, or if was he still a novice learning the high art handed down by Chaacha Khidr.

Chaacha straddled his bicycle, his feet barely reaching the ground.

"Ready when you are!" he shouted.

I looked at Pir. His earbuds were back in his ears and his lips moved without making any sound. He gripped my shoulder with his large hand and gave it a shake.

"No matter what happens, don't panic."

Was he kidding? Then he slapped me on the back and headed back toward his room without another word, the jinn boys close on his heels.

Without a word or warning, somebody killed the lights in the courtyard, plunging the whole place in darkness. I saw a pair of eyes suspended in the dark about five feet from me. It was Chaacha. The sight of him would have scared the hell out of me before, but tonight it was strangely comforting.

I hopped sidesaddle on the back of Chaacha's bike and immediately his pedaling was fast and furious. My legs dangled to one side as I sat on the carrier behind him. It was the only position that allowed me to maintain my grip on the bag that teetered precariously in my lap.

There was nothing to see or hear besides the rustling of Chaacha's robe as he pedaled deeper into the sightless void. The sheer audacity, style, and scope of this adventure had punched a gaping hole through my logical self. My right foot found the footrest just in time as Chaacha bore down on the handlebars and we picked up even more speed.

"Hold on!" Chaacha shouted, glancing back at me.

In the next moment, we were rocketing down a steep slope in free fall. I let out a scream—the kind you hear out of people strapped to a rickety seat on an evil roller coaster ride; half terror, half ecstasy. The bike plunged several hundred feet before finally leveling off. We must have been barreling along at a good hundred miles an hour.

The air had become stifling hot and dry as we hovered weightlessly. The dark was less intense here too. The sky shimmered with the warm glow of that mystical hour just before dawn. Soon we were enveloped in a gray mist that was lit from below by a crimson glow. I looked down and the scene below jolted my every nerve. My first thought was that only a miracle would get us out of this alive.

Like a bird in a nosedive we plunged into a vast chasm that opened beneath us. I was numb with shock when I saw the steel cable as thick as my wrist on which our bicycle sped through open space. The bottom loomed a good mile below and swelled with a scintillating river of boiling blood-red magma. It was a monster of a canyon with its distant rims shrouded in darkness. My cheeks burned and my throat contracted as a sulfurous heat blasted us from the floor of the abyss.

"Are you enjoying the view, Babu Ismaeel?" Chaacha asked.

"Was—was this the route you took to bring us the tea?" I stammered.

"I cross over every day, Babu, often several times," he said.

"So this is what Pullsiraat looks like," I said, still numbed with fright.

Instead of answering my question, Chaacha began humming a tune—an old pre-Partition Indian song, one about princesses and unrequited love. Black smoke rose from the bubbling river of liquid fire and the air smelled of sulfur. Chaacha's sack was weightless in my lap. Fear began to fade with the retreating darkness and I resigned myself to whatever was to assail my senses next.

Steep canyon walls emerged through the mist revealing tall spires of twisted black rock rising toward the sky like minarets. Some of them reached as high as the cable, while others disappeared above our heads.

"Chaacha, was this the route you took to bring us the tea?" I repeated my question.

"No Babu, that is the long way. There are many other routes. The cable chosen for your journey was shorter than that," he explained as I struggled to hear him over the noise.

"I thought Ismaeel Babu could use a little adventure! You're not in any big hurry, are you?" Chaacha asked, as another mighty gust of blistering wind shot up from below and almost swept us off the bike and into the chasm. I began to shiver uncontrollably.

Looking into the distance I saw a black bird the size of a small plane rip through the air and plunge toward the bottom. Chaacha hugged the handlebars and I hugged Chaacha.

"We better stop—the winds are getting worse and we could get blown off the wire."

"Stop? Where? Is that possible?" I screamed, watching in amazement as the gigantic bird surged up from the bottom of the abyss, its enormous red-tipped black wings carried on the brutal blasts of superheated air.

"There's a rest area just up ahead," Chaacha said, pedaling faster. "Don't panic."

Don't panic? Just get me off this bicycle. Now.

"How far?" I asked, still watching the massive bird ride the currents up the canyon. "Do they serve tea there?"

The bird shifted its angle of flight and turned right into our path. It came up alongside us and hovered about twenty feet to our left. Up close I say it had the face of an owl, but its long pointed beak was that of an egret. Fresh blood dripped from its beak and talons. I wondered at its prey, and shivered. The bird regarded us closely with black, jewel-like glittering eyes.

"Chaacha, are you seeing this?"

"Here we are!" Chaacha announced as if he hadn't heard me. The bike stopped moving. Seeing the ground beneath my feet, I jumped off the bike, and so did Chaacha.

The ground was solid volcanic rock, black and jagged as broken glass. We were on the flat top of a rocky column not more than a hundred feet in diameter. The bird was now circling us. Chaacha started walking toward the edge of what looked like a broad mesa, and, keeping an eye on this winged thing from hell, I followed, my legs shaky and my feet wobbly.

The bird emitted a shrill cry, folded its wings back against its body and plunged back into the abyss. I laid the sack down and walked over to the edge where Chaacha stood staring after it. Together we watched the bird's descent. It sped down in a spiral arc and then crossed the burning river of fire and landed on a rocky ledge a couple of hundred feet above the floor of the canyon. Black smoke continued to rise from the pit and obscured both the ledge and the monstrous raptor that perched there.

"Ismaeel Babu, this is Lookout Point," Chaacha said.

I realized we were standing next to a rusted pipe fixed to a pole. Touching the pipe it was quite warm, but not infernally hot like everything else in this place.

"Chaacha, what the hell is this thing?"

"Telescope!" he said pulling the thing toward him and bringing it up to his eye. "What's the point of touring Hell if you can't have a Lookout Point complete with telescope?"

"Hell!? I'd always thought—"

"Yes, that's right. At this very moment you're looking at one of the tiny tributaries of Hell."

The Lookout was the tallest rocky spur that rose from the floor of the grand canyon of Hell. It was no more than a needle in that boundless space but it afforded a staggering panoramic view of the pit of horrors and despair.

"God Almighty—!" I gasped. "Who built a telescope in a place like this?" Was Chaacha going to point out the roasting bodies of the sinners with the help of this metal tube engraved with the word *Galileo* next to the viewfinder?

"It's been here ever since Hell came into being," Chaacha said, peering into the canyon.

"Chaacha, telescopes were only invented a few centuries ago," I said. "And Hell is supposed to be older than humanity."

"Time is only important because things need to happen one after the other, Ismaeel Babu," Chaacha replied. "Or at least, it has to look like they do," he added with another of those infuriating winks of his.

Directing the device at the bottom of the canyon, I looked through the lens and adjusted the glass until everything came into sharp focus. I gasped and jumped back, bumping into Chaacha. The old man just cackled and held his sides.

"Looks close enough to reach out and grab it!" he cried.

That was actually an understatement. The surface of the river of fire was so clear, I could see bubbles and geysers forming on the surface and then exploding to emit jets of gas and plumes of debris.

If Hell was real, Paradise had to be real too. At that moment I knew with certainty that I'd been done with my doctoral thesis trying to prove otherwise. Would I be given a glimpse of the latter at some point?

I slowly moved the glass over the distant wall of the canyon, searching for the basalt ledge where the raptor had perched.

Finding the spot, I scanned the area looking for the creature. What I saw instead stunned me. Where the bird had been, there was now a man just standing there. He was tall and muscular, his body chiseled like a statue. The copper-colored skin glistened with sweat and his face was as red as the flames that licked the earth at his feet.

I shuddered in alarm when I saw the guy wasn't just standing there at all; he was bound to a pole. His hands were chained high over his head and his ankles were lashed one over the other by a heavy manacle. A dark liquid oozed from a deep gash in his side.

Movement on the other side of the ledge caught my attention. The bird waddled out from a cave in the wall of rock. The man's head slumped on his chest at a sickening angle. Waddling over to the captive, the bird thrust its enormous beak into the gaping wound on the man's ribcage. The raptor shook and twisted its beak with such terrible ferocity it would only be a matter of minutes before it ripped the poor fellow apart.

The man looked up, his face a mask of unspeakable torment and pain. For a moment, our eyes met and I stopped breathing. He opened his mouth and screamed in agony as the bird ripped deeper into his tortured flesh. Sweat poured from my body and I gagged. I tried to tear my eyes from the horrific spectacle below, but it was impossible.

At last the monster pulled its beak from the man's side. It swallowed whatever hideous trophies it had extracted from its victim and then it lifted its massive body and took flight. Beating its enormous wings twice against the volcanic currents, the hideous creature disappeared into the smoke rising from below. I turned and looked for Chaacha, but he was no longer at my side.

Nearly panicked at the thought of being alone in a place like this, I almost cried out with relief when I saw him standing next to the bike, gripping his ghastly burlap sack. The bird reappeared and soared upward across the canyon toward us.

"Chaacha, what's going on down there?" I demanded, trying with little success to stifle the terror in my rising voice.

"Time to feed the birds," Chaacha replied, flashing me his nearly toothless grin.

I heard a rustling noise overhead and looked up. I held my breath as the raptor from Hell descended above our heads. Chaacha rushed to the far end of the mesa and dumped the rotting contents of the sack onto the ground. Then he turned and dashed back to where I stood.

We watched in fascination as the bird dropped its enormous bulk next to the carrion, its wings still held aloft. The sword-like beak contained hundreds of dagger-sharp teeth that still dripped blood from its recent feasting on the captive below. "Let's go!" Chaacha gave my arm a tug.

A gust of wind lifted what looked like a scrap of paper from the remains of the corpse and dropped it next to us. I picked it up and looked at it. It was a Certificate of *Shahadaat* or martyrdom. The bottom of the paper was scorched but I could still make out most of it. It read: Fida Muhammad, resident of Farid Kot, embraced martyrdom for Allah and entered Paradise on.... The date and place of his death had been burned away. I tossed the paper into the scalding wind.

Chaacha was perched on his bike ready to go, so I jumped on behind him as before, my eyes still glued to the bird. The creature clasped the severed head by the beard and swung it back and forth in its enormous beak like a pendulum. It gained momentum with each swing. The skull cracked like a gourd. With ravenous eyes the bird pecked on the emulsified brain, its long black tongue scouring the inside of the skull.

"It loves brain," Chaacha said solemnly.

Fighting sensory overload and the urge to vomit, I succumbed to a light sleep for much of the next part of the trip. I had no idea how long we rode or what surrounded us, but I awoke with a start, clutching Chaacha's waist.

"It's time for tea," his voice chimed within my dreamless reverie.

Opening my eyes I saw a tent large enough to sleep a dozen people set up on a large grassy field. The tent's faded green cloth was patched at many places and reminded me of a dervish's robe.

Chaacha parked the bike and we made our way over to the tent. The grassy area looked down on a lush beautiful valley in one direction and the broad sweeping canyon of Hell in the other. Not far from the tent, a rectangular wooden table and a pair of benches were set on a patch of grass, so we sat down.

The place smelled of roses and an occasional whiff of sulfur and the air danced with golden beams of light filled with sparkling dust. Rolling green meadows stretched out below and a grassy slope drenched in mauve was ringed with waterfalls. Birds of all kinds soared in flight over the valley. At the far end, a dark band stretched across the horizon. It took me a moment to realize that I was looking at a massive wall that, given its immeasurable distance from us, must be hundreds if not thousands of times taller than the Himalayas.

"Wow! Is that really a wall?" I asked Chaacha. "What's behind it?"

"Paradise," Chaacha replied, retrieving a pack of cigarettes from his pocket. He looked old and weary now, and I wondered again about his true age.

Before I could learn anything more about the place, a man holding a tray emerged from the tent. His face was radiant and his eyes were as bright as two moons.

"Welcome to the Bihishti Tea Corner. My name is Ibrahim."

Chapter 14
The Mission

IBRAHIM SET A PAIR OF TEACUPS and a plate of biscuits on the table in front of us. The tea was the same delicious tincture that Chaacha had served at Pir's compound. But this time it didn't rejuvenate me as it had before.

Ibrahim sat down on the bench next to me and took out a flute. As I sipped my tea, he lifted the slender reed to his lips and began to play. It was such a hauntingly beautiful and sad melody that I was soon overcome with inexplicable grief.

Time seemed to have stopped. When Ibrahim finished his tune and set his flute down on the table, I was absolutely heartbroken. I could've spent the rest of my life sitting there listening to the sad cries of Ibrahim's flute and staring into the verdant meadow that lay below like an exquisite silk carpet.

"How far is Paradise from here," I asked Ibrahim, certain that his flute had carried me half the distance at least.

"It depends how fast you ride your stallion, and what challenges you meet," he replied.

"Where do you get stallions around here?"

"From the country down below," he said, pointing to the rolling green slopes.

"Let's say you've got the speediest horse, and there are no obstacles to slow you down, how long would it take to get to Paradise then?"

"Seventy years, if you go by human time."

"Seventy years?" I cried in shock. I'd be almost a hundred years old if I set out for Paradise right this minute.

Suddenly, coming out of nowhere, a rush of shrieking cries filled the air. The light was fading. My head felt hot and beaten like an anvil, and it was getting harder to keep my eyes open. I heard Chaacha's voice behind me.

"Look up, Ismaeel!" Chaacha shouted, pointing to the sky in joyful agitation. "The Ababeels!" he cried.

A black cloud of birds stretched across the sky. The massive flock undulated sensuously as the birds turned as one unit and darted back and forth across the heavens.

"They were last used fifteen hundred years ago on earth," Ibrahim shouted over the din, which was so loud I could barely catch what he was saying.

"They're used only in the direst emergencies," Chaacha chimed in. "And here they are!"

I wanted to be part of the conversation but felt too drained and overwhelmed to speak. I knew that they were talking about the incident that'd occurred a decade or two before the birth of Prophet Muhammad. It was even mentioned in the Quran. According to the legend, a flock of ababeels, carrying stones of baked clay in their beaks and talons, descended on the mighty army of Abrah Al-Ashram—the king of Abyssinia, who'd attacked Mecca in order to destroy Kaaba—discharged their payload turning everything into husk.

"I think he couldn't hold out any longer." I heard Chaacha say from somewhere.

Overpowered by sleep at long last, I let my chin drop to my chest and just zoned out.

"Wake up, Ismaeel, we're back in Lahore." A familiar excited voice broke through the thick silence. I opened my eyes. I was still seated behind Chaacha on his bike, my hands gripping the fabric of his robe. It was dark and we'd come to a halt.

I jumped off and rubbed my eyes, feeling strangely refreshed and rested. We were back in the exact same spot where we'd begun our ride—the ledge overlooking the courtyard in Pir Pullsiraat's compound. Tarzan was still on the wire pedaling his bike. It looked like we'd never even left.

"Chaacha, what time is it?" I said.

"Time is always *now*!" he declared, pushing his bicycle toward Pir's sanctuary.

I walked by his side, recalling the night's journey. It was as vivid and fresh as a blustery day in a monsoon rain. The shamans of Lahore were clearly operating on a whole different level of reality. Whoever they were, they were worthy of far more respect than I'd given anyone before.

Entering Pir's candlelit room, we saw him sitting at the table, one leg over the other with a cigarette in his mouth and a black leather book in his hand. Two of the jinn-cats lounged on the carpeted floor at his feet. Pir jumped up when he saw us and threw his arms in the air, the black book still clutched in his hand. He gave me a firm hug, slapped me on the back, and smiled.

"So the prodigal son returns! Welcome! So, you're a believer now?"

I had no idea how to respond. The crazy ride on Chaacha's bike had shredded my concept of reality to pieces. There were so many questions; many more questions than I'd had at the beginning of my trip to Hell. I looked back on the moment I'd first arrived at this compound as the good old days of innocent simplicity. I realized that I'd done nothing but wasted all that precious time writing my dissertation on a topic I had no freaking clue about.

"Would you like some more tea?" Pir asked.

"No, thank you," I said, even though I craved its rejuvenating effects and otherworldly taste. I had no desire to send Chaacha back across Hell's abyss just to get me a cup of tea.

"I think you need to get some sleep."

It was time for me to leave, and I was being, at least for the moment, dismissed. I wondered when the potion that would make me remember the Quran would take effect.

"The recall of Allah's word is a tricky business," Pir explained. "Each word, each dash, every dot must be checked and rechecked many times before it's restored to its original place within the mind of the hafiz."

I looked at Chaacha. He stood by his bike and nodded in agreement.

"Babu, the smallest error and your brain could be permanently damaged. Try not to force any recall tonight," Chaacha said placing his warm hand on my shoulder.

"It'll happen on its own when the time is right," Pir added.

I felt naked in Pir's presence. The man read me as easily as the most elementary volume in his library. He tapped my chest with the black leather diary he held in his hand.

"This is a very special Quran. Always keep it on your person. As they say in America: 'Never leave home without it,'" Pir said.

I took the Quran from his hand. Its pages were burgundy parchment with a fine hand-lettered text penned in lustrous gold. The text stood out from its dark background and almost hovered over the page. This was clearly the work of a master calligrapher. It radiated an ineffable but palpable energy that pressed upon me like an unseen hand.

"This is the most beautiful Quran I've ever seen," I said, staring at the golden text as it glittered in the soft candlelight. It was unbelievable that I used to recite the whole of this book from memory, sometimes in one sitting, but without knowing what it really was—a miracle in its own right.

"It's yours now," Pir said.

I opened the Quran at random and silently read the first line of the page. Then I closed my eyes and tried to recall the next line. But it eluded me like a shy mistress avoiding my gaze.

"I told you not to force it!" Pir barked. "You've been warned.

You'll lose your mind if you aren't careful, if you don't follow my instructions to the letter," he said.

"Patience is the fastest way to achieve one's goal, Babu," Chaacha said.

"I understand!" I apologized, though feeling annoyed and embarrassed.

"This Quran is the key to our mission's success," Pir continued. "The secret will reveal itself when the time is right," he said, taking his red headband off and handing it to me. "Wear this."

I took the headband and slipped it over my forehead, wishing he'd stop being so cryptic and tell me the facts and the truth.

"I'm not the only one who can read your mind," Pir said, glaring at me. "Some of the Khalifa's people are trained to do that too. They're damned good at it, too. That's part of Khalifa's impenetrable security system. It's the most sophisticated system ever developed. For now, the less you know, the safer we'll all be."

"How can someone read minds?" I asked. I was kind of creeped out, yet intrigued, by the idea.

"It's easy. All you need is a medium," Pir said, bending down and stroking one of the cats. It responded by standing up and rubbing the side of its head against his leg. There was no doubt in my mind that these two cats of Pir and the torch bearing boys were one and the same.

"All animals are telepathic—not just the jinns. It's in their nature. The big cats bred by Khalifa are used especially for this very purpose," he said. "They are the most perfect telepathic medium known to man. There's no information so private, so guarded and protected, so deep, that they can't easily lift it from your skull."

"Wow, that's wild!" I said, thinking that every goddamn thing about this place was weird in the extreme.

"The animals are innocent in all this, of course," Pir continued. "They aren't conscious of their mind reading ability, nor are they aware of giving such information to those whose job is extract it."

"It's unbelievable!" I said. "Very sophisticated indeed!"

Pir smiled and looked at me without saying any more. I was startled to hear him speaking within my mind.

"One day this Quran may have to be ripped apart to activate its power." His voice sifted through the folds of my mind like a warm hand.

"I don't want to die so young," I replied, just thinking it to see if he heard me. The thought of ripping up a Quran in a place like Caliphate of Al-Bakistan stopped the blood in my veins.

Pir threw back his head and laughed out loud. Chaacha joined him from behind me where he'd been standing as a silent witness to our discussion.

"The tele-band worked," Pir said aloud with a smile. "It passed the test."

"I don't like it when people laugh at me," I shot the thought out at both of them, squeezing my brows; but they only laughed harder. I wasn't sure what Pir meant by the tele-band. Did he mean the headband I wore?

"I'm afraid you'll still have to be blindfolded on your way out," Pir said out loud. "It's better that way—for you, and for us. This place is under constant surveillance and threat of our cover being blown by Khalifa."

I turned around and looked at Chaacha. There was a worried look on his face, but he just shrugged when our eyes met. The cats snarled once, flicking their tails and baring their canines. I heard footsteps and knew my escort had arrived.

"Babu, whenever you encounter a suspicious cat, empty your mind of all thoughts," Chaacha said. "It doesn't work all the time, but it may give you some protection."

"Put the tele-band over your eyes," Pir said. "Keep it with you all the time, along with this Quran, and put it on when you find yourself in trouble."

"Thank you Pir," I said, also nodding at Chaacha.

"You've been wanting to ask me something. Just ask," Pir said.

"Since you've been more than kind to allow me a visit to Hell, would it be possible to arrange a visit to Paradise?" I said. "With Chaacha, I mean."

"Life arranges things according to one's intention, capacity, and performance," Pir said. "We're here only to help you accomplish the task we'll soon set before you."

I had the uneasy feeling I might never see any of these unusual people ever again. A thought that saddened me intensely.

"Your request will be considered depending upon how you perform this time around," Pir smiled. "Desire alone will not take you there. There has to be a need for such a visit to take place."

I looked at Chaacha. He was scratching his temple as if considering my request.

"Chaacha, I'll never forget the ride over Pullsiraat," I said, sliding the headband over my eyes.

"Let Tarzan know where the book is—I need to have it in my possession as soon as possible," Pir's voice resounded in my ears. Startled I uncovered my eyes and looked at him. He was a brilliant mind reader.

"The book with blank pages!" I said. "Don't worry it's safe."

"If it's not with me, it's not safe!" he barked. "Nobody is safe."

"What could be so important about a book with blank pages?" I asked.

"Its pages aren't exactly blank," Pir said. "That book is loaded with enough power to take a whole village to..." He paused for a second and then continued. "We don't have time, Ismaeel. I must have the book in my possession as soon as possible."

"Take a whole village to where?" I insisted.

"Paradise," he replied.

"How is that possible?"

"It's only a matter of time before Khalifa finds it." He'd ignored my query.

"He'll never find the book," I said, casually, and immediately realizing the idiocy of my statement.

"Don't be a fool!" Pir said, exploding from his chair. "We can never underestimate Khalifa's power."

"All right. Okay, I'm sorry," I said, all my smugness deflating in the face of Pir's anger. "I'll tell Tarzan where the book is; he'll know exactly how to get there." I said. "But it's in a place that would be impossible to stumble upon, and I really don't think—"

"No, you really don't think! You *really* don't think that trained psychics you know nothing about could possibly find that book?" Pir said glowering at me like I was a child who'd just ruined everything.

"Oh, all right," Pir said, his voice softening and the warm smile returning gradually to his face. "But you tell Tarzan I want that book, *NOW*. And Ismaeel, don't ever hold information back from me again, or we're finished."

"I understand. Mind reading aside," I said, fully recovered from Pir's outburst with a closed-lip smile on my face. "I need to know more, a lot more, about my mission."

"There's no harm giving some basic briefing to Babu Ismaeel," Chaacha said. "It's a fair request."

Pir and Chaacha exchanged glances for a moment.

"All right." Pir took a deep breath, looked me in the eyes and continued. "What you need to know is that over the years Khalifa has been systematically contaminating the water supply of the entire country; city by city, town by town, making all water in the country undrinkable. He now produces his own brand of water, the only clean and drinkable water available, and it has become his private monopoly. Then there's the Hoor Afza, his very lucrative side-business.

"The water he bottles under the brand name Paradise Water is laced with a tasteless, odorless chemical which, when consumed in sufficient quantities over time, starts to work its sinister brand of magic. It puts people into a trance-like state that allows them to go about their normal daily lives while becoming obsessed with thoughts of Paradise, and how to get there as quickly as possible. It makes them volatile. Emotionally unstable." He paused and watched me intently. "Do you follow me?"

All I could do was nod at this troubling revelation. I understood a lot about this place in that moment. The people's obsession with Paradise had basically turned them into a nation of bloodthirsty zombies. They had become disconnected with reality; people like Wali, his mood swings; *that* family of five oblivious to their obvious brush with death in *that* accursed martyr-vest shop; not to mention the hordes cheering the bloody sport called Cricket and being blown to bits; beheadings and stonings; car trunks fitted with martyr tanks; and of course, my father's business that had become a household name.

"And now, Khalifa has something very special planned, a real spectacle," Pir said, cracking his knuckles. "If he's not stopped very soon, this world and the Next will need a major cleanup that will stretch into the not-so-foreseeable future. Without that book, he won't be able to bring his plans to completion. Your job, Ismaeel, is to help us stop the man. And that's all you need to know for now."

"So if you get the book, it's all over for him, is that it?" I said, feeling dazed by the scope of the mission at hand.

"No. But it gives us an opportunity to strategically insert you into the scheme of things," Pir said, giving me a mischievous smile. "He'll get another such book soon—the backup copy. He's relentless in his pursuit of Paradise."

Pir's words left me speechless and in the grip of more questions than ever. There was still so much unexplained.

"So am I being strategically placed for you to get to the Khalifa using my father as a bridge?"

"Don't think too much," he said. "Just do it."

"Is that the price I've got to pay to walk the Path to High Knowledge?"

"Certainly." Pir's eyes brightened, his mouth stretched in a grin. "And remember: the basic reminders still apply, especially the *lust* part. You're expected to perform better this time around."

"I'll try my best." I knew that he was referring to the *basic reminders* he'd jotted down for me in the *note*.

It was time to leave. I couldn't wait to get back to the car to sort myself out. I needed to make sense of my mission. Most of all I needed to recover from everything that had happened in the last however many hours, weeks, or centuries that had elapsed since I'd landed on this godforsaken continent of wonders and horrors, of heaven, and hell.

I covered my eyes with the tele-band. His large hand firmly grasping my shoulder, Pir walked me to the door and handed me off to somebody who led me back into the real world of ordinary heroes and monsters. The world I knew.

It was Tarzan who pulled the headband off my eyes. We were back in the courtyard and the buzz of dozens of hushed conversations filled the air. Men were still hunched around their fires under thick clouds of smoke, and the yard was as thick as ever with the heavy pungent fragrance of Cannabis. Nothing had changed. As we walked back to Wali's car I told Tarzan about the black book and the exact location where he could find it. He laughed when I told him Pir wanted the book NOW!

"It might be tricky getting back in there again tonight. But I'll try. Pir can be, *persuasive*. Don't you worry, sir," Tarzan said.

Half a dozen armed men dressed in black followed us, all but invisible in the murky shadows. Outside the walls of Pir's compound I spotted the car parked under the giant Bunyan tree. The cats, roused from their slumber by our approach, resumed their haunting symphony overhead. I saw a cluster of glowing yellow eyes moving within the huge tree.

The thing was alive with cats. They crawled along the thick branches, their howls piercing the air like the voices of the Sirens. I wondered if they were all jinn cats, or the especially bred psychic variety, or a mixture of the two. I figured they were probably the former guarding the shrine of Shah Jamal from the latter. Everyone in Pir's entourage seemed to have his task, his mission and sacred duty.

Wali, completely indifferent to the cats by now, lounged as before on the hood of the car, smoking his *biree*, his eyes glued to the bright crescent that hung low in the sky. An empty teacup sat beside him. He gave me a surprised look and slid off the car.

"We took care of Wali while you were gone," Tarzan whispered in my ear, as one of the guards picked up the empty cup from the hood.

I wondered what he'd meant by that. Had they spiked Wali's tea? And if so, why? Without saying a word, Wali opened the rear door of the car for me. Tarzan and I shook hands and then I slid into the back seat.

Tarzan waved goodbye and flashed me a warm smile, his teeth white as ivory. Two armed men stood a few feet behind him, their faces obscured by shadows. Wali turned the headlights on, momentarily flooding the two guards' faces in light. One of them looked vaguely familiar, but I couldn't place where I'd seen him.

We'd only driven a few feet when Tarzan dashed towards the car and beat on the window. Wali braked.

"What's up, Tarzan?" I asked, rolling down the window.

"Your watch!" he said, grinning and dangling the watch in my face. "And here's a phone number of one of my associates," he said in a whisper. "If you need to reach me." He pressed a small folded piece of paper into my hand. As I slid my phone into my pocket, I noticed it was 1:38 am.

"Thanks!" I said, tucking the paper into my wallet. "We'll be in touch."

Wali picked up speed as I rolled up the window.

"Wali what's the time?"

"Sir ji, my watch always runs ten or fifteen minutes late," he said, turning on the overhead light and bringing his wrist to his face. "It's half past one."

"And what's the time on the car's clock?" I said.

"The car's clock stopped working five years ago, sir ji."

"How long was I gone?" I asked, feeling completely disoriented.

"Gone where, sir ji?" Wali sounded alarmed. "You never left the car since I picked you up from the airport."

"Wali, we stopped at the fortress stadium for shopping, watched the game, then we were at the hospital, remember, and..." I said, baffled by his answer.

"Sir ji, I think you need some rest. You had a long trip, and I know this place can drive anybody mad," he said.

His answer was like a slap in the face. I understood exactly what Tarzan meant when he said they'd taken care of Wali.

They'd wiped his memory of all traces of the night's bizarre collection of curious and inexplicable events. He looked oblivious to the fact that he'd picked me up from the airport seven and a half hours ago. Wali was also oblivious to the fact that we were still barely halfway home, and on a route far afield of our expected route.

Chapter 15

The Blast

WALI WAS SILENT AS WE NAVIGATED over the guttered remains of Canal Road. But then, that was just fine by me. Clutching the Quran Pir had given me like it was my only hope of survival, I struggled against my jagged nerves to understand my mission. Other than tossing a couple of vague and disturbing hints, Pir had done nothing to give me a foothold to speculate upon. His message was clear. All I needed to know was, the less I knew the better it was for all of us. I just had to live with that, for now.

A hundred questions tumbled around in my head. How could a goddamn book, which at the moment was resting peacefully at the bottom of a dried-out water tank, transport a whole village to Paradise? Assuming Pir got the book by tonight, and I was pretty sure that he would, what was up with this *backup copy*? What did he mean by having me "strategically" inserted into the scheme of things before Khalifa got his hands on the backup copy? What sort of spectacle had Khalifa been planning for? How would his plan, if executed successfully, require a major cleanup not only in this world but also the Next?

The more I tried to fathom the mystery surrounding my mission, the more baffled I became. My personal quest to understand the realities of Paradise and Hell, which apparently kickstarted all this craziness, felt insignificant in relation to what Pir and Chaacha were up to. Clearly, if it weren't for my father, one of the most important men in the Khalifa's inner circle, I wouldn't be here. How would I feel when I finally laid eyes on Abba after such a long time? What would his reaction be? Would I be able to convince him, of all people, that I was all of a sudden a true believer? And I just couldn't wrap my head around the fact that my father was the owner, the mastermind, behind Mujahid Vests Inc.

My rumination came to a sudden halt when Wali slammed on the brakes at the roundabout of Kalima Chowk. The car was surrounded by several men armed with high-powered flashlights and the ubiquitous Kalashnikovs, all of which were trained on the car. Hammering their fists on the hood of the car, the men gestured for us to roll down the windows.

"Sir ji, we're in big trouble. These guys are the *shikaree*, the hunters; they travel around at night in packs," Wali said. "I hope you still remember a little bit of your *deen*."

"Hunt for what?" I said, covering my eyes with the Quran to hide my panic.

"They hunt for infidels. Every kafir they kill will earn them the next level of Paradise," Wali said.

I recalled the sharp cold edge of Wali's knife pressed against my throat. He too was a *shikaree* deep down. Fortunately, thanks to Tarzan's concoction, Wali himself had no recollection of that particular event.

"But isn't everyone around here trying to advance to the next rung of Paradise—by killing those they consider to be infidel?" I asked. The men were now beating on the windows with their knuckles and the car was rocking back and forth.

"Yes, sir ji, it's the duty of every believer to aim for the highest heaven. But most people, like me, have to work all the time just to make ends meet. The *shikaree* don't do anything but this, they've given up the world completely," he explained, rolling down his window. "Just keep calm, and let me do the talking."

"Where are you heading?" One of them barked at Wali through the open window, his face hidden behind the glare of flashlights.

"Faisal Town," Wali said.

"Who's that in the backseat?" the man demanded. Several flashlight beams hit my face, blinding me.

"Sir ji Ismaeel," Wali announced.

"Wali, don't give them any more information about me," I whispered harshly, hoping he'd heard me, and the others hadn't.

"Tell your sir ji to get out of the car, now!" the man bellowed in rage.

"Wali, let me handle this," I said, pushing the door open and stepping out of the car, the Quran pressed to my forehead for shade against the blinding glare.

"Hands up!" one of them shouted. From his voice I could tell he was probably only about twenty years old.

I raised my arms above my head.

"What's in your hand," the same voice shouted.

"The Quran, Alhamdolillah," I tried to sound confident and relaxed.

"Never heard of a brother who could read the holy book in the dark," the man said, his voice lilting with sarcasm. "We've seen many like you before. Out of fear, you try to deceive us by merely pretending to be a believer."

"I'm a hafiz," I said, and immediately regretted it. What if they decided to test me?

"Which sect?"

For a moment I didn't know what to say. My father had always been a hardline Sunni of the Salafist variety. I considered declaring my sect, but what if these guys turned out to be part of a Shia gang? Very few Shia remained in Pakistan after the Revolution, but those who did were known to be active, striking Sunnis wherever they could. Statistically, telling them I was a Sunni seemed like a safer bet.

"Alhamdolillah, I'm a Sunni," I said. "Who are you people and what do you want?" I said, hoping I seemed both indignant and calmly respectful.

"Who we are is none of your business. What you need to know is that if we find a non-Muslim reciting the holy text of the Quran, his blasphemous crime is punishable by death. Now, you will tell us which sect of the Sunnis you belong to."

"Alhamdolillah, brother, I watch the beheadings on the Umer Media. My hero is Dandy Chowdry of the UK." The guy was likely tricking me into choosing a sect, but that was all I could think of at the moment.

"Oh, Hazrat Dandy Chowdry. The man who's helping spread Islam in the West!"

"Yes, exactly," I said with excitement.

The beams of light retreated from my face. I took a deep breath and stared at the patch of darkness that descended over my eyes like a veil.

"Tonight, I believe I'm in a mood to listen to Sura Al-Bakrah from a hafiz such as yourself," a raspy older voice I hadn't heard so far demanded.

Damn! Al-Bakrah was the longest sura of the Quran. Even if recited at a breakneck pace, it would take a good part of the night to complete. I remembered this sura to be the most difficult one to memorize, even in the heydays of my hafizhood. I berated myself for opening my big mouth and foolishly declaring myself to be a hafiz.

"I would love to say this most beautiful part of the Quran, but I'm so very tired at the moment, and I've got work to do early in the morning," I knew it sounded lame and I feared it wouldn't work, but things had already spun out of control. If Pir's DSL didn't kick in soon, I'd be a dead man walking. Then I remembered Pir's headband. I was instructed to wear it whenever I was in trouble.

Without warning, the ominous cadre of figures parted and a man of medium height elbowed his way toward me. I took the opportunity to reach in my pocket and grab the headband.

Standing at arm's length, the new guy scrutinized me from head to toe, aided by a flashlight in someone's hand. The headband was out of my pocket and in my hand, like some magical cloak of invisibility. I needed to somehow get that thing onto my forehead.

"What kind of work you do, sir ji, bedsides being a hafiz who makes pitiful excuses when asked to recite the holy words?" he demanded with an arrogant toss of his head. Clad in a black robe, he was barely distinguishable from the darkness around him. I could hear a few muffled chuckles ripple through the group. The man cleared his throat and dislodged a huge wad of phlegm onto the ground at my feet.

It would be suicidal to let him even suspect I found him disgusting, or that I'd just arrived from the US. Should I invoke my father's name? As the maker of the hottest selling brand of martyr vests, my Abba must be almost a household deity to this crowd. Accept no imitations!

"Are you really a hafiz?" he asked, digging his hand through the huge beard that sprouted from his face like a thicket of bramble.

"It's not advisable to recite the holy text under stress," I said, quickly putting the headband on my forehead.

"What are you doing?" he bellowed, thrown off by my sudden move. A few more of the flashlights further illuminated my face.

"It's just a headband. I sweat when I'm exhausted and under stress," I touched the cloth and adjusted the Nike logo over my brow as Pir had done.

"Al-Bakrah!" he roared. "Now!"

"I need some light here," I said, fumbling with the Quran in my hand.

"Recite!" The menacing figure moved closer to me, coughed, and let out another ball of muck that landed about an inch from my shoe.

Feeling like a cornered animal, I closed my eyes and almost gasped with surprise. Something warm poured from the top of my head and my brain swam with a circling wheel of sparkling light. Radiating outward, points of golden luminescence breathed like living creatures then morphed into the shimmering words of the Quran.

Shocked, I started reciting the text. My eyes closed and I was afraid to open them. What if I lost sight of the words as they danced into sentences behind my eyelids? Line after line of spun gold streamed from the swirling circle of lights as if from Rumpelstiltskin's enchanted spinning wheel.

What poured from my lips was clear and powerful; each word recited with perfect enunciation and musical grace. I relaxed and was momentarily startled as my hands rose to my chest, palms up, in the gesture of ritual supplication.

My volume increased as the words tumbled from my lips like the waters of blessed Zamzam. As my voice soared through the darkness, a hushed stillness descended around me and the men who held me at gunpoint. The more I recited, the more confident I became. The desert melody tore my heart. Time itself paused as if listening with rapt wonder to the Word as the tears flowed from my eyes.

I had no idea how long I went on like this, but I must have recited at least five pages. When I opened my eyes the *shikaree* had vanished. They'd slipped away into the night, though I hadn't heard them move out. Wali sat beside my feet, his head bowed and his body swaying from side to side. I placed my hand on the top of his head. He jumped up and hugged me so hard I almost couldn't breathe.

"Sir ji, I beg your forgiveness," he said, his palms held together in front of me.

"Forgiveness? What for?" I asked, touched by his sudden change.

"For not giving you the respect you deserve," he said, wiping his eyes with the back of his hand. "I assumed you'd forgotten your religion while living in America."

"Let's go Wali, it's getting late," I said, not exactly sure what all had just happened.

The rest of the drive to my father's house was uneventful. As we entered Faisal Town, I was struck by the startling transformation of the houses. There was a dome on top of every house as though it were a mosque. Not a flattop or pitched roof remained. Every gate and entrance was flanked by minaret-shaped pillars.

I thought back on the run-in we'd had with the *shikaree*. It was absolutely mind-blowing to have been able to recall any sura of the Quran at will, with or without the headband. I still marveled at the sight of the luminescent text forming with perfect clarity in my mind's eye. By the time Wali turned into the street where my father lived, I was able to see the text with my eyes wide open, and able to close the vision at will. This was way more than the usual recitation of a hafiz. I wondered how long the effects of Pir's prescription would last, or if this would be a permanent feature of my new skill set.

Wali pulled up in front of a multi-domed building where once had stood the house of my childhood. The place was lit by gas lamps that lined its periphery. The house had been constructed from the ground up to look like a mini replica of the Blue Mosque of Istanbul.

"Wow!" was the only word I could summon up, startled by the transformation of the house I'd been born in. "When did Abba build this house?"

"It got completed last year—took three years to build," Wali said, looking at me through the rearview mirror, his eyes glistening with reverence. "Allah has blessed Haji sahib with a noble son and an exalted business. He is indeed a winner in this world and will be in the Next."

I glanced at my watch. It was 2:40 am. I was glad my father wasn't home, since I'd need every minute of the next two days before he returned to repair what was left of my sanity.

Wali honked and someone opened the gate from inside. The car rolled into the grounds toward a broad wraparound veranda lined with columns. Ghulam Rasool—my father's cook for as long as I could remember—pulled open the door on my side.

He'd aged since I'd seen him last. Under the harsh white light of the gas lamp at the entrance of the house his wrinkled face looked emaciated and pale. He welcomed me with a warm smile as he held my arm and helped me out of the car. I hugged him. He was skin and bones. Wali stood by his side and whispered something in his ear.

The two men stared at me wide-eyed, their hands clasped over their navels. Ghulam Rasool dragged my suitcase down from the camel's hump and carried it to the front entrance while Wali gently shouldered my backpack as if it belonged to a beloved saint.

At the front door, paneled in exquisite woodcarving, Wali handed Ghulam the seemingly precious backpack and said goodbye. Then he took off toward the servant quarters. Ghulam Rasool pushed the front door open and stepped aside.

"After you saab," he said.

"Thank you," I said, as I entered the mansion. The palatial residence looked like that of a Turkish sultan of a bygone era. Gone was my expectation of some big emotional turmoil, upon entering my childhood home. This place bore absolutely no resemblance to the place I'd grown up in. All I really felt was a sad detachment. It was only the warm presence of Ghulam Rasool that reminded me I was indeed home.

The place smelled of stale smoke, old rugs, and tribal leather. There seemed to be no one home.

"Has Abba got any more children?"

"No, saab. You're his only son," he said, as he led me under a massive crystal chandelier with dozens of real candles hung over the foyer. "I thought you'd never come back, saab."

"Whatever happened to Sophie?" It was the question I was most afraid to ask.

"She was never found. We believe she died long ago," he said, shaking his head sadly.

"Where are Abba's wives?"

"They all live in Islamabad."

"Then who lives here?"

"Nobody. Wali and I take care of it. Haji sahib stays here whenever he comes to Lahore for his business." He led me into a large living area. "He's given us this car for the upkeep of the house, the one Wali drives."

A monumental landscape painting dominated the entire surface of the wall over the fireplace. The work depicted a crimson mushroom cloud over a miniaturized Indian subcontinent on one side, and the

Middle East bordered by the Mediterranean on the other. The sky was suffused with billowing clouds of smoke rising from the lower half of the painting. In the upper right corner, a monstrous black bird with bloody eyes and wings of fire spiraled toward earth.

As if the mural's message weren't clear enough, a gleaming crescent and a sword dripping with blood hovered over the scene like some Masonic all-seeing eye. Despite the horrific vision, I could not deny the exquisite workmanship evident in this masterpiece. This was not the work of some heavy-handed zealot. The calm, reasoned execution and masterful brushstrokes made the image all the more chilling and almost impossible to turn away from.

The other walls were covered with equally beautiful paintings, either of mosques or Arabic calligraphy. Ghulam Rasool led me over a seemingly endless succession of fabulous Persian rugs that had not adorned the floors of my boyhood home. I was in absolute awe of a collection that was easily worth as much as the house which displayed them.

It seemed the martyr business was truly heaven-sent for Abba. He'd never been a poor man, but I remembered our living rather simply.

I wondered if the carpets represented a newfound aesthetic passion, or a pragmatic desire to keep cash-on-the-hoof on hand in case of unexpected emergencies. I also wondered if my father had a cache of blood diamonds lying around somewhere behind a secret panel in the wall. Maybe under the portrait of Armageddon over the fireplace.

"How are Uncle Umer, and his sons Tariq and Khalid?" I asked, remembering my father's younger brother and my cousins who lived in Defense Housing Society. Uncle Umer exported handmade rugs to Europe and was known for his not-so-secret liberal views. Abba had always detested him for that reason.

"The mob burned their house while they were still inside, saab" he said, as he led me into my room.

The news upset me and I said a silent prayer for them.

After making sure I was comfortably ensconced, Ghulam Rasool said goodnight and returned to the servant's quarters. My room for the duration matched the grandeur of the rest of the house, but the only rug in sight was a threadbare prayer rug at the foot of the bed; my prayer rug when I was a kid. Message noted.

The room was lit by a brass lantern on a mahogany nightstand next to a king-size bed. On a table near the window sat a jug of water and a glass.

I stretched out on the bed and put the Quran and the Pir's headband under my pillow. The cheery flame of the lantern danced feebly with the movement of my breath and eased me into a delicious drowsiness. Sleep overtook me about sixty seconds after my head hit the pillow.

My dreams were a disjointed mess; too fragmented and hazy to piece together or hope to remember. I woke up around noon, my throat feeling like sandpaper. I drank water, a lot of it, and then fell asleep again.

The room was sunk in total darkness when I opened my eyes. I jerked upright, not sure where I was when I felt Ghulam Rasool's hand on my shoulder nudging me awake. I got up and he turned the lights on and showed me the tray of steaming tea and hot snacks he'd made for me. I looked at my watch. It was 9:00 pm. The day was Wednesday, and the year 2050; that would be 12:00 noon in New York. I had slept for 17 hours straight. It felt as if my circadian rhythm had been permanently damaged due to the surreal events of the past day.

"Saab, just to let you know, the electricity will go off in twenty minutes," he said, setting the tray on my bed.

"Oh, great! They used to have generators. What happened?"

"They have been banned, saab, for both residential and commercial use. Only mosques are allowed to have them. For one thing, the noise— you could hardly hear the call to prayer when they were running. And they prevented people from practicing their *deen,* their religion in its true spirit according to the natural times of day decreed by Allah."

I understood the first reason well enough. I had my doubts about that second one though, but it seemed awkward to ask for an explanation.

"Your father called—he told me to wake you. Saab, you've been sleeping all day without any food or drink in your stomach. It's not good for your health," he said, putting the morning paper, *The Daily Khalifaa e Waqt,* in front of me beside the tray.

"This country has been inviting the wrath of Allah for a long time—I'm glad you left," he added, pressing the folded paper flat with his hand and smiling to himself. "I'm really happy to see you, saab, but you should have stayed abroad, if I may say so."

I rubbed my eyes, looked at the headline, and almost fell from the bed. *Blast At Shah Jamal.*

With a surge of panic, I picked up the paper, my hands shaking, and scrolled through the details. Someone had martyred himself at the shrine of Shah Jamal killing seventeen people. The explosion had occurred around 2:00 am, according to eyewitnesses.

My lips trembled as I stared at the picture under the headline; the severed head of the suicide bomber nestled within a wreath made of red roses. I'd seen that face before, but where?

And then it came to me like a flash flood racing down a mountain gorge. I knew where I'd seen that face! It was that of the man who'd been standing behind Tarzan outside the shrine, one of the two armed guards who'd escorted us to Wali's car. And in another flash, I realized that it was also the same bloody face I'd seen being thrashed against the rock by Hell's winged minion; the face of Fida Muhammad.

But how could that be? How on earth was it possible to see the bomber's carrion, which Chaacha Khidr fed to the bird, before the man actually exploded himself?

I broke into a cold sweat and the bile rose in my throat as I recalled Chaacha Khidr's words: *It likes brain.*

Clutching the paper in my hands, I held back my tears. Had

Tarzan been killed?

I remembered his handsome, smiling face as he stood at my window handing me my watch along with the phone number of one of his associates. He might have survived, if he'd gone to retrieve the book right after I left.

"Saab, you look as if you are ill," Ghulam Rasool said, his face contorted with alarm.

"Ghulam Rasool, I need to make a phone call." I said, remembering the words of Pir: *We can never underestimate Khalifa's power.*

"I'll get the phone. It's in the kitchen," he said, hurrying toward the door.

He brought me a cordless phone. I dialed the number Tarzan had given me, but there was no answer. I gave up after a few more tries.

The blast was obviously directed against the head of the Resistance Movement, Pir Pullsiraat. Did he and Chaacha Khidr survive the attack? As I recalled, Pir's abode wasn't located right at the shrine, where the blast had taken place. I remembered walking blindfolded for a good five minutes, and then going down nineteen steps to get to his quarters. I dropped the paper on the bed.

"Ghulam Rasool, please arrange for the car. I need to go see someone."

"Saab, are you all right?" Ghulam Rasool asked. "Wali will take you anywhere you want to go," he assured me as he refilled my cup.

"I can drive myself—I don't need Wali with me."

"Saab, I made a club sandwich for you, still your favorite I hope. You'll enjoy having it with your tea. Let Wali go with you saab, it's not safe to drive alone at night in Lahore these days."

"Please go and arrange for the car. I promise I'll eat," I said, regaining my poise. "I know how to take care of myself."

Ghulam Rasool left the room looking puzzled and shaking his head, probably worried about what my father would say if I was not well cared for and coddled.

My perception of reality had taken another huge hit. I had no appetite. Sipping tea, I took a few bites of my favorite club sandwich just to fill my stomach. My mind coiled around the shocking tragedy. Stop, I told myself. Nothing was going to get solved by my sitting here on my ass and becoming paralyzed with anxiety.

Slowly thoughts were replaced by black rage. I loathed my father, and everything he stood for, with all my heart. I could envision all the martyrs out there, high on Paradise Water, using his brilliant invention to beam themselves up to the next world. How about if I blew myself up by wearing his vest when he gave me the obligatory hug?

The phone rang. I knew it was he. My father. Gritting my teeth, I picked up the phone from beside the bed.

"Hello."

"Assalamualaikum, Ismaeel. I hope you had a good rest?" my father asked. "I was busy last night and could not call you."

"I'm good," I said. "My phone was stolen anyway."

"Happens all the time. Wali will take you in the morning to the market. I'll call the store in advance. You may go and pick whatever you like. Do you use Droid or Apple?"

I didn't say anything, but he didn't seem to notice and just kept on talking.

"I'll be back in Lahore tomorrow evening. Until then you have a driver and a cook at your disposal. This place is not as bad as it may seem on the surface. Did you like the house?"

"I love what you did to the house."

"Allah has never been so gracious and kind. When I see you, we'll talk, Inshallah!"

"Okay—until then Allah Hafiz." I tried to sound bright and friendly.

"Allah Hafiz," he said, and the line went dead.

I was glad he was in no more of a mood to chat than I was. If my father was such a big honcho in the Khalifa circle, his phone was likely being tapped by the security of the Khalifa. And I was probably already a known entity somewhere high up in the Caliphate.

I felt frustrated by the absurdity of a mission that required me to gain the trust and affection of someone like my father. The whole thing would be a lot easier if he was a complete stranger. If I didn't pull it off, the fact that I was the man's son would do nothing to help me and would probably hasten my spectacular demise. Pir and his crew had taken extraordinary measures to make a seemingly unthinkable task seem possible. All this for what?

I had never been a man of faith as far as its ritualized version was concerned. I'd taken the religious text as a manufactured narrative that had been propagated over centuries without having to face any serious examination, but in all honesty, I'd never given a serious thought about God. I'd considered myself agnostic, in the sense that I wasn't sure what IT was I had to deny or believe in. But now I couldn't deny that I'd been shown Hell, and I'd also seen the luminescent golden light that bathed the lush country studded with waterfalls, and across from it the walls of Paradise, some 70 years far away on the back of a horse. I'd sipped tea with Chaacha at the Bihishti Tea Corner, and listened to the haunting melody from the flute of Ibrahim. And I'd seen ababeels. Was some mysterious divine intervention at play here, and I being a part of it?

Ghulam Rasool barged back into the room carrying a milkshake.

"Another favorite of yours, saab!" he said with obvious delight.

Not wanting to disappoint the old man who was taking great pains to please me and make me comfortable, I took the glass and tasted his confection.

"Delicious as ever," I said, giving him a smile. "Is my car ready?"

"Saab, Wali will take you anywhere you want to go," he insisted.

"Tell him to get the car ready, I'll be out in fifteen minutes," I said, heading to the bathroom, and then suddenly remembering the water situation.

"Is it okay to take a shower?"

"Not good, saab. There's a bucket in there I just filled with warm water for you. I've put an extra dose of Gentian Violet. But it may still smell though."

"Thanks! So very thoughtful of you. So everyone around here uses the bottled Paradise Water for cooking and drinking?"

"Of course, saab. What else would we use?"

I stood in front of the mirror surveying my appearance of facial piety when the lights went out.

At 9:40 pm I was back on the road, thankfully alone except for the Quran and Pir's headband tucked in my pocket. It was a pleasant night, a bit chilly but not unseasonably cold. Wali, of course, had insisted on coming along. Except he had no choice but to obey my order and remain behind.

I left instructions with the two of them that I would probably return around midnight. But no matter how late I was out, they were not to panic and start calling my father. They both insisted I take their cell phones along, their faces reflecting grave concern for my safety, but I refused. I didn't want to be tracked.

The streets were a disaster, having suffered everything from prolonged neglect to roadside bombings. The upside was that traffic was light and confined to emergency travel and dire necessity. I got to Shah Jamal without incident and parked the car in the same spot Wali had used the night before.

As soon as I got out of the car, I was welcomed by the piercing howls of the cats as they moved about in their massive Bunyan tree. There seemed to be many more of them gathered now than on the previous night. I looked around for the emergency barricades you'd expect at the scene of a violent crime, but there was no sign of any police activity.

The place was deserted and dark, but it wasn't difficult to guess why. These ferocious animals, in such numbers, could terrorize a whole town if they wanted to. Oddly I felt relaxed and quite alert. The trip to Hell seemed to have done wonders for my fears. I slipped Pir's headband over my brow and started toward the entrance.

I was a few feet from the arched gate when I heard a soft thud behind my back. I froze in my tracks. Then I heard another thud. I turned around and saw two of the cats standing about ten feet from me. I held my ground as they padded silently toward me. Their steps were slow, deliberate, nonthreatening. I recognized them; they were Pir's jinn cats.

They stood at my side, regarding me with those mesmerizing yellow eyes. As I stroked their smooth fur, they rubbed their bodies against my legs. The howling had stopped and I pushed on to the entrance of the shrine. The cats accompanied me as they had Pir when he made his rounds about the courtyard housing tighropes.

The shrine's courtyard was strewn with broken glass and scorched debris and resembled a ruin from antiquity. A creepy silence gripped the place, punctuated by my footsteps.

A lone figure sat hunched beside a meager fire near the staircase. The man looked up when he heard my footsteps crunching over the broken masonry. His haggard face and long braids caked with white dust made him look like a statue.

"Ya Mushkil Kusha!" he shrieked, shaking his head from side to side and throwing his hands in the air. A cloud of ash flew off his body as he turned to look at me.

"Come sit here with me brother," he pleaded, turning his bloodshot eyes toward me. I could see there was dried blood on his face, but I saw no visible wounds and wondered what horrors the man had witnessed, or participated in, during the last night's activities.

I squatted by his side and stared into the flames that had begun to die out.

"I'm very sorry about what happened here," I said, my feelings truly sincere.

He just sat there, staring into the fire and digging absently at the crumbling embers with a stick, but said nothing.

"I'm looking for Pir Pullsiraat and Tarzan," I said. "Do you know anything about what happened to them?"

"It's all over, Ismaeel," he said with a hoarse voice.

It startled me to hear my name. I looked at him closely. His face was obscured by ash and grief, and tears streaked the wearied flesh. Then I knew who this man was. This was the dhol player whom Pir had invited into his quarters after I'd swallowed the contents of the yellow vial.

"Please tell me, did Pir survive, or was he killed? I must know!" I begged, gripping the man's arm. "If he's alive, I need to see him, please! I'm sorry; I don't know your name."

"My name is Pappu. Pappu Saien."

"Help me Saien."

"I can't help you, Ismaeel. The bastard has taken down the best of our people."

"Saien, do you know Tarzan? Is he alive?"

"Only Allah knows if he's alive or dead. Ahhhh! I live to see this day!" He sighed, rubbing his head with his palms and dislodging more ash from his hair.

"Saien, please, if Pir is alive, take me to him," I pleaded. "You know where he lives."

"No one can enter Pir's abode without an invitation," he said solemnly.

"Not even in emergencies?"

"No."

"Not even in catastrophic times like these?"

"Pir's abode can only be found by going into the intermediate world—the world between this one and the next," he said. "Unless you're escorted there, you cannot find it. Those who could have escorted you, they are all dead, Ismaeel," he said softly, his voice choked with tears.

So Pir had survived. I was elated with relief. The revelation only confirmed what I already suspected: Pir, like Chaacha Khidr, was no ordinary earthly personage. He hadn't been speaking in metaphor or poetry when he'd told me he was hybrid. He was neither jinn nor fully human, that much I knew. But I had no clue what kind of hybrid he was.

I touched the headband on my forehead, remembering the headphones in Pir's ears, the big military style black boots he wore, the pack of John Player's Gold Leaf cigarettes in his extended right hand, his coppery skin that glowed in the light of flames, his fiery gaze, and his not-so-secret dislike for the best of creation, the humans.

I left the courtyard in complete emotional disarray. The cats accompanied me back to my car. Tarzan was likely dead as far as I knew, blown to pieces by his own bodyguard. If *that* was the case, the black book probably still needed to be retrieved from the water tank back at the hospital. After all, it was the thing on which Khalifa's power rested, his ticket to Paradise, as Pir had put it. But how?

Standing beneath their tree, the cats waved their tails in the air. Waving back at them, I sat behind the wheel and rolled down my window.

"I wish you guys could tell me how to find Pir," I said as I turned over the ignition. By the time I got the headlights on, the cats had vanished. It was then I heard Pir's voice.

"Ismaeel, can your hear me?" he was saying, his voice loud and clear inside my mind as before. It felt so weird I almost forgot to breathe.

"Hello Ismaeel, it's Pir Pullsiraat," he said. Stunned, I touched my headband. I almost pulled it off of my head without thinking when he spoke again.

"Your headband is a telepathic headset, we're going to be using it to communicate," he said.

"Pir! Hell! Can you hear me?" I was elated to hear his voice.

"You don't have to shout. You don't have to speak at all. Just keep calm and think."

"Pir, how is this possible?"

"Everything is possible, Ismaeel. We have our own ways of communicating with one another," he said. "Like you have yours."

"I must say, this is pretty outrageous," marveling at something that would put even Google to shame. At that instant, the face of Don Miguel rose in my memory. I remembered how he'd tapped his headband over his temple and told me: *The people of the spirit world have their own special methods of communication.* Had he been in touch with Pir and Chaacha through his headband while I was tripping on Ayahuasca under his supervision? It had to be, for why would he say: *A great task has been given to you, Ismaeel. Make yourself available to it, no matter how strange it may appear.*

"Pir, is Tarzan dead?" I asked and held my breath, afraid of the answer.

"Tarzan's here with me."

"He's alive? Yes!" I yelled, punching the air with my fist at the news. A sense of relief coursed through my body and I smiled. "Did he get you the book?"

"That's what you're going to do for me right now. I want that book."

"That's exactly where I was heading, after hearing about the blast and thinking maybe Tarzan hadn't made it. I'm shocked at the loss of so many lives Pir, I'm deeply sorry." I really was.

"We're living in a war zone, Ismaeel," he said. "If we lose this war, the world will be counting its dead for a very long time."

"Where will I find you once I have the book?" I asked, remembering the dhol player's shocking news that all the guides who could take me to Pir were dead.

"Once you get the book, send me your thoughts and tell me of your success—make sure you have the headband on. I'll let you know what the next step will be," he said, and then he was gone—just like that.

"Pir, Pir, don't go!" I cried, but there was just echo of my own thoughts.

I looked down at my watch. It was 10:40 PM. Once I got the book I probably could make it back to my father's house by midnight.

Chapter 16
The Book

PIR'S WORDS PLAYED OVER AND OVER in my head during the twenty-minute drive from the shrine to the hospital. I could only marvel at the telepathic headband that enabled psychic telecommunication between distant parties. Was the thing pure technology, with some chip embedded that was capable of things I'd only read about, and which had been rumored to be used by the Green Berets?

Or, could I be having some kind of auditory hallucination thanks to the multiple concoctions I'd been given to ingest, Hoor Afza included? Or was this something even stranger; something that sprang from a world only Pir and Chaacha Khidr could understand?

Whatever the explanation, it was Pir's voice that had resounded within my head over my left temple with the best news of all: Tarzan was alive. The boy had a bright future under the tutelage of someone like Pir. His death at such a young age would have been a terrible loss. Besides, I just plain liked the kid. And what of Chaacha Khidr? He had to be alive. He was clearly even less of this world than Pir and had probably defied death a thousand times.

I drove through the gate of the hospital, looking for signs of any suspicious activity I should worry about. All the lights were out and the place looked deserted. To make sure someone driving through the gate couldn't see my car, I parked it at the far end of the empty parking lot.

As I walked across the tarmac to the hospital entrance I tapped the headband over my left temple. I also wondered if Laila was on duty tonight at the reception desk.

"Pir, hello! Are you there?" I whispered but got no answer.

I climbed the steps to the emergency room entrance and paused. It'd be damn near impossible to find my way in the dark once I was inside the building. And I'd never be able to navigate through that tunnel of junked furniture piled outside the bathroom door.

I was thinking about going to the drug store across the street for a flashlight, even a keychain mini-light would do, when the door swung open. I was pleasantly startled to see Laila barreling through the darkened doorway.

Her huge black-lined eyes widened when she saw me. She had an unlit cigarette in one hand and a Styrofoam cup in the other. We just stared at each other in silence for several very awkward moments.

"I love the headband, Ismaeel," she said, grasping for something to say.

"Good to see you again, Laila," I replied, flashing a broad smile. It was the truth. I couldn't remember one girl out of many whom I'd slept with, once upon a time in New York, who'd made me want her with the passion I was feeling at this minute. This shrouded beauty in black, with her big black gorgeous eyes said all that needed to be told. I was more than delighted to see her again. But a part of me also knew that this girl was trouble.

"I'm on my break. Come have a smoke with me." She said it like a dare, sensing I probably wouldn't refuse her offer. Not waiting for my reply, she glided over to the service ramp and leaned back against the cement railing.

I knew I'd never reach the bathroom unless I smoked with her. The challenge of getting the book had suddenly been bumped to the next level.

"Sure, I could definitely use one." I followed her down the ramp.

Laila sighed, lifted the edge of her veil, and took a sip from her cup, then set it on the ledge beside her. Pulling a white pack of Marlboro Lights cigarettes out of the folds of her burqa she tapped one halfway out and pointed it at my navel.

I shivered with excitement; to be in such close proximity to that dazzling pair of eyes was sheer bliss. She flicked her lighter and lit my cigarette first.

Hey. The girl got style! With a smile on my face, my instincts triggered, I leaned back against the railing next to her, our bodies just inches apart. I took off my headband, stuffed it in my pocket, while starting to brood. I was *expected to perform better this time around*, and I was already failing. Regardless, I didn't want Pir to intrude into such private moments of my personal life.

"I had a feeling you'd be back," she said, as she slid her veil from over the corner of her mouth by about an inch, and pressed the cigarette between her lips.

She slid her body closer to mine but still not touching, and lit the cigarette, which looked as if was suspended in darkness by magic. She looked toward the sky, and took a long drag. I wished she would just take the damn veil off.

"I don't know—it feels like I've known you for a long time," she said, exhaling into her veil. In an eerie effect, smoke rose through the thin black fabric of her burqa.

"It's uncanny. I feel the same way." I slid towards her, and stopped when our bodies touched.

"I liked your headband. The red looks good on your face. Why did you take it off?" She gently pressed herself against my side.

"To cool my head."

"I love the Nike slogan."

"Yes, me too!" Was our conversation going to stay so inane?

"Just do it!" She turned to face me. "Life's too short."

"Just do it!?" I cried, unsure of what she was up to. Even in New York City such careless sprints to the finish line were frowned upon as not the best idea.

"Yes," she whispered, closing any distance between us and pressing her shoulder into mine.

I clasped my hands in front of me and stared at the glowing tip of my own cigarette, watching it rise slowly away from my body. Damn, the girl didn't stand on formalities.

"Can I see your face, Miss Night," I said, swallowing hard. "I'm not really into anonymous sex," I added with a smile, unable to find anything else to say.

She flicked her cigarette away and watched it roll down the ramp into oblivion. Laila's lips brushed the rim of her cup as she slid in front me. Her veiled face was just inches from mine now, and her breath, despite that black curtain over her face, warm against my cheek. Her eyes were aflame with passion and bore into mine.

I lowered my head to give her a kiss where I thought her lips would be but she turned away. Then she turned back and embraced me with such hunger that I felt as if she was going to devour me, her body pulsating with raw energy. The large firm points of her breasts against my chest flared my own fire to a new high. I was burning with desire. Any sense of control I had was gone. Feeling my hardness, Laila pressed her crotch against my cock and swayed her body with mine.

Holy shit!

"Just do it," she pleaded in my ear, biting my earlobe through the fabric of her burqa.

"You're a dangerous woman," I panted, breathing hard into her ear as my arm encircled her waist and I pressed her body tightly against mine. I knew I'd fallen headlong into the pit of my lust, and now only a miracle could keep me from fully indulging in it. Unlike fear, this lust deal was proving too hard to get a good handle on; it needed my active participation to die down. Where the hell was my willpower? It seemed to have gone to sleep somewhere. I had to try to give my red-hot desire a fight.

"Would you please take your goddamn burqa off?" I said. Inside the voluminous black covering, her body felt like that of a girl in her mid-twenties. Slim, toned, hot. But I could be terribly wrong in this land of strange uncertainties.

"Janu, this is not New York City! We'd be crazy to do it right here," she whispered with a deep sigh.

I wanted to tell her that wasn't quite what I'd had in mind when I commented on her burqa. All I wanted was to see her face. But I didn't say anything. I relaxed my grip on her waist and she pulled away, her small hand dragging across my chest.

"Come with me," she said, the voice of a confident tease returning. Grabbing her cup from the railing she started back up the ramp.

"I know a secret place," she said over her shoulder.

"You're playing with fire, Miss Night." *But I'm the one getting singed.*

"Night has to seek fire to become illuminated," she said.

"Uh-oh...They're selling a variety of stones for people like us in the market," I said, struggling to slow things down.

"Yes, we're good for the economy," she quipped. "Come on, let's get out of here."

Suddenly I was hit by another strange kind of déjà vu. I felt like I'd already lived a lifetime with this girl, as if I knew her all the way down to the root of my soul. I shook my head to dispel such fluffy notions.

"Not tonight. I've got things to do."

"Ah! Men! Scared of getting stoned."

Now the girl had challenged my manhood.

What if she turned out to be the agent of some secret society? What if her crowd didn't jibe with *my* secret society? Under the circumstances, any goddamn thing was possible. I was afraid to touch my headband, which at the moment was safely tucked in my pocket. I was afraid to put it on lest Pir started barking orders in my head. What if he called while we were making out? He'd surely wonder why I didn't have it on. I'd assumed that it had to be on my head for the communication to occur. What if it was communicating right from my pocket? What if Pir could not only talk, but also see all my activities through this telepathic headset of his. Was it just plain stupid and dangerous to assume anything at all about Pir? I was thinking, *yeah, pretty much.*

"Hey listen..." I said, as she headed for the door, its glass reflecting flashing red lights. Damn! The Commaqaadis!

"Stay quiet and follow me," she whispered.

"Yes, ma'am," I dashed behind her, as the flashing red lights neared the hospital gate.

The power was still out as we walked past the glass paneled entrance down the dark hall toward the rear of the building, skirting along the wall separating us from the emergency room waiting area. I knew exactly where we were headed.

A minute later we stood in front of the ten-foot wall of rusting hospital junk. Laila's lighter came in handy and I was able to make out the twisted cabinet Tarzan and I had used the night before. The girl was taking me closer to the object of my mission. So far so good. My desire was in harmony with my mission, geographically speaking. I was on the right track. Could I resist her? I wasn't sure. *Be strong*, I told myself. *You can do it.*

We crept through the same tunnel he'd led me down, and we exited by the same broken closet door. The bathroom still smelled of Tarzan's handiwork on the briefcase. The flame from the lighter began to splutter just as we reached our destination.

"I can't keep it on—it's burning my finger," she said, closing the lid and extinguishing the flame, and my hope of seeing her face.

We stood in pitch darkness, listening to our breath, ready to devour each other. My desire for her was like a blaze that had all but consumed whatever was left of my sense of duty.

If this was going to happen, it'd happen in a standing position, unless I could find myself a chair or a bench from the pile of junk.

Laila threw herself into my arms. Mustering the last bit of my will power, I jerked away.

"Wait!"

"What's the matter, janu? What's happening?" Laila asked, touching my face with her fingers.

"I'm going to go look for a chair or something," I said, heading toward the door. "Just stay put. I'll be back," I said, heading towards the door.

"What? Where are you going?" she asked, obviously confused.

"We don't need a chair," she said, sounding annoyed.

Without replying, I opened the door and dashed out of the bathroom, making sure to close it behind me.

I stood in the dark by the pile of junk, my mind racing. I had the feeling that Pir must be trying to get in touch with me, so I took the headband out of my pocket and put in on.

"Where have you been, Ismaeel?" Pir roared in my head.

"Sorry, Pir. Can't explain right now—but I'm right next to the book," I whispered, hoping Pir couldn't pick any of the savory details of the moment from my mind.

"Are you sure?"

"Yes." I moved away from the door and stuck my head under what my probing fingers told me was a wooden desk balanced atop the steel beams of what looked a bunch of IV stands and end tables.

"Waiting for further instructions, Pir," I whispered into the underside of the desk.

"All right, now, I'm not going to repeat myself, so listen very carefully."

"Go ahead," I said, taking the measure of the desk with my hands. It seemed perfect for the intended purpose.

"First, find a quiet place where no one will disturb you, someplace where you can lie down for ten to fifteen minutes. Then open the book and examine its pages closely. You'll see scored indentations dividing each page into small squares a centimeter in size."

"Yeah, I know exactly what you're talking about," I said, remembering the look of the pages. They were all blank and scored.

"Good. With the book in your hand, carefully tear one square from the page, and then close the book. Next, remove the headband and slide it around the book as if it was your head. Make sure it fits snuggly. Did you get all that?"

"Yeah, got it. Go ahead," I said, feeling a little annoyed and confused.

"Then lie down on a comfortable spot and put the torn piece of paper under your tongue."

"And then?" I muttered apprehensively.

"There is no then, then."

"Not another drug, Pir! Please! I'm still not over my jet lag or the other chemicals," I said, feeling exhausted and dejected.

"Well, what can I say? Your desire to see Paradise was so heartfelt and sincere it moved heaven and earth. See you soon," he said and then closed off his thoughts. He was gone, just like that.

"Paradise!" I said, moving the desk and banging it against the pile to let Laila know I was still out there. Did he mean he was going to see me in Paradise?

I slowly straightened up using the top of my head to lift the desk off the broken poles. Steadying the bulky weight with my hands, I inched toward where I thought the door was. Thankfully, Laila was standing there to guide me through. She flicked her lighter on just in time and I managed to get the desk through the door by tilting it slightly. In the light of her flame my weirdly distorted shadow jerked across the floor of the bathroom revealing exactly how precarious the maneuver was.

"We needed something really sturdy to support our weight," I said, trying to catch my breath and thinking the only way to get rid of this girl would be to satisfy her *now*. I had no choice but to do it for the sake of my mission.

"Janu, passion doesn't need any external support," she added, locking the door from the inside. "Do you realize the desk only has three legs?"

"Would you please help me?" I said, kneeling on the floor, feeling stupid as hell.

She scrambled to help get the thing off my head then stepped back. Once the desk was on the floor, it fell on its missing leg the moment I let it go. She turned on the flame, her gorgeous eyes staring at me quizzically.

Still kneeling on the floor in a humbled state of genuine despair, I felt torn between my duty and my desire. This burqa-clad temptress, whose face had remained elusive to my hungry eyes, had proven to be as formidable a force as Pir. I was pretty sure he wasn't listening at the moment.

Maybe it would work if the desk, which was about four feet tall, was moved closer to the sink and we used the latter as a support for the missing leg. What if the height of the desk and the sink turned out to be uneven?

"Janu, what's wrong?" She came over and threw her arms around my neck and crushed her body into mine. Suddenly, I regained my wits. There was something really weird about her behavior; even her movements seemed crazed. She came off as too horny and over the top for my taste. At the very least, I had to see her face if I was going to allow her to suck up any more of my time and energy. My desire began to wane.

"Sorry," I said, disentangling myself from her arms. "I just can't do it, not like this, not until I see your face," I said, gently placing my hands on her slim waist to show her we were still in negotiations. Just then the girl beneath my hand began to vibrate.

She pulled away from me and dug a cell phone out of her burqa. She looked at the number.

"I'll be there in a minute," she said to the phone. Hanging up she touched my face with her fingertips.

"You stay here, love. I'll be back. They've brought in a head-injury case. I have to go."

"I guess we're calling it off for the night."

"It's not even midnight yet, my love" she said. "Ismaeel, please don't go! It won't take me more than ten or fifteen minutes at the most," she pleaded.

Ten or fifteen minutes. That's exactly what I was looking for.

"Okay fine—I'll wait."

"See if you can find something sturdier than that desk. I have to run," she said, heading toward the door. "And keep the headband on your head. It looks so sexy on you."

"Leave your lighter with me, if you don't mind—you can use the light on your phone to get out," I said.

"Janu—I'll do anything for you." She handed me the lighter. Without another word she disappeared out the door and into the dark maze of junk.

I flipped the lighter on and climbed on top of the commode. Reaching with my hand into the tank and feeling around, I breathed a sigh of relief. The book was there; lying on the bottom of the tank, right where I'd dropped it.

Going over Pir's instructions, I looked around the room for a place where I could sit and lean against the wall. The most suitable spot was a six-foot wide area between the door and the sink.

Laila had left her Styrofoam cup on the sink. I picked it up, smelled it, and cautiously took a sip. As soon as the vile liquid touched my tongue I spit it out into the sink and wiped the back of my hand across my mouth in disgust. Holy crap! Laila had been drinking the goddamn Hoor Afza. No wonder she'd been acting so provocatively.

Making myself comfortable beside the sink, I opened the book and tore one of the little squares from the top corner of the first page. Then I pulled my headband off and slid it over the book's leather-bound cover from top to bottom—the only way to get the thing to fit snugly. I looked at my watch. It was now 11:30 pm. I extinguished the lighter, said my *bismillah,* and put the little square of paper under my tongue.

Immediately an effervescent sweetness bubbled across my tongue and flowed through the roof of my mouth into my brain. My forehead tingled as if a host of butterflies fluttered behind my eyes. Saliva ran over my tongue and my heart pounded in my chest as a delicious vibration washed through my body from my head to my feet. Feeling a little apprehensive, I flicked on the lighter and looked at my hands and arms. No sign of shaking; the flame in my hand was perfectly steady and surrounded by an intense multicolored halo. Taking a deep breath, I flicked the lighter shut and the room collapsed in darkness.

The inner shaking intensified and my head swelled with a roaring noise. I felt as if I was suspended in vast space and immediately the noise surged into a shrieking wail. Then all sound and sensation melted into a brilliant white light that shattered like glass into a million diamond-tipped arrows that plunged toward the core of my being. My body felt so heavy it was as if I was weighted down by a massive boulder.

Keeping my eyes shut I allowed the arrows of light to pierce my body. Then something hot and fleshy shot into my mouth and started moving about. I heard Laila's voice from far away. I tried opening my eyes but my eyelids refused to budge.

"Janu, you're all sweet and honey."

I almost gagged when I realized Laila was on top of me, her tongue hungrily exploring the interior of my mouth. I tried twisting my torso to get her off me, but my body felt paralyzed. I'd lost all power to resist and my limbs dangled at my sides like those of a dead man. I tried to speak, but my tongue refused to move. I panicked, realizing I wasn't even breathing.

"Janu, come back!" Laila screamed.

That was the last thing I heard before I lost consciousness.

Chapter 17

Laila

THE THUNDEROUS ROAR OF WATER crashing over rocks jolted me awake. I opened my eyes to a clear blue sky overhead and a waterfall to my left. The air was warm and humid, and the scent of cinnamon drifted on a light breeze. Except for a faint sweetness from the magical potion that clung to my lips, the bizarre scene in the bathroom seemed nothing more than the lingering tendril of a bad dream.

I looked at my body and bolted upright. I was completely naked. I wasn't even wearing my watch. A woman was lying beside me wearing nothing but her radiant wheat colored skin and a veil of jet-black hair thrown over her face. She was asleep; her arms were spread out, her breasts displayed like golden dunes rising from a desert ground.

Mesmerized, I let my gaze follow her luscious curves until it fell on the black book pressed between the grass and her right hip. The red headband had slid to the edge of its cover and was about to fall off.

Laila? I wasn't sure because I'd never actually seen her face. I remembered zoning out in the bathroom after dissolving Pir's tiny square of paper under my tongue. I'd been unable to move as Laila had pinned me to the ground and her hot tongue ravaged the inside of my mouth.

The woman stirred in her sleep, her beautiful face looking up at the sky. Her shaved pubic area was as smooth as a baby's belly. An insistent stirring in my loins made me look around for something to cover myself.

We lay in a grassy sloped meadow. One side merged into a bay bordered by the steep blue granite cliffs of an inlet that led to the sea. Near the shore, a hundred feet or so from us, the huge waterfall spilled down the face of the cliff and crashed against the rocks sending plumes of mist and spray into the air. On the other side of the meadow, rocky cliffs were crowned with a knoll covered with shrubs that shimmered as if backlit by the sun.

Except that no sun hung in this strange monochromatic blue sky. Luminescence seemed to be radiating from the ground. Everything glowed as if lit from within. I got to my feet and stood marveling at the stark alien beauty of this dreamlike terrain and the unknown woman who slept at my side, oblivious of her surroundings.

Could this beauty be a *hoor*; one who'd drifted away from her sisters? I glanced at the girl's ankles looking for the signs described in the traditional Islamic texts; but her ankles were not translucent. I walked over to a patch of vegetation, my feet relishing the exquisitely soft grass beneath my feet, but my mind scattered like beads of mercury. Something had gone very wrong. There was no sign or word from Pir. Hopefully he was on his way and would appear at any moment. It was 11:30 PM when I last looked at my watch. But I had no idea what time it was here, if there even was a here.

I broke off several leafy shoots from the shrubs and wrapped them around my waist, tying each in a knot. Satisfied that the leaves had adequately covered my private parts, I thought of taking some for the woman but decided against it. I was in no hurry to give up the vision of a beautiful naked woman.

By the time I got back, she was awake. She sat like a yogin with her back straight, her radiant black hair tumbling over her breasts and her hands covering her face except her eyes. They were Laila's eyes. In her lap lay the black book.

"Ismaeel! Is that you?" she asked, keeping her face covered with her annoying hands and pretending not to see me. "Where are we?"

"Laila! What the hell are you doing here?" I demanded, drawing near to her.

"You're supposed to be attending the head injury back in the emergency room," I said, realizing how ridiculous it sounded.

"Is this a dream?" she asked. "Everything here is so—so beautiful." She gazed at our surroundings with bewildered eyes.

"Yes, it is. In a dream, you know, you're permitted to unveil your face."

"No!" she hissed. "You won't like me if I let you see my face," she cried, her head buried in her hands and thrashing back and forth like a village mourner. Her reaction completely baffled me.

"Why would you say such a thing?" I knelt beside her.

"See this side of my face?" She pressed her right cheek with her fingers without lifting her palms off her face. "The first stone hit me here," she said through her tears. "It blew my cheekbone and knocked me out. That's the only reason I'm alive today. They thought I was dead. They left me there to rot." Her shoulders shook.

"My God!" I placed my hands on her head and stroked her hair.

"It took a long time to heal, leaving this ugly scar under my eye. That's why I refused to take my veil off when you'd asked me to." Her sobbing continued.

I held her wrists and gently moved them away to find an impeccably beautiful and unblemished face.

"But your face is perfect and lovely. I don't see any scar. What are you talking about?" I wished I had a mirror.

As she touched her cheek and slid her trembling fingers over the soft flawless skin, her eyes widened and she gasped in happiness and covered her mouth.

"You're right! Oh my God! Ismaeel, how can this be?"

"May I have the book, please? Actually, just the headband."

She slid it off the book and handed it to me without uncovering her lap.

Pulling the thing over my head and adjusting the logo I collected my thoughts and beamed them to Pir, my brows furrowed with the effort. But there was no reply.

"Hello! Can you hear me? Pir, can you hear me?" I said, tapping my temple this time.

"Who are you talking to?" she asked, her voice filled with curiosity and amusement.

I stayed silent, for if I mentioned the name of Pir, I'd have to then explain a whole lot more, and the last thing I'd want to do was to compromise Pir's mission. I struck my temple several more times in order to establish the connection but without success.

"Look, I'm really sorry about last night," she said. Her cheeks were flushed. "I couldn't control myself, and when I came back and saw you lying there on the floor, I just couldn't help it."

"I thought it was illegal for women to drink Hoor Afza."

She turned her face away without saying anything.

"You see this," I took the headband off and held it in my hand. "This is a special kind of phone. If we can't make it work, we're struck here forever."

"The minute I saw you in the emergency room that night, I knew you were different. Special," she said, her eyes searching mine.

"Well, thank you," I slid the headband back over my head, giving my temple another tap. "Hello, Hello."

"Ismaeel, it's so strange. It feels as if it all happened such a long time ago."

"What happened a long time ago?" I asked, listening for the sound of Pir's voice in my head.

"The stuff in the bathroom—the time when we met. It all feels as if it happened in another life. Do you feel that way?"

"I need to make this thing work," I said, ignoring her questions. I took the infuriating piece of red fabric off my head and lashed the air with it several times before putting it back on.

"So what's next, boss?" She was composed and her lips curled in a smile.

Her beauty was mesmerizing; the supple skin radiated vitality and her eyes were suffused with a calm, steady desire.

"I'm going to take a walk up that hill and see what's on the other side." I pointed towards the grassy knoll. "It looks like about a ten to fifteen-minute walk."

"Ismaeel, you are a true gentleman. How many men would keep their cool with a naked woman sitting right beside them?"

Had she known what was stirring beneath the canopy of leaves below my waist, she would have thought otherwise.

"You want to come along?" I asked, jumping to my feet and quickly turning away from her.

"No. I want to go look at that waterfall. It's so magnificent! You go on up. We'll meet back here. Sound good? And please, don't forget to bring some leaves back for me," she added, rising to her feet with an effortless grace and making sure the book still concealed her sex.

I wondered what would happen if the book got soaked with water? It could wash away whatever its pages were coated with. Then it occurred to me: why not tear out a couple of the tiny squares and put them under our tongues. That would probably get us beamed out of here. It was a wild thought, but was certainly worth a try—but only if Pir and I failed to make contact, say, in the next twenty-four hours.

"Would you mind trading that book for my leaves?" I asked, thinking that on my way up the hill I'd harvest another eco-friendly organic loincloth, and take the concept of edible garment to the next level. Smiling to myself again, I decided not to *go there* just yet.

Laila pursed her lips and stared at my canopy of leaves as if giving the trade a great deal of serious thought. I felt uncomfortable under her mischievous gaze as it wandered over my not so well hidden private places. I wished I had used a few more leaves to make my cover a little denser.

"Sure, that works. Here," she said, thrusting the book toward me and locking her eyes on mine in case I allowed mine to drop. "Now, may I please have my leaves?" She demanded with a smile and an outstretched hand.

Keeping my eyes on hers I smiled and untied the precarious foliage from my waist and extended the leafy strands to her. A few leaves had fallen off during this maneuver. We exchanged our hostages without allowing our eyes to take unfair advantage of the awkward tradeoff. As soon as I got the book in my hand I turned and sprinted off in the direction of the hilltop, savoring her hot stare on my bare ass.

"Wait!" she yelled. "Would you be kind enough to loan me the headband of yours? I need something to tie my hair with." Her request was innocent enough, but I knew not to part with it. What if Pir tried to contact me?

"You can have it when I get back," I said, turning to look at her. She had her hands on her waist and looked ablaze with an inner light but was modest as hell. She'd certainly made better use of the leaves than I had. She nodded, then turned around, and headed toward the waterfall.

I continued on toward the top of the rise, the book held firmly in my hand. Had Laila been accidentally transported here because she was kissing me as I passed out? Or did she appear as a trap? I remembered her soft hot tongue probing the inside of my mouth. I tried to block the memory as it rose to demand the renewed attention of my cock.

I stopped by the shrubs and took my time making a new garment for myself. To my satisfaction it turned out to be a significantly improved design over the earlier version.

What I'd thought would be a fifteen-minute hike to the top was turning into what felt like an hour. The sound of the waterfall had faded to a distant hum and the light had dimmed. The once-blue sky had faded to a pale mauve. I had trouble locating Laila near the water, but then I spotted her running in my direction. I stopped and waited for her to catch up with me. When she reached me she was out of breath, her face beaming with joy. Quite a few leaves had fallen away thanks to her sprint.

"What's going on?" I said, stealing a glance at her breasts, at the rosy orb of flesh around her nipples that showed through her hair.

"I was looking at my reflection in the water. My face really is fine, perfectly normal!" she cried. "Ismaeel, I want to stay here forever."

"Are you crazy?" I said, resuming my walk up the hill and adjusting the leaves around my waist.

"Ismaeel, we can live a perfect happy life here—just you and me," she said, following me. "We'll make love—day and night. We'll have lots and lots of children."

"And then what?" I asked, without looking back at her.

"Then we'll grow old, watching our children grow. We'll play with our grandchildren, and then one day we'll just move on to the next world," she explained as though I should be delighted at the proposition.

"I'm afraid we're already in the next world," I said, wondering where the hell these grandchildren of ours were going to come from, barring incest. A very creepy idea.

She remained quiet as we ascended the grassy slope, zigzagging our way toward the ridge. Just below the summit we stopped to catch our breath. Standing before me, she clasped her hands under her chin, closed her eyes, and started moving her lips.

"What are you doing?"

"Praying," she said, opening one of her eyes.

"That may be the only way we get out of here. Maybe I should join you."

"I'm praying to Allah to keep us here forever."

"Isn't that like meddling with his plans?" Not liking where this was headed.

"He's known to change his mind if you ask sincerely." A model of piety, she touched her face with her palms and blew her breath over her chest.

"How do you know for sure what's right for you and what's not?" I asked, trying not to show the irritation I felt at this line of talk.

"Allah has given us the ability to know right from wrong."

"Oh. The moral sense!"

"Yes, the moral sense."

"So you seriously believe that staying here is right for you?" I thought she must have gone completely out of her mind.

"Yes."

"What about me?" I threw my hands in the air, growing more and more disturbed.

"Man doesn't know what's right for him. That's why Allah created women to help men out." She stated this way too forcefully.

"I don't agree."

As the words left my mouth, the sky darkened over the inlet and the air exploded with a crescendo of noise. A black undulating shape filled the chasm over the water and advanced in our direction. The shrill screeching was unbearable and we had to cover our ears with our hands.

Ababeels!

It was the exact same sound I'd heard just before I'd zoned out drinking tea at the Bihishti Tea Corner.

We stood in awe and watched as a vast flock of tiny black birds zoomed over our heads. And then it became still, silent, and the sky returned to its previous shade of mauve.

"What was that?" She had her hands over her temples, her eyes widened.

"Ababeels," I said.

"Ababeels? So frightful!"

At that instant, the text of the sura Al-Fil shot across my upper visual field in blazing red-gold Arabic script: *Have you not seen what your Lord did with the companions of the elephant? And send on them birds in flocks. To throw on them stones of baked clay. And He made them like eaten straw.* It was one of a handful of sura I knew the translation of.

I recited these lines silently, imagining the sea of bloody carnage in the wake of Abraha's army as it advanced upon the Kaaba with its legion of elephants some 1,500 years ago.

We continued walking, watching as the treetops came into view over the crest of the ridge. One of the trees shook and something moved within the rustling canopy of leaves.

"Did you see that," I shouted, pointing toward the tree.

"What was it?"

"Not sure. Maybe some animal."

The rocky cliff on each side of the knoll formed a natural pass that separated the stark landscape of the inlet from a strangely contoured country on the other side. It was like standing on a rim of a bowl and looking into it. Brimming with an exotic array of plant life and dotted with waterfalls, a seemingly interminable slope led our gaze toward a hazy green at the bottom of the valley before ascending again. There it was, forming the opposite rim, occupying the elevated horizon like a band of dark clouds. The Wall—the perimeter of the most coveted real estate in the universe, Paradise. Laila gasped at the sight and gripped my arm, her body trembling briefly against mine.

"All praise to Allah! This surely is Paradise." Her face was illumined by a peaceful glow of love; not passion this time, but love.

"Not exactly, technically speaking."

"Look at that massive wall! None other than jinns could have constructed a wall of this size. How far do you think it is from here?"

"Seventy years on the back of a horse," I said, remembering my conversation with Ibrahim at the Bihishti Tea Corner.

"Seventy years! How do you know that?"

"I just know. I also know that the Paradise you're talking about exists behind that great wall."

"Really?"

"That's all I can tell you."

"Ismaeel, it's time for you to explain how we got here."

"It's complicated."

"Try me." She stared at me with eyes wide, unblinking and demanding.

I considered her request for a moment. She looked too innocent to be a trap. And the truth itself was so wild, that it'd only make her laugh. I decided to spill the beans and held the book up in front of her.

"See this book? It contains the tickets to Paradise. Literally."

"Tickets to Paradise?" she asked with a hint of amusement in her voice. "You mean those little coupons?"

"Yeah, the *coupons*. They're good for a free ride," I said shaking my head and starting off down the slope and away from the cluster of trees where I'd spotted suspicious animal activity.

"I'll explain everything. I promise. First let's find someplace comfortable to sit down."

She followed me silently.

Hoping Laila wouldn't notice, I tapped on my headband repeatedly, visualized an SOS in big bold letters, and beamed the image at Pir, but no luck.

After having walked downward a couple of hundred steps, absorbing the surreal vista of a bowl-shaped landscape of staggering dimensions, we came upon another cluster of gigantic trees, each a hundred or so meters tall; their roots rose off the ground like ledges. A natural seating area. We sat face-to-face and drew a few deep breaths.

"Are you ready for my story?" I asked, leaning toward her, drawn by a strong magnetic current. She radiated intoxicating warmth and my loins rippled with desire.

She bit her glistening lip and brought her face closer to mine. Our lips met and hers parted in a hot intake of breath.

Putting the book down on the root, I stood up with her wrist in my hand, pulled her up, and in the next moment we collapsed and were rolling on the ground, wresting like wild animals, the leaves tumbling from our heaving bodies. Without warning she pulled out of my arms and sat upright. She stared at me, her eyes huge and haunted, her knees drawn up to hide her breasts.

"Ismaeel, do you accept me as your wife?"

"What kind of question is that?"

"You'll have to say yes, if you want to have me. Let's not risk our chance to enter Paradise."

"For heaven's sake, last night you were on top of me in that goddamn bathroom. Now all of a sudden you need to marry me before we can make love?" Ravishing as she was, I was in no mood for tying a knot with a strange, possessive woman I didn't really know, especially under these circumstances. Deep down I knew I'd failed Pir thanks to my unbridled sexual urges. Lust. Women. My greatest weakness. For such a refractory case as I, death would be the only cure from this affliction.

"Circumstances alter cases." She smiled mischievously. "So what's your answer?"

I looked at her in disbelief. And then a thought occurred. Why should I care when I had the option that would be perfectly halal according to the precepts of Sharia, and I saw no reason why it shouldn't be acceptable to this newly minted Muslimmah.

"Okay fine. Let's do the *Mut'ah,* the temporary marriage."

"Although I'm not a Shia, for now that'll do." She smiled. "We can always convert it to a permanent one later."

"Our contract will hold until we get back to our previous lives, or, as long as we're stuck here."

"It's a deal."

So she asked me three times: "Do you accept me as your lawful wife?" I answered her each time: "I do."

"We are now husband and wife. Promise you'll never cheat on me."

"For God's sake, Laila!"

She climbed on top of me, her knees resting on the ground. Her nipples touched my chest as she played with my hair. Her breath on my face was hot, a fevered and rhythmic chant of desire.

"Ismaeel, I don't ever want to wake up from this lovely dream. Do you really love me?"

I lay hypnotized, staring at her ecstatic face as she took the whole of me into the hot moist folds of her body. She winced, then swung her head and threw her hair back as she started to grind on top of me. I took my headband off and put it on her forehead. She licked her lips and my fingers and I shut my eyes. In mid stride she screamed then collapsed on top of me, her pelvis, filled with my throbbing cock, still moving.

I heard a rustle over my head. Looking up I saw the huge red bulbous ass of a baboon retreating nimbly into the branches of the tree. In his hand the creature gripped the black book.

"Hey!" I yelled, writhing under Laila's body in the throes of my orgasm and hers. "Come back! Hey, you fucking little shit, come back here! Shit!" I screamed. The monkey just kept climbing hand over hand and soon disappeared into the dense green covering overhead.

Laila kissed my cheeks, her breath still hot with desire. Her body twitched as I lay beneath her, spent. I lamented the loss of our tickets to get out of here, not to mention the chance of entering Paradise. Most importantly, what would Pir say? He seemed pretty adamant about a lot of things, but chief among them was this: he wanted that book.

I finally disentangled myself from Laila's body and jumped to my feet. Berating myself, I climbed the tree trunk up through the heavy branches as far as I could, but there was no sign of the mischievous baboon thief.

Later, as we lay side by side on the bed of grass staring up at the vault of space overhead, dusk crept over the hillside and bathed everything in radiant light. The air felt exquisite against our skin. The heavens were dotted with tiny lights, like the tips of a fiber optic bundle dangling from the hand of some celestial being as he watched from above. We made love again; gently this time, and then fell asleep; each surrendering to our private dreams.

When we awoke, the air was colored with a pale golden light and the trees were full of birds in song. And we were starving.

After making love so wildly that our bodies were covered in bruises, we set off down the interminable slope toward the valley. Along the way we gathered more leaves and fashioned new garments for ourselves. There was fresh water in unlimited supply and the air was sweet, warm, and fragrant.

The trees were heavy and drooping with many varieties of unfamiliar but delicious fruits and we took our fill of many of them. Still no sun appeared, if there was a sun in this peculiar land; and the daylight lasted only a short while. Dusk returned rather quickly, and to our amazement dusk turned to dawn without any intervening night. It was disorienting initially, but after experiencing a few of these sunless cycles we got used to it.

If this was how the punishment for my cardinal sin was going to look, then I wasn't complaining. However, the realization that my chances of getting out of here alive were pretty slim was making me increasingly anxious.

We slept whenever we pleased; we ate whenever we felt hungry; we made love at each rest spot; and we continued our descent toward the valley. Along the way, we spotted several black monkeys squatting among the branches of the trees. But there was no sign of the book among this tribe. Eyeing us with curious looks and emitting low-pitched screams they stood their ground without abandoning their perches, and made no attempt to approach us.

It didn't take us long to realize we'd lost all sense of time. Our descent along the slope continued for what felt like a lifetime. Laila's hair began to show streaks of white, and so did my beard that had now reached my navel. The soles of our feet, after repeated blistering, had become thickly callused, and our knees were swollen and throbbing with pain from the exertion of our perpetual downward march. To ease the discomfort we made walking sticks of fallen tree branches.

When we finally reached the floor of the valley we followed a winding creek and at dusk came to a broad trailhead. Too exhausted and wracked with pain to go any further, we made our bed among the tall soft grasses and went to sleep.

We were awakened to the excited chatter of a gang of twenty or so wild-haired, topless women with white skin, extraordinarily beautiful faces, and long legs. They spoke in a monosyllabic tongue, which sounded quite musical and pleasing. They had us surrounded and each woman carried a wooden spear pointed just inches from our throats.

Each of these beauties wore a palm-sized green leaf over her pubic area.

Rubbing our eyes we bolted upright and stared at the newcomers. Laila looked distraught seeing so many strange looking women around us. They had radiant skin, translucent over their ankles, through which the marrow could be seen as a tint of red within the core of their bones. It was the strangest thing to see, but in no way diminished the otherwise beautifully shaped legs.

Hoor! That was the only logical thought that came to my mind, for the women's ankles fit the description of a *hoor,* the woman of Paradise, as stated in Islamic theology. Had we after all landed in some forlorn corner of Paradise that happened to exist outside its boundary wall?

Chapter 18
The Dump

DRAGGING US TO OUR FEET, the women lashed our hands behind our backs using coarse vines as strong as rope. They marched us at spear-point over a thick, moss-covered trail that snaked through a humid forest of gigantic trees with smooth red bark and trunks twice the size of Sequoias.

We passed several thundering waterfalls and crystal-clear ponds teaming with fish whose bodies glowed from within. We spotted a three-legged fox, a double headed deer, antelopes with horns mangled together in an ungainly mess, and a pair of winged horses white as snow.

After what seemed like several hours on this forced march, we entered a dark, narrow, rocky canyon that opened on a clearing about the size of a city block. Ensconced within a circular ring of red and black volcanic rock that jutted from the earth like a massive ridge of broken teeth, the place resembled an ancient coliseum. The rocky face was cut in broad uneven steps, both horizontal and vertical, and was dotted with dozens of caves. At the far end of this amphitheater another huge waterfall emptied into a pool where several women were bathing, playing, and splashing. Their laughter rose over the sound of the falls.

The women chattered in their melodious voices as they tied Laila and me to the gigantic trunk of a solitary tree whose canopy could easily shade a whole village. It stood at the center of the clearing, a lone guard watching over the settlement.

Suddenly a hush fell over the women as a gust of wind hit my face.

Everyone looked up. My eyes blinked uncontrollably as I followed their gaze.

A winged creature, the hideous unnatural blending of man and bird, glided through the air about fifty feet above us. Its wings flapped unevenly as if with great exhaustion while it descended and landed just a few feet from us. The bizarre personage wore a tattered off-white cloak and stood about five feet tall with a bowed back and drooping shoulders. He seemed to be in the advanced stages of some wasting illness.

He could've been three hundred, or three thousand years old. Folding his wings against his back, the man-creature stared at Laila and me with beady black eyes with hardly any white in them. A sweeping elongated forehead and large hooked nose that appeared hard and beak-like were remarkable features on his otherwise human face. The creature was bald except for patches of fine gray feathers that grew out of his temples against the side of his face.

Moving his shoulders from side to side and clearing his throat, he seemed about to say something when the crowd parted and a stunning long-legged, luminous beauty emerged and stood before us. All I could do was stare in horror and fascination.

The woman's chest was dominated by a mammoth single breast, both taut and supple, without a hint of sagging. Her demonic nipple pointing straight at us, the woman stood beside the winged old man. Her tongue swiped her upper lip a few times, as her big black eyes stared unblinkingly at me.

The woman whispered something in the old man's ear. He nodded in response then bowed as if in supplication and clasped his hands in front of his body. He resembled a statue; the classic image of humility. The woman stepped closer and stood in front of me, her feet spread apart. I glanced down and saw that, unlike the other women, who wore the green leaves, she wore a red heart-shaped leaf over her sex.

"I am Queen Xenobia!" she declared in perfect English with just a trace of an accent I couldn't place. "Language?"

"English—Urdu—and Punjabi," I said, turning to look at Laila. She nodded her head in agreement.

"Some Arabic, as well," I added.

"Ah! Excellent. I've always had a fondness for Arabic," she said tossing her head.

"Uh... Well, I can read and write in Arabic, but I can't understand it," I hurried to correct her lest she started off chattering in Arabic.

"Oh? How is that possible?" she exclaimed, wrinkling her nostrils and narrowing her eyes.

"It's very possible," Laila chimed in. "That's how it's always been done in my country."

"And just which country would that be?" Xenobia demanded, skewering Laila with an icy glance.

"Never mind. I don't really care," she continued, turning from Laila and looking back at me. I could see she had made Laila simmer with rage at being dismissed like that.

"Here, we speak all languages known to man. However, we have no capacity to understand women. I am one of the few, very few, who does understand their prattling." Her glance swept over the hushed crowd that seemed to be growing as we spoke.

"We mean no harm," I said.

"Where are we?" Laila asked.

"You were caught trespassing in the Dump," she said.

The winged creature shook his head as if in disagreement but didn't lift his eyes from the ground.

"Dump?" She'd just negated my suspicion that we might be in Paradise. "We never intended to trespass onto your settlement. We were just lost while hiking down the big green slope—we're from other side of the ridge," I explained, thinking the Dump she was referring to meant this particular settlement of hers, and, or perhaps, its adjoining jungle.

"This side or that side, it doesn't matter. It's all part of the Dump we hate," she said with a stern look in her eyes.

"I wouldn't call it *that*," the old man protested, speaking for the first time.

"You've never been dumped, Fukraeel," the queen barked, looking over her shoulder at him. "There's a difference between retiring here by choice, and being discarded like a load of trash just because we didn't come out perfect."

"Who are we to question our fates?" the old man said meekly.

"What are you talking about? Where are we?"

"You," the queen said looking at me with an appraising eye. "You may consider yourself to be in Paradise." She glanced again at Laila and smiled with her mouth but her eyes remained cold and distant. "I'm not too sure if I can say that about you, my dear. Paradise is for men only."

Laila straightened up, the rope around her torso tightening. She fixed Xenobia in an angry glare with the red of her enraged face indistinguishable from the color of my headband she wore.

"He's my husband," she growled. "Don't you dare put your dirty hands on him."

"Laila, please! Stay calm," I whispered in her ear.

"I don't like this place, Ismaeel. You'd better not do anything stupid here." She started to sob.

"It was you who prayed to Allah to keep us here forever. And I warned you not to ask for something you've no frickin' clue about. That's why I don't pray." I said. "Now be quiet and let me do what I can."

Queen Xenobia turned and began addressing the assembled women in a language unlike anything I'd ever heard before. The group had grown considerably since our arrival and now several dozen women crowded around their queen. Most of them had conspicuously uneven breasts and a few had no breasts at all.

Some had very large breasts and no nipples. I spotted one woman whose buttocks were without a cleft in the middle; some had six fingers, and some had toes missing. All the women had some bodily defect, except for their faces and legs, which were ravishingly beautiful with creamy unblemished skin.

When Queen Xenobia finished her address four women stepped forward from the crowd, followed by four more. They put their spears down, untied Laila, and dragged her away towards the forest. Entangled in the eight pairs of hands, she convulsed like a fish out of water. Her screams, piercing my heart, faded as she was dragged from the canyon and swallowed by the dark crevice within the rocky massif. Horrified, I slumped against the rope and brooded over my fate, still under the curious stares of these hauntingly beautiful women.

Soon, they untied me from the tree and made me march under the shadow of their spears behind Queen Xenobia. She led the procession up the rocky steps into a large and luxurious cave that was decorated with a king's ransom of beautiful things.

Her three-room dwelling opened onto the waterfall and was pervaded by the atmosphere of the rain forest: misty, green, and dark, and well stocked with a profusion of exotic fruits, nuts, and fragrant flowers. Situated on a ledge next to the mouth of the waterfall, the queen's perch enjoyed a commanding view of the whole settlement. It was truly an aerie worthy of a great chief. I was told in no uncertain terms that from now on I was to be her sex slave and I'd be killed without hesitation if I ever attempted to escape.

For the next couple of days, despite her best efforts, she couldn't turn me on.

"I can't perform under stress." I told her, still feeling frightened and heartbroken at the loss of Laila. Besides, it was that hideous breast of hers that'd independently turned me off.

"No worries. We've arrangements for all sorts of stresses." Xenobia smiled and poured me a tablespoon of thick white liquid.

"What the hell is that?" I took the spoon from her and stared at the creamy liquid.

"Sex nectar, courtesy Fukraeel."

"Do I have to?"

"You've no choice, my dear Ismaeel."

I emptied the spoon into my mouth without further argument.

The potion tasted like honey-sweetened kefir.

As I'd soon discover, this sex nectar thing, which she had me swallow three times a day, was a remarkably potent aphrodisiac with addictive properties, and which had been smuggled out of Paradise by Fukraeel; the winged old angel in retirement.

Fukraeel lived a one-room nest made of twigs on top the encampment's only tree. From the mouth of the queen's cave the aerie could be seen and afforded a clear view of the old angel's comings and goings.

Xenobia told me that, before his retirement, Fukraeel had served as a minor functionary in the lowest rung of Paradise. He possessed no sex organs, but he wasn't without a fine aesthetic sense and libido. To exercise that sense, he'd become adventurous and resorted to illegal means to compensate for his congenital impotency. He dosed himself on this illicit amorous nectar on a daily basis; something many angels did during the golden years of their retirement.

Since he had no competition and the women had never encountered a real man, Fukraeel had been enjoying every moment of his retirement. That is, until I showed up. He was devastated by my arrival, especially after discovering that his stash of illicit sex nectar had been stolen. He'd stored it away in the airtight bowling-pin-sized clay gourds in his nest.

From then on he despised me. But he was too fearful of Xenobia and her gang of Amazons to harm me in any physical way. In a state of learned helplessness, Fukraeel's spite towards me only intensified with each passing day. I pitied the old guy, and of course that only made things worse.

"He's utterly useless—doesn't even deserve your pity," Xenobia said one day as she sucked my toes, her breast tucked between my calves. "He's just a dirty old angel who should be spending his remaining days worshipping."

Xenobia kept me in her cave for what seemed like a good month. Her wild company helped me cure some of the gloom and despair that had overtaken me after having witnessed the cruel ejection of Laila from the settlement. But I missed her terribly. I felt so alone.

During these strange times of surreal sex and otherworldly orgasms, I noticed a gradual but conspicuous weakening of my memory, which I suspected to be the side-effect of the nectar I'd been ingesting religiously three times a day. Alarmed at the peculiar loss of my precious faculty, I'd made a habit of starting each day by reminding myself who I was and where I came from, how I landed in this place, my meeting with Pir Pullsiraat at Shah Jamal, Tarzan's smiling face, and my trip to Hell on Chaacha's bike over the Tightrope. I remembered my first love-making with Laila, the red-assed monkey that ran away with the book, my obscure mission whose success depended upon my gaining trust of Abba whom I'd yet to meet. And there was my own quest—to know whether Paradise and Hell were real, and the refractory nature of my weaknesses, indiscretions, and stupidities. This few minutes of daily recollection was my only hope for keeping my sanity, my identity, my purpose, and my quest alive. It was like a rope that connected me to my past life, and I needed to hold on to it as long as I could. But the loss of my headband was a constant reminder that I might remain here forever.

Who knows how long I would have remained there in Xenobia's cave had she not detected an impending mutiny brewing in the settlement over her exclusive rights to my concubinage. She reluctantly released me, and it was clear the women had things all figured out.

Including Xenobia, there were seventy-one women in the colony. They had divided themselves into ten groups—seven in each—and they had a plan. With the guarded blessing of Xenobia, I was to spend one day with each of the ten groups, and then move to the next the following dawn. Then I was allowed to sleep for a few hours before facing the next cohort of ravenous, albeit defective, hooris.

On the eleventh day of the cycle I would return to Xenobia where I would remain with her as before. Only with her was I allowed the luxury of orgasm. The girls protested against this injustice, but Xenobia stood her ground. This naturally shifted the onus onto my ingenuity to violate the queen's command as I saw fit.

"Time is a curious thing, Ismaeel," Xenobia said to me one day after I asked her how long they were planning to feast on my immutably hardened manhood. "Before you know it, we'll all be old and withered. Enjoy it while it lasts."

"The way things are going, the supply isn't going to last much longer," I replied. I had no idea what would happen when the nectar ran out and sure as hell didn't want to grow old here. It was not my desire to die in the Dump; especially without ever seeing the real Paradise.

Time raced at a dizzying frenzied pace, thanks to the shortened days and the absence of real night. In order to keep track of the passing days I began carving lines in the bark of the tree that housed Fukraeel's nest.

Weeks flowed into months and months into years as I got used to living in a state of perpetual orgasm which was impossible to describe, except that it took a toll on my daily practice of recollection. Past life memories I'd been holding on to so dearly began fizzling out at an alarming rate. For example: all I remembered of Pir and Chaacha Khidr was their hypnotic eyes; Tarzan, his perfect white teeth; Laila, her embrace; Abba, his temper. My quest, engulfed by my heightened lust raised to the power of infinity, had been reduced to a state of jello, an amorphous mass of incomprehensible propositions and conjectures.

Xenobia marveled at my prowess and rolled back her earlier strict limitations. The queen learned to share me with her subjects unreservedly. In some strange way it only increased her power over them. So nourishing and potent was the milky white elixir I consumed daily that I'd go for long periods of time without eating anything else. My body stopped expelling waste altogether, including semen.

Before my arrival, the girls, whose congenital bodily defects had rendered them unsuitable to be inhabiting Paradise, had been unable to perform their only function, the sole reason they'd been created—that of providing carnal pleasure to the men. This had resulted in their suffering from various mental illnesses. They had been devastated by having been condemned to an utterly useless existence in this godforsaken place as well as being in the company of an equally useless creature, Fukraeel. My arrival had changed all *that*.

By the end of the first year, I'd become so proficient in the art of satisfying multiple partners simultaneously that I was taking all seventy-one of them in the span of a single day.

Despite possessing a superhuman sexual stamina, reserved only for the men dwelling in the real Paradise, I was aging at an alarming rate. By the third year my hair was snow white and thinning and my muscles had become soft and flabby. By the fourth, my back stooped, my fingers became knotty and arthritic and my skin wrinkled and sagged from my starved frame.

By the end of the fifth year—the year I'd given up my desire to get out of here alive—most of my teeth had rotted and fallen out. Like an old man I was hobbling around with a cane. Thanks to the nectar, whose end now looked inevitable, I remained very much functional, discharging my duties of those of a sex slave. In order to reach Xenobia's cave, I had to be hauled up in a litter constructed for that purpose.

The virgins aged as well, but at a slower and less alarming rate. Their skin, once translucent, became dull and opaque, their breasts sagged, their legs and buttocks became flabby and developed ugly stretch marks, their vaginas turned lax and stopped lubricating. Xenobia even started carrying her breast in a sling hung around her neck.

The supply of the heavenly nectar ran out in the beginning of the sixth year, plunging the whole community into a downward spiral from which it never recovered. Deprived of the potion, I began regaining my childhood memory, but it was too late. I was already an old man heading for the grave. Xenobia tried a host of different herbs to treat my erectile dysfunction, but with no success. I'd lost all interest in sex forever.

Once I was officially out-of-service, the colony lost its immune system and quickly lapsed into decay and disease. Xenobia developed a festering sore on her breast. It enlarged and eventually spread over her entire chest. It oozed yellow pus and smelled of a rotten corpse. Soon she stopped venturing out of her cave at all. All the women were afflicted with disfiguring ailments, with leprosy and gangrene of the arms and legs being the most common. Soon the ground was littered with their blackened, rotted-off body parts. Their once charming little caves became graves from which the afflicted women never emerged.

Feeling like a shriveled, empty husk, I spent my time beneath Fukraeel's tree, valiantly fighting off his mocking amused gaze and waiting for death. The bastard had not aged a bit; perhaps he'd already aged as much as he ever would by the time of his retirement.

Every day around dusk, he'd flutter down from his nest, his wings quivering behind his drooping shoulders, to honor me with his sweet company. He briefed me extensively and in lavish detail on all the various tortures I'd soon be experiencing in my grave for all the debauchery he'd been a witness to and that I'd so willingly indulged in.

Sensing the imminent approach of my last breath, Fukraeel began digging the grave he took such delight in telling me about. The old angel told me that he had known both Munkar and Nakir—a pair of terrifying angels whose sole job it was to inflict torture on the damned within the grave. In him I saw a reflection of my father. I remembered the bedtime stories which Abba used to tell me. His favorite characters indeed were Munkar and Nakir, his favorite plot, torture in the grave.

Within a matter of days, Fukraeel had excavated a hole large enough to accommodate me without any undignified squashing of my sad corpse.

Finally, the day Fukraeel had been waiting for all these years, arrived.

"I'm very concerned about you Ismaeel," he said morosely. He stood tall beside me, using the wooden shovel as a cane, sweat pouring out of his forehead. I lay on the ground, flaccid, bathed in cold sweat and gasping for air. It took a supreme effort to sputter even a few words.

"I've done nothing wrong," I said with as much conviction as I could muster while wiping the spittle from my lips. My chest started rattling and wheezing with the effort.

"It is I, Fukraeel!" he roared, straightening his back and glaring down at me with contempt, his wings now flaring behind him. "It is I who bears witness to all sins great and small that you, Ismaeel, son of Ibrahim, have committed before these, my eyes!" He stood before me, vengeful and defiant, and I saw a shadow of the angel he must have been, once upon a time. Then he sighed, just a tired old man again.

I wanted to tell him that he was nobody, and that no one had ever heard his name where I lived. He wasn't documented in any of the theology books I'd read. But I remained quiet. I didn't want to waste my last breath on him.

He squatted down beside me and looked into my eyes.

"The hedonism, the debauchery, the mistreatment of women. Each and every act of yours has been recorded by each and every one of your organs. In the grave each part of your body will declare its sins, and Munkar and Nakir will be standing nearby, taking notes. Even I shudder thinking of what they will do to you."

"My witnesses," I said, pausing to catch my breath. "Are going to be these seventy-one lovely hooris..."

"They're not allowed to be witnesses," he screamed angrily, putting the flat of his palm over my closing eyelids. "So long Ismaeel! Remember, no one knows torture better than Munkar and Nakir. Say hello to them from me when you meet."

I wanted to reply, but my tongue just lay in my mouth and I stopped breathing as my head slumped to one side. The last thing I saw before the darkness closed over me like a cold shroud was that grave; dark and wet like the mouth of the earth waiting to swallow me.

Chapter 19
The Grave

AN EXCRUCIATING PAIN shot across my chest. I opened my eyes and saw two owl-faced beings staring down at me. Standing on either side of my head, they folded their trembling black wings against their shoulders. The dank grave that had held me was now a four-walled cell. My decrepit body lay on an inclined bench a few feet off the ground—my feet above my head.

The angel standing on my right jabbed his knuckles into my ribs, causing a fresh round of unbearable pain. Devoid of any white, their eyes looked like black marble. Their bodies were covered with fine shiny black feathers like a crow's, but their limbs were completely human.

"Hey, man! That hurts," I said. "I'm up! I'm up." As I tried to sit up, an elbow slammed against my chest and forced me back down, knocking the wind out of me.

"Not so fast."

"Look," I said, throwing my right hand in the air, forcing a smile. "My name is..."

"American?" Removing his arm from my chest, the angel shook my hand, giving it a squeeze that almost snapped the bones in my fingers. I let out an inarticulate wail.

"I'm Munkar." His voice had a fluttering quality, as if he spoke through an electric fan.

He grabbed my balls and squeezed them tightly. I let out another scream. "Welcome!" he said.

It took me a while before I was able to speak.

"Easy, easy!" I said, moaning, and raising my hands in the air. "Let me get oriented to the damn place first. Okay?"

Without warning, Munkar put his hand on my throat and squeezed until my eyes bulged and I started coughing violently.

"First question. Who is your Lord?" Nakir demanded, as flames leapt from his tongue and singed my cheek. His thundering voice was so loud that dirt and a few pebbles dropped from the ceiling and landed on Munkar's wings.

"My Lord is the same as yours," I sputtered through my teeth.

"No! You are lying! Tell the truth!" Munkar bellowed.

The two angels looked at each other, their brows raised and their eyes roving within their sockets. Before I had time to protest, they had my wrists and ankles manacled to heavy iron rings built into the bench I was lying on. Nakir stood behind my head and laid a damp cloth over my face. Then Munkar poured water over my covered nose and mouth. I choked and gagged as water trickled into my bruised windpipe. Just before I passed out they stopped and uncovered my face.

"What is your religion? Say it!" Munkar roared.

I coughed and spit the last of the water from my throat.

"I want to talk to your superior!" I gasped, then coughed some more and struggled to get my breath.

"Superior?" Nakir said, giving me a puzzled look.

"The head angel who makes all the policy around here," I demanded.

"Policy?" Munkar said, furrowing his brows and rubbing his forehead. He looked at Nakir. "Do you know what he's talking about?"

"I think I do," Nakir said, staring at me, his hand absently stroking the feathers where his waist would be if he were a man. "Policy! Hmm! Would you like that hot, cold, orally, or rectally? Your pick?"

Before I could answer, my body began to vibrate, filling the grave-cell with a low hum, which soon became a tremulous twittering. Panicked, I lifted my head and looked around. The sound originated in my fingers, toes, lips, nose, even my eyes and earlobes. The loudest of the noise poured from the area below my navel and from my genitals.

Oh shit! I thought, figuring I was really done for now as Fukraeel's explicit warnings reverberated in my head.

Both angels now held quill pens and notebooks in their hands; black leather-bound volumes in which they furiously scribbled all the noise of my past deeds. They began with my upper torso but rapidly moved to the lower and more offending regions. When they reached my groin, their pens became a blur and their eyes bulged with excitement.

Standing on either side of my hips, they scrawled at a dizzying pace until they ran out of pages. For a brief moment they looked at each other, their eyes darting back and forth, before they extracted a fresh set of notebooks from under the bench. These also proved woefully inadequate to fully contain the breadth and depravity of my escapades in the Dump. Throwing away their quill pens and notebooks, they stared at my penis that still buzzed loudly. The two just shook their heads in disbelief.

"Have you ever seen anything like it before?" Munkar asked Nakir.

Nakir rubbed his chin, gritted his teeth, and shot me a fiery glance.

Realizing that I was in serious trouble, I shouted in desperation.

"I'm a friend of Fukraeel! He asked me to say hello to you," I said. "He told me all about you."

"How the fuck do you know Fukraeel?" Nakir shouted.

"What's your name, brother?" Munkar said, a hint of gentleness creeping into his trembling voice.

"Ismaeel."

"Profession?"

"It's complicated," I said, my eyes following his movements behind my head. He opened a scroll before his face. The light in the room brightened and Munkar came and stood next to Nakir.

Putting their heads together they stared at the parchment, Nakir's fingertip sliding over the text from top to bottom.

"His name isn't on our exit control list," Nakir announced to his partner. "And he knows Fukraeel. Very strange!"

"Yes, very strange indeed!" Munkar agreed, nodding his head.

"I told you, I'm not your ordinary run of the mill dead guy. Now can I talk to your supervisor?"

Instead of replying, they disappeared from the room with a whoosh, leaving a trail of smoke that smelled of something long dead. They weren't gone long when my cell started filling up with rats. They materialized by the hundreds out of the dirt walls and dropped from the ceiling, some landing on my chest and then skittering away. Soon the ground was a black undulating carpet of screeching rats, their numbers swelling by the minute.

Still shackled to the bench, I watched in horror as their mass surged like a wave. Soon their jagged yellow teeth and razor-sharp claws would be ripping into my flesh. I closed my eyes and prepared for the most hideous death imaginable. I doubted this would be the last amusement Munkar and Nakir would draw from their arsenal of devilish divertissements. I wondered how many deaths of unspeakable agony and torment I'd have to endure before I would be deemed fit to proceed to the next stage of purification.

With another swoosh of feathers and flap of ebony wings, Munkar and Nakir reappeared and surveyed the room that was now bursting with the deafening squeal of the rats. Hovering over my head, their wings a blur, the feathered duo removed the manacles and pulled me to my feet.

"Congratulations, my friend! It seems you're on your way to Paradise after all," Munkar said warmly, his eyes tearing up with emotion.

"I'm extremely sorry for any pain or discomfort we may have caused you, sir," Nakir said crisply. "You know how it is. We must do what is part of our job."

"Paradise?" I asked, looking at Munkar in near shock.

"We've been told that you've passed all the necessary steps to gain entry into Paradise," Munkar said, now sporting a kind and affectionate look. "And that included a little taste of torture in the grave."

I was speechless and couldn't trust what I heard. It had to be a mistake or something.

"Lucky bastard, I'd say!" Munkar said, wiping his tears.

"Now close your eyes—we're leaving," Nakir said.

Before I even had the chance to react, I exploded into a million tiny sparks of golden light.

I awoke to the sound of a pleasing feminine voice—speaking in English—over a telecom system.

"Welcome to the VIP salon of the Intiqaal Lounge," the voice was saying. "Your orientation will begin shortly. We'll make every effort to ensure that your stay with us is as enjoyable as possible. Please feel free to ask any questions that you may have."

Covered with dirt, my decrepit worn out body lay on a white marble floor beside a rectangular pool of clear blue water under the compassionate gaze of seven ravishing, black-eyed beauties. They kneeled over me like the fruit-laden branches of some heavenly tree, their skin shining through their gauzy diaphanous robes as if lit from within.

A number of white-winged angles flew about overhead. They carried all sorts of things: chairs, chaises, bedposts, mattresses, pillows and cushions, trays with food and drink, towels and robes, shoes, plus many strange looking objects.

"My lord, welcome," one of the women said, massaging my hand and smiling with a mouth full of beautiful white teeth. She had very long jet-black hair, eyes that glittered like polished onyx and moist red lips curled in a charming coquettish smile.

"I'm Veena," she said, and introduced me to the rest of the pack. They bowed their heads and smiled when their names were mentioned. Veena continued. "We're here to help you turn back into a young man again."

"How is that possible?" I asked, raising myself up feebly onto my elbows, and looking at my horrid-looking self.

"My lord, you leave that to us," a woman chimed in, in a voice that sounded like the tinkle of a tiny crystal bell.

"You must be a very special man—a saint perhaps. We've never seen Munkar and Nakir fast-track someone in here with such urgency," Another woman named Tina added.

"Special men deserve special treatment," she whispered in my ear.

"The procedure we employ to make you young again is completely lust-free," Veena pronounced in her sweet voice softly rubbing my chest with her fingertips. "Just relax, sir. Let us do our scared duty."

They took off their robes and then carried my tired old body to the pool. The water was warm and oily and smelled of sweet herbs. The girls took turns scrubbing my dirt-clogged skin using an abrasive sponge made of some plant material. After the bath, they dried me with perfumed towels and rubbed fragrant oil into my hair.

I was made to lie down on a divan draped with crimson silk and piled with colorful pillows. Forming a circle, the women kneeled on the floor beside me and told me to close my eyes. Then they applied a cushiony blindfold over my eyes. I felt their hands, and later tips of their tongues, lapping gently at my withered flesh. Soon my entire body was vibrating with vitality, and I was drenched with their saliva.

My blindfold was removed, and I was then taken into the pool a second time. Instead of water it was now filled with cardamom-scented milk. My skin now glowed with youthful radiance. As the girls washed the saliva off of me, I could feel my bones growing stronger, more substantial.

I was brought back to the same divan, blindfolded, and guided, without any effort on my part, through seven orgasms without once losing my erection, and the pleasure only heightened with each successive act. The last one, by far the longest and most stunning, didn't produce any fluid from my body.

"In Al-Jannah one doesn't produce any waste," Veena spoke quietly in my ear, as if telling me a secret.

"But what happens to the food one eats."

"It changes into musk," she said. "Your body will ooze musk in place of sweat—it drives the virgins crazy."

I emerged from the pool feeling buoyant. A pair of handsome

young male angels landed beside me. They carried fresh garments folded over their arms: a blue robe of silk, its neck and cuffs studded with diamonds and rubies; a gold turban speckled with thousands of tiny iridescent five pointed stars; a pair of leather sandals, and a finger-sized glass vial of perfume which smelled of moist earth.

I was then served a thick green beverage in a white china cup. It tasted like cough syrup and made me groggy. I lay down once again on the divan and closed my eyes. Immediately memories of my past flooded in. They were vivid but fragmented, like the pieces of a moving three-dimensional jigsaw puzzle. Slowly the fragments started to coalesce.

"What the hell did you put in my drink?" I asked one of the angels as my speech began to slur.

"My lord, it's restoring your memory," Veena said. "You may feel a little tipsy during this phase of your restoration. Take a nap if you like."

Then it all came crashing down onto me. So intense was the complete and sudden recall that I bolted upright, my palms on my temple and my eyes blinking uncontrollably. A gentle fragrant musk exuded from my forehead.

It all had happened only a moment ago; the ruined bathroom in the hospital; the book bound in black leather; the red Nike headband; Pir's instructions for my journey. I was supposed to meet with him in Paradise, to hand over the book. Where is the book? I panicked until I remembered the monkey. What if he had chewed it up, ripped it apart? How was I going to face Pir after all that had transpired? Laila! Whatever happened to her? She had my headband! Abba! He must be returning home from Islamabad today.

Had I died for real? Suddenly, the last seven years spent in that celestial dump—the place never visited by night; the retirement outpost of Fuqraeel whose dream of attaining manhood with the help of the smuggled nectar was shattered by my arrival—felt like a fleeting moment in that one vast span of my now eternal life.

My brooding came to an end with the arrival of my escort, a middle-aged dark-skinned angel with a graying beard and stiff smile who wore a green turban and a plain yellow robe. His wings were dull gray color and his name was Braqeel. The women bade me farewell. Braqeel took my hand.

"First stop, Hoz e Kausar," he said, his powerful wings bristling with a nervous energy.

Chapter 20

Paradise

"**H**OZ E KAUSAR! I've been longing to drink that sweet tasting water ever since—"

Before I could finish my sentence, I disintegrated into a cloud of light. The next moment I materialized beside a heart-shaped pond filled with sparkling water. Not much bigger than a twelve-person hot tub, the pond was set in a grassy mound a couple of feet off the ground. It was bordered by a dazzling array of exquisite tiles depicting intricate Arabian geometric patterns in blue, white, and gold. Water flowed from a golden faucet in the shape of a spray of gathered palm fronds and collected in a round bowl of white marble. Several rough clay cups lay scattered on the overgrown grass beside the marble bowl. The pond was cordoned off by Day-Glo orange hazard tape stuck to wooden posts with flashing lights.

"Alas! Hoz e Kausar is no more," Braqeel said in his morose voice. "It's been off limits for quite some time."

"What happened?" I asked, stunned by the revelation.

"It's the water." Braqeel said sadly, shaking his head side to side. "Not fit to drink anymore."

"But it looks so clear?"

"Clear but not clean—it's contaminated."

"With what?"

He refused to divulge anything more other than that it had been under investigation for quite some time. He successfully derailed the discussion by diverting my attention to the famous virgins who awaited me.

"Don't think that seventy-two is all you're going to get," he said, as if trying to allay my greatest and most natural fear. "If you desire more, all you've got to do is tell your ladies to introduce you to their slave girls." He flashed a mischievous smile. "They may not be as beautiful, but you'd be surprised by what they can do to heighten a man's enjoyment of the heavenly sphere."

"How many slave girls are we talking about?" I asked, scratching my head.

"Each of your seventy two virgins has been granted seventy two slave girls," he said, his wings quivering with excitement.

"That's an awful lot of women!" I said, feeling a bit overwhelmed.

"Never say that again!" he hissed, arching his thick brows and piercing me with his black eyes. "Never heard that complaint before. You've a problem with women?"

"No, that's not what I meant," I added quickly so as not to offend him.

I wanted to tell him about my insanely vibrant sex life serving a horde of wild women in the Dump. Been there, done that. I wanted to tell him that I wasn't your ordinary pious Joe from earth who'd start drooling at the promise of unlimited sex with countless women because he hadn't gotten much in his earthly existence.

Thinking carefully, I decided not to say anything. It would be more interesting to check the place out, like a tourist, without having to go native or anything. For me, the place had always been a mere metaphor, a work of the human imagination. I just stared at the sad limpid pond before me that was in dire need of the immediate attentions of a Hazmat team. The thought crossed my mind that if I ever made it back to New York, I'd ditch my thesis in favor of something more fruitful. Though what, I didn't know. The sight of ugly orange hazard tape dripping from this glorious pond that was supposed to be filled with the sweetest tasting water in the whole universe, made me feel inexplicably sad and defeated.

Our next stop was a vast green parkland at the center of which stood a palace of gleaming white marble. The magnificent edifice was topped with a number of steeples and towers of various sizes and was so monumental in scale that it would probably take a lifetime on the back of a swift horse to circle its perimeter.

The delicate crowns of the lofty turrets disappeared into another radiant purple sky with gigantic orbs emitting soft soothing vibrations circled around each of the towers. Overhead, angels drifted in formation like migrating swans carrying packages and bundles. The air smelled of jasmine and my skin tingled.

"My job was to bring you to the Guest House of Al-Jannah," Braqeel said, pointing toward the colossal mansion. "I'm not allowed to go any farther."

"Guest House?"

"It's for people traveling back and forth between Al-Jannah and other worlds," he said. "You're on your own from here on."

"What am I supposed to do now?" I asked, feeling alarmed at the prospect of being left to my own devices in such an incredibly vast space where just to get to the entrance of the Guest House might take me years, if not decades.

"To move from one point to another all you have to do is will it," Braqeel said, as if reading my mind. "See that entrance?" He pointed towards the center of the building where a gate like a glittering reflective mirror stood open and waiting.

"You are expected in the welcome tent just to the right side of the main gate. Now it's time for me to get back and pick up my next passenger." He opened his wings and flapped them a few times like a runner warming up for a sprint. He then rose into the air and became a brilliant white streak across the sky.

Keeping my eyes to the right of the gate where the tent was supposed to be, I willed myself to be there. Nothing happened with the first two attempts, but the third time I disintegrated into a flash of light.

When I opened my eyes, I was standing in the doorway of the marble estate.

Hundreds of women draped in diaphanous multicolored silks stood around on the lush grounds like exquisite statues. About two hundred feet ahead, against the horizon, I saw a large red awning supported by poles: the welcome tent. Lounging under this canopy on divans were a number of people wearing colorful robes.

So this was the Guest House of Al-Jannah, the Muslim Paradise. I wondered how many other kinds of Paradises were there, and if this one was exclusively for Muslims.

A coterie of dark-skinned beardless youths clad in red loincloths milled around outside the red canopy as if waiting for orders. Dazzled, I wandered through the dreamy gardens toward the red canopy, lulled into a peaceful reverie. The air was heavy with the smell of night-blooming jasmine. On my right a delicate pink marble fountain gushed a stream of milk, and on my left a stone-lined trough filled with fragrant honey meandered through flowerbeds of white lilies and red tulips. A multitude of trees dotted the lawns as far as I could see. Their branches drooped under the weight of ripe fruit, their blossoms dripping nectar. Even the grassy areas were manicured to perfection.

I was about a hundred feet from the awning, pleasurably immersed in the otherworldly serenity of my surroundings, when a swell of agitated voices rose in the air. The severed head of a bearded man landed about twenty feet from me. It rolled across the ground like a bowling ball and stopped beneath a wall of stones supporting the stream of flowing honey. I froze where I stood.

A moment later, a human leg sailed through the air and landed just a couple of feet from where I was standing. I dropped to my knees retching, and then I heard a woman's voice shouting my name. Getting to my feet I saw a woman wrapped in a flowing black burqa racing towards me. She halted just a few inches from me and lifted her veil. I gasped when I saw her face.

"Laila!" I whispered. She looked ravishingly young and beautiful.

"Ismaeel! Where have you been?" she said, throwing herself in my arms, sobbing and burying her face in my chest.

I stroked her hair and surveyed the area which was teeming with women laughing and talking in small groups. They seemed unfazed by the flying dismembered appendages, as if it was all just business as usual around here. Laila pulled out of my arms and repositioned her veil over her face.

"You'd better stop looking around. They won't dare lay a finger on you here, not as long as I, your lawful wife, am with you."

"Looking around?" I yelled, as if she was an idiot. "Didn't you see what just landed here? Look at that!" I barked, baffled by her indifference and pointing to the carnage at my feet. Also, I wasn't too happy to see her clad in a burqa in Paradise of all the places.

"It's a big problem here in Jannah," she said.

I wasn't sure what to make of the information. To be honest, her burqa bothered me more than any problem Al-Jannah may be having at the moment. Last time I had seen her she was practically naked.

"Why in the hell are you wearing that burqa?"

"Married women must wear full hijab here in Jannah, Ismaeel," she said quite seriously. As I started to speak, I caught sight of Chaacha Khidr over her shoulder. He was sprinting toward us with a burlap sack in his hand.

"I'm just so happy to see you, Ismaeel," Laila said. "I know it'll be a little confusing for you at first, but soon you'll—"

"I'm happy to see you too, but I'm not so sure about that burqa. How did you get here?"

"Your headband. It worked. Pir Pullsiraat tracked me down, but we couldn't find you. Xenobia and her bitches had that den of theirs camouflaged by methods known only to them."

Upon hearing the name of Pir, I was filled with a mixture of excitement and terror. I had a lot of explaining to do, for having arrived in Paradise without the book and headband.

"Where is my headband?" I asked.

"Pir had it."

I remained quiet. The meeting with Pir wasn't going to go well, that much I knew.

"How did you do in my absence?" She narrowed her big black eyes in an interrogative stare.

The last thing I wanted to be reminded of were my days as a sex slave of Xenobia.

"I survived by dying." I avoided her gaze and looked over her shoulder at Chaacha. "Look what Chaacha is doing." Laila turned around, and we both watched as he gathered up the human remains and put them in his sack. Once all the pieces were stowed and the sack was tied up, he walked over to a stream of fresh water and washed his hands. His appearance hadn't changed a bit. Nor had his job!

"Now you see the scope of the problem, Babu?" Chaacha said aloud, looking at me with the sparkling eyes I remembered.

"Wait a minute Chaacha." I walked over to him. "Are you telling me that all those knuckle-heads blowing themselves up on earth are actually landing here in Paradise in bits and pieces?" I was acutely aware of the fact that Abba's Mujahid Vest probably had been used in about two third of such cases.

"Not all, but those whose desire for Jannah has become greed. Desire, if not coupled with need, becomes destructive," he said, standing up and hoisting the sack over his shoulder. "The world is not some place which is located over *there*, far away from *here*. Jannah exists within the world, but behind an invisible curtain." He turned and began walking toward the awning then stopped and turned around.

"Now you've seen with your own eyes the kind of mess we must deal with over here. You're going to help us clean it up," he continued, patting his sack. "Follow me. Pir is waiting for you." He started walking away.

I recalled his words when I met with him for the first time in my Ayahuasca journey back in New York: *Babu, you're going to help us clean up a big mess.* I remembered him emptying his sack on the floor of the

Pir's quarter in Shah Jamal. *Delicate and subtle! I am fed up with being delicate and subtle. It's time for action. A military action.*

What felt so gratifying was the fact that despite all my spectacular failures on the Path to High Knowledge, I was still in play and still relevant to the mission, whose details had just begun to emerge out of the thick fog of my adventures.

Next I remembered the words of Pir: *Khalifa has something very special planned, a real spectacle. If he's not stopped very soon, this world and the Next will need a major cleanup that will stretch into the not-so-foreseeable future. Without that book, he won't be able to bring his plans to completion. Your job, Ismaeel, is to help us stop the man in his tracks.*

I began to sense the scope of my mission. It was a big deal for sure, though how big, I had no clue. What was I going to tell Pir about the book? Considering the number of waffled pages in that thing, it surely looked to be packed with enough power to help transport a whole village to Paradise. Had I not bumped into Laila the other night, I'd have landed straight here in Jannah after having ingested just one tiny stamp off its page. And then there was this *backup copy* that was still on the loose somewhere in that hellhole of a place that was scarier than the real Hell. Was Khalifa planning a mass exodus to Jannah? If that was the case, how could I, single-handedly, stop that from happening?

As Laila and I strolled behind Chaacha, I wondered if his human carrion could be put back together again in the form of a living, breathing human. But there were more important things to think about. I took a deep breath and braced myself for Pir.

As we neared the red awning, the dark-skinned boys arranged themselves in a single line, their hands clasped over their navels and their heads bowed. We strolled past them and stepped into the shade of the canopy. Inside I saw Tarzan and Pir Pullsiraat sitting on a richly draped divan that looked like the throne of some legendary emperor. Like Ottoman sultans they lounged among cushions of red velvet, their backs resting against bolsters of rich golden brocade.

A couple of legless marble slabs floated in the air around the lounge. These were laden with baskets filled with fruits of all kind: pineapples, apples, guavas, mangoes, bananas, and pears; cut watermelon, red and white grapes, cherries and multicolored berries. There were platters of dates, figs, and olives, cheeses of countless varieties; jars of jams, honey, juices and wines; breads of all shapes and sizes. It looked like the gourmet section of some celestial high-end grocery store.

Tarzan had grown. He was taller and more filled out. Dressed in a purple robe with intricate gold embroidery around the collar and cuffs, he looked like the prince in a fairytale; one where everybody lived happily ever after. Only a couple of days ago, he was a handsome teenager with a bright smile, selling bhang pappurs out of his carry-on stall in Fortress Stadium, as he repeatedly pulled the loop of his fake martyr vest. I also remembered his expertise with explosives and his ability to control as stubborn a mind as Wali's.

Tarzan's face broke into a broad smile when our eyes met. For some odd reason I felt sad deep down looking at him.

Draped in his voluminous shimmering green robe, Pir smoked a cigarette and looked us over. But unlike Tarzan, he wasn't smiling. He wore a black headband without any insignia and looked quite worried.

"Welcome to Paradise, sir," Tarzan said, standing up and throwing his arms in the air. His face was radiant with joy.

As I hugged Tarzan, my eyes caught sight of a metal cage sitting on the grass beyond the far end of the awning. It was surrounded by a dozen or so heavenly beauties who giggled and stared at whatever was inside the cage.

"Thank you Tarzan. I'm so very glad to see you." Cautiously, I moved over to Pir, who didn't get up to greet me. After shaking my hand he gestured for me to sit on one of the divans across from him. Laila slid beside me while Chaacha bounded over the lawn toward the cage.

"Ismaeel, do you know why you are here?" Pir said in a low angry voice as he nailed me with a look that was more than furious.

"I am here because of you."

"Correct!"

"Do you've any idea what it took to get you here?"

I remained silent.

"I was forced to lie to get you out of the hands of Munkar and Nakir." I was pretty sure I knew what he meant. I recalled my grave, my water-boarding session at the hands of Munkar and Nakir, the ceaseless buzzing of my penis, and the squealing mass of rats about to devour me. And then how things changed. I remembered the teary eyed Munkar's words: *We've been told that you've passed all the necessary steps to gain entry into Paradise.*

"I'm sorry." I was damn well aware he knew what I was thinking.

"You've screwed up seriously. Not once but twice."

"I am the one who screwed up," Laila spoke, her voice cold and flat. "Ismaeel can't be blamed for something he had no control over."

"Lady, I am not addressing you. Please be quiet. This is between him and me," Pir said, picking a tattered book from the divan beside him and holding it toward me. The book's black leather binding had been chewed up pretty badly.

"Thanks to your brilliant work, Jannah is now populated with monkeys."

"But—" I opened my mouth to speak.

"There's no *but!*" Pir roared, skewering me with his glance. Then he looked at Laila and his expression began to soften.

"Not that I have anything against this lovely lady, but Ismaeel," he continued, pausing for a moment as if considering what to say. "You were supposed to come here alone, by yourself, not with a companion. Your only task was to deliver this book to me safely and in one piece." He flicked the ash off his cigarette into a white porcelain ashtray.

"I want to know exactly what happened," he demanded. "Don't leave out even the smallest detail,"

I glanced at Laila. Her face was composed but her eyes looked terrified.

"Go on, tell them the truth. It's okay. He can't do anything, for we're a married couple now," she whispered to me. "Just don't mention Hoor Afza."

Recalling the events of the night in that ruined bathroom was like viewing the past through a stereoscope, for they seemed to have transpired simultaneously both a lifetime ago and also just last night. I told him how I'd run into Laila—whom I'd known from my earlier visit to the hospital—outside the emergency room, and how I was about to get myself a flashlight from the drug store across the street, when the red lights appeared on Jail Road. I was left with no choice but to run inside in the dark, hoping to find the book before it ended up in the wrong hands, and how Laila helped me with her lighter. Without light I would never have found my way in the dark.

I paused and scratched my head, trying to conjure some plausible scenario that would explain Laila's presence in the Dump. But everything just sounded lame. I knew Pir wasn't buying any of my explanation.

"And then you started moving furniture," Pir said. "Right?"

Lowering my gaze I bit my lips. Thankfully, Laila came to my rescue, breaking the painful silence which was punctuated only by Pir's searing gaze. "Please. I'll tell you exactly what happened." Laila stood up and faced the divan where my two benefactors sat.

"Leaving Ismaeel in the bathroom, I was called to the emergency room to register a head injury case which had just arrived. When I got there they told me the patient had died. I don't know where it came from, but a strong feeling occurred to me that Ismaeel's life was in danger so I ran back to the bathroom. And I was right," she said, nodding with satisfaction.

"I found him lying on the floor. He wasn't breathing so I'd no choice but to start giving him mouth-to-mouth resuscitation for he was dying right before my eyes! What else could I do? The next thing I knew, we were lying completely naked beside a waterfall in some wilderness."

Laila's answer startled me. She seemed to be telling the truth. And if she was, it was more than likely that we both had died in that accursed bathroom. But if she was lying, wow, she was really good at it.

"Interesting," Pir muttered, glancing at Tarzan, not certain if he believed her. "What do you have to say about all this, lieutenant?"

"I think they crash-landed in the Dump because the power of a single ticket meant for only one person, which sir Ismaeel put under his tongue, got split between two people during mouth-to-mouth resuscitation. One ticket wasn't strong enough to propel two bodies all the way to Paradise," Tarzan proclaimed.

"Excellent point," Pir replied. Then he glanced at Chaacha Khidr who was involved in an animated conversation with a knot of houris beside the cage. "But that's only a partial reason," he added, looking at me and shaking his head. He looked disappointed.

"You create the kind of world you've been intending, secretly or otherwise. Sometimes an intention lurks in one's mind like a snake in a thicket," Pir said without taking his eyes off me.

I knew what he was trying to say. I wanted to tell him that it wasn't my fault that I harbored the kind of intention he was referring to; of having an unlimited supply of virgins in the afterlife. First, I wasn't conscious of it. Second, it was Abba who had embedded his indelible footprints on my mind ever since I was a child.

"Perhaps the intention you're talking about is part of my genetic makeup, my upbringing, or my fate, about which I can't do anything," I offered, in a bid to absolve myself of the guilt he was trying to impose on me.

Pir seemed ready to reply but he looked at Laila, and then settled back on his cushion. I figured he didn't want to say anything classified in front of her.

Why was sex so jealously regulated on earth and so utterly unregulated in Jannah. The memory of my seven lust-free orgasms in the Intiqaal Lounge was still fresh in my mind. Clearly, having sex was not the issue. It was all about where preferably one should be having it. I knew Pir was reading my thoughts and would enlighten me at some later point. And where were the male equivalents of *hooris?*

"Those monkeys in that cage have probably taken a few squares each from the book. That's how they ended up here," Pir explained, his anger was gone. "Tarzan, any idea what we should do with them?" Pir narrowed his eyes as his face broke into a mischievous smile.

I breathed a sigh of relief at the change in direction the conversation was taking. If Pir grilled me on how the damn book got into the hands of the monkeys, I'd have to concoct another elaborate lie, one thing I clearly wasn't very good at and, of course, I feared Pir was reading my mind. Pir stood up and walked over to me.

"Ismaeel, now we've got the book, and you, out of the hands of Munkar and Nakir. We wasted time. We must get back to work immediately."

"Yes, sir," I was relieved to be safe with Pir and back on track.

"And don't forget, you still haven't been reunited with your father yet," Pir said, attempting to orient my short-circuited existential GPS.

"Yes, sir."

An angel in a white robe appeared overhead, circled once, then landed beside Pir. He was a good six feet tall, fair, young, with trimmed red beard, and very handsome. The red tips of his otherwise white wings matched the color of his cowboy boots.

"Apollo!" Pir said, turning toward the angel. "What are you doing here in Jannah on a fine day like this?"

The angel whispered something to Pir then took a couple of steps away to stand erect like a guard with his hands clasped behind his back while he stared unblinking past us.

"Ismaeel, someone from the Greek quarters would like to meet with you," Pir said.

"Greek quarters!?" I said, feeling Laila's fingernails biting into my arm.

"That's where the pagans live," she whispered in my ear.

"Pagans? In Paradise?" I asked.

"There're all kinds of paradises in Paradise," Pir said. "There's a Christian Paradise, that's where most angels receive their education.

There's one for the Jews, then an Islamic Paradise you already know about. There's one for the Hindus, one for the Buddhists another for the Zoroastrians and so on. And there's one called the Greek Quarter."

"Who wants to see you in the Pagan Quarter?" Laila asked.

"I have no idea." I squeezed her hand and stood up. I was excited, but at the same time also a little anxious at this new development. If I made any wrong moves, chances were better than even I'd spend another lifetime wandering the crazy halls of high weirdness. God help me, I muttered to myself. God help me.

"Your ride is here," Pir said as he pointed at the angel and grinned through closed lips. Finally, he'd cracked a smile.

"I want you back here soon. You've got work to do," he added.

"I'll be back—soon," I said, and wondering about the meaning of soon. For my current location was clearly outside Time.

Apollo did look like an honest and hardworking being—as opposed to Fukraeel, who radiated contempt for all things human and oozed with a fondness for anything shady and unwholesome. As soon as Apollo took my hand we became streaks of light across the horizon.

Chapter 21
Sophie

WE REAPPEARED BESIDE A thundering waterfall, surrounded by a growth of old pine that covered a steep mountain slope. Before I could orient myself, Apollo rose into the air and waved goodbye. He thrust his arms forward then exploded in a shower of light.

The place looked strangely familiar. Like déjà vu times twenty familiar. My heart began to race in anticipation. There beside the waterfall I spotted her; my Sophie. She stood in the exact same spot where I'd kissed her *that* first time on earth. It was the same rainbow that had formed behind her on the curtain of mist over her shoulder.

The water crashed against the same boulders and roared down toward the exact same valley. The mauve flowers that covered the green slopes were the very same, as was the deafening sound of splashing water and the electrified air filled with passion. But the rest-house where I'd stayed with Abba more than a lifetime ago was not there.

Sophie seemed to have matured by half a decade; she was curvaceous and more ravishing than ever. However, she wore the same black skirt, the same golden hair and beautiful body. In her hands was the same bouquet of violets she'd held *that* day so long ago.

This stunning replay of time had completely blown me away. I pinched my arm to make sure I wasn't dreaming. Sophie broke into a radiant smile as she walked toward me, slowly, with teasing steps. For several moments I forgot to breathe.

Transfixed by her beauty I was entrapped within a timeless web of love. And then in a flash I saw within me, lurking like an anaconda in the misty thicket of a dark forest, the truth that had been guarded jealously by my subconscious ever since she'd become my father's bride.

I knew beyond the shadow of doubt that she had died. I remembered my willed vision of her, after having drunk two bottles of Hoor Afza in the backseat of the car. I'd seen her strolling through the violet hue of a green meadow, unaware of her stalker, the dark-skinned, bearded man who'd taken her into the underworld.

She stood just inches away, her breath warm over my neck, her eyes twinkling like the brightest star in the northern sky. In a daze, I kissed her. She tasted the same, like fresh apricots.

I wrapped my arms around her and drew her into me. For a brief second Abba's face floated in my mind. The realization that Abba's face and that of the dark skinned bearded man carrying Sophie off were one and the same tortured me and made me enraged. But the dark face dissipated like a foul mist as soon as I willed it away, and I kissed her deeply and without guilt. *If I could just take her back with me to earth the world would be such a great place to live.*

I thought of Laila, my temporary wife. She was certainly beautiful, caring, and in all, I liked her a lot. She was great in the sack, but I could never connect instantly with her on the deepest level as I had done with Sophie.

We exchanged not a single word, allowing our tongues and fingers to communicate all that was necessary in the language of passion. In the next minute we were rolling on the ground, our clothes discarded in the tall grasses that hid our bodies from all eyes but our own.

Later, exhausted and at peace, we lay naked on a bed of green moss. Still entangled in each other's arms, not a word had been spoken between us. The experience of making love to her had been a completely earthly one. In sharp contrast to the mechanical, utilitarian coupling of the women in the Dump that I had performed, fueled by the illicit nectar from Al-Jannah, the Muslim Quarter of Paradise. I shuddered when I thought of the red rock compound of Xenobia and her cohorts as they lined up on a conveyor belt of perpetual sex, to ravage me with their insatiable appetites.

Sophie rolled over and put her head on my shoulder.

"This has to be a dream," I said. "I love these pagan quarters of yours."

"It is rather unbelievable that you're here," she agreed, nuzzling my neck with her face.

"How come we're in Kafiristan?" I said, combing her hair with my fingers.

"I willed it that way," she admitted, playing my earlobe with her lips.

"Willed it that way?" I asked, wondering at the implication of what she just said.

"Yes—the same way people will things on earth and they happen, except there they happen over a period of time. Here, they happen instantly."

"Mind creating matter!" I said.

"Without the help of time," she explained. "It needs a little practice to create things exactly the way you want them."

"Like creating Kafiristan in Paradise,"

"Yes, you can say that," she said, smiling mischievously.

"But seriously, you guys are supposed to be in Hell—the kafirs I mean."

She raised herself up on one elbow, and looked into my eyes.

"Who says?"

"The books!"

She laughed softly.

"Well, now you know that's just not true," she said. "Paradise is for all who do good things in life, regardless of their faith."

"That's what I've always thought!" I hoped that someday I'd be able to convince Abba of that.

"How did you discover I was in Paradise?" I asked.

"I've got my connections," she said.

"Really?"

"Really," she whispered, and kissed my cheek.

"You died then? After you left Abba?"

She nodded without a hint of sadness in her eyes.

"What happened?"

"I don't want to talk about it. Why don't you tell me how you died?"

"I'm not exactly sure what my status is at the moment, but I do know I'm being sent back into the world."

"I always felt you were special, Ismaeel." Her eyes sparkled like the water of a clear mountain lake. "I'll wait for you," she continued. "When you return, we'll build a little hut down there in the meadow."

"But only if I can make it back here. I'm not too thrilled about living in the Muslim Quarter for all eternity."

"Oh yes! I heard there's an epidemic going on over there," she said.

"What epidemic?"

"It's just a rumor. They say it's polio. I've heard all kinds of weird things are happening there."

"Oh!" I said, remembering Hoz e Kausar had been shut down due to some undisclosed contamination. Was the source of contamination an infected body-part that might have landed in the sacred pond?

She climbed on top of me and kissed my forehead, her braids brushing against my face.

"Why doesn't everybody just live in one big Paradise?" I said putting my hands on her thighs. "Like one nation under God, one big happy family?"

"People have different tastes. You create your Paradise according to your nature, or your own vision of things," she said, bringing her face to mine and staring into my eyes. "As a man you should be very happy. In your quarters there are a million naked women who want nothing but sex."

"Oh please! Don't talk about them." I cringed at the thought of the meaningless sex I'd had with the equally meaningless women of the Dump.

"Why? What happened?"

"I just want you," I said. "I love the natural look of a woman's body and I can't stand burqas."

"Where did the burqa thought come from?" She rubbed her breasts against my chest.

"Accident."

"Must be a serious one." Her tone was playful and light.

"It is—kind of," I said, feeling a sudden irresistible tenderness for Laila.

"I wish you a quick recovery."

"Thank you but I can handle it," I said, feeling rising apprehension and guilt.

I could easily, or legally, say goodbye to Laila whenever I wanted, since ours was a temporary contract to fulfill a specific purpose. That purpose had been served and it was time to move on.

"Promise me something," she said, putting her chin on mine. "That you'll stay with me when you return."

"I promise."

After we had dressed, Apollo appeared and landed beside us on the soft grass.

When Apollo dropped me back at Pir's lounge, everyone was sitting quietly and the place was enveloped in a heavy and serious atmosphere. Tarzan looked at me quizzically and Pir's face was an unreadable mask as I took my seat on the divan next to Laila. Her eyes brimmed with a nervous curiosity.

"Who did you see, Ismaeel?" she whispered in my ear. "And why are your clothes such a mess?" She was looking at the green smudges on my blue silk robe.

Before I embarrassed myself by trying to concoct some transparent lie, Pir, who'd been watching closely, stood up and motioned for me to join him.

"I need to have a word with you."

I looked at Tarzan for a clue but he just shrugged and raised his brows.

Laila shrank away from me as I stood and followed Pir to the edge of the canopy.

"This isn't the time for you to sort out your love life," he said in a flat tone that would tolerate no opposition or buts.

"Yes, Pir." I had no doubt that he read me like a book.

"Good," he said. I was almost certain that he was appreciating not what I'd said, but what I'd just realized.

He smiled and put his hand on my shoulder as if I was an old friend, or a son who'd just been gently, but sternly, corrected in his ways.

"Your quest to know if Paradise and Hell existed may be over, but our mission is not. While you were gone, another book has been shipped to the Khalifa, just as we'd predicted. This backup copy is identical in its potency and power to the original book, the book you were sent to retrieve."

"That doesn't sound good," I said, avoiding his intense gaze. An understatement to be sure.

"We have to prevent Khalifa from exploiting the power of the book," he continued, his hand still resting on my shoulder.

"Pir, if you don't mind," I broke in, sensing he was in an unusually receptive and friendly mood. "If I were you I'd go after the person who's making all these books," I said.

"You can't go after the master chemist," he stated, shaking his head from side to side. "You can only try thwarting his tricks, like playing a game of chess with the grandmaster. Don't worry. There are no more books to come after this."

"The master chemist—who is he?"

"Instead of knowing who the master chemist is, you'll serve yourself better by knowing that if you play your cards right, the world may be saved from a catastrophe," Pir said, as he moved toward the cage.

His face was creased with worry, and something else I couldn't quite place. Was it fear?

"What catastrophe?" I asked, walking by his side.

"You can't be told more than what you already know, and that's more than enough for now. We've spoken about this before. The Khalifa's security forces include the mind-reading cats whose expertise is in particularly painful and thorough methods of wet data retrieval, if you get my drift," he said sternly.

"If you knew the whole breadth of your mission before the time of executing it, you'd be a huge security risk for us. A risk that's just not worth taking merely to satisfy your curiosity. The information would be hacked out of your brain as if from a computer hard drive. Then you wouldn't be able to be present where you need to be in order to pull the plug." He refused to elaborate further.

"Pull the plug?"

He ignored me.

"You'd be arrested the minute they got wind of any such information floating around in your brain." He pulled a black headband from his pocket and handed it to me.

"Here's your new tele-band. The red one you gave to Laila is no longer effective. And by the way, where is the Quran I gave you?"

"In the pocket of the robe I was wearing back on planet earth, or wherever *that* was before I came to wherever *this* is," I said, realizing I was about to leave Paradise, probably for good. I took the headband and stretched it over my head.

"I'd like to stay here a bit longer," I said. "If that's possible, of course."

"Good to know you've been following my instructions," Pir said, ignoring my request completely. "Tarzan will take you back now."

"What about Laila?" I asked, sensing that something ominous must have happened to her back in that bathroom in the hospital.

"You can ask her yourself," Pir said as we headed back to the lounging area.

Tarzan and Laila sat deep in conversation and I heard Tarzan saying, "I know, I miss Lahore too, a lot."

Pir dropped down onto the divan beside Tarzan and I beside Laila. She touched my arm, her eyes glistening with tears. The air was heavy with the scent of fresh-ground cinnamon.

"I'll be right here waiting for you, Ismaeel," she said. "I know you'll come back for me one day so can be together forever."

Her words stung deeply and filled me with sadness. She'd been good to me; possessive definitely, but she was one hot woman under that awful black burqa. I felt sad that I'd cheated on her with the love of my life; but hey, this was Al-Jannah, the Islamic Paradise with its liberal sexual mores, the last place in the universe where one was expected to behave like a saint. And no matter how much I wanted to change, I still wasn't one to pass up a good time.

Tarzan came over.

"Time to go, sir."

Then Chaacha shouted from afar.

"Stop, don't leave yet." Dropping his bulging burlap sack on the ground by the cage, he ran to us.

"Be safe, Babu Ismaeel," he said giving my shoulder a friendly shake.

"Wait!" I barked. "Not so fast! I've got questions—a whole lot of them."

Without any warning, Tarzan grabbed my hand. The air was filled with the crackling sound of static electricity and then we were swallowed by empty space.

We landed just outside the entrance of a familiar green tent; the Bihishti Tea Corner, by the same picnic table where I'd drunk tea with Chaacha Khidr in what seemed like a lifetime ago. I still wore the clothes given to me in the Intiqaal Lounge.

It was as if Ibrahim was anticipating our arrival. He emerged from the tent all smiles the moment we touched down. He carried a tray with two steaming cups of tea and a plate of biscuits whose taste had remained as crisp in my memory as if I'd had them only yesterday.

A red bicycle was parked a few feet from the table, leaning on its kickstand. The towering walls of Paradise flanked the sky far on the horizon. Behind those walls lurked the unfinished business between Sophie and Laila that would have to be sorted out one day; between the black burqa and red shawl; between the heavily regulated world where beauty was kept hidden, and the world in harmony with natural laws and expressive beauty. Laila was my companion in a time of need which had served its purpose, and Sophie was my inspiration, an anchor to the bottom of my being. I realized now that I had loved Sophie all my life.

"Welcome back, Babu," Ibrahim said, as he set the tray on the table.

"I missed your tea, Ibrahim," I said, sitting across from Tarzan warming my hands on the cup and breathing in the fragrant steam.

"Once you are done with your tea, you may go in the tent and change." Ibrahim looked at us with a warm smile.

"Tarzan, please tell Chaacha that I could use a helper-boy," Ibrahim said.

"I'll certainly let Chaacha know."

As soon as Ibrahim left, I bombarded Tarzan with questions.

"Tarzan, did you survive the blast at the compound?" I asked pointedly. I'd been dying to ask that particular question.

He shook his head from side to side and then up and down, all the while with a broad toothy grin on his face.

"I wish I'd get a straight answer on occasion," I said, feeling frustrated and fighting rising irritation.

"Sir, there's no such thing as death—you move on to the next world when you die in the one you're born in," he said, sipping his tea.

"Tell me what Khalifa is up to, and who is this master chemist providing him with all these books?"

"Sir, one day you may get the answers to all your questions. But remember, the success of this mission doesn't hinge on you knowing very much about it."

"But I know nothing."

"Less is more. You've the headband, and you've got the Quran. That's pretty much all you need. Remember, the headband is for telepathic use. Whenever you can't talk, just think, but think clearly, and you'll be able to get the critical communication you'll need." Tarzan pushed the plate of biscuits towards me. "Have some."

"Who is Pir Pullsiraat, really? And Chaacha Khidr? Where do they come from?" I asked, taking a bite off the biscuit.

"Smuggled goods," Tarzan said, holding the cookie in front of his face and examining it.

"Tarzan, please, I'm asking you an important question."

"I will explain what I can. Chaacha—he's been around a long time, and he has seen it all. As for Pir, well, there are different theories about him."

"What kind of theories?"

"Chaacha told me—not that I necessarily believe everything he says—that Pir is the IGP."

"IGP?"

"Inspector General of Paradise."

"And what's another theory?"

"That he's a former prophet who left the comfort and luxury of the highest level of Paradise to take matters into his own hands," Tarzan said. "Some say, he's the Messiah everyone down there has been waiting for, and who is cleaning the place up before he declares himself in the Middle East."

"Interesting! Which theory do you believe in?" I probed, sipping my tea and wondering which Messiah he could possibly be— the Jewish Messiah or the Islamic one.

"Neither," Tarzan replied with a toothy grin on his face.

"So you don't know?"

"Sir, I'm more interested in eating mangoes than counting them," he said. "I've got a good life here, though I'm not too excited about it, but still—I don't ask questions whose answers I have no use for."

As we finished our tea, the sky grew dark. A shrill noise rose in the air, intensifying as it drowned our conversation. A gigantic dark cloud of ababeels appeared overhead that took several minutes to pass out of sight.

My gaze followed the tail of the vanishing cloud.

"It's best if the mission is accomplished without having to turn everything into husk," he said, leaving me more confused than ever. "Time to change clothes, sir. My cycle is ready. It should be a short ride."

"How come we can't beam ourselves to earth, like we've been doing here in Paradise?"

"Because we can't. Because Hell lies in-between, and only Chaacha and Pir know how to move about between the spheres directly."

"Oh, I see," I said, nodding. But of course, I really didn't.

After having changed into a single length of unstitched white cloth, large enough to be worn as a toga, we hopped on the bike. Waving goodbye to Ibrahim, Tarzan put the tires on the cable. A stench of sulfur hit my nose and Tarzan began peddling.

"Ibrahim, I'm going to talk to Chaacha about the tea-boy for you," he looked back and shouted.

Although the novelty of seeing Pullsiraat over a river of magma wasn't as strong, the ride was as horrific and terrifying as before. Thankfully the ride was short, and we crossed over quickly without incident. We rode over a flat surface in complete darkness and then Tarzan braked.

We got off the bike and walked for a minute or two in the faint glow of his eyes until we were standing by the door of the hospital's bathroom. Compared to where I had been, this world seemed completely real. I touched my forehead to see if Pir's headband was still there. Happily, it was. Tarzan passed like a ghost through the solid door into the bathroom. I followed, gliding through the wall and feeling only a slight resistance against my body.

Once inside the bathroom, I saw the hazy outlines of two bodies lying on the ground. One of them was mine; clothed in my unmistakable patched robe. The other, draped in a burqa and lying beside me, was Laila's. The sight made me sick to my stomach. I shook uncontrollably and felt I was going to pass out.

"Now what?" I asked, my voice shaking and my teeth chattering loud enough to be heard.

"Sir, be calm. All you have to do is lie down on top of your material body and you'll sink into it. It's better if you keep your eyes closed." The strange glow of Tarzan's eyes was enough to dispel the darkness around us, but it had an unsettling effect on me.

"Sir, good night, and best of luck. Make sure you keep the Quran on your person at all times."

"Tarzan, don't leave yet. One last question, I promise," I said.

"Yes?"

"Who is this master chemist?"

"I've never gotten a straight answer out of anybody on that question myself," Tarzan said. "My guess: Iblees, the Devil. But I've also heard that it's the Almighty Himself, and He likes to play chess. No further questions. Good night!"

He broke into a million particles of brightness before disappearing from view. I was left standing in my toga in pitch darkness and feeling more unsure of things than ever.

Had I not seen Hell and Paradise with my own eyes, I'd have taken his answers to be mere metaphors at best and a big joke at worst.

Still shaking a bit, I sat down on the dirty cold floor beside my body and made myself stop trying to analyze what was happening. I laid my hand on the forehead of my inert form. It was warm, except my hand passed through the skull as if I was made of smoke. Without daring to indulge in any further experimentation, I laid myself on top of my corporeal body as instructed, closed my eyes, and surrendered to whatever was going to happen.

A sound like the whine of a chainsaw filled my head, growing louder by the moment. It felt really weird to be back in my earthy body.

The noise subsided and I opened my eyes.

It took some serious effort to raise myself up from the floor. My body shambled as if it were filled with lead. Laila was still lying beside me. Her skin was warm, but she wasn't breathing and she had no pulse. I looked at my watch. It was 11:35 pm. I'd made the whole of the celestial journey in just under five minutes.

Before I left the scene of the crime, I pulled the burqa away from Laila's face and let my fingertips feel the asymmetry of her cheekbones. She'd been telling me the truth. This was reality. My eyes welled up with tears. The woman had given her life for me. I kissed her lips, then gently put her head on the floor and covered it with her veil.

I got back to my father's house at 1:10 am, feeling like burned celluloid. Had it not been for the potholes which kept bouncing me around the car and rattling my teeth, I would've fallen asleep at the wheel.

Faisal Town was steeped in darkness due to a power outage when I arrived at my father's house. Ghulam Rasool, a gas lamp dangling from his hand, opened the gate and I parked the car near the porch. As I climbed out, the old man eyed me suspiciously.

"Salaam Saab. Are you feeling all right?"

"Please get me some water, I need to go to bed."

Thankfully, he didn't ask more questions but just quietly followed me into the house.

Wali was asleep out in the servant's quarters so I didn't have to deal with his giving me the third degree. I stumbled into the living room and tripped over the curled-up edge of the carpet. Ghulam Rasool raised the lamp above his head and white-hot light splashed across the painting over the fireplace where it loomed larger than life. It writhed with hideous energy and I stared at its hypnotic beauty, marveling at its size, the impeccable brush strokes, and its ominous foreboding mood. It was indeed a masterpiece worthy of any museum on the planet.

Ghulam Rasool led me into my bedroom, lit a candle on the bedside table and pointed to a jug of water and a glass.

"Saab, if you need anything just call out to me," he said. "There's water in the jug and just so you know, the lights may or may not come back on tonight."

"Thank you. Please don't wake me for breakfast. I'll call when I'm up."

As soon he left, I took out the Quran and the headband from my pocket, and tucked them under my pillow. I put on my pajamas, and the second my worn and exhausted body hit the mattress I was out like a light.

Chapter 22
Abba

I AWOKE AT AROUND NOON from the dreamless slumber of the dead. My head felt like it used to after an all-night party. I dragged myself to the bathroom, emptied my bladder, then stole a quick glance at myself in the mirror. I looked like I'd been in a fight; dark circles under both eyes looked bruised and swollen, and my cheeks were sunken and hollow beneath a stubble that was verging on downright pious and fully legal. I was starving.

Ghulam Rasool delivered a tray with a hearty breakfast of French toast, a glass of milk, and tea. I ate in bed as he hovered over me. With hands clasped on his navel the old man watched with obvious approval as I feasted on this manna from heaven. My praise of his cooking skill brought smiles of delight to his care-worn face and I had to plead with him not to bring me another stack of the dessert-like confections.

"Haji sahib is expected sometime this evening, saab," he informed me, sweeping the breadcrumbs off my bed into the tray with a small whisk.

As soon as he was gone I went back to sleep. This time however, my sleep was cluttered with dreams that were chaotic, vivid, and populated with the usual suspects. From time to time Laila entered my dreams wearing various dresses, masks, and makeup. And Sophie was always strolling in a meadow, and always being stalked by some unknown man. I was awakened at dusk by the sound of my father's voice.

"It's just the jet lag. Get him some more tea."

Startled, my eyes shot open and I instantly recognized his six-foot frame outlined dimly in the open doorway. He stepped into the room and his loose white robe flared as if on unseen currents of power he carried about his person. He had gained some weight but not much, and his fist-length beard, once jet-black, had become a wizened gray.

Though obviously older, my father's face was almost devoid of wrinkles, and his eyes possessed the same penetrating glare which had always made my heart sink. Suddenly, it seemed as if I'd never left home. I was that same eighteen-year-old kid again. I jumped out of bed the same way I used to—terrified, when he'd walk into my room un-announced.

He stopped at the foot of my bed, his eyes scanning me from head to toe like a laser beam.

"Salaam, Abba," I muttered, scratching my chest and feeling a churning in my stomach. "It's been such a long time."

"Ismaeel! How did the miracle happen?"

"What miracle, Abba?"

"Wali told me about what happened the other night but he is given to exaggeration. Tell me, did it really happen?"

"I know my Quran, Abba," I said, feeling a prickle on back of my neck.

"You've always been full of surprises—you haven't really changed, Ismaeel." There was a faint smile on his face. I detected just a hint of warmth in his otherwise cold stare.

A rustle behind my back made me turn around. A large brown long-haired cat stood on my bed, sniffing my pillow. My heartbeat quickened and sweat poured from my forehead. Pir had said that the Khalifa was using his specially bred cats to extract the deepest inner thoughts from anyone he was suspicious of. I held my breath and tried to keep my mind as blank as possible.

"Don't be scared," Abba said, looking at the cat affectionately. "Nofel is a good cat."

Nofel growled and shoved my pillow onto the floor, revealing my Quran and headband. Abba stared at these items, his eyes narrowing.

"So, what are you reading these days?" Picking up the Quran and flipping through its pages, Abba parted his lips and I heard a sharp intake of breath.

"What a magnificent copy of the Quran you have in your possession, my son!"

"It's great to see you, Abba," I said, thrusting my hand toward him.

"Where did you get this?" he asked, ignoring my hand, his eyes locked on the book.

"Oh, you know, I got it from an antique store down in the East Village, Manhattan, owned by a Moroccan friend of mine." I stammered. My arm had started to shake.

"Never seen anything quite this beautiful," he whispered seemingly to himself. His eyes glittering with undisguised greed as they darted snake-like over the book's surface.

"It's my constant companion in this transient world of ours, Abba, By the way, I got something really nice for you." I was about to withdraw my hand when he reached out and gave it a squeeze. Damn! I shouldn't have said anything about his gift. Since Wali had no recollection of our visit to Fortress Stadium, it could complicate things.

"I've got everything I need," he said. "I still can't believe that you've really come back—to faith." Thankfully, he didn't seem too interested in his gift.

"I missed being with you, Abba," I said, feeling the cat's furry torso against my legs.

"Ismaeel, please say something believable," he said, staring at the cat.

"Abba, would you please ask Nofel to leave the room?" I was holding my breath.

"So you missed being with me?" He let out a laugh and shooed the cat away.

"I swear by Allah…"

"Do not try to fool me, Ismaeel. You are known to swear falsely."

"Abba, people change—and twelve years is a really long time," I said, feeling a cramp in my stomach. "How's the family? Where is everyone?"

"Alhamdolillah. Everyone is well." He handed back my Quran "For the most part, I'm in Islamabad these day. I have two houses there now. One for Farzana, and one for Ruskhsana," he explained.

He had always been unapologetic about his love of women, especially really young ones. I wondered how many times my father had married and divorced in my absence.

"Any more kids, Abba?"

"It hasn't been the will of Allah—so far. Man can only try," he said with a shrug. "I've never once thought you'd see the light of faith."

"Who can question the Allah's will?"

He opened his mouth to reply but before he could utter a word the *maghrib azaan* filled the air. The loudspeakers of a dozen neighborhood mosques were soon joined by even more mosques that turned the call to prayer into a senseless wall of meaningless noise.

The power came back on just as the azaan stopped. Abba walked over to the light switch by the door and flipped it on. I felt exposed in the bright light hanging over my head. My stomach churned again and I desperately wanted to run to the bathroom.

"Where did you go last night, Ismaeel?" Abba demanded, his eyebrows raised. "I was told you didn't return until one in the morning."

"Just wanted to drive around and see Lahore. Get some fresh air. The roads are pretty bad."

He looked directly at me. Nofel, rubbing its body against his legs, stared at me with its large, unblinking yellow eyes.

"Hmm. Why didn't you take Wali with you?" I felt like I was undergoing some kind of interrogation. But I couldn't tell if I really was, or if this was just the old man's way.

I shrugged my shoulders and kept my mouth shut while forcing my mind to be completely blank.

"It's time for maghrib," he snapped. "Why don't you take a quick wash and join me in the drawing room for the namaaz? Don't be late." He opened the door and walked out, Nofel at his heels.

"Sure thing," I muttered under my breath as I dashed to the bathroom.

I took a hurried bath and put on my freshly laundered robe that Ghulam Rasool had hung over the chair next to the bed. Unfortunately there wasn't time for the leisurely bathroom time I was longing for.

Putting my headband on, I went to the drawing room. There by the fireplace Abba, Wali, and Ghulam Rasool sat on their respective prayer mats, waiting for my arrival, their heads covered with white skullcaps. They stood up as I entered the room, their curious eyes staring at my headband. Thankfully Nofel wasn't around.

"It's a substitute for the cap," I said, touching my forehead to soothe their obvious anxiety over my headband.

"Sir ji, faith requires complete covering of the whole head while praying, otherwise it can easily leak out; especially through such a big hole as that American style cap you're wearing," Wali declared through pursed lips.

He turned without waiting for my reply and started intoning the *niyyath*, the pre-namaaz prayer. My father nudged me towards the prayer mat placed in front of the other three.

"Ismaeel will lead the prayer tonight," Abba announced.

"Subhan-Allah!" Ghulam Rasool cried. "I am a happy man who has lived to see the day when our saab Ismaeel will lead the prayer."

Reluctantly I stood on the leading prayer mat and assumed the role of the imam. They all stood behind me in a line, their shoulders touching. The mushroom cloud in the painting loomed imposingly over my *qiblah*, the direction of Kaaba. My stomach cramped violently a couple of more times as I waited for Wali to complete his recitation. I deeply regretted having postponed my private gastrointestinal ministrations when I had the chance.

I took a deep breath and mustered all of my willpower to bear the burgeoning agony in my belly. I touched my earlobes. As soon as I said

Allah hu Akbar, the text of the Quran streamed across my eyes like a fiery ticker tape. Since I could shuffle the text with the force of my will alone, I chose some obscure verses to impress my father.

My pronunciation was flawless. Feeling happy that my stomach seemed to have eased up, I was doing the second of the three rakaat of *maghrib* when the lights went out. On the third and final rakaat, I was struck violently by a renewed urge to hit the restroom. It happened when I was kneeling, my hands resting on my knees: a small amount of gas escaped from my ass, despite my superhuman effort to stop it. It wasn't loud, but it was clearly audible.

A commotion erupted behind me but I continued the namaaz as if nothing had happened. Out of the corner of my eye, I saw Wali standing beside me. Clearly he'd broken his namaaz.

"Sir ji, what are you doing?" he snapped. "You have to stop praying! Once the *wudu*, the ablution, is broken the namaaz becomes invalid."

Startled, I turned around and saw my father staring at me angrily, his fists knotted on his thighs. Ghulam Rasool had stuffed his skullcap into his mouth and his eyes bulged like he was in mortal anguish.

"I'm so terribly sorry," I said. "My stomach hasn't been right since I landed."

"Go do your wudu again," my father commanded like I was his servant. "We still have a few minutes before the time for maghrib runs out." Then he turned to Ghulam Rasool and growled, "Get your cap out of your mouth and light some candles."

"We've got to do the whole namaaz again, sir ji," Wali said.

"Who says we have to do the whole namaaz?" Ghulam Rasool asked as he lit a large candle on the fireplace mantel. "We have to do only one rakaat and we're done."

"You don't know what you're talking about, Ghulam Rasool," Wali said, his voice trembling with rage.

"Be quiet, both of you!" my father's voice boomed. "I'm not taking sides here," Abba continued. "It's best if we consult the book of fiqah, and not go by mere opinions."

As he walked over to the bookshelf in the far corner of the room I darted out of the room and headed for the bathroom. After having relieved myself, I was doing my wudu squatting on the floor beside the water bucket when I heard someone clearing his throat in my head. I reflexively touched my forehead.

"Pir, is that you?" I whispered.

"Hope everything is moving along smoothly, Ismaeel," he said.

"Kind of," I whispered, as I continued my wudu in the dark.

"You can't afford to be on your father's wrong side, ever. Tell me what happened."

"A minor mishap but I think I can handle it."

"Good! Remember, though, you really don't have to speak out loud when we're talking—just use your thoughts. It'll feel awkward at first, like learning to ride a bike," he said with a chuckle. "But you'll get the hang of it. And it's safer too."

"Got it!" I told him by projecting my thought.

"Your father leaves for Islamabad tomorrow morning. Go with him, and stick to him closely at all times. Do you read me?" Pir asked.

"I read you clear!"

"We want you to be there in Islamabad with him. Your Quran should be with you at all times. Did you get it?"

"Yes."

"Last time you went off course, you crashed in the Dump. There's no margin for error this time," Pir said. "Do not try to contact me. Wait for my call."

"Yes, Pir," I replied, while washing my left foot.

"Ismaeel, think of this mission as traversing the Pullsiraat, the Razor's Edge." With that, Pir went offline.

I dashed to the candlelit drawing room where Wali and Ghulam Rasool were engrossed in a heated argument and about to come to blows. They lowered their voices as soon as they saw me. My father sat on the carpet pouring over a large, thick book that lay in his lap. At his knee was a candle.

"So what's the verdict?" I asked, taking my position on the imam's mat.

"Fiqah is silent on the matter," Abba said, with a look of resignation on his face. "It's an unusual case since it involves the imam himself."

"Why don't we do *ijtihaad*—decision making through personal effort," I said.

"Ijtihad?" Abba looked at me incredulously, shaking his head from side to side.

Ghulam Rasool had stepped on his mat behind me.

"Go ahead, saab. Let's do one rakaat and get it over with," he said. "I'm not saying one additional rakaat, if it's not needed."

"Sir ji, ijtihad is not applicable in this situation," Wali replied.

"Why not look up in the fiqah to see if it's okay to do ijtihad in a situation like this?" I looked at my father.

"Time has passed for the namaaz-e-maghrib," Ghulam Rasool said. "Look outside. It's already night."

They continued arguing over the cutoff point of when it's too late to say Maghrib.

"It's not night as long as you can see a plucked hair held to the sky," Wali added.

I had the longest hair in the room so I plucked one and handed it to him.

"Why don't you go out and check for yourself," I said.

"Everyone, stop!" my father stood up, his eyes flashing. "I say, there's still time."

Both Wali and Ghulam Rasool abruptly walked out of the room, heading in opposite directions. Wali went outside and Ghulam Rasool disappeared into the kitchen.

"Islam is the simplest religion there is," Abba said. "Alas! Only if we know how to follow it properly."

"Exactly, Abba," I said.

"Since we've got very little time left, maybe it is best if you do your own namaaz and I do mine, separately so we can finish it quickly."

"It's all my mistake, Abba," I added sincerely. "If given another chance, I'll make up for it."

"What happened was not a good omen," he said, pulling his mat away from mine. "You haven't changed, Ismaeel."

"Abba, please!"

He said nothing but just started his namaaz about five feet from me so I followed his cue and began mine. I was indeed on the Razor's Edge, where even a light gust of wind could initiate a hurricane and blow everything to hell.

Having finished our respective namaaz, Abba and I remained seated on our mats; our hands raised in prayer, our lips moving without uttering a sound. Shadows danced about the room and over the painting, making the canvas seem like a living, breathing tableau and no mere work of art.

Abba blew on his chest and rubbed his palms over his face and I copied his gestures.

"That's a great painting, Abba. It must have cost a fortune," I said. "A bit frightening, though. Where did you get it?"

He stared at the painting, rubbing his temple, as if considering what to say.

"It was a gift," he finally replied. "A gift from Khalifa ji to me."

"Wow! From Khalifa ji! Really?"

He nodded his head in affirmation, his eyes shining with pride.

"Who made it, Abba?"

"A certain retired general—his last masterpiece before he died. I'm blanking on his name at the moment." I could tell he had deliberately censored the name of the artist.

"Well, it's clearly a museum-quality piece," I said.

He grinned and scratched his neck. He was about to say something when Ghulam Rasool entered the room rolling a food cart topped with tea, samosas, and shami kebabs. He must have been eavesdropping on our conversation.

"Saab, your Abba ji is very, very close to Khalifa ji—not many people are aware of it," he said, smiling with satisfaction as though bathing in the glory that spilled over him from his master. Then he composed himself and returned to pouring the tea into our cups.

"You must be a very important person, Abba. You always were a leader."

"Tomorrow I'm meeting with Khalifa ji in Islamabad" he said, straightening his back.

"Abba, didn't you just come back from Islamabad? That's a lot of travel."

"If you have a good car, the distance doesn't matter," he said, his face tightening in a smug self-satisfied smile.

"Oh? What kind of car are you driving these days?"

"Mercedes Benz SE505X, custom made." Lifting his eyebrows he stared at me, as if trying to read my reaction.

"Abba! That's an expensive car."

"Bought and paid for by the state. I'm certainly not wealthy enough to afford it otherwise."

"Well, Khalifa ji is very kind to you, it seems."

"Anyway, one day I'm in Islamabad, one day in Lahore. Khalifa ji has entrusted me to communicate his message in person with certain important people."

"I see."

"The Day of Judgment is upon us, saab," Ghulam Rasool interjected with excitement as he handed me a cup of tea. He looked at my father. "Am I right, Haji sahib?"

"Ghulam Rasool, your eyes and ears are too sharp for your own good."

"Saab, I've been with you for the last thirty years. I don't need my eyes and ears to know what is happening," Ghulam Rasool said, handing my father his cup.

"What's going on, Abba?" I felt as if my *mission* was about to be revealed at long last through this innocuous master-servant conversation. My heart started thumping against my ribcage.

Before my father answered, Nofel appeared in the room and curled up on the carpet beside him. The cat's yellow eyes were radiant in the light of the candles and his tail swayed back and forth like a cobra. I immediately emptied my mind of all thoughts.

"Help yourself to the shami kebob, saab. I've made them especially for you." Ghulam Rasool held a plate of warm round patties in front of my face, his eyes seeming to float above the plate in the steam. I could feel their mushiness and taste their meaty flavor in my watering mouth.

It was time to change the conversation lest Nofel tag onto my stream of thought.

"How's your business these days, Abba?"

"By the grace of Allah, business is very good," Abba replied, sipping his tea.

"What kind of business are you in, exactly?" I asked casually, as I poured green chutni on the kebob. I wanted to see if he would tell me the truth.

"Transportation," Ghulam Rasool chirped, but my father threw him a cold stare.

"A couple of years after you left," Abba began, as though launching into one of the great desert tales. "I bought a new chemical plant in Kala Shah-Kaku. A few years later I added a garment factory to my holdings. By the grace of the Almighty, we now manufacture and export quality products to China, Russia, and to the far end of the Maghrib," my father continued, taking a bite off the samosa in his hand.

"Saab, orders have started to come from Europe and even America," Ghulam Rasool chimed in. "Why don't Wali and I give you a tour of the factory, if that's okay with Haji saab?"

The prospect of visiting a plant manufacturing suicide vests with Wali and Ghulam Rasool gave me the shivers.

"Abba, I'd rather go to Islamabad. I came here to spend time with you, and don't want to be here in Lahore by myself."

"For that, I'll have to get approval from Khalifa ji," my father said, as he slid his palm gently over Nofel's spine.

"Please, Abba. Otherwise, I'll be wasting my time in Lahore doing nothing," I said, taking the succulent kebab into my mouth.

He quietly sipped his tea, smoothing his eyebrows from time to time. He was thinking.

"Please, Abba."

"Ismaeel, I just heard you reciting the Quran with my own ears. Wali saw you doing the same the other night. Your turn-around is all the more mysterious and remarkable considering that you've been living and breathing the same air as the infidels for so long. And now you somehow defy all logic. Not only have you apparently rekindled something I was certain you never had to begin with, but now you are able to do it so very, very well. This whole thing has to be a miracle, some kind of sign."

As my father spoke, his eyes became teary, glistening in the dancing flames of the candlelight. He fell silent, then looked up and contemplated the painting. He seemed to be trying to collect his thoughts and regain his composure.

Turning to Ghulam Rasool he said, "Go and see what Wali is doing outside. Tell him to prepare my car. We'll be leaving for Islamabad early in the morning. And make sure you feed Nofel—he hasn't eaten anything all day."

Nofel trotted behind Ghulam Rasool as he left the drawing room. The front door of the house creaked open and then slammed shut behind him. Once Nofel was out of the picture, I relaxed and let my thoughts wander beyond their self-imposed dark prison.

If the Khalifa was planning a spectacle, as Pir had called it, then Abba was part of it for sure. Whatever *it* was. My curiosity gnawed at me like a dog with a bone and I wondered what role I was supposed to play.

In all this darkness, there was one small bright spot: a leisurely drive in my father's custom-made Mercedes Benz through the two-hundred-plus miles that snaked through the lush plains of Punjab and merged with the foothills of the Himalayas, the Margalla Hills. These low-lying hills, hardly reaching more than a thousand feet in elevation, provided a picturesque backdrop to the otherwise flat capital city.

"I'll be calling Khalifa ji shortly, asking if I can bring you along," Abba said as he stood up. "I'll be very busy tonight."

"Thank you, Abba."

"Perhaps he will let you join the Friday Prayer as well," he added without looking at me as he stood and walked over to get his shoes at the edge of the carpet.

I had no clue what day this was. I looked at my watch. It was Thursday.

"What's happening on Friday, Abba?"

"Allah, out of His infinite mercy, has brought you here to be with me, Ismaeel, to witness history in the making."

Something was going to happen tomorrow, the very something Pir had said would have serious consequences for this world and the Next. I also knew that without his mysterious book, the Khalifa couldn't move forward with his plans.

If tomorrow was to be his big D-Day, then the Khalifa must have gotten his hands on the second book Pir mentioned that had already been shipped. Was he planning a mass exodus to Paradise by having himself and his associates ingest the stamps, the so-called Tickets to Paradise—the same trip Pir had sent me on via the black book?

Or did he have something else in mind; something that sent dismembered body parts flying through the air and landing near Chaacha Khidr's ominous burlap sack? If that was the case, then how was I supposed to stop him from carrying out his plan?

"I'll see you tomorrow at the morning prayer, at *fajr* namaaz," Abba said, slipping his feet into his sandals. "Let Ghulam Rasool know if you need anything. I'm not going to eat dinner tonight. I've got a lot of work to do and many phone calls to make."

"I'm not hungry either, Abba. See you at the fajr prayer, Inshallah."

When he left, I stared at the painting where it loomed darkly from the mantle, its mushroom cloud over a vast swath of land looking like a swirling vortex in real-time. Was Abba in on the scheme of Khalifa? It seemed pretty obvious that the answer was a resounding, *yes!*

The mystery surrounding my mission was driving me insane. Sitting in my room I was wide-awake; my mind afloat with inescapable thoughts, fears, and misgivings. I needed a distraction that would occupy my mind and soothe my jangled nerves. I decided to take a long dive into the namaaz of ishaa—the longest of the five daily obligatory prayers.

I chose some of the longest passages of the Quran because I wanted Abba to peek in and catch me in the act of flagrant piety. It was past midnight when I heard his footsteps and felt his presence at the door. I continued to pray without letting on that I knew he was watching me.

He left without saying anything, returned an hour later, and found me still praying. I wasn't even halfway done yet. He stood at the door for at least five minutes before wandering back down the hall. And when he showed up again around two in the morning, I knew he had been moved by my reverence for Allah, though only slightly. Sitting with my legs folded under, I blew on my shoulders. I still had two final *rakaat Nafil,* considered optional but spiritually beneficial, to go before concluding my prayer. I looked at his dark figure standing in the doorway, and felt thankful for not having to have eye contact with him.

"In all my sixty-plus years of life, I've never seen anyone who'd spend so much time in one *rakaat,*" he said. "Are you taking any medications, Ismaeel?" Abba had always been good at sniffing trouble.

"Of course not, Abba," I said. Of course it was a huge lie, considering the assortment of novel chemicals which must be flowing in my bloodstream and bathing my brain at the moment.

"Khalifa ji would like to meet with you in person." His voice betrayed excitement.

The news struck me like a projectile piercing my forehead. For the next few seconds I couldn't breathe.

"Khalifa ji wants to see me? Are you serious Abba?"

"Yes. He believes you're one of the signs he has been awaiting. The sign first shown to him in a dream."

"Me? The sign?"

"Who taught you your faith, Ismaeel, in America?"

"I'm my own teacher, Abba." I was feeling a surge of confidence. I'd be going to Islamabad with him. One of the critical tasks of my mission had been accomplished, though I was far from winning Abba's heart and mind.

I looked at Abba in a daze. He stepped forward and sat on the bed, staring at me with great interest.

"No man can learn his faith with such perfection as you have without divine guidance," he said, studying me with his eyes. "You have to tell me, Ismaeel, who brought you back to your faith? I must meet this man, and kiss his hands."

Chapter 23
Three Guests

MY FATHER PRESIDED over the *fajr* prayer amid a sea of flickering yellow candles. When it was concluded, Ghulam Rasool was sent to fetch tea, Wali to find Nofel, and I was instructed to remain seated on my prayer mat for a chat. Having served us, Ghulam Rasool scurried back to the kitchen to prepare breakfast for five. My father was expecting guests.

These guests were Abba's business partners. They also happened to be high ranking VIPs within the Caliphate. After breakfast, the five of us would be traveling to Islamabad together in my father's car; a vehicle that also seemed to be a high-ranking notable within the regime. The three guests had been wanting for some time to experience for themselves the otherworldly luxury of my father's car.

The distinguished guests were: the Chief Qadi of the Sharia Court Punjab, the Imam of the Badshahi Mosque, and the Grand Mufti of the Fatwa Council. The thought of being trapped in a car with three such strangers on a long road trip put a serious damper on my already precarious spirits.

The plan was to head straight to the Faisal Mosque in Islamabad to attend a historic Jumma congregation with various handpicked luminaries of the Caliphate. The Khalifa himself would be there to honor the ceremony. Admission to the auspicious occasion was by invitation only. I'd been to the mosque only once before; on a school trip when I was just a boy.

I remembered being completely blown away by the size and scale of the place. To my boyish imagination it had looked like a huge space station. It was actually intended to resemble a Bedouin tent. The design was the brainchild of Turkish architect Vedat Dalokay. Four minarets shaped like sharpened pencils towered hundreds of feet above a triangular prayer hall that resembled a massive tent pitched on the green foothills of the Margalla Hills.

From what Abba said, or rather hadn't said, it didn't sound like even he knew the exact purpose of this mysterious gathering. It could be that he just didn't want to divulge any secrets he'd been privy to. The conversation then turned back to his infamous car, which of course I was dying to see for myself.

Abba told me how much he loved racing along the Motorway because there was no speed limit. He loved driving this car so much that he'd refused the official driver that had come as part of the deal. The Benz could make the trip to Islamabad in two and half hours—a distance of about 230 miles. Abba's record was just under two.

My father's eyes widened when he described the 100-mile-an-hour warm-up, how the car hugged the road at 120, and how you never felt out of control even at speeds in excess of 150-miles-an-hour. Describing a cruise along the Motorway, my father had used words like "freed from time and space," and "the cares and worries which belong to the world."

"This is the closest one gets to experiencing Jannah while still on earth," he said in a serious tone. He remained silent then for a good ten seconds, as if gathering his thoughts.

"Owning the best possible ride one can get in life is *sunnah*, which in my case basically means that every mile I drive the closer I get to Jannah."

I lowered my head, thinking of Sophie living in the pagan quarters of Paradise. What would he do if he ever found out that I'd consummated my love for his seventh wife in Paradise? He was the epitome of greed— greed for Paradise.

"Never thought that earning swaab could be as easy as slamming on the gas pedal," I said. I felt happy about my decision to leave this bizarre world of his when I was 18, and I couldn't wait to get the hell out of it once my mission here was accomplished.

"Yes, it is so, son. Allah's ways are indeed mysterious."

This was the first time he'd called me "son." I must be doing something right. He was definitely beginning to soften.

By the time he went to change for breakfast, the candles had fluttered in the morning light that spilled through the open windows. I wandered outside to take a look at the magical car and there she was—a gleaming black Mercedes-Benz SE505X. Parked alongside was the ravaged looking Corolla with its fake camel top. Compared to the black beauty, the Corolla could easily have passed for a pile of scrap. A palm-sized green flag bearing the Caliphate logo was tethered to the circular coat of arms of the Benz at the end of its hood.

I stared at the smooth sleek lines, marveling at the unapologetic disparities life was capable of displaying, the incongruous nature of reality, the lopsided nature of cause and effect, and the deceptive linearity of time. Before I was finished contemplating Wali, carrying Nofel in his arms, appeared through an opening within the front gate.

"The moment this bastard sees a female cat, he loses his mind." Wali looked angry. "Sir ji, I've asked Haji sahib many times to get him neutered."

"And what did he say?" I said.

"It's against the sharia."

"I think he's right."

"Sir ji, I can prove that he's wrong," he said, putting down Nofel who dashed back into the house. I kept my mouth shut so he wouldn't launch off into some new tirade on religion.

Before Wali could say another word, a car blasted its horn outside the front wall. He raced toward the gate and threw both sides wide open and then stepped aside and bowed deeply.

A black top-of-the-line Toyota Land Cruiser with tinted windows and not a hint of chrome rolled ominously into the driveway and braked within six inches of my shins. Three men wearing identical starched white robes and headdresses emerged from the plush interior of a vehicle that seemed suited to Darth Vader. Or someone who admired him greatly.

As soon as the Toyota had discharged its passengers it retreated silently and disappeared from the compound. Wali closed the gate and ran back inside the house. Ignoring my presence, the guests started fingering their mobile phones.

A moment later, rubbing his palms together, Abba came rushing out of the house, his face radiant with happiness. Once he finished hugging his guests, he turned to me. I could tell from his face he didn't like what he was seeing. Maybe because it was the first time he'd seen me in the daylight, but I must have looked like a wreck. In the hooded glare of my father's disapproving gaze I somehow felt unclean, impure. Of course! I was wearing the same patchwork denim jellaba he had hated when I bought it twelve years ago.

"Meet my son, Ismaeel, he's just returned from America," Abba said, sounding awkward and looking just slightly embarrassed. The three wizened grey-beards stared at me with narrowed eyes. None of them smiled.

"It's a pleasure to meet you all," I said, standing still.

"My son lived in the belly of the Great Satan for a decade so pardon his appearance. What's important is that his faith is stronger than all of us put together," Abba said, as he tried to regain his bearing. "Ismaeel, come, let me introduce you to my friends."

As I shook their warm flaccid hands one by one, Abba introduced them by their names and titles, all of which were long and complicated. In my mind, I assigned them each a nickname according to their job description. Qadi, or the Judge, was six feet tall with broad shoulders and a head that was too small for his body. Imam, fair skinned, looked impossibly round and reminded me of a grenade that was about to pop. And Mufti, the issuer of fatwa or rulings according to Islamic law, was a little guy, barely five feet tall, thin as a blade of grass and wearing a black patch over his right eye. I had no doubt the patch was well earned and worn to strike respect and awe in the hearts of all.

Once the guests were seated in the drawing room, Abba asked that I follow him to his bedroom.

"Didn't you bring anything to wear besides what you have on right now?" he asked as he closed the door of his bedroom behind us. He made no attempt to hide his anger.

"No."

"Is this how the believer dresses in the land of the pure, and out of all the days, on a Friday?" he demanded.

Without waiting for my reply he flung open the double doors of a huge walk-in closet. Inside was a vast collection of robes, headdresses, and pre-wrapped turbans hung neatly from hangers and hooks and laid out on countless shelves; all arranged by seasonal wear, color, fabric, and importance of occasion.

"No one, no one, wears denim jellabas here anymore," he growled. "Only liberal extremists used to wear robes like yours," he said, carefully extracting a light brown robe of high quality cotton from one of the covered hangers. "This one is tight on me now so it should fit you fine."

"I'm sorry, Abba, I honestly didn't have the time to shop." I took the robe from him along with a white keffiyeh and a coil of black tasseled rope to keep it in place.

"Abba, if you get tired from driving, I could take the wheel," I offered, trying to distract him and lighten the mood. "Just let me know." He gave me another of his long hard looks.

"Maybe on our way back."

His answer made me wonder again how much he actually knew about the Khalifa's plan. If he was in on it, he probably wanted to enjoy the last ride of his life by driving his own beloved car. Why not? If I were he, I suppose I'd want to break my previous record too.

Wearing authentic Arab dress, the thobe, I joined everyone in the dining room. It was a little loose on me, but didn't look too bad. My face was washed, my beard combed, and I wore Pir's psychic headband tucked under my headdress and ready to transmit.

God knows what Abba was saying about me, because when I took my seat next to him his buddies were all smiles, their faces radiating warmth.

I sat across from Imam, who pushed a plate of sticky halva toward me. Qadi, seated next to him, held out a basket of steaming pouris, and Mufti, sitting at the far end of the table, shut his solitary eye for a little while longer than a blink would take, as he took a sip of tea. It could have been a wink, but I wasn't too sure.

"So, Ismaeel," Imam said, clearing his throat. "If what your father has told us about you is true, I'm truly impressed. I would very much like to see a demonstration of your ability."

"It's unbelievable that after living all these years in a place like America, created for the sole purpose of keeping the Satan busy, you're able to hold onto your faith," Qadi said. "Quite remarkable, indeed!"

Abba's face glowed with pride as he listened to their comments. He was in for a huge surprise—provided my mission was a success. I tried to feel sympathy for him, but I just couldn't find any.

"In honor of this auspicious repast, I propose that Ismaeel describe for us the kinds of foods we'll be eating in Al-Jannah," Mufti suggested, looking me in the eyes as his face broke into a mischievous smile. "Hint: it's in the Quran."

The pointedness of his request startled me at first. Surely, I could recite any part of Quran in Arabic. That did not mean I understood the meaning of what I was reciting. Pir's download hadn't come with a translation. Feeling at a loss for the answer and a little panicked, I tried recalling the food I'd seen lying on the floating slabs of marble under the red canopy in the Guest House of Al-Jannah.

Overwhelmed by the sheer variety of food I'd seen, I lowered my head and thought of where to begin. Then I saw Nofel sitting beside my chair, staring at me with his piercing yellow eyes. I immediately shielded my thoughts, straightened up, and looked around the room.

"Abba, would you please send Nofel away?" I asked shaking my head and feigning confusion. "I just can't concentrate with him staring at me like that."

"Where's Wali? He should be feeding him. We've got a long journey ahead.

"Ismaeel, go ask Wali to take Nofel into the kitchen."

"Excuse me, sir," I said to Mufti, as I stood up from my chair. "I'll be right back."

As I came out of the dining room, formulating my answer to Mufti, Nofel followed me. In the hall I bumped into Ghulam Rasool as he rushed out of the kitchen carrying a basket of fresh pouris.

"Abba said to keep Nofel out of the dining room. Please tell Wali to feed him," I said. "The cat's coming with us to Islamabad."

"I'll never understand what your Abba ji likes about this cat." He headed toward the front door, coaxing Nofel to follow him. I was about to return to the dining room when Pir Pullsiraat's voice sounded inside my head.

"Hello. Can you hear me."

"Yes," I whispered. "Loud and clear."

"Make sure you satisfy Mufti. He isn't too comfortable with your presence. Just so you know, he knows how to read information off the cats. Your father doesn't."

It was comforting to know that Pir was hacking into our conversation.

"Nofel was planted in your father's house by Khalifa's men. He's trained to keep an eye on your father. But be careful of him. He's also trained to smell trouble."

"Thanks for the heads-up," I thought toward him. I could feel the connection and his silent nod.

"That's what friends are for," he added, and then broke our connection.

When I returned to the dining room, Abba was talking animatedly and enjoying the unwavering attention of his guests. He was speaking about Khalifa's dream. I sat and helped myself to some more halva, savoring the delicious sweetness as it dissolved on my tongue. When Abba was finished describing the dream, they all looked at me as if I was some kind of holy relic. All but Mufti. He just sat dabbing his lips several times with his napkin as his solitary eye roamed in its socket like a yoyo. Unlike Imam and Qadi, Mufti seemed wholly unconvinced of my lofty status.

Time to deliver him the fatal blow. I cleared my throat, poured myself a cup of tea, and looked Mufti in the eye. I was ready for the knockout punch.

"Mufti sahib, first of all, no human can ever hope to grasp the sheer variety of foods that are available to the believer in Jannah," I said. "Gently flowing streams of milk, honey, pure water, and other nectars crisscross lush rolling grounds that stretch to eternity. The celestial palaces there are so large that one needs the full lifetime of an old man to circle their grounds.

"Trees grow there in abundance that are so large, a fleet horse must gallop for seventy years and beyond to escape the shadows of even their saplings. A magnificent purple sky lies overhead like a priceless carpet spun of the purest silk, and the air drips with a heady intoxicating fragrance.

"There under a red canopy the truly faithful will be lounging on costly divans and leaning against soft cushions. The pious will be served pure sparkling wines without alcohol by beautiful youths wearing red loincloths, their skin glistening as if massaged with priceless oils. As for beautiful women, they are scattered about like butterflies by the scores; all with big round eyes, voluptuous breasts, and translucent ankles through which the marrow may be clearly seen. Their skin is radiant as if lit by the heavenly fire from within. Some of these beauties play the harp, all for the pleasure of the purest among the faithful.

"Around you will be placed lovely baskets overflowing with ripe fruits of all kinds; cheeses of numerous varieties, olives, dates, and figs, as well as nuts in great and varied abundance. For your ease and convenience, all will be near at hand on floating slabs of marble." I stopped here, realizing they'd gone into trance-like states, with their eyes out of focus as if gazing upon some far distant scene. No one said anything for a long time. Finally, Imam cleared his throat.

"Subhanallah! Mashallah! What a recitation!" he said, swaying his massive ball-like torso and smiling at my father. "Haji sahib, here is the kind of son every father dreams of having. I congratulate you for having already attained the highest level of Jannah—thanks to Ismaeel."

"Very impressive!" Qadi nodded his small head. "A bit improvised, if I may add."

I eyed Mufti out of the corner of my eyes. He was squirming in his chair, waiting for his turn to comment.

"Not merely *a bit*, but rather profusely improvised," he announced, leaning forward, his hands gripping the table in front of him. "Some of the things you've mentioned, like the purple sky, red canopy, the cheeses, the floating tables of marble, the red loincloths on the youths, the women playing harp, *etcetera*, are not mentioned anywhere in the Quran. I'd be very happy if you'd give us some references which specifically mention these things. I must humbly submit that some of the information you have given us is quite new to me."

Suddenly Pir's voice thundered in my head, making my skull vibrate like a tuning fork.

"Tell him to fuck off!" he roared.

"It may not be possible," I said, addressing Pir, not realizing that I had said it aloud.

"Indeed!" Mufti said sitting up stiffly in his chair, his eyes shining victoriously. "One must be very careful when speaking of such important matters without proper reference to back up one's claims of special knowledge."

My father came to my rescue.

"Ismaeel, show them your Quran."

"Abba, some other time, please," I said, feeling uneasy about his suggestion. I tried changing the subject. "I can assure Mufti sahib that the things I have mentioned do indeed exist in Jannah, and Inshallah all references will be provided to him in due time."

"Enough discussion, son," Abba said, turning towards his guests. "I bet none of you has seen anything like this." He nudged me with his elbow. "Come, you may show us now."

Reluctantly, I took the book out of my pocket and held it in the air. I cringed when Imam reached for it with his glistening fingers still smeared with the oil from the pouris. He held the book in his hand and kissed its leather cover with his glossy lips before beginning to examine its pages.

"Where did you get this, Ismaeel?" Imam hissed, a look of astonishment lighting up his round face.

"From an antique store in Manhattan," I said.

"Subhanallah! My Allah can make a flower sprout from a rock," he said.

He swayed his head several times and then passed the Quran to Qadi, who turned out to be a gentleman. He wiped his fingers on his napkin before taking the book into his hands.

"Truly unique!" Qadi said. "Amazing calligraphy! Never seen a Quran with burgundy pages and golden, handwritten text."

The book then went to Mufti who sniffed it first before putting it on the table in front of him.

"Quite unusual! An antique book retaining the smell of fresh leather," he said, staring at the pages.

My heartbeat quickened as he took a magnifying glass from his pocket and held to his eye and began examining the text.

"This ink looks fresh, as if it was put on the page only a few days ago. May I check it a little more closely?" he said, steadily looking at me.

"Please go ahead, Mufti ji. Go ahead." Abba's face quivered with excitement.

It was when he dipped his fingertip in his glass of water that I threw my hands up in alarm.

"Mufti sahib, I'm not sure what you're trying to do, but this book you're holding in your hands is a living, breathing being. No tampering please."

I knew I was on solid ground with this one. Tampering with the holy text, even the intention of doing so, in any shape or form, was punishable by death—provided the intention could be proved to be so.

Mufti recoiled at my abruptness as if shoved from his chair by physical force.

Qadi gave me an approving look.

"I'm afraid Ismaeel's statements carry weight," he said. The comment made Mufti cross his arms over his chest and avoid looking Qadi in the eye.

Before the situation could get any worse, Ghulam Rasool came into the room carrying a tray topped with five tall glasses of sweet creamy lassi, another from his arsenal of specialties. He served my father's guests first, beginning with Imam who gulped down more than half of his glass in the first swallow. He paused for a breath and as he emptied his glass, he threw his head all the way back. Slamming the empty glass down on the table, he wiped the white foam from his mustache with the palm of his right hand.

"This young man speaks the truth, Mufti ji," Imam said, glancing at me and nodding with approval.

"My intention has never been to tamper," Mufti said curtly, passing the book to Abba, who handed it back to me.

"Khalifa ji's dream has come true, as far as I'm concerned. Don't you think, gentlemen?" Qadi said, taking a sip of his lassi.

"Without a doubt, *that* young man is Ismaeel; and the light in his hand is this most glorious Quran he just showed us," Imam said.

"Exactly! It's a divine green light. The Almighty is letting Khalifa ji know all is well. He's telling him to go ahead with his plans," Abba said, looking his guests in the eye one by one.

I wanted to know more about Khalifa's dream but wisely refrained from asking about it. This wasn't the right time or place.

Abba's comment made Mufti restless and he shifted in his chair. Qadi lowered his head and massaged his temple. Imam however, remained unperturbed. He gave Abba a sharp nod, but didn't say anything.

For several minutes, a long and uncomfortable silence hung over the table that was broken only by a rather loud and prolonged belch from Imam. A rancid odor filled the air and clung to my nose for a painfully long time.

It seemed Abba, unwittingly or deliberately, had tried to let me in on the secret they all shared. He might be testing the waters to see how his guests would respond to his casually uttered remarks about the Khalifa's plan while in my presence. After all, I had come from America, the enemy number one, and a country known for planting spies within the Caliphate, even though so far there had been no success.

"Seems like we're going to be attending a very special Jumma Prayer," I said, smiling into the friendly face of Imam. "Would you please hand me that bottle of mango pickle, Imam sahib."

"I think we should start to hurry," Mufti said. "We have a long journey ahead."

"You may relax Mufti ji. We have plenty of time," Abba said. "You leave that up to me."

Once Abba and his friends were finished eating, I excused myself from their esteemed company and retired to my room in hopes that Pir might contact me. I was dying to know more about the Khalifa's plan. I was pacing back and forth when Ghulam Rasool walked in.

"Anything I can do for you, saab?"

"Do you by any chance know what's happening in Islamabad today?" I asked, trying to sound as casual as possible.

"Something that's to change everything, saab," he said shutting the door behind him lest our conversation be overheard. "Something that will make Khalifa very very powerful."

"How do you know that?"

"I heard your Abba ji talking to someone on the phone a few days ago."

"Come on, Ghulam Rasool," I said. "Please tell me what you know."

As Ghulam Rasool opened his mouth to speak, there was a knock at the door. He opened it and Abba walked in.

"I was looking for you in the kitchen, Ghulam Rasool," Abba said. "Go and load the trunk with food. We won't be stopping to eat along the way."

Ghulam Rasool hurried off.

"Ismaeel, we're leaving in ten minutes," Abba said. He paused. "Why do you look so distracted?"

"Still jet-lagged Abba. Would you please tell me exactly what's going on in Islamabad?"

"What time is it?" he asked.

"It's quarter to eight," I said, looking at my watch.

"By 2:00 this afternoon, all will become clear," he said nothing more, just gracing me with a quick smile before he left. I couldn't tell if the smile was sincere, or merely a long practiced affectation for throwing his prey into confusion.

I went into the bathroom, which was filled with sunlight that poured through a small window fitted with a wrought iron grill. I was standing at the sink looking at myself admiringly in my new clothes, when Pir spoke in my head.

"We won't be in touch until you get inside the Faisal Mosque. Until then, under no circumstances are you to attempt to contact me," he said.

"Yes, sir."

"Chaacha Khidr sends his blessings, and Tarzan is giving you thumbs up."

"And Laila?"

"She says she's praying for you."

"Wait! Don't go!" I began to panic.

"It's not safe to talk now," he said.

"But I'm alone in the bathroom."

"Are you sure?"

I looked around and then froze. Nofel was sitting on the outside windowsill staring at me through the grill.

"Holy shit!" I grabbed a towel and snapped it against the grill, hoping the damned thing would run off. "Get lost, you motherfucker!" Nofel growled as he jumped off the ledge and disappeared.

"It was Nofel. Sorry. He's gone now."

"Nofel? This is what I mean. You cannot, and I repeat, you cannot, under any circumstances disregard my instructions. I've told you before: you're on a tightrope—one slip and gone."

"But I didn't do anything," I protested.

"We have to do something about Nofel. He probably already knows too much," Pir said and then closed the connection.

I headed to the porch with a growing sense of unease. Ghulam Rasool was loading a crate containing a couple of thermoses and cups into the trunk of the car. Wali, orange cloth in hand, circled the car in search of wayward blemishes to eradicate.

"One thermos has tea and the other lassi," Ghulam Rasool said. "The drinks can be reached from inside the car." Opening the rear door he showed me a passage between the middle of the seat through which the cups and thermos could be retrieved without having to stop the car.

"Where is Nofel going to sit?" I asked.

"He usually sits in the backseat, but also likes the trunk. He goes back and forth though the opening in the middle of the backseat"

"You have to put him in the trunk," I said firmly. "That's where he's going to go."

At that moment, Abba and his guests came out of the house. As they stood beside the sparkling black Mercedes where it lounged near the porch like a panther, there was a palpable tension in the air. Each man naturally felt it was his right to command the front passenger seat next to Abba. But they all knew there was no way Imam would fit in the backseat with two other passengers and they looked at each other without saying anything. Wali broke the tension by opening the rear door and gesturing me to enter first. I slid into the middle seat, feeling content with the wide-angle view I had through the windshield.

Imam opened the front passenger door and sank into his seat, filling all available space between his corpulent form and the dashboard. His massive back blocked half of my visual field. Mufti sat on my left and Qadi on my right. Nofel was put in the trunk. Thankfully due to Mufti's diminutive size there was ample space for all of us in the back.

We were zooming down the motorway by 8:30 am. It looked like a deserted runway that stretched to infinity just for us. Imam had dozed off and begun snoring with an incremental crescendo of noise—his chin bobbing up and down on his chest. With a frown on his face, Abba pushed the gas pedal. A sudden powerful acceleration slammed me back against my seat. This deliberate maneuver failed because the Imam's ample girth was able to absorb this sudden impact quite well. It did, however, transform the character of the snores that now overwhelmed the cabin like a buzz saw, much to the dismay of all.

Qadi spoke. "He drank a whole jug of lassi." He and Mufti were clearly annoyed by this breach of propriety.

"Haji sahib, please do something," Qadi pleaded.

Abba was doing 90-miles-an-hour but it felt like we were going no more than about forty. He jacked up the volume on the music system and flooded the cabin with Quran recitation in an attempt to drown out the snoring. He kept increasing the volume while slowly pressing the accelerator to the floor. By the time he reached the maximum sound tolerable by the human eardrum, the speedometer read 149-miles-per-hour.

Things outside flew past in a blur, probably more from the sheer physical impact of the sound than from the speed itself. The Imam did not wake up, and his snores became even more annoying. During the necessary pauses in the holy text a reciter of the Quran must observe, the noise was downright unbearable.

Lowering my head, I pressed on my temples and gave Imam a forceful nudge with my forehead. He awoke and looked around the cabin in a daze. Abba lowered the volume without slowing down the car. By then he was doing 155-miles-an-hour and overtook an eighteen-wheeler that at first I'd thought was coming at us from the opposite direction.

"Ismaeel, would you please get Imam ji a hot cup of tea?" Abba asked, looking at me through the rearview mirror.

I was in no mood to put my hand in the compartment currently occupied by Nofel.

"Yes. I need a cup of tea. That lassi was a bit too heavy for me," Imam said, leaving me no choice but to access the trunk through the back of my seat. *Damned cat.*

"Anyone else for the tea?" I asked.

Both Qadi and Mufti politely declined.

Reluctantly, I folded my seat down a bit. All I saw was Nofel's snarling face as he tried to squeeze past the opening and get into the cabin.

"No, no! Stay there!" I tried to shoo him back into the trunk.

"Why don't we just let the poor animal ride up here? It must be suffocating back there in the trunk," Mufti said. "It can sit on the floor next to my feet. There's plenty of space for him here," he added, allowing the cat to enter the cabin. Of course Nofel took advantage of the opportunity. Squeezing through the opening the animal curled up beside Mufti's feet.

I grabbed one of the thermoses from the basket—luckily it turned out be the one filled with tea—and handed Imam his cup. Putting the thermos back in the trunk, I closed the opening, leaned back in my seat, and emptied my mind of all thoughts. Mufti petted the cat's lush fur and stared into his eyes. After several moments he leaned back in his seat, scratched his neck, and glanced at me sideways. At that moment, I knew Nofel had communicated something damning about me to the man.

No one spoke for a long time while Imam noisily slurped his tea. This was only slightly less obnoxious than his incessant snoring. Abba set the cruise control at 130-miles-an-hour and then started swaying his head as he listened to the sacred recitation.

Keeping my mind empty for such a long time proved to be quite a strenuous exercise. Soon I started to doze, but I felt too lethargic to make the effort to get myself a cup of tea. They were all talking about the intrinsic qualities of the water of Hoz e Kausar, when sleep over-powered me.

I woke up when the car decelerated abruptly and stopped at a security check post on the exit ramp of the Motorway. Under an azure sky, the green peaks of the Margalla Hills topped the horizon. I glanced at my watch to find it was 11:00 am. Abba had made it to Islamabad in about two and a half hours.

Six gunmen draped in black robes ran up and surrounded the car. Abba rolled down his window.

"What can I do for you?" he asked politely, looking at the man standing beside his door.

Slamming his heel against the asphalt, the gunman gave Abba a stiff salute.

"Sir, just making sure, sir!" he cried, looking straight over the car, his hand glued to his temple.

"Good job," Abba said with a smile.

"Let them pass!" the man shouted, turning about on his heels.

As the barrier rose, the soldiers snapped their salutes in our direction; whether to Abba and his august companions, or to the flagged black Benz gleaming in the sun, I couldn't tell. Abba floored the accelerator. In a matter of seconds we were cruising along the Kashmir Highway at 100-miles-an-hour and heading toward the heart of the capital city.

Chapter 24
Islamabad

WE WERE STOPPED THREE more times at heavily armed checkpoints along the Kashmir Highway. It seemed like more of a formality than a security necessity but it was a stark reminder of the charged atmosphere, and a way different feeling than when I left years ago. At each stop I also got the distinct impression that Abba and Company really enjoyed watching those kids squirm when they recognized the car.

Once we turned north on Faisal Avenue toward the Margalla Hills, the place began to look more like a military garrison. Army vehicles with olive drab and green camouflage lined the avenue. Pickup trucks mounted with machine guns and manned by robed men with black bushy beards tore up and down the roads leaving dusty trails.

There wasn't a single civilian vehicle in sight. At the far end of the avenue, partially hidden by dense foliage, stood the massive edifice of Faisal Mosque, highlighted against the rolling green hills.

"Mashallah!" Imam exclaimed, waving at a knot of men clinging to the top of a camouflaged Toyota pickup truck. He was still waving long after they had disappeared in the rear view mirror.

"Khalifa ji has better security than the president of America," I observed, eyeing the brown armored vehicles parked at the side of the road, their guns raised at a 45-degree angle as if saluting the morning sky.

"Of course!" Mufti said proudly. "He's more important than your president in the eyes of Allah."

"My president? Mufti sahib, I've left America far behind and I do not care about its president."

"The young man knows how to speak his mind," Imam replied with a smile.

"It's called the American style," Qadi added as he winked at me.

"You know, I had almost given up on my son," Abba said, his face bristling with pride. "Deep indeed are Allah's mysteries!"

"Haji sahib, those who are guided by the Almighty Himself can't go astray," Qadi added.

"The chosen ones are directly plucked out by the sanctified hand no matter where they are," Imam said, clucking with approval and nodding to himself in agreement. "Mere mortals like us can never hope to understand the divine secrets."

I could tell Mufti wanted to say something, but he kept quiet and simply rolled down his window and stared at the distant hills. The air hitting my face smelled of petrol.

A few seconds later, he rolled the window back up and squirmed in his seat. His solitary eye stared at Nofel who was lying at his feet, pretending to be asleep with his head on his paws.

The closer we got to the mosque, the heavier the military presence became. We were stopped at the intersection of Khayaban-e-Iqbal, which was thickly barricaded by tanks and desert cammo Hummers. The mood of the men manning this checkpoint was very different than at previous stops where the guards were noticeably younger. These men were seasoned and aloof, tense, and thoroughly unimpressed with anything or anyone.

They were robed in desert cammo fashioned into Saudi-style thobes strapped with black leather belts with brass buckles in the shape of a crescent; the official symbol of the Caliphate. They didn't care about the kind of car we were driving, or about the Caliphate's flag stuck on its hood, or about the rank and identity of its occupants. The invitation to step out of the car was in the form of a barked and authoritative command.

Having thoroughly searched the cabin and the trunk of our vehicle twice, they swiped its underside with long-handled mirrors and bug-detecting devices. Finished with the car, they patted us down roughly and a little too intimately for my liking. Then they requested Abba present his papers and ID.

At the end of the intersection I spotted a line of anti-aircraft guns, partially camouflaged by shrubs, flanking grassy strips that ran along the avenue. Nofel had sprung from the car and raced off to do his business. He emerged growling from a clump of bushes and stood at a distance as if waiting for us to pass muster. The cat dashed toward us the moment we were cleared by the guards and leapt back onto the floor where he curled up and pretended to go back to sleep. Everyone was quiet and Abba drove on with a grim face.

I closed my eyes and remembered the words of Pir Pullsiraat: *Khalifa has something very special planned, a real spectacle. If he is not stopped very soon, this world and the Next will need a major cleanup that will stretch into the not-so-foreseeable future.*

Bloody hell! The *real spectacle* couldn't just be a few hundred Caliphate diehards storming the gates of Heaven. It had to be much more than that, considering this huge military presence. What the hell was Khalifa planning? And what exactly did my handlers, who surely didn't look as if they were from this world, have in their minds about how to stop him? Was I part of some mysterious divine intervention which was coming into play?

Clearly, I was in the midst of a military-grade mayhem of cosmic proportion. And I was the one chosen to put a stop to all this madness. But how could I achieve it all alone, unless I was like a guided missile carrying a mysterious payload, which ought to be delivered at the right time, at the right place. I had no doubt in my mind the place was the Faisal Mosque.

Something soft touched my knees, something warm. I opened my eyes and gasped when I saw Nofel's curious eyes peeking over my knees and boring into mine. Mufti had a mischievous smile on his face, his eyes focused on the cat. All thoughts came to a screeching halt. It was like stopping on a dime at 110-miles-per and my eyes blinked in rapid succession from the shock.

"It looks like we're preparing for war," I said, laying my hand on Nofel's head and trying to pet him. He growled and jerked away but continued to stare me down. I tried to keep my thoughts to myself and not convey my mounting apprehension.

"Today the promise of the Caliphate of Al-Bakistan is going to see its fulfillment," Abba said. "What do you say Imam ji?" He gave the Imam's enormous thigh a slap.

"Jazaak-allah! Haji sahib. You've indeed spoken the truth," Imam said, grabbing the door handle and shifting himself about in his seat. "Mashallah!" He rolled the window down but immediately rolled it back up while I held my breath.

"Abba, I don't understand," I said, smelling a pungent odor that filled the cabin. Qadi lowered his window and frowned and Mufti and Abba did the same.

"Mufti sahib, why don't you give Ismaeel the details," Abba said.

"Haji sahib, we've sworn by our lives not to talk about this matter in front of anyone, regardless of his or her relationship to us," Mufti said. "Unless, of course, the person is authorized by Khalifa ji himself."

"Mufti is correct," Qadi said.

Abba scratched his temple but kept quiet. We were trailing a black Bentley by fifty meters or so and seemed to be in the midst of a motorcade of vehicles fit for a gaggle of Saudi princelings.

At the end of the Faisal Highway, separated by a series of manicured lawns, rose a gigantic, white tent-shaped structure of modern design which was the main prayer hall of the mosque plus its four towering minarets. The unadorned tapered caps glittered in the midday sun. The central complex was fronted by a broad courtyard large enough to accommodate 40,000 worshippers.

We turned onto a side road that was streaming with even more fabulously expensive cars than ours. The whole structure and its grounds were lined with armed military personnel standing at attention, their ubiquitous Kalashnikovs held tight across their chests. Abba pulled the Mercedes around the rectangular courtyard of the mosque and slowed at the main entrance. He parked about ten feet behind the Bentley that was already swarming with armed guards.

The guards pulled the Bentley's doors wide-open, guns trained and ready. Out stepped four men wearing black robes, red headdresses, and sunglasses. They were followed by a huge Siamese cat with thick lavish fur and an elegantly pointed face. The youngest among them pointed in our direction and said something to his companions. They all stared at us, as if trying to determine our identity.

"You know who they are?" Abba elbowed Imam.

"The Chairman of the CPVPV, and his three sons," Imam said.

"CPVPV?"

"Committee for the Promotion of Virtues and Prevention of Vice," Qadi answered firmly.

"Oh!"

Once the men and their cat were escorted to the entrance to the mosque and their Bentley valeted, the guards approached our car and pulled open the doors.

"Abba, are cats allowed in the mosque?" I asked.

"Of course! It has been so for centuries," Abba said, climbing out of the car and handing his keys to one of the guards.

As we waited to be escorted into the mosque, the roar of a monstrous engine ripped through the air. Heads snapped around as a black Ferrari with red stripes approached the reception area. It shuddered to a halt behind our car and the driver gunned the engine once more before killing it. A hush fell over the crowd as its gull-wing door rose silently toward the sky.

A tall, dark skinned man clad in a tight black leather robe, orange headdress and a pair of reflective wraparound sunglasses climbed out of the cockpit. He must have been at least in his fifties as his tight pointed goatee was snow white. Leaning his tall frame against the hood of the Ferrari he gave us a wave. We all waved back.

I whispered. "Who is this dude?"

"He heads the Ministry of Women's Affairs," Abba said, without taking his eyes off the man.

Standing beside Abba, Mufti swayed his head from side to side as if reciting scripture. His solitary eye glanced at me from time to time and made my flesh crawl. Nofel, as if in love with him, rubbed his torso against the man's legs. They seemed to have bonded all too well during the trip. And their proximity was making me increasingly nervous.

Suddenly a gust of wind swept through the area. Robes fluttered around bodies and headdresses fluttered in the air over everyone's head. In the next minute all was calm again and the wind died down as quickly as it had appeared. Nofel parted with Mufti and started to meow while staring at a cat with silky white fur. It seemed to have materialized out of nowhere. It wore a red collar and stood its ground about twenty feet from us and was the most beautiful cat I had ever seen.

Waving his tail, Nofel approached the newcomer, taking measured steps. The cats stood nose to nose looking into each other's eyes, then turned and sniffed each other's butts. Mufti looked restless.

"Nofel! Come back," he shouted.

Startled by Mufti's shout, the white cat dashed off and disappeared into a waist high green hedge that bordered the roundabout. Nofel threw a defiant glance at Mufti then took off after his newfound girlfriend and vanished into the hedge.

"Mufti ji, let it go—that's Nofel," Abba said. "He's not returning until he's had his way with her."

I overheard Qadi whispering into Imam's ear: "A pet's behavior is a reflection of its owner's."

Imam said nothing but gave a quick nod at Qadi as he tried to hide a sneer.

Mufti rubbed his palms, looking remorseful. He'd lost his telepathic buddy, his only witness to the inner workings of my mind. I was relieved to be able to think without somebody, or something, sifting through my deepest thoughts.

A couple of armed guards escorted us through the main entrance into a colonnade beneath the courtyard. This was the ablution area fitted with dozens of faucets. On the wall above the faucets was a sign: No Mobile Phones Beyond This Point.

We took off our shoes and handed them over to a lad who was too young to grow a beard, but who wore a 9 mm Uzi over his shoulder. He reminded me of Tarzan as he handed each of us a numbered token in exchange for our shoes and cell phones. He tucked each phone into the shoe of its respective owner and then looked at me expectantly.

"I left mine at home," I stated firmly.

He stepped forward and patted me down from head to toe to make sure I was telling the truth.

After doing our wudu and drying ourselves with towels brought on a silver tray by another armed beardless lad, we were taken upstairs to the courtyard. At the far end stood the triangular Prayer Hall guarded over by the four imposing vertical shafts, each 90 meters tall.

And then it came to me in a horrifying flash. What stood before me was the same structure which, in my dream, I'd taken to be a huge tent. I'd seen myself standing in this very courtyard at dusk, light in my hand, facing a veiled, black robed man whose overwhelming shadow concealed the light in a large dark band. Even though the place had begun to spook me out, I knew my mission was about to be revealed at long last.

In the porticoes bordering the courtyard stood hundreds of clone-like armed and bearded men who looked like ranks of toy soldiers from this distance. The party of the chairman of the CPVPV, including their cat, was more than halfway across the courtyard when we were told to proceed.

A gentle breeze blew from time to time making the midday sun pleasant against my face. As we walked on the cool tiles, escorted by a cortege of armed guards, I marveled once again at the size of the minarets, as they remained just as impressive as they had been in my boyhood memory.

The minarets looked different somehow today, though they still were very modern. A silvery metal covered their tapered heads, something I didn't remember seeing before. I was about to ask Abba about this innovation when a crescendo of noise rose in the air. Halting in our tracks we looked up, but the sky was clear as far as I could see. Suddenly, a dark cloud appeared over Margalla Hills and swiftly descended across the plain. In the next moment, the hills disappeared behind a wavy black curtain and I was swallowed by a wave of déjà vu.

"Ababeels!" I shouted.

Mesmerized, everyone watched the opaque black mass plunge toward the mosque, spiraling, swelling, and contracting. The noise became deafening as the sky continued to darken and the minarets disappeared from sight.

"Whoa!" I gasped. "Will you look at that!" I yelled, glancing at my companions for confirmation that this was indeed an astounding sight.

Mufti uttered a shriek, his hands covering his head and his lips moving rapidly. The ababeels cleared the mosque and flew south toward the city. The dark mass spiraled around once again then zoomed toward the mosque with incredible speed and dexterity. This time, the swarm passed overhead at a higher altitude, retreating back toward the hills, leaving behind a multitude of terrified faces and a loud recitation of the sura Al-Fil from the quivering lips of Imam.

Abba stared at me, opened his mouth to say something, but was too stunned to speak. Qadi had his eyes closed, his lips muttering a prayer.

"It's a sign," Abba finally managed to say.

As the party began moving again, all clearly shaken, I recalled my previous sightings of this mythic flock of ababeels: once in the company of Chaacha Khidr, another in the Dump at the edge of Paradise, and then once with Tarzan. All three were undeniably auspicious occasions well outside the confines of anything approaching normal reality.

The wide columned entrance to the Prayer Hall was flanked by more gunmen in the same modified thobe-camouflage as those outside. They stood at attention, shoulder-to-shoulder, and stared straight ahead. An opening in the middle of this formidable wall of security was manned by a different breed of guard. The monster cats, about twenty of them, were each restrained on leashes by handlers robed in hooded cloaks.

Our escorts brought us to a sudden halt about fifty feet from this final checkpoint. The Chairman of CVPVP and his three sons—their cat nowhere to be seen—walked into the grouping of cats. They made it through this living-breathing mind-reading scanner without incident. Once they had disappeared into the hall we were motioned forward. I emptied my mind as we began walking toward the phalanx of cats and their disquieting handlers.

Mufti led the party. I was the last one who followed just a few feet behind Abba. I avoided making direct eye contact with any of these peculiar creatures. All had dark coats and fierce golden eyes. They seemed restless in my presence with a few pulling on their leashes. Some hissed as I passed. By the time I was three-quarters of the way through the passage, every single cat had stood up snarling at me.

I held my breath and continued to move ahead purposefully. One large gray cat with bloodshot eyes broke rank from his comrades and approached me from the side. One of the guards raised his hand.

"Stop, right there!" he commanded.

I froze in my tracks. The cat stood on its hind legs, rested its forepaws on my chest and began sniffing me all over. The guard holding the leash of this red-eyed cat stepped forward and gestured for me to empty my pockets. As soon as I took out the Quran he grabbed the book and began flipping through its pages, his face twitching with a nervous energy.

"What's your name?" he demanded with a piercing look.

"Ismaeel."

"ID?"

I extracted my US passport from inside my robe and handed it over.

"American?" he asked, scratching his chin. "The mosque is off-limits to anyone not a citizen of the Caliphate."

Mufti gave the guard a knowing look and nodded his head approvingly.

"Correct. That has been the decree of the Khalifa for many years," he said.

Imam and Qadi exchanged glances but kept quiet.

Abba cleared his throat and glared at the man. He took a folded slip of paper from his pocket and held it between his fingertips in front of the guard's face.

"I'm Haji Ibrahim, a close friend of Khalifa ji," Abba said. "Ismaeel is my son and is here by the personal invitation of Khalifa ji."

The commotion caused a stir among the other cat-handling guards. They drifted over and eyed me curiously. The cats growled and strained at their leashes. Sweat broke out on my forehead but luckily was absorbed by my headband. Clearly, the self-induced draining of my mind had failed to do the trick. Even Chaacha had warned me the technique wasn't foolproof.

The guard returned my Quran, swiped the paper from Abba's hand and then disappeared into the Prayer Hall.

Feeling like a mouse in a trap before these angry cats—which still growled and strained on their leashes as if longing to pounce on me—I began to recite the surah Al-Nas under my breath. This sura was believed to be the most effective way to repel bad spirits.

At that moment something remarkable happened. The cats settled down and turned away from me. Out of the corner of my eye, I saw two enormous black cats standing unattended a short distance away. As soon as I made eye contact with them, the pair let out a howl. It took me

only a moment to recognize them as the same cats that had accompanied me to the shrine of Shah Jamal after the blast that killed Tarzan.
They were the cats of Pir Pullsiraat. Pir had left nothing to chance.

All eyes were on these two black newcomers when the guard with
Abba's piece of paper emerged from the hall.

"Let him go," he shouted over the howling match that had ensued
between the Pir's cats and the Khalifa's. Restraining their animals, the
guards stood down and moved away from me.

Taking my hand, Abba led our party into the Prayer Hall. The
sweeping interior was devoid of a single column and could easily accommodate 10,000 worshippers at one time. A profusion of geometrical
cutouts dotting its multifaceted walls let in plenty of light and ensured
the place was well illuminated. The hall looked strangely empty, except
for a cluster of about two hundred men gathered before the famous
book sculpture. The mihrab, carved in the image of the Holy Book,
indicated the direction of the Kaaba and was set against the qibla wall at
the far end.

Except for the massive chandelier with its golden wheel of
twinkling lights which hung over the center of the hall, the structure
was amazingly devoid of curved lines—a sharp departure from the
tradition.

"Abba, what was that piece of paper?" I asked, walking over a vast
blue carpet that was divided by parallel golden lines indicating rows.

"I knew it would be useful," Abba said, winking at me. He then
looked at Mufti. "Don't you agree Mufti ji?"

Mufti remained quiet. Abba put his hand on my shoulder.

"I had Khalifa ji fax me the letter of invitation for you—with your
name on it," he said aloud for the edification of everyone in the party.
Abba was known to always play his cards right.

"Excellent thinking, Abba," I said.

Abba knew a good many people in the crowd, as did his three
companions. Mufti, Qadi, and Imam drifted away and mingled with
their many acquaintances. Abba took me around and introduced me to

a bunch of his friends, mostly in their fifties and sixties. The Emir of Punjab was a solemn-faced, short stocky man with a squarish black beard that framed his large, round face; General Hajjaj Hijazi of the Caliphate Army was tall and lanky with big bushy eyebrows, a right eye that never blinked, and a blow-dried beard dyed unnaturally black. There was also a minister with a paralyzed arm and dimmed eyes, a group of four pompous-looking industrialists, and a handful of other assorted self-important luminaries with long meaningless titles.

Invariably, their welcoming smiles fizzled and turned into uncomfortable stares as soon as Abba informed them that I had just returned from America. The General stared at me fixedly, biting his lower lip as Abba described my miraculous skill as a hafiz, despite my prolonged and unsupervised immersion in the Great Satan. He merely nodded his head without comment, which made Abba look awkward and uncomfortable.

Later, as Abba was introducing me to a famous retired cricketer with a long conical beard and no mustache, I caught sight of Mufti standing beside the General, whispering in his ear and glancing at me as he rubbed his lips.

Presently, the sound of the azaan—the call to prayer—pierced the air and the crowd fell silent though there were many stragglers still wandering in. Abba gestured to me to follow as he walked along the qibla wall away from the gathering. Once the azaan had been said, Abba halted and began saying his four rakaat of Sunnah; the non-obligatory portion of the Friday Jumma Prayer. Standing about ten feet from Abba I began saying my namaaz too. Thoughts of Pir, who hadn't contacted me in some time, filled my head.

"I'm right here." His calm reassuring voice was like a sweet healing breeze. I was able to relax and take a deep breath.

"So good to hear your voice," I replied silently, bowing in *rukoo* with my hands on my knees and the cloth of my keffiyeh like a curtain over my cheeks.

"I've been worrying about you," Pir said.

"What were those ababeels for?" I raised myself briefly before going into prostration, my forehead touching the ground.

"On a day like today, all options are on the table," he said. "Extraordinary times call for extraordinary measures."

"What the hell is happening that's so extraordinary?" I hissed, straightening up on my folded knees, and then going into prostration again.

"I'll let you hear it directly from the horse's mouth," Pir said. "How is Mufti, by the way?"

"He thinks I'm a mole," I whispered, my lips touching the carpet. "He's let a friend of his in on this too," I said.

"Which friend?"

"General Hajjaj."

Pir remained quiet for a good five seconds before he continued.

"The mission has remained fluid," he said. "It's not over until the fat lady sings, as they say in America."

Chapter 25

The Khalifa

REALIZING THAT I'D BEEN in sajda for an unusually long time, I stood up. Abba had already finished his prayer and had left his spot. I'd been curious to know if that beautiful white cat was in any way connected to Pir.

"It took me quite an effort to find a willing candidate for Nofel," Pir said, responding to my unformed thought. "Now, no more questions."

"Thanks for sending your jinn cats," I whispered, but I could tell that Pir had gone off line.

As he broke the connection I heard people talking behind me. Hearing my name, I turned and saw Mufti, General Hajjaj, and Abba deep in conversation about fifty feet away. Sensing that I was looking at them, they stopped speaking. Then Abba said something to Mufti, pointed at his chest with his finger, and took off in my direction. My heart sank seeing the angry look on his face. Mufti must have said something compromising about me. Whether Abba believed Mufti or not was something yet to be determined. Mufti and General Hajjaj had become a threat faster than I had anticipated.

As Abba and I made our way back to the assembly, which had swelled considerably since we'd left, he touched my arm.

"Mufti thinks you're a spy," Abba said grimly. "And General Hajjaj seems to agree."

I shook my head and didn't say anything.

"I'm serious," he said tersely.

"He just doesn't like me for some reason."

"Just say it's not true," he halted in his tracks and gave my arm a squeeze, all the while staring into my eyes.

"Abba, please! Do you really think I'm a spy? Why would I be?"

"I don't know what to think anymore, Ismaeel. Just don't embarrass me in this place. It's all I ask."

"Abba, I'm sorry I asked you to bring me along. I was better off staying in Lahore."

He opened his mouth to say something but became distracted by a sound rippling through the congregation sitting shoulder to shoulder in seven perfectly even rows in front of the sculpture of the Holy Book. Abba seated himself next to the last man in the front row and gestured for me to sit next to him. To my dismay both Mufti and General Hajjaj, who had been walking parallel to us all this time, hurried to join the end of the second row, positioning themselves right behind me.

Suddenly, a hush fell over the assembly. The chandelier and circle of lights surrounding it dimmed, softening the room with a golden glow. Everyone stood up and looked expectantly toward the entrance of the hall.

Leading the procession that appeared were a dozen or so masked gunmen who marched crisply through the entryway, machine guns angled across their bodies and pointing toward the ground. Then a lone figure walked in carrying a black briefcase in his right hand. He was of medium height with a plump body, voluminous black robes, and a huge black turban.

"Long live al-Amir ul Momineen," the crowd chanted in unison, punching the air above their heads.

"Khalifa ji," Abba whispered sharply in my ear.

The Khalifa wore a brown shawl over his shoulders and glided over the carpet with such fluid motion that he appeared to be floating a few inches above the ground. He was trailed by a dozen men in plain khaki robes and stiff green peaked caps, their chests medaled, their collars decked out with bronze stars. These were pushing six flatbed trolleys piled with large black suitcases and boxes of various shapes and sizes.

The next wave in the procession consisted of a second team of masked gunmen. As the procession drew near, the crowd parted and the welcoming chant was replaced the shouts of *Allah Hu Akbar*. Following Abba's lead I threw my arms in the air and roared the battle cry.

Standing this far from the center it was hard to see Khalifa's face. All I could see of him was his big black turban bobbing among the curtain of arms. Khalifa took his position in the center of the first row of the assembly, flanked by his masked bodyguards.

I had to move several steps to my right to accommodate these new entrants. The men in khaki robes pushed their trolleys around the crowd then parked them beside the exquisite marble mihrab. The chant died away as Khalifa seated himself on the carpet, folded his legs under him and laid his hands on his thighs.

"What's in those boxes?" I whispered to Abba, as the men in khaki robes unloaded the carts.

"Only Khalifa ji knows," Abba whispered back.

When the whole assembly was seated, Imam, who'd been missing in action along with Qadi ever since we arrived in the hall, stood up at the far end of the front row and made his way to the minbar just to the right of the book sculpture.

"Masha-Allah!" Abba said, beaming with pride. "Our own Imam ji."

Imam stood on the first step of the minbar and began reciting the Friday *khutbah* into the microphone in Arabic. This was the most boring part of the otherwise colorful Friday Congregation I remembered from childhood. Everyone enjoyed it when the imam entertained us with miraculous stories about saints and prophets, jinns and angels. Then he launched into the khutba part of the ceremony and those who could get away with it caught a nap.

Meanwhile, the men handling the boxes had taken out a couple of large-frame computers from the suitcases, along with rolls of cables and wires and motherboards. Another suitcase contained a half dozen laptops, which were turned on and booted up by a team of four men. The unpacking and setting up of the equipment continued through the drab khutbah. By the time it was over, two spotless white screens had been unrolled and applied to each of the two marble pages of the book sculpture. I marveled at the incongruity of the display in here, in the sweeping interior of this magnificent edifice constructed for prayer.

The screens matched the exact dimensions of the diagonally held panels, and hiding behind their opaque whiteness the Kufic script of the surah Ar-Rahman engraved in gold. The rectangular column in the middle, separated from the screens by just a few inches and engraved with the name *Allah*, remained uncovered. The set up reminded me of a giant white bird with its wing folded preparing for flight.

"Abba, any idea what's going on?" I whispered, sensing a rising anxiety coursing through the crowd.

"Patience!" he hissed, jabbing my knee with a bony finger.

Imam finished his khutba, stepped down from the minbar and waddled back his to his place in line. Khalifa, raising his hand, gestured for Imam to halt.

"I, the Amir ul Momineen, command you to lead the Friday Prayer," Khalifa said in a thundering voice.

With his hands clasped in front of his belly, Imam turned around and stood on the leading prayer mat, placed about five feet in front of the Khalifa's spot, which was in line with the central column of the mihrab. An eerie silence griped the room. This was broken by a loud beautiful voice uttering the *niyyath*, the intention, which came from somewhere in the back rows.

Then everybody rose to their feet. The technicians stopped working and took their places among the worshippers. Imam said the takbir, touched his ear lobes, and began the two rakaat of *farz*, the obligatory portion of the Friday Jumma Prayer. I went through the motion of the namaaz without thought or feeling. The apprehension was driving me crazy.

The namaaz turned out to be a brief affair, followed by a boilerplate *dua* when everyone just sat with their palms up. Everything was business as usual up to this point.

As soon as Imam stood up and vacated the leading prayer rug, the techno-wizards in khaki robes and green service caps resumed their work and the assembly erupted into hushed chatter. A wooden divan with a Persian rug and a pair of black cushions resting on one side was placed a few feet in front of the book sculpture. A wooden table holding a laptop was placed at the right side of the divan.

"Abba, seems like we're going to be given a presentation," I said, looking at the pen-sized laser projectors being affixed atop a pair of tripods placed in front of the screens.

"It took us more than a decade to re-acquire the capability," he whispered.

"What capability?" Finally, he was opening up.

"To make bombs," he said in my ear.

"Really?" I said, feeling terrified of the prospect of Khalifa in possession of nukes again. And what did it have to do with the presentation? Though, it seemed clear that at last the pieces of the mystery were coming together and my questions were being answered.

Many years ago, the nuclear stockpile of the country along with its nuclear reactor had been disabled by spyware launched from a foreign government. It had been all over the news at the time. No government had taken responsibility, but everyone suspected either the U.S.A. or Israel—or both—of being the culprit.

"None can defy the will of Allah," Abba said.

"But how did we manage to escape detection, considering all these satellites spying over us day and night?" I leaned into him and glanced back over my shoulder. Mufti and General Hajjaj locked their eyes with mine, their jaws clenched in anger. They were watching my every move. Thanks to the background noise, my conversation with Abba was immune to their eavesdropping.

"Khalifa ji always thinks beyond the obvious," Abba said with a broad smile on his face. "He is the man who possesses special knowledge and strange powers."

The chatter died as Khalifa rose to his feet, the briefcase still clutched in his hand. Flanked by his bodyguards, the man glided forward, seated himself on his throne, and placed the briefcase in his lap. One of the khaki-robed technicians adjusted the microphone height for him.

Despite appearing a bit stooped, Khalifa was an imposing figure. His lush black beard reached the middle of his broad chest. It was dramatically marked by a four-inch wide stripe of stark white running from his lower lip to the beard's pointed tip. He craned his neck forward, throwing a sweeping glance over the crowd.

Without the customary prayer: *In the name of Allah, the Most Gracious, the Most Merciful,* the Khalifa began reciting the holy scripture. And as soon as he did, the same text started running across the upper portion of my visual field. I saw he was reciting from the last third of the surah number 9.

I wished that Pir could add on a translation feature to this clever program.

Khalifa paused, closed his eyes, and murmured something under his breath. Glancing at the audience, he resumed speaking in his native tongue in a clear and measured voice.

"All praise be to Allah, the Lord of the universe, without Whose command not a leaf would move. I, al-Amir ul Momineen, the commander of the faithful, the Khalifa of the Caliphate of Al-Bakistan, hereby declare that those who are present under this magnificent roof at the grandest of the houses of Allah outside Hijaz, the blessed land of Saudi Arabia, have been chosen to witness and be part of the miracle allocated to me by the Most High for the purpose of bringing an end to an era.

"I, al-Amir ul Momineen, the Khalifa of the Caliphate of Al-Bakistan, have been given the task of ushering the faithful into a new epoch to be marked by a worldwide jihad against the followers of the Great Deceiver, ad-Dajjal. On this blessed Friday, in this holy mosque, by the grace and will of the Most High, we intend to set forth a chain of events whose impact will continue until the world enters into yet another era—the time of peace—when the faithful will have conquered the world and declared Allah its sovereign ruler." He paused, his eyes sweeping the hushed crowd like a beacon. Then he threw his right hand into the air.

"Begin!" he cried, tossing a glance over his right shoulder.

Suddenly the screens sprang to life with multiple still images of the Faisal Mosque. The screen on the right displayed an aerial view of the mosque and seemed to originate somewhere in the adjacent Margalla Hills. The screen on the left was divided into four equal squares, each showing a close-up of the gleaming top third of one of the four minarets. It was only when a helicopter flew across the right screen that I realized the images were live.

As I leaned into Abba to ask about the metal coverings of the minarets' tops, Khalifa began speaking again.

"How many of you know what is going to happen today?"

Everyone except me raised his hand. Khalifa's head rotated back and forth as he surveyed the crowd. It stopped when his chin touched his left shoulder and his eyes fixed on me. My pulse quickened and my breath caught in my throat as he slowly raised his finger and pointed it directly at me. My back stiffened when our eyes met. I was a rat caught in the gaze of a cobra.

"Wonder of wonders! Haji Ibrahim's own son, Ismaeel, the carrier of light," he cried out, like it was an auspicious declaration of the greatest import. "This young man seems to be the only one who knows that he does not know. The rest of you know nothing." His voice thundered.

A nervous murmur rose then fell as hands were retrieved from the air, heads turned in my direction, and glances fell upon me like arrows from all sides. Holding his head high, Abba put his hand on my thigh. The warmth of his palm felt pleasant and comforting through my robe against my skin. Mufti and General Hajjaj whispered behind my back, but I couldn't make out what they were saying.

Khalifa looked over his shoulder again to where the men in the khaki uniforms and green service caps were still busy working on the computers and other devices. I exhaled and thought about Pir. I needed help. Where was he?

"Are we ready?" Khalifa addressed the men at his back.

The men nodded. Khalifa turned around and brought his lips to the microphone.

"This auspicious occasion requires me to offer my deepest regard for those who are not with us anymore. May Allah grant them the highest Jannah!

"It took seven years, seven long arduous years, and more than five thousand dedicated souls, to accomplish what you're going to witness today. They were the brightest and best the Caliphate had to offer. This is a true miracle." Khalifa looked back and extended his arm toward the men setting up the equipment. "These are the few who have been left behind to complete the miracle."

Khalifa looked at his bodyguard on the right. Obviously on cue, one of the men handed him a bottle of Paradise Water. A hushed whisper broke out behind me and Abba's face was unreadable except for a blank incredulous stare. I leaned toward him.

"Abba, do you know what he's talking about?" I whispered.

"Five thousand men have been transported to al-Jannah, and the very man who runs the transportation business for the Caliphate doesn't know a thing about it," he said, sounding absolutely mortified, confused and even angry. His answer left me shocked. I swallowed several times and cleared my throat as I tried to fathom what he had just said.

"Abba, I thought you knew everything about what's going on here."

"We were told it would be an underground atomic test somewhere in the desert of Sindh, to be broadcast live for the select few." Abba now sounded quite disturbed.

After taking several swigs from the bottle, Khalifa wiped his mouth with the back of his hand and continued.

"Before we move on, it's my duty to remind you: the higher one's station in the eyes of Allah, the harder it becomes to stay the course. If today you find yourself thinking too much about the task at hand, remember this verse of our great poet, Hazrat Qibla Llama: *Mad love jumped into the blaze without fear, while the Intellect stood by watching the spectacle from afar.*"

Khalifa opened the briefcase and brought out a black leather-bound book.

"Have I ever told you a lie?" he asked, bringing his lips close to the microphone.

"No!" the crowd roared in unison.

Khalifa nodded several times then raised the book over his head.

"I swear by the One in whose hands is my life that this book contains the keys to al-Jannah. One key for each of you." He opened the book, and waved it in an arc over his head. "O you people, would you believe me if I were to tell you that the book which I hold in my hand is soaked with a powerful invisible energy?"

"Yes! Yes! Yes!" the crowd chanted.

"Do you have faith in me that I will never lead you astray?" Khalifa said.

"Yes!" This time the affirmation was even louder.

"Would you all like to live an eternal life in al-Jannah and enjoy its delights?" Khalifa asked.

"Yes! Yes! Yes!" Again the words were deafening.

"Then, know that each page of this book is laced with enough power to transport fifty of you straight to Paradise—no questions asked along the way, no meeting with Munkar and Nakir, no accounting of your sins, no walk on Pullsiraat, no pits of boiling pus and no raging fire of Hell's inferno. Just an immediate route to Paradise."

He paused, took a swig off the bottle of Paradise Water, and glared at the stunned congregation. Abba's jaw had dropped almost to his chest, his brows almost touched his hairline and his eyes bulged. A combination of déjà vu and a flood of real memories overpowered me.

The whole thing seemed as if it had happened in a far-off time. My mind raced over the image of Tarzan and his exploding briefcase in that bathroom in the hospital. Next to him, I'd been holding a book just like the one Khalifa now raised in his hand. Shit! It was all making sense.

"Yes! Shit," Pir's voice slid through my cranium. Before I could respond, Khalifa began speaking again.

"Such is the reward for those who follow their Khalifa, those who believe in him. Why? Because they know that Khalifa represents the will of Allah. Now, I'm going to ask the last row to stand up and come to me one by one to receive their ticket to Paradise. They're to recite verse number one-one-one of the sura nine, which says: *Indeed, Allah has purchased from the believers their lives and their belongings in exchange for what they will have in Paradise. They fight in the cause of Allah, so they kill and get killed.*

"After each one of you has received the ticket, let it rest on the palm of your right hand, and wait for further instructions." Khalifa stood before the congregation.

I counted forty or so men who had gotten up from the back row. With their hands clasped below their navels, and their lips moving without making any sound, they walked single file along the edge of the assembly toward the khalifa who received each man with a handshake. Then he tore pieces of paper from the pages of the black book and placed one in each waiting palm.

"This is serious, Abba."

"I have no idea what Khalifa ji is doing today," Abba said, his voice now filled with anxiety. "But I can tell you this new technology often concerns an old fashioned businessman like me."

"Abba, are we all going to die?"

"Death comes at the appointed time—not a second late, not a second early."

"What happened to the minarets? What's that metal on their tops?"

"Khalifa ji had them modified a couple of years ago. Don't you think the sheen of the metal highlights them nicely?"

"Yeah, sure, nice work," I mumbled, wishing more than anything in the world that Pir would just beam me the hell out of here.

It didn't take long for the entire congregation to stand one at a time before Khalifa and receive his psychedelic benediction. From time to time a chopper or two flew across the screen on the right, the one with the aerial view of the mosque. The screens showing the minarets against the clear blue sky were devoid of any movement. Staring at these four odd looking metal tipped spires on the screen, I pushed my thoughts to Pir.

"Pir, what's going on?"

"You're in a better position to see what's happening. I'm just listening."

"We're all getting ready to take off. I don't want to die another death."

"Once you're part of Chaacha's team, you'll survive a hundred deaths."

"That's good to know, but small comfort," I said, brooding over the meaning of his answer.

The front row rose to their feet; I was the last one in line. Abba, having already received his potion stepped in reverse towards his seat, lest his back turn accidentally on Khalifa. Now it was my turn to stand face-to-face with al-Amir ul Momineen. His eyes had a hooded, dreamy quality yet were flecked with a fierceness that made him look crazed and otherworldly. He looked at me without blinking, his lips stretching ever so slightly in a smile. Then he extended his hand for the handshake.

"So it was you," he whispered, giving my hand a painful squeeze.

"It's a great honor to be invited by the Khalifa, al-Amir ul Momineen, on such an auspicious occasion," I said to acknowledge his position.

He turned around and took his seat on the divan, and picked up the microphone to speak. I was left standing in front of the not-so-friendly crowd. I had not been dismissed, nor had I been given the key to Paradise.

"Today, I've received two clear and righteous indications from the Most High. The first: the ababeels, which some of you might have seen on your way here today. Never before have they been seen in such large numbers. Remember, these same birds once turned the mighty army of Abrah into pulp. Today, their presence in the vicinity of this mosque is the clear and precious sign we have been waiting for."

Keeping his eyes on the crowd, Khalifa raised his hand and pointed toward me.

"The second auspicious sign is this young man standing here in front of you. He was shown to me in a dream; a dream in which he carried the *noor* in his hand, the light of Allah. By his presence with us here today, my dream has become a reality. Those who have eyes to discern the divine signs need no further reassurance that Allah has graciously accepted our hard work."

He put the book down on the divan and struck the keyboard of the laptop in front of him.

Standing in front of so many people, all of them staring at me, was an unsettling and terrifying experience to say the least. My legs felt like they were filled with lead and my mind was a chaotic frenzy of energy. It was almost impossible to have a clear thought. Everyone had their right hand held in front of their navel, the stamp-sized ticket to Paradise resting in their palm. They looked to be in a trance.

Khalifa nodded twice at the men in khaki uniforms who were seated at the outer edge of the screens. The men, waiting for this signal, began furiously typing on their laptops. A hum filled the air. I felt a deep rumbling vibration under my feet as if far underground, the earth was being moved about by heavy machinery.

Vertical cracks appeared in the metal shields over three of the minarets. The fourth remained unchanged. The cracks widened and the six distinct metal plates moved away from the minarets like the petals of a flower. My heart began to pound. Khalifa's voice boomed across the hall.

"Today is the Day of Judgment for our enemies and our enemies' friends. By the grace and decree of the Almighty, I, the Khalifa of Darul Islam, declare Jihad against Darul Harb—the land of the infidels."

Chapter 26

Ababeel

HOLY SHIT!

"Stay strong, Ismaeel," Pir's cool even voice purred through my head.

"I'm trying," I replied silently, turning to look at Abba. My father, like every other man in the room, had his eyes fixed on the screen and his fist pressed to his side.

Stunned, I stared at the screens as the surreal blooming continued atop three of the four minarets. The metallic panels continued to slowly fall away to reveal missile warheads rising toward the sky like giant tubes of lipstick. It was all so simple and obvious. Damn!

Khalifa began speaking again.

"What you see on the screens are indeed as they appear, missiles, the fruit of the labor of those who are no longer with us in body, but who remain very much with us in spirit through their sanctified work. Each of three missiles is loaded with a very powerful nuclear warhead."

With a pointer he scribbled across his laptop screen. Names appeared in red on the top of each of the four images: Abu Bakr, Umar, Uthman, Ali—the four Caliphs of Islam who succeeded Prophet Muhammad—the name Ali was on the image of the tower that had not opened.

"Abu Bkr will be heading for Israel to annihilate the eternal enemies of Islam. Umar is destined for Iran, the troubled land of the Shias, the apostates who, according to my intelligence sources, are preparing right now to fire their own atomic missile, the Mehdi, on us.

Uthman is headed for India, the land of the polytheists and conspirators. We did not have enough raw materials for the tower of Ali, but if we had enough uranium, Ali would have been aimed at the Americans in the Strait of Hormuz."

He paused. The ominous vibration coming from under my feet had gotten a lot louder and my whole body quivered. The missiles continued their rise into the sky and Khalifa glanced at the live video feed for a few seconds before turning back to his mesmerized audience.

"O you who believe! Know that the time has come for the Final Battle. O you who are faithful! Know that Allah has prepared a great reward for you in the Next world, and a grievous punishment for those who rebel. O you who desire none other than Allah! Know that I am commanding Ismaeel, son of Ibrahim, to recite to you the surah Al-Qiyamah."

My head snapped. He was addressing me! I ran through the holy text as it streamed across my eyes. I pulled up the desired surah in less than five seconds and gasped when I saw the English translation running beneath the Arabic text. Pir had indeed thrown in the upgrade for my edification.

"That's exactly what I need!" I thought, beaming my thanks to Pir.

"Since you've wished for it."

"Do you think I can pull it off?"

"Shush!"

Khalifa's voice was booming over the crowd again.

"All missiles will fire simultaneously, bringing our sacred jihad to the enemies of Allah. Once they disappear from sight, everyone here must recite their *shahaada* three times, and then place the ticket to Jannah under their tongue. Am I clear?"

The crowd started chanting *Allah hu Akbar* over and over.

"After the recitation of Al-Qiyamah, I will push the button and seal the fate of all the evil-doers forever." His voice sliced through the deafening battle cry. "O Allah accept our sacrifice as you have Hazrat Ibrahim's."

The Khalifa stood up, glided over the carpet toward me, and tore off one of the tiny paper squares from the last page of the book. Keeping my eyes lowered, I opened my right hand and prayed it wasn't shaking enough for him to notice. Without a word he pressed the little paper into the palm of my hand and then closed my fingers tightly around it.

"I can tell from your face that you're dying to wet your tongue with the sweet water of Hoz e Kausar," he said.

"Surely, your eminence, surely," I muttered, keeping my gaze fixed on the floor and remembering the orange Hazmat tape stretched around that most famous of ponds, with its contaminated water spilling over the ground.

Suddenly, a solid wall of noise consumed the place, growing louder by the second. The sunlight pouring in through a multitude of skylights and cutaways in the walls dimmed as if behind a bank of dark clouds. The warm glow of indoor light was transformed into a sickly piss-yellow haze. Khalifa's head shot around as the whole congregation stared upward.

"Here they come again," Khalifa hissed in a low voice.

A look at the screens showed the missiles had disappeared behind a dense black wall. Ababeels!

"It's time, Ismaeel," Pir's voice gave me jolt. "Take your weapon out, now!"

"Weapon?"

"The Quran! Take it out of your pocket. Pretend you need it for inspiration. Even the best of hafiz can forget a line or two."

With a fluid motion my hand disappeared into my robe and slid the Quran out of my pocket and pressed it to my navel.

"Done."

"When you're half-way through the surah, open the Quran and rip out the opening sura, al-Fatiha, then tear out the last page, sura, Al-Nas. Rip them right out of the book. Drop the pages. Raise the book above your head and close one of your eyes. Use your hand to cover it if you have to. And that's all there is to it."

Shit! I remembered his words from a long time ago: *One day this Quran may have to be ripped apart to have its power activated.*

I remembered how he and Chaacha Khidr had laughed at me for having expressed my fear of dying young. At the time, I thought they were joking.

One thing was certain; I wasn't getting out of here alive, one way or the other. I stared at the little square of magic paper in my hand. The option of getting beamed out of here and straight into Paradise was starting to look really good. The alternative, of course, was getting torn to shreds by the mob for the crime of blasphemy. I wasn't too keen on that either, particularly since it would probably involve Abba's enraged face leading the pack.

"Ismaeel, remember. You are on Pullsiraat—one slip and you're gone. Failure is not an option."

"I know. I know." Unfortunately, I knew quite well.

The noise of the birds died away. As their mass sped from the mosque, the full light of day returned. The missiles had risen a good fifty feet above their point of exit and stood fully unsheathed against the clear blue sky.

My heart began to pound inside my chest. Dying for a glass of water, I glanced over at Abba who sat at the far end of the first row staring at me. His face was twitching; never a good sign even at the best of times. He gave me a series of quick nods. The poor man genuinely seemed to have no clue about the elaborate proceedings Khalifa had underway. If we survived, Abba would banish me forever, or shoot me in the head, or better still, have me wear a Mujahid Vest and detonate myself at the time and place of his choosing.

The pirate-faced Mufti, sitting behind Abba in the second row, looked restless. He elbowed General Hajjaj whose face was a mask of resignation. They whispered to each other while glancing back and forth at the screens. Did they know what was going on? Or were they just as clueless and out of the loop as my Abba?

"Khalifa is master at keeping his real intentions to himself. No one in this hall knew the full scope of his mission," Pir elaborated.

"But that's not possible."

"It's possible when you've made a pact with the master chemist."

"The Devil? But that can't be." *But why not*? I thought. If Hell and Paradise were real, the Devil had to be real as well.

"Concentrate!" Pir commanded.

Khalifa returned to his divan, sat down and stared into the screen of his laptop. I craned my neck forward and brought my dry quivering lips to the microphone. After clearing my throat a couple of times, I weakly uttered the *bismillah*: In the name of Allah, most Gracious, most Compassionate. Then I began reciting, as the surah's text slid across my eyes from right to left. Underneath, the English translation ran from left to right. Pir's attention to detail was absolutely marvelous.

I swear by the Day of Resurrection.
And I swear by the reproaching soul.
Does man think that We shall not gather his bones.
Yes! We are able to make complete his very fingertip.
Nay! Man desires to give the lie to what is before him.
He asks: When is the Day of Resurrection?
So when the sight becomes dazed,
and the moon becomes dark,
and the sun and the moon are brought together,
Man shall say on the day: Whither to fly to?
No! There shall be no place of refuge!
With you Lord alone shall on that day be the place of rest.
Man shall on that day be informed of what he sent before and what
he put off.
Nay! Man is evidence against himself, though he puts forth his excuses.
Do not move your tongue with it to make haste with it,
surely on Us is the collection...

"Surely on us is the task to deny these lustful bastards the Paradise," Pir's voice echoed in my head. "Now, let's see some action, Ismaeel."

Continuing the recitation, I opened the Quran and tore its first page and then the last from its leather-bound spine. The torn pages fluttered to the ground along with my ticket to Paradise. A scream shattered the air.

"What are you doing?" somebody shouted from the front row.

"Unbelievable! Did you see what he just did?" Mufti bellowed in rage as he sprang to his feet. "He has torn the pages of the Holy Book."

General Hajjaj stood up and fixed me with stares of rage that pierced my resolve.

"Did you all witness what he has done?" he roared. "Blasphemy!"

The disordered chaos ignited and spread through the assembly like a brushfire. Everyone leaped to their feet, their faces writhing and red with anger and barely contained as they stood like the feral jinn cats. I just stood there, not even able to draw a breath or move a muscle. There was no means of escape.

Only Pir could come up with such a freakish scheme. My legs trembled and I looked around for something to hold on to.

"That's Haji Ibrahim's son!" someone cried out. "Where is Haji Ibrahim!" somebody else demanded hoarsely.

"The blasphemer must be killed first. Now!" a voice screamed hysterically from the back row.

Every man in the room was on his feet and heaving with rage. The crowd was ready to spring, all except Abba. He just sat there with his head in his hands as he stared at the ground in front of him. He couldn't even bear to look at me.

Sweat poured from every inch of my body. Panicked, I looked over my shoulder at Khalifa who sat on his divan a few feet behind me. He gritted his teeth and his lips moved over them like an animal. His face quivered and his brows arched as he stared at me.

Bolting up, Khalifa lunged at me while his bodyguards trained their guns on my head. The ominous click of a dozen *safeties* being switched off was the only sound in the place. Every heartbeat in the room waited for al-Amir ul Momineen to give the sign as to what to do next.

"Shit!"

"Shut one of your eyes, Ismaeel! Do it now!" Pir screamed inside my skull.

As Pir's voice faded the sound of static short-circuiting came from the Quran in my hand.

"Put the Quran in your palm and raise it over your head," Pir said, as a luminous crack like a miniature lightning bolt appeared in the black binding of the book. With one eye shut I raised the book over my head.

Khalifa grabbed my arm and screamed in my ear.

"What the fuck are you doing?"

"It's the light..."

The moment I uttered these words, the book burst into brilliant white effulgence. Millions of tiny laser-like bands of molten light shot out in every direction. The air shimmered with palpable energy and crackled with what sounded like a bug zapper going to work on a hapless swarm of mosquitoes. The rage, which a moment ago had seized the crowd, was replaced by stunned nervous confusion. It was one step from utter pandemonium.

Khalifa let go of my arm. Dazed, he looked around and then staggered for a moment before dropping to his knees. His eyes had stopped blinking and he just looked ahead with an empty gaze. Oblivious to my presence, he sank onto his folded legs, his hands placed on his thighs. He might have been praying. Two of his bodyguards lurched ahead and fell flat onto their guns, their noses smashed against the ground.

The men in the khaki robes, who had been hammering away at their laptops, slumped where they sat. In a matter of seconds the stupor spread through the entire assembly. People staggered, their knees hitting the ground with a thud. They were oblivious of their tickets that had fallen to the ground.

In less than a minute, everyone had slumped into the same posture as Khalifa with their palms resting on their thighs. Everyone, except Mufti and General Hajjaj. Curiously, they had remained standing and seemed unaffected by the light. Mufti raised his arm and pointed his finger at me.

"Sorcerer!" he screamed, and then fled toward the entrance followed by General Hajjaj close on his heels.

"Pir, what the hell is going on?"

"Phototherapy—designed to give the mind a hard reset," Pir said.

"Hard reset?"

"It's the light of the higher spheres concentrated in the book form. It'll purify their minds, so their brains can resume working like those of normal human beings," Pir said.

I kept my hand over my shut eye, and grappled with the meaning of what he had just said, as I watched Mufti and General Hajjaj cutting through the radiant beams illuminating the Prayer Hall.

"Well, apparently it didn't work on Mufti and General Hajjaj— just so you know."

"Because they both are one eyed," Pir said. "For the light to work, it has to enter both eyes."

I remembered how the right eye of General Hajjaj didn't blink when Abba had introduced me to him. Now I knew why.

There was long pause, before he continued. "We'll worry about them later. Let's get the job done. You must abort the launch. Now!"

"Yes," I said, returning to where Khalifa kneeled like a statue, his body prickled by hundreds of tiny points of light. He didn't respond, even when I waved my hand in front of his face a few times.

Holding the book over my head, I went over to the divan, sat down, and examined the screen on Khalifa's laptop. It displayed the same shots as were projected on the bigger screens behind me. At the bottom of the display were two thumb-sized buttons: the red one on the right was labeled with the words *Allah hu Akbar* in black letters. The green one on the left had the word *Inshallah* on it. Sliding my finger over the track pad, I moved the pointer to the green button. Inshallah; *God willing*, could very well mean the same as Allah hu Akbar; *God is great* under the present situation. I moved the pointer to the red button and scratched my head.

"It has to be the green button," Pir said.

"What do you mean by, has to be?" I said aloud.

"Do what you think is right?" he said. For a fleeting moment I saw myself tightroping over Pullsiraat: one wrong move and all would be blown to hell.

I moved the pointer to the green button, said a prayer, and clicked on it. A dialog box appeared: Are you sure you want to quit? I clicked yes. A faint humming vibration shook the room. Then the missiles started to slowly retract into the modified silos of the minarets. I exhaled a sigh of relief, though shaking uncontrollably.

"Done!" I cried, noticing the glow of the book dimming.

"Congratulations! You've saved the Caliphate from becoming a mountain of radioactive ash," he said.

"Caliphate? I thought we've just saved India, Iran, and Israel?"

"I'm not sure if the Khalifa's nukes would have even worked, to tell you the truth, but the retaliatory strikes would have killed a hundred million people in the Caliphate alone," Pir explained.

"Would you please guarantee me a place in Paradise now? I mean for real."

"We're not done yet," Pir said. "Now you must help Khalifa get to Paradise."

"What?"

"Put one of the little squares in his mouth."

"But he should be in Hell!"

"Just do it."

Feeling confused, I walked over to Khalifa, with the faintly glowing Quran in my left hand. I picked up the book of tickets lying beside his knees. There was still half a page of little squares left in it. I tore one off and shoved it in his mouth over his teeth. He showed no signs of consciousness. He shivered for a second or two then his eyes rolled up and turned white.

Khalifa fell backward and began convulsing like a fish in a skillet. Saliva poured from his mouth and his face was a mask of agony as his labored breath rattled in his chest. The master chemist's Paradise Potion was certainly not for the faint of heart. As I watched the poor wretch flailing around, I remembered my own experience in the bathroom of the hospital. Had I suffered like this? There was no way to tell. The mighty had surely fallen.

The missiles had fully descended back into the silos and the huge panels were slowly closing. A few seconds later and the minarets were just harmless minarets once again. Then the book stopped emitting light and went out like an extinguished candle. In my hand was a weightless mound of black ash. I blew on it and watched the tiny flecks swirl into the air.

Khalifa was completely still, his eyes were closed and his chest ceased heaving. I put my thumb on his jugular. He was dead!

"Done." I said, turning my palm and pouring the remainder of the ash over Khalifa's face. It was impossible to fathom that the mission might be coming to a successful end.

"Mission accomplished," Pir said.

"What's going to happen to the rest of them?" I asked, glancing at Abba, who, like everyone else, looked like he was under some kind of spell.

"They'll be detoxed from all those years of drinking Paradise Water, but not without losing some of their memory. You've been drinking it too, by the way. We'll need to get you into rehab, too," he chuckled.

His words made me realize that never before had I felt such an urge for Paradise. It wasn't exactly a burning desire, but it was there—an unmistakable, insinuating presence, like an itch you don't really want to scratch. I could only imagine the intensity of longing these men must have had for Paradise after having drunk the stuff for so many years.

"How am I supposed to get out of here, Pir?" I asked, picking up my own tiny slice of Paradise from the blue carpet where it had fallen during my Quran-shredding session. If push came to shove and in my experience it usually did, and I was captured by the Khalifa's men, this

Asif Ismael | 325

could just be my only way out.

"No! No!" Pir said. "You're not to do that."

"I deserve it," I said defensively, staring at the corpse of Khalifa where it lay in an inglorious heap on the floor. How on earth this man, who'd planned to destroy half of the world, was being given a free pass to Paradise was an affront to my already boggled imagination. Not fair!

"First of all, no human has ever been tested for using the ticket twice, and you surely don't want to be a lab animal on this one. Secondly you can't be leaving your body at the scene of the crime for reasons too complicated to explain right now," Pir said.

"So what is going to happen to me? What do you have in mind?" I said, as I heard a familiar noise growing louder. The ababeels were back, darkening the sky over the mosque once more.

Suddenly the air was filled with the howling of the cats. They poured into the Prayer Hall in waves, hundreds, perhaps thousands of them. They were gigantic and reminded me of the rats materializing off the walls of my grave. They were followed by armed men in black uniforms.

"They're here! Pir!" I screamed in my mind. "I'm willing to take full responsibility for cashing in on my ticket. I want out!"

"Don't! I'm dispatching someone to pick you up. Meanwhile, take refuge behind the Holy Book," he ordered.

Still clutching my ticket, I dashed towards the book sculpture. Once behind it, I looked through a vertical chink of its central column. The cats and their handlers had advanced halfway through the hall.

"Pir, I don't think I'm going to make it." I stared at the ticket pinched in my fingers.

"Patience."

Suddenly, it looked as if night had fallen over the place and the cats' cries were drowned out by a deafening screech. Like an arrow, a long dark band shot through the wide entrance of the prayer hall. The stripe widened into a flying carpet of black feathers. I tried to see the traditional stones they carried in their talons and beaks. I remembered how the ababeels had rained them down upon the elephants of Abrah's army and turned them into pulp. But these birds were far too swift for me to be able to see if they carried the mythic stones.

A flash of light momentarily illumined the marble of the sculpture. Startled, I looked back. Chaacha Khidr was standing about three feet from me, his eyes shining as bright as ever, his solitary tooth sticking out of his gummy smile. He wore his usual clothes; the white dhoti and kurta with a long white cloth around his neck like a shawl.

"Babu Ismaeel, your ride has arrived," he said, greeting me with a big smile.

Speechless, I stared at his bright, happy face. Then he stepped forward and peeked through the opening.

"Pir likes to play rough," he said.

The birds, now obscuring the ceiling, formed a huge black spiral overhead which began to circle the interior of the hall at a dizzying speed. Under the golden glow of the chandelier hanging from the center of the place, Mufti appeared with his hands over his temples as he stared above.

The cats halted in their tracks. Overhead the feathered mass of pure energy broke off into many spirals like coiled springs ready to crush the mighty cats.

"It's going to take a lot of cleaning to dispose of all that cat pulp," Chaacha said in a matter of fact tone. He put his hand on my shoulder.

"Come. Let's go!" he said, as we burst into light.

Chapter 27
The Beginning

WE LANDED ON PATCH OF SOFT GRASS, enveloped in a cloud of haze. Chaacha Khidr was standing next to me, his hand on my shoulder. My ears still roared from the screeching of the ababeels and my head felt like it was caught in a high-speed blender. I rubbed my eyes and tried to focus on where I was.

A hundred images crashed over my brain like a tsunami; nose-diving black birds taking out an army of snarling cats and leaving a sea of red pulp in their wake; nuclear tipped rocket minarets armed with a deadly payload rising into the sky and readying for lift-off; Pir's genius in thwarting a global nuclear holocaust without shedding so much as a drop of human blood; and countless more visions all surreal and unfathomable to the rational mind.

My vision cleared and I continued to feel overwhelmed. I was standing beneath the arched entrance to the Guest House of Paradise. As I gazed at the place, I realized that, except for the headband around my forehead, I was once again stark naked. I darted away from Chaacha who was fully dressed, of course, in search of some leafy vegetation to cover my private bits.

"Ahem!" Chaacha uttered behind me, clearing his throat. "You may use this for the time being," he said, taking the white cloth from around his neck and waving it like a flag.

Taking the fabric, I recognized the two unhemmed sheets of white cotton which were the sacred garb of the Hajj pilgrim, the *ihram*. I wrapped one sheet around my lower body and the other around my upper, leaving my right shoulder and arm bare.

"Much appreciated, Chaacha," I said, tightening the knot over my waist so the thing wouldn't swing open as I walked.

"We haven't used ababeels in a long time so it is good you were able to witness them in action."

"I've got to give you people a lot of credit for destroying Khalifa's planned event without spilling any human blood." I could not stop wondering about the aftermath of such a brilliantly executed operation. My head was whirling.

But it was with mixed feelings that I realized I'd never see my father again. A small price to pay, I suppose, considering the scope of the mission which essentially was saving a good chunk of humanity from mindless annihilation.

A smile rippled over Chaacha's face, once more exposing the solitary shark tooth on his lower jaw.

"Take a few deep breaths before we move on," he said slowly.

I did as instructed, taking in more of my surroundings with each breath as I calmed down bit by bit. A breeze carried the delicate strains of a harp being played nearby and the air was infused with the *Night Blooming Queen*. My body was warm, light, and expansive. I flowed into and filled the space around me, merging with a connectedness I had never before experienced.

"At last that ordeal is over." Part of me still wondered if any of it was real. A wave of pleasure coursed through my body like a gentle orgasm. I thought of Sophie, of the time I would be spending with her in the Greek Quarters by that waterfall of Kafiristan; and of Laila, the woman of unreal passion, with or without Hoor Afza, who'd died while kissing me in that dark dilapidated bathroom. I wanted her as well. With time, she would understand how important Sophie was to me. I hoped that Laila would have no objections to my seeing her and that one day the three of us could make a home together where Laila wouldn't have to wear the burqa.

"The end is just the beginning, Babu," Chaacha said, waking me from my reverie. He wasn't smiling now. This was the first serious expression I'd seen on the kindly old face since our descent on the Pullsiraat over the fiery abyss. I didn't quite get what he meant and, once more, I began to feel uneasy.

"Let's go and see Pir," he added, motioning me toward the red canopy on the green slope that merged with the horizon.

We followed a stone path that meandered through the grass and watched as a huge orb slowly rose from the horizon into the radiant purple sky like a gigantic balloon. A tumbling brook of fragrant milk flowed nearby and a lazy stream of scented honey glinted in the morning light. The melody of the unseen harpist became clearer as we made our way over the soft grass. Butterflies fluttered on the delicate petals of iridescent flowers, bird-song filled every fruit-laden tree with pleasing melodies, and angels darted about or hovered in delightful formations.

My pleasure intensified when I beheld a host of gorgeous women running about playing hide-and-seek amidst a large area of gardenias. Their skin glowed with ethereal light, their ankles were translucent, and their laughter like tinkling petals that echoed the cosmic music of the spheres. Beauty of unlimited varieties rose to greet my eyes like mist from the lake of eternal spring.

Passing by the dark skinned lads in their red loincloths, we stepped onto the marble floor of the Guest House. They were all there, seated on their divans: Pir, Tarzan, and Laila still in her burqa. They all stood as I approached.

"Good job, Ismaeel. I'm very proud of you" Pir said, shaking my hand warmly.

"Thanks." I looked into his jubilant eyes, hoping there would be no sign of rebuke about any of my behavior lurking within. My journey had indeed been marked by my own stumbles and indiscretions. "I know I could have done better."

"Enough. You can't argue with success," Pir said.

Without saying more, I moved over to Tarzan who seemed eager to speak to me.

"Sir, the world can never thank you enough," he said while he gave me a big bear hug.

"Tarzan, you're the real hero. In that jungle down there, you did justice to your name."

"Thank you for saying that, sir," he chuckled before letting out a roar of laughter.

I left him and made my way over to Laila, who grabbed my arms, her big black eyes locking onto mine with intense love. Tears moistened the veil over her gorgeous eyes, her chest rising and falling heavily as she looked at me.

"It feels like you've been gone for an eternity," she cried. "I'm still not used to how time passes here."

"I know. It feels so strange." Glancing over her shoulder I saw the crowd of women gathered around the cage that sat a hundred meters away. The last time I was here, that cage had been filled with big black baboons from the Dump; those bothersome creatures that'd chewed the book and somehow landed in Jannah. I wondered if they were still here or if Pir had managed to do away with them.

I joined Pir and the others on the divans, while Chaacha took off toward the cage. Halfway there, he turned and waved at us.

"Babu, when you're finished you should come take a look," he shouted, pointing at the cage.

I waved back. My mind bubbled like a pot on the boil, one forgotten for an eternity. I was overpowered by the need to understand all that had happened. The first thing I wanted to know was "Dead, or alive? Which am I?"

One of the boys handed me a chilled goblet made of transparent gold that dripped with condensation and overflowed with an effervescent pale liquid that tasted just like champagne. Pir lit a cigarette and held the red and white Gold Leaf pack to me. "Smoke?"

"No thanks," I said, thinking that a person of his stature should be above the earthly addictions.

"When you involve yourself with the affairs of the earth, you become addicted to combustion." His voice rose inside my head, reading my thoughts again. I pulled off the headband with a snort of laughter.

"I see there's excellent reception here! I believe this is yours."

"You can keep it," he said with a smile. "Think of it as a souvenir."

"With pleasure." I wrapped the headband around my left wrist.

Suddenly quite serious, Pir asked, "Is something bothering you, Ismaeel?"

"Just wondering if the mission was completely successful."

"Of course! Most definitely"

"But the rockets are still there," I said, not able to believe my part of the mission was finished.

"Not to worry. They'll be eliminated in phase two, which will all be divulged in good time."

"Ah!"

"Anything else?"

"Well, I was just wondering what my 'living arrangements' are going to be."

Pir let out a deep roar of laughter that rippled across the serene air of the Guest House.

"Well, what exactly did you have in mind?" he asked, flashing a barely contained grin.

"I don't mind staying here," I said, glancing at Laila though feeling tense and awkward since I had to tell her about Sophie—the sooner, the better.

Pir shook his head, giving me another closed mouth grin.

"Why would you want to live a meaningless existence?" he asked in a gentle voice. "A life without a worthy goal is all but wasted. You'd be bored to death here."

Shocked by his answer, I glanced at Tarzan who was smiling and nodding in agreement.

"Life on earth is so much more interesting, sir," he said. "Much more fun. You don't know from one minute to the next if you'll even be alive, or dead. What better place to live than always on the edge? And here—boredom alone would drive you crazy! Here we live without a calling.

"Everything you want is handed to you. Anything imaginable is created for you instantly just by willing it. After a while, everyone starts missing earth. Trust me, sir, I'm telling you from personal experience. Believe me, I'd go back there if I was allowed to," he said, scratching his sideburn.

"There's a lot going on down there that you're an integral part of, Ismaeel," Pir said, ignoring Tarzan's not so subtle hint. His voice was calm but firm.

"I'm not sure if I'm ready to see my father," I admitted to him and myself. I had no desire to return and face Abba after everything we'd been through, even if the so-called *Phototherapy* had given his brain a hard reset.

"You're going back to your work," Pir said.

"My work?"

"Ismaeel, it's time for you to understand something; something that is a critical. Right now, you are in a world that exists parallel to the world you started your journey from," he said.

"Parallel world?"

"Yes. There are countless possible outcomes to each and every moment that passes in the material world, and each outcome is creating a unique world of its own," he said. "And every now and then, these worlds intersect, making it possible to have the outcome in one altered by affecting the other. Do you understand?"

"I'm not sure," I said, as I tried to tease the meaning out of what he'd just said.

"Okay, let me make it simpler," he said, rubbing the side of his neck and thinking. "We wanted to follow some of the logical outcomes along a linear time, if over at the Caliphate certain things or events were to proceed uninterrupted, or without the higher intervention."

I'd begun to understand, feeling somewhat uneasy. Parallel worlds of all possible outcomes. How was that possible? The sheer number of such worlds could be staggering. Was he talking about infinity?

"You were sent in order to preempt the catastrophe the Caliphate was rushing headlong into; the logical, disastrous, and inevitable outcome when people confuse the letter with the spirit of faith."

"So you're telling me that I'd been sent into a world that didn't exist in the normal sense, except in the domain of possibility?"

"All kinds of things are employed to ensure the smooth running of the most screwed up of all places in the universe, the earth. You must remember: there's nothing out there except a luminous dark emptiness. It's all within."

We were interrupted by Chaacha's shout. Standing next to the cage, surrounded by a coterie of women, he was waving his arm in the air.

"Ismaeel! Come!"

"Let's go take a look," Pir said, standing up. "Walking will do you good."

Like a zombie who was running out of juice, I walked alongside Pir and Tarzan. Laila had remained seated. I could feel her gaze on my back like a warm presence.

"How did you make Khalifa and me share the same dream?" I'd been wondering about that for some time.

"Admittedly, that was Chaacha's big idea in order to make the mission foolproof. Thanks to that little trick, Khalifa, already a highly superstitious man, took you as a genuine sign from the Almighty."

"But Pir, how's it done?" I was overwhelmed with curiosity.

"Oh, come on now! You can't expect a magician to give away his tricks." Nearby, Chaacha giggled and nodded enthusiastically.

The cage was surrounded by a dozen or so girls. Their translucent garments had a warm pinkish hue that made their skin look deliciously creamy. They were beautiful with their huge eyes and sleek voluptuous curves. Giggling mischievously among themselves they parted to let me stand next to the iron bars between Chaacha and Pir, who seemed oblivious to their presence.

In the far corner of the cage sat a gloomy-looking young man in his twenties, stark naked and covered with black hair. His chin rested on his knees and his black beard flowed over his shins. His arms were clasped around his calves and his face was a mask of haunted bewilderment.

"Khalifa!" I gasped, staring at the unmistakable but a good three decades younger-self of Khalifa. When I'd seen him last back in Faisal Mosque, he'd looked to be in his sixties.

"Yes, Khalifa," Pir said in my ear. "Chaacha wanted him here."

"But—but why?" I stammered.

"He can work at the Bihishti Tea Corner. The place we had tea together. You know our Ibrahim? He needs a boy to order around," Chaacha responded. "I promised I'd get him one."

"I'd rather have him turned into a monkey and tossed into the Dump with his own kind, his only chance at rehabilitation," Pir stated definitively with more than a hint of anger in his voice.

Chaacha and Pir looked into each other's eyes without blinking, and I had no desire to get in the middle of it. There was no way to tell for sure who was boss here. Maybe Pir was being truthful when he told me a lifetime ago that he was the deputy of Chaacha.

"Give him a chance," Chaacha said softly, without breaking the fierce gaze he held with Pir.

Pir shook his head and exhaled an exasperated breath.

"Humans are beyond rehabilitation, as far as I'm concerned," Pir said, then skewered me with his eyes.

"You'll pick yourself up wherever you find yourself to be—that's the golden rule of life," he continued. "You're ready for the journey, Ismaeel. You've been initiated into the mysteries of the universe. You are now part of Khidr's hand-picked elite guard."

Feeling dizzy, I grabbed the bars of the cage and rested my head against the cold steel. Khalifa stared at me, his eyes twitching in confusion. He looked like he was trying to place me in his memory.

Chaacha Khidr put his arm around my shoulders and pulled me closer. His body was warm and radiated vitality.

"Babu, stop writing your silly paper about Paradise and Hell," he said, and then gently gave my arm a squeeze. "But write!"

"Write what?" I was confused.

"Your story—the story of your journey," he said. "You start writing as soon as you get back, because memory is transient and the world impermanent. Only stories have permanence."

"Your polio vaccine is tucked inside one of the cold packs on your kitchen counter," Pir said. "Don't forget to take it before you start your journey."

"What kind of a hybrid are you?" I asked, beholding the glowing face of Pir.

"Will of the Almighty. And matter." He smiled, his gaze remaining fierce without a hint of anger.

My mind ground to a sudden halt. Then I understood. It was vast, staggeringly complicated yet so very simple. I almost laughed out loud as the gnawing confusion that had weighed so heavily on me dissipated and lifted from my heart like a flock of vultures. There was no ending, and no beginning either. It was there, all along, all of it simultaneously. I looked at Pir. He nodded his head, his smile broadening. Even without the headband, he knew exactly what was going through my mind.

"I'm going to reverse him just to see what he will look like," Pir said, fixing his cold stare on Khalifa.

"No harm in giving it a try," Chaacha chimed. "But I need him for Ibrahim."

Suddenly it was dark all around, except the spot occupied by Khalifa, which was lit with a beam of light that made him look like he was on stage. Startled, I looked around but everything was pitch dark and the Guest House and its residents had vanished. Then the bars of Khalifa's cage melted away out of my hands. My body shuddered and I had to take a deep breath to steady myself.

With a look of sheer horror on his face, Khalifa jumped to his feet.

He shot me a fiery glance, lifted his hands in the air and then dropped them back on his head. I stared in pity and fascination as his forehead shortened and bulged outward; his nose flattened; and his eyes became smaller, deeper, and beadier under bushy brows that now overhung his face.

In shock and disgust I realized I was staring at a Neanderthal. Continuing his regressive biological collapse, Khalifa's head became even smaller and I was unable to tear my eyes away from the spectacle. The whites of his eyes were gone and he stooped as his arms lengthened. Within minutes, the thing's entire body was covered with dense black hair and his apish hands hung to his knees. He had turned into a big black baboon! I held my breath, absorbed in this mesmerizing reverse evolution of what was once a good looking homo sapiens.

The ape let out an agonized scream and started beating his chest. Then he charged, shrieking my name in a vile mockery of a human voice stretched over a monkey's primitive vocal cords. I froze with terror. He rammed into me with his shoulder, lifting me off my feet. I fell backward into a smothering emptiness.

I had no idea how long I'd been in free-fall, but I slowly realized I was floating. I was nothing more than awareness, a weightless presence in a void. I stayed suspended for what felt like a million years. Countless worlds were ripped out of the immense black sea of nothingness I had floated in, in a seemingly great cosmic womb. Galaxies came into existence for the blink of an eye, only to be sucked back into this luminous dark void. Species without number crawled from the primeval mud, blossomed to unfathomable greatness, and then succumbed to complete extinction.

Then a thunderous crack sounded across the vast black sheath of eternity, shattering all visible things into countless pieces as if all of reality were nothing more than a sheet of glass. I became aware again of my weight, my posture, my surroundings, and my body. I was sitting down somewhere, my ears abuzz with the sirens of an ambulance speeding down the block. I opened my eyes.

I was staring at a spider web on the ceiling of my studio apartment. A moth, trapped in its filaments, was fluttering its wings trying to break free. I was in a daze, drenched in sweat, my mouth parched. The bottle of Heineken was on the coffee table. I reached out to grab it and stopped. Wrapped around my wrist was the headband of Pir Pullsiraat. The Heineken was still icy cold. I took a swig and looked at my watch. It was quarter to midnight, it was Sunday. I got up and stumbled toward the kitchen counter, my head spinning like a centrifuge overloaded with vials filled with God knows what.

The note was there on the table. The empty vial of polio vaccine was there; so was the Styrofoam cooler. I took both the cold packs out of the cooler and extracted a sealed single dose vial of polio vaccine.

Remembering the last words of Chaacha Khidr, I pulled the stylus out of my phone and began writing, my hand trembling: *It was a balmy Saturday night late in October of the year 2050. The southbound A-train arrived fifteen minutes late at Columbus Circle, forcing me to make a run for it as soon as I hit the street. Breathless when I arrived at Yage Yoga Center—a sprawling...*

I looked at my watch, and then stared at Pir's black headband, still wrapped around my wrist, for a long time. An exquisite sense of well being began to wash over me. I got up and opened the window. The air was balmy and there was no sign of snow. I understood that the snow I'd witnessed right after taking my so-called polio vaccine, had fallen in another dimension, in one of the countless parallel universes. Vaccine, it was not.

I'd toiled twelve years of my life to understand religion. That toil was nothing but a ruse that enabled me to avoid my inner struggle with my father, a fight between my world and his. The cover was blown. I felt light and totally free. I was at ease when I picked up the phone to call him, to let him know of my imminent arrival in Lahore.

As the phone jangled on my father's end, the text of sura Al-Qamiya started running across the upper part of my vision with the handy translation underneath. The brush with eternity had surely left its fingerprints.

I was done with my thesis, with being an atheist, like I'd been done with being a believer ever since I was a child. I'd ended up being a knower.

I smiled remembering the words of Pir Pullsiraat: *It's all within*. It was a great feeling to be a member of the elite guard of Chaacha Khidr, and I wondered what my next mission would be. I was ready to take on my father, but most of all, I missed Sophie.

"Hello!" my father said into the phone at his end.

"Abba, it's Ismaeel."

THE END

About the Author

BROUGHT UP IN Lahore, Pakistan, until the age of 20, Asif Ismael has been living in the United States for the last 25 years. Currently, he resides in New York City, and is working on his next novel. To contact Asif Ismael, email him at: overthetightrope@gmail.com.

26705621R00210

Made in the USA
San Bernardino, CA
03 December 2015